Praise for

DEATH WITH A DOUBLE EDGE

"Timely . . . and engaging . . . another terrific mystery."

—*Bookreporter*

"[A] veritable page-turner . . . Perry is a skilled craftsperson, and she delivers an exciting and satisfying resolution."

—*Historical Novel Society*

"Brava Anne Perry—long may we continue to follow the exploits of the Pitt family."

—*Criminal Element*

"Tying family connections with intrigue is one of Perry's strengths. . . . [This is a] fast and fresh story that will satisfy readers of the series."

—*Mountain Times*

Praise for

ONE FATAL FLAW

"*One Fatal Flaw* is at once a courtroom thriller, a psychological-suspense tale, and a novel of manners (with Ms. Perry being especially sharp on class distinctions)."

—*The Wall Street Journal*

"Reliable Edwardian legal suspense, liberally flavored with contemporary feminism, from an old pro."

—*Kirkus Reviews*

"Characters are rich and multi-faceted, and their development skillfully merges details from the past with hints of the future. Young women, in particular, are fleshed out in unexpected-of-the-times ways. . . . [*One Fatal Flaw*] captivates with both major and minor characters that readers will look forward to following."

—*Historical Novel Society*

"*One Fatal Flaw* is like a set of Russian dolls. . . . Anne Perry is a masterful writer and this series just gets better and better."

—*Criminal Element*

Praise for
TRIPLE JEOPARDY

"Readers may find themselves smitten with Daniel and with the dauntless Miriam fford Croft. . . . [Anne Perry is] primarily identified for her authentic period sets and well-rendered characters. . . . This book is an excellent example of her craft."

—*Booklist*

"Veteran Perry dials back the period detail and the updates on the lives of the continuing characters to focus on one of her most teasing mysteries, this time with a courtroom finale that may be her strongest ever."

—*Kirkus Reviews*

"Another deftly crafted and original mystery by a true master of the genre, *Triple Jeopardy* . . . is ideal reading for all dedicated mystery buffs."

—*Midwest Book Review*

Praise for
TWENTY-ONE DAYS

"Set ten years after *Murder on the Serpentine*, [Anne] Perry's excellent new series launch expertly takes the Pitts into a new century and makes use of the scientific advancements of the time, fingerprints and X-rays, to add fresh drama to the courtroom scenes. . . . Fans of Perry's long-running [Charlotte and] Thomas Pitt series will delight in following the adventures of a new generation."
—*Library Journal* (starred review)

"Readers will quickly fall in love with [Daniel] Pitt, following along as he investigates a gruesome murder and chuckling as he throws those involved off kilter. Perry is a master at bringing setting to life, and readers will be taken in by the time and place as they get to know Daniel Pitt and those close to him in this engaging novel."
—*RT Book Reviews*

"The maven of well-crafted Victorian mysteries and author of both the William Monk series and the Charlotte and Thomas Pitt mysteries introduces the Pitts' son, Daniel, junior barrister, in this first of what proves to be an intriguing, entertaining, and character-centric new series. . . . In a story that's nicely tied to the characters in the Pitt series, Perry introduces Daniel and his cohort, the brilliant Miriam fford Croft, and raises the knotty question of whether some clients are truly undefendable."
—*Booklist*

"[Perry] seems just as comfortable in 1910 as she ever did back in Victoria's day."
—*Kirkus Reviews*

BY ANNE PERRY

FEATURING DANIEL PITT

Twenty-one Days

Triple Jeopardy

One Fatal Flaw

Death with a Double Edge

Three Debts Paid

The Fourth Enemy

FEATURING CHARLOTTE AND THOMAS PITT

The Cater Street Hangman

Callander Square

Paragon Walk

Resurrection Row

Bluegate Fields

Rutland Place

Death in the Devil's Acre

Cardington Crescent

Silence in Hanover Close

Bethlehem Road

Highgate Rise

Belgrave Square

Farriers' Lane

The Hyde Park Headsman

Traitors Gate

Pentecost Alley

Ashworth Hall

Brunswick Gardens

Bedford Square

Half Moon Street

The Whitechapel Conspiracy

Southampton Row

Seven Dials

Long Spoon Lane

Buckingham Palace Gardens

Treason at Lisson Grove

Dorchester Terrace

Midnight at Marble Arch

Death on Blackheath

The Angel Court Affair

Treachery at Lancaster Gate

Murder on the Serpentine

FEATURING WILLIAM MONK

The Face of a Stranger

A Dangerous Mourning

Defend and Betray

A Sudden, Fearful Death

The Sins of the Wolf

Cain His Brother

Weighed in the Balance

The Silent Cry

A Breach of Promise

The Twisted Root

Slaves of Obsession

Funeral in Blue

Death of a Stranger

The Shifting Tide

Dark Assassin

Execution Dock

Acceptable Loss

A Sunless Sea

Blind Justice

Blood on the Water

Corridors of the Night

Revenge in a Cold River

An Echo of Murder

Dark Tide Rising

FEATURING ELENA STANDISH

Death in Focus

A Question of Betrayal

A Darker Reality

A Truth to Lie For

THREE DEBTS PAID

Anne Perry

THREE DEBTS PAID

A Daniel Pitt Novel

BALLANTINE BOOKS • NEW YORK

2023 Ballantine Books Trade Paperback Edition

Copyright © 2022 by Anne Perry
Excerpt from *The Fourth Enemy* by Anne Perry
copyright © 2023 by Anne Perry

Published in the United States by Ballantine Books, an imprint of Random House, a division of Penguin Random House LLC, New York.

BALLANTINE is a registered trademark and the colophon is a trademark of Penguin Random House LLC.

Originally published in hardcover in the United States by Ballantine Books, an imprint of Random House, a division of Penguin Random House LLC, in 2022.

Originally published in hardcover in the United Kingdom by Headline Publishing Group, London, in 2021.

This book contains an excerpt from the forthcoming book *The Fourth Enemy* by Anne Perry. This excerpt has been set for this edition only and may not reflect the final content of the forthcoming edition.

LIBRARY OF CONGRESS CATALOGING-IN-PUBLICATION DATA
Names: Perry, Anne, author.
Title: Three debts paid / Anny Perry.
Description: First edition. | New York : Ballantine Books, [2022] |
Series: A Daniel Pitt novel ; #5
Identifiers: LCCN 2021044260 (print) | LCCN 2021044261 (ebook) |
ISBN 9780593358757 (trade paperback ; acid-free paper) |
ISBN 9780593358740 (ebook)
Subjects: LCGFT: Novels.
Classification: LCC PR6066.E693 T48 2022 (print) |
LCC PR6066.E693 (ebook) | DDC 823/.914–DC23
LC record available at https://lccn.loc.gov/2021044260
LC ebook record available at https://lccn.loc.gov/2021044261

Printed in the United States of America on acid-free paper

randomhousebooks.com

2 4 6 8 9 7 5 3 1

To Keith Stern

THREE DEBTS PAID

One

"COME IN."

Daniel answered the swift, light tap on his office door. He knew it was Impney, the chief clerk at the fford Croft and Gibson chambers. Daniel had been here for three years now, and it was all familiar.

Impney came in and closed the door behind him. He was a middle-aged man with immaculate appearance and manners. "There is a gentleman to see you, Mr. Pitt. His name is Professor Nicholas Wolford. I believe modern European history is his subject. He says he knew you at Cambridge, sir?" There was doubt in his voice.

Daniel had studied law, or else he would not have been here, in this excellent position. The firm of fford Croft and Gibson did not employ anyone without both a first-class degree from a reputable university and a personal recommendation.

Daniel did not have to think for more than a moment or two: he remembered Wolford clearly. The man was striking in appearance, moody in nature, a fine scholar, and beyond that, a brilliant teacher. For Daniel, he had made history seem more alive and urgent, more compelling, than any current affairs. Modern history was considered to have begun about the year 1500, and Wolford was interested in all of it, but he was especially passionate about the French Revolution. The 1789 one, before the uprisings all over Europe—with the exception of Britain—fifty years later. In the France of 1848, it was a revolution born and then crushed.

Impney was waiting patiently.

"Yes, yes, I remember him," Daniel answered. "What does he want?"

"He has a case that I believe he wishes you to take, sir. A matter arising from an instance of . . . *plagiarism*." He said the word as if it were the name of some obscene minor disease.

"Someone has plagiarized his work?" Daniel was not surprised. Wolford's style was unique and, in its own way, brilliant.

"No, sir. I believe the matter is somewhat more complicated than that," Impney answered. "It concerns a new book he has written. Something to do with the French Revolution. He wishes you to represent him. But I believe there is more."

"Really?" Daniel was startled. "What do you mean by *more*?"

Impney's face was impassive. "I am not certain, sir, but Professor Wolford is very clear that he wishes you on the case. He says an old friend recommended you, an Inspector Ian Frobisher, whom he says you know."

Daniel was surprised. He had not thought of Ian for so long. They had been to the same prep school together and then both gone up to Cambridge, Daniel to study law and Ian to read modern history. After graduation, their paths had gone in different ways. As for Wolford, he remembered the man only from the single year he had taken modern history. "Well, you had better send him in, if you please?" he requested.

"Yes, sir." Impney withdrew.

A few moments later, Nicholas Wolford strode through the door and closed it behind him. He was exactly as Daniel remembered, but then it had been only five years since Daniel had last seen him. Wolford still had his magnificent mane of black hair, now touched with silver at the temples and forming a bright streak at the front. He retained those strong features: a wide mouth and dark brown eyes, almost black. He was of average height, but he appeared taller.

Daniel rose to his feet, more from habit than courtesy. He held out his hand. "How are you, sir?"

"I'm well," Wolford replied, "but angry." He spoke with the same strong, precise voice he had used in his lectures as he related fascinating and terrifying stories to the roomful of students—true stories that made the days of yesterday seem far more alive than today. Daniel knew that many of Wolford's students found his lectures life-changing, opening up their eyes to the past. Wolford had a devoted following among his ex-students, many of whom stayed in touch for years after they left Cambridge.

Daniel indicated the chair on the other side of the desk. "Please, sit down and tell me the salient points. Details can come later."

"The salient point is that the man accused me of having copied his work," Wolford said between gritted teeth. "But the actual charge I am facing is one of assault," he added, before sitting down and leaning his elbows on the desk.

His manner irritated Daniel. It was too close, too familiar, but he could see the rage building inside Wolford. He remembered the man more and more clearly as the moments slipped by, and he believed in his sincerity.

Wolford's arrogance had always been as clear as his passion for the drama of the past. Daniel could not imagine him borrowing words from anyone else, much less stealing by imitation. He listened intently, memories flooding back of the classroom, the hush of enraptured silence as everyone was caught up in Wolford's stories.

Wolford laid out the specific passages that formed the body of the plagiarism accusation. "He used exactly the same words as I did to describe Charlotte Corday," he said angrily. He was speaking of one of the heroines of the Revolution who had gone to Paris specifically to murder Jean-Paul Marat in his bath. Of course, she died on the guillotine. "'She was tall and she walked with a grace that verged on arrogance,'" Wolford recited from memory. "'Her features were not beautiful, but she had a clear and radiant complexion. Not surprising. She was a country girl. And she had beautiful hair.'" His hand clenched into a fist on the desktop. "Exactly what I had written. But I got it from the words of those who were there, who saw her as close as I am to you! And I can prove it."

"So can we presume that you and your accuser have got it from a common source?" Daniel asked, realizing that there was no point in asking about the physical assault Wolford was charged with until he knew the whole story.

Wolford's black eyebrows rose. "I can see you've not forgotten everything I taught you! Of course we got it from a common source." His fist on the desk opened and clenched. "Except the bit about her complexion. But then, we all know she came from the country, so it is a reasonable deduction. I did not copy that oaf!"

"What is the oaf's name?" Daniel asked. "I had better know."

"Linus Tolliver."

Daniel wrote it down. He had not heard of the man. "Young?" he asked.

"Why do you ask?"

"It seems rather a juvenile thing to do," Daniel replied. "To copy someone else—possibly someone whose work you admire—and then, when you think you are going to be caught, blame them before they can blame you. Since you are charged with assault, I presume you hit him?"

"Yes," Wolford said.

"Before he struck you?"

Wolford smiled. It changed his face completely, taking years off his age. "Yes," he replied. "He tried, but he missed. I'm wondering if anyone put him up to it. His editor, maybe?"

"Any reason to suspect his editor?" Daniel asked.

"Yes. Slimy little toad. Looking for publicity for Tolliver's book. A nice, juicy case, true or false, would make the newspapers. Especially with the added titillation of violence. That was stupid of me. Now he can trade on my name in the worst possible way." He drew his brows together in a frown. "Some men will do anything for money—and perhaps do even more for a few weeks of fame." The contempt in his voice burned like acid.

"It's a high risk," Daniel pointed out. "Your style, your choice of words, are unique. If Tolliver is copying you, it might well be apparent to anyone who studies the subject."

"Hardly the general public!" Wolford snapped. "Passion, injustice, violence, slaughter, and betrayal are the stuff of great drama! The more so if it is based on truth! Think, man. What would Shakespeare have written if he had not plundered history to draw his inspiration? A few comedies, perhaps." He shrugged his shoulders dismissively. "Fairies. Mistaken identity. Love stories of mere infatuation. But the great dramas, the giants among all the works of literature, were drawn from history, true or false. *Hamlet*, *Macbeth*, *Caesar*, *Lear*, *Richard III*, *Titus Andronicus*." His voice shook with emotion. "What would Shakespeare have made of Charles I and Cromwell? The immovable king and the irresistible puritan! How I would love to have seen his art reimagine the trial of the king, which was in fact as much a trial of Cromwell. Think of it, Pitt! What a work that would have been. Any trial is a test of the judge, as much as of the accused . . ."

He stopped, staring at Daniel with brilliant eyes, as if he could see the drama playing out in real life, contained within the bounds of the room they were in.

Thoughts raced round Daniel's mind. He drew breath, ready to argue that the accused was charged with a crime, while the accuser—through the representation of their lawyers—was charged with seeking the truth of it. But then he glimpsed what Wolford was getting at. Yes, in a way, the accuser was as much on trial, in that their legal team conducted the proceedings. They set the rules. They chose what to present and what to leave out. And perhaps the jury was in the same position. How much did their own fears and prejudices decide the verdict they returned?

Wolford must have read Daniel's thoughts on his face, because he smiled slowly, as if the young barrister's understanding of his supposition was visible to him. As if all he had wanted was for the breadth of the issue to be understood by Daniel.

"I will get all the information for you," Wolford said. "My publishers will send you the original draft, with editing details, of course. And my sources, although I don't have all the books in my personal possession. Some of them are in reference libraries." He shrugged. "Many are in Paris, as you might expect, but I can name them all, even to the page number. One would need to speak French to understand them. But you can get expert witnesses for that, if you need to. Some documents are sitting in museums. But these, too, are verifiable." He gave a brief smile. "Since Tolliver is accusing me of plagiarism, he will have to prove his sources first!"

"Thank you. They would all be most helpful." Daniel accepted the professor's offer. "But as you say, Tolliver is making the accusation, and he will have to prove his case. With a copy of your manuscript, and the reference works you used, I should be able to prove the originality of your work. But that doesn't vindicate you from the charge of assault. It merely serves to explain the cause of it. Anger, even righteous anger, is not a justification for violence."

"He hit me first, or at least he tried to," Wolford repeated.

"Then why is it that you are being charged?"

Wolford shrugged very slightly. "I hit him harder. I broke his nose."

"But he did hit you?"

"Like I said, he missed."

"Then you admit to actually striking him first?"

"Yes, with just cause."

"And you will apologize?"

It was a long moment before Wolford responded. "I suppose so. But only for hitting him, not for refuting the accusation of plagiarism."

Daniel smiled.

Something in Wolford's stance eased. It was a very slight movement, as if a shadow had passed from him. "Then you'll take the case?"

"Yes, of course," Daniel agreed.

He had never felt comfortable enough with Wolford to like him. The man was brilliant, and he knew it only too well. Despite his overly confident manner, Daniel had always found him interesting, and more alive than any other teacher. Nicholas Wolford was passionate about his subject and his students' pursuit of that passion; he had a way of bringing the past to life and making it pulse with vitality.

Sometimes, in the excitement and bustle of the new century, with its amazing innovations, the giant steps of the past were forgotten, as was the price others had paid for the privileges of today, even laying down their lives in the pursuit of their ideals. It was already 1912, a modern era filled with new ideas. There were motorcars in the street, along with horse-drawn vehicles; London was crisscrossed by stations for the ever-expanding underground railway; new notions of medicine were being espoused, not only for the body, but for the mind. Women were clamoring for the right to vote. Their voices seemed somehow passive beside the foment of revolution so vividly described by Wolford. Daniel thought how English it all was—leaden-footed, even unimaginative, compared with the French. A blessing or a curse? He wasn't sure.

Wolford was watching him. "I've sparked your interest, haven't I?" he said quietly. "You're a good man, Pitt. Using your brain. Up to a challenge." He stood up slowly. "I'll send a messenger with the materials you need. I'll speak to your clerk on the way out."

Daniel stood, too. "Yes, sir," he replied firmly.

Wolford was right: this was an interesting challenge.

Two

Two days later, Daniel walked quickly along the city pavement, with nothing further from his mind than Nicholas Wolford's case of assault. His speed was not because it was late in the afternoon, or because the wind was rising with an edge of ice to it. That was normal for London in early February. His step was fast because he was looking forward to where he was going, which was the laboratory attached to one of the city's morgues.

He crossed the street, dodging his way between horse-drawn carts and motor-driven automobiles. The gutters were already filling from the rain that had been falling, on and off, all day. The gas lamps made everything appear shiny and sharp-edged, and in the mist, they were haloed with light.

Miriam fford Croft had come home two days ago, and Daniel had not yet managed to see her. At the firm, he was currently doubling for his friend and immediate senior, Toby Kitteridge, who was taking a walking holiday in France. So Daniel was spending long days in chambers, where he worked all the hours he was awake. Added to that, he had received Nicholas Wolford's papers, and had stayed even later to begin studying them. Now, at last, he felt he could spare some time to focus on other matters.

Miriam had been away for well over a year, studying forensic pathology, the subject closest to her heart. She had previously studied as much as she could in England, but however excellent her examination marks, and despite completing all of the course work, she would not be granted the professional status to practice. Not in England, nor in Scotland or Ireland. Or, for that matter, anywhere in Europe . . . except Holland.

The magnificently eccentric Dr. Evelyn Hall, the only woman pathologist in Britain, had earned her credentials in Holland and encouraged Miriam to continue her studies there. She believed in Miriam's passion and skill and had given her every help she could— including urging her to pursue her final degree and certification and assisting her to secure a place in one of Holland's most prestigious science institutes.

The move to Amsterdam had not been easy, but Miriam was determined. None of the subjects were new to her, but it had taken over a year to sit all the examinations and return with her credentials. Now that she was home, and working with the woman they called "Dr. Eve," Miriam was a fully accredited pathologist in her own right.

In pursuing her own career, Dr. Eve had taken advantage of the fact that Evelyn was both a man's and a woman's name, so her applications were not questioned. The head of the institute where she currently worked had been prepared to give her a chance, and she proved herself beyond qualified.

Dr. Eve chose to assume masculine attire, and her manner was more outspoken and braver than that of most men; she also smoked stronger cigars than any of them. Daniel had learned that the vile-smelling cigars were a defense against the overpowering odor of some of the bodies she was called upon to examine, not an uncommon practice among those working around death.

Dr. Eve was also brave, open-minded, and a patron of lost causes. Daniel would have liked her just for how she'd helped Miriam, but he also liked her for herself. She was utterly honest, and that was a welcome change from the law, which seemed always to be about equivocating and finding one more argument.

The morgue was only one crossroad ahead. Daniel leaped over a swift-running gutter and hurried along the pavement, avoiding the chipped edges of uneven stones.

He was soon there. He went in through the heavy door and was aware of it closing behind him. The smell enveloped him immediately, carbolic and lye not quite masking the odor of death. What could not be covered up was the way Daniel's imagination dwelled on everything his mind did not perceive but knew was there: memories of other visits, bodies to identify, the dread that it might be someone he knew. Perhaps, worst of all, the knowledge that he might have to take the news to parents, families, friends. Knowing there was an empty space where a loved one had been only a short while ago.

Daniel stopped at the desk of the attendant, gave his name, and asked for Dr. Hall. He was directed to her laboratory, thanked the man, and found himself quickening his step along the bare passageway.

At the door he stopped, gathered his composure . . . and then knocked.

"Come in!" The voice was deep, hearty, but a little rough-edged—whether with weariness or emotion, it was hard to tell. But it had to be Evelyn Hall.

Daniel took a deep breath, turned the handle, and pushed the door open. The white light hit him immediately, hard and brutal. He saw Dr. Eve first. She was tall for a woman and heavy-shouldered, but curiously shapeless. She was wearing trousers, a man's shirt and waistcoat. Her sleeves were rolled up, baring muscular arms and strong, curiously beautiful hands, supple and graceful. Her hair was gray, and she wore it cut short and ragged, like a man who had forgotten his barber's address. Her face conveyed a burning intelligence, and there was nothing in it willing to compromise. The emotions displayed there were naked: pity, anger, horror. All the theory and knowledge in the world could not mitigate the darkness of death, whether by accident or illness. And if that death had been caused by murder . . . doubly so.

"So, you've shown up at last," Eve observed. "Thought you were never coming!"

Daniel ignored her, and his eyes went to Miriam. She was exactly as he remembered her. First, the bright auburn hair, now pulled back tightly and secured with a woven net to keep it under control. Her face was paler than he recalled. Was his memory at fault? She stood very straight, a little stiff, as if defending her new position. Or was she too tired for any pretense at all?

He smiled at her, a sudden, wide smile that he knew lit all his face, the warmth of it coming from deep inside him.

Her face softened and she smiled back, her eyes bright and gentle.

"Well?" Evelyn interrupted the silence. "Are you here to see one of us?" Her face wrinkled with unhappiness as she looked down at the naked corpse on the table between them. "Poor little beggar," she added, almost under her breath.

Daniel did not want to look, and yet he could not help it. Against every instinct, he stared at the white and bloodied body of the woman on the table.

"We've hardly begun," Eve said quietly. "Sorry, Daniel. It won't wait. It's . . ." Her face was bleak, all expression drained from it now.

"She just came in," Miriam spoke for the first time. "I'm . . . sorry. It's good to see you." She looked straight at him.

He had forgotten that her eyes were so blue—not the lighter color he would have expected, but deep, almost navy blue. He found himself smiling, even though, looking at the unknown woman on the table, stripped of her clothes and daubed with her own blood, what he felt was a mixture of pity and horror at what had happened to her. Still, warmth welled up inside when Miriam looked in his eyes.

"Got time?" Eve challenged him.

He turned to her blankly, no idea of what she meant.

"It must be dinnertime," she went on, as if that were an answer.

"I thought you were too busy," he began.

"Rubbish," she answered. "Go to the pub along the street. To the left. And get us some sandwiches. Roast beef. Light on the mustard."

"Oh . . ." He had been about to blaspheme, and only just stopped himself.

"Get cheese for yourself, if you'd rather," Eve said with weary patience. "You can have a cigar, if you want."

"Cigar?" he said with disbelief.

"Best thing I know to overcome a smell you'd rather not know about," she said, staring directly at him. "This poor girl just arrived. She was"—her voice was suddenly tight in her throat—"killed earlier this afternoon. Just after dark."

Daniel did not know how they could deal with such violence and tragedy. It was not by dismissing it, he knew that. Even a glance at their faces, in this harsh white light, would have told him that they were moved. Some people imagined that women were weaker than men, but Daniel knew better. Perhaps it was what people wanted to think? Or needed to?

"Roast beef," he repeated, then looked at Miriam.

"Ham and cheese," she answered. "And apple cider, for both of us. And . . ." Her face softened into a half smile. "Bring some for yourself, if you don't mind eating here?"

He smiled back, a little crookedly. "Not at all. Just put a sheet over her, poor soul." He nodded in the direction of the dead woman, but still did not look at her. He turned to leave.

"Hey!" Eve said peremptorily.

He turned back.

She was holding out money. "We are not entirely barbarous. We invited you to dine with the corpse, but we don't expect you to have to pay for it yourself."

He did not know what to say. Things had gone well for him lately, with several excellent cases. He could easily afford it. But this was not about money, it was about friendship. And professional respect.

He took the money. "I'll be back soon," he promised.

When he returned twenty-five minutes later, the body was covered with a sheet. It could have been anything under that blank white cotton. In his absence, Eve and Miriam had washed their hands. They were drying them now, and taking off the aprons that had protected their clothes.

"Excellent," Eve said. She accepted the paper bag and opened it, exposing three thick and crusty sandwiches, three fresh oatcakes, and three fairly large bottles of cider. "Thank you," she added, with evident satisfaction.

The question flickered through Daniel's mind of when she had last eaten. He sat down at the makeshift dinner table, a surface normally covered with instruments and now cleared for the occasion. There was another white sheet over it, but this was spread as if it were a tablecloth. Daniel tried not to think what it usually covered. They had very thoughtfully invited him to sit on the stool that positioned his back to the corpse.

He ignored the hard, white light, the stacks of jars and tins of various chemicals, the pieces of equipment, the sinks with their metal taps, the containers holding God knew what! He concentrated on the food, with an occasional glance at Eve and Miriam.

Eve Hall's features were strong, bold, her expression almost blank, as if she had washed all the tragedy from her mind.

Miriam's was so different. Grief was sharp in the lines of her cheeks and jaw, the muscles she could not control.

Daniel understood the fine line between her emotions and her scientific knowledge. The theory she knew to perfection: she could answer even the most complex questions in her mind, recite not only facts but also formulae. But the silent presence of a real woman, younger than she was, dead and naked in her final vulnerability: that was a different matter. In truth, all the examinations in the world were different from this. It was a test he knew no one was ever prepared for; if they were, perhaps they should not be doing the work.

They ate their sandwiches in solemn silence. At first, Daniel found his a little difficult to swallow. It seemed indecent to eat in the presence of a woman who had been alive only a few hours ago, and who now lay silent and hideously injured a few yards away. But not to eat was pointless. None of them was of any use if faint with hunger.

Besides, the young woman was oblivious to anything now. If she could care, she would want them to find who had done this to her. Did she have family? Did they even know she was dead? Or how she had died?

"Do they know who she is . . . was?" he asked, and then wished immediately that he had thought of something else to say. Should he apologize?

It was Miriam who answered quietly. "She had a small purse with her. There was a note inside it, with the name Lena Madden."

"She looks to be about twenty-eight or -nine, at a guess," Eve added.

Daniel wanted to ask if the woman had been sexually assaulted, but he did not know how to approach such an appalling subject with any tact. Since they had found her purse, it did not seem as if the intent had been robbery.

"No, she hadn't," Eve said, looking straight at him and meeting his eyes.

He could feel a warmth spreading across his cheeks.

"You were wondering if she'd been violated, weren't you?" she correctly surmised.

He thought of evading her question, then realized how childish it would be—and ineffectual. Miriam would think he was such a boy! "And she wasn't robbed," he said instead. "Unless she had something of value that we don't know about?"

"Precisely," Eve agreed, taking the last of her sandwich in one bite. "Thank you," she said, chewing. "Very good." She picked up one of the oatcakes and bit into it hungrily, then took a long drink from the cider bottle.

Daniel wanted to stay. Not to watch the post-mortem examination of the young woman, but to spend a little more time with Miriam before he had to leave. He had seen her only once in the last year, when she had returned home for a very brief spell, during her father's illness. As soon as Marcus had recovered enough to expect a good outcome, he had insisted she should not miss any of her time in Holland, particularly not her exams.

Now Daniel felt her watching him. Had she missed him, too? Or was that just a touch of impatience, waiting to see if he realized he was interrupting them?

He turned a little in his seat and looked directly at Miriam. She caught his movement and returned his gaze, her dark blue eyes curious, with a faint light in them that was surely a smile.

He wanted to say something, at the very least something intelligent, if nothing more constructive. "Could it have been an accident?" he asked, glancing indirectly at the body.

"No," Miriam answered. "The only decent thing about it is that it must have been quick. A moment's terror, then pain, then nothing."

He wondered if she might be trying to hide her feelings for his sake.

"The first blow killed her," she added. "The others were either a kind of signature, or a hatred so deep he couldn't help himself."

"How do you know that?" He hoped she would give him a definite answer, not just hopeful conjecture that the woman's death had been mercifully swift.

"The first wound bled badly," she answered. "It was fatal. The others were inflicted afterward."

He was puzzled. "Why would anybody do that?" he asked. "And why was she killed, anyway? She wasn't assaulted and she wasn't robbed—at least, not of her purse."

"A good question," Miriam said quietly, her face puckered a little. "There's no obvious reason. Personal enmity? Revenge for something? Something she knew about her attacker, dangerous enough that he had to silence her? A rival of some sort?"

"So many possible reasons," Daniel mused. He shook his head.

"It's the police's job, not ours," said Eve, as she drank the last of her cider. She put the empty bottle on the table and looked at Daniel quizzically, as if she were going to add something but was weighing up how to phrase it.

He looked at Miriam. She seemed a little thinner than before. Knowing her, she had been working very hard indeed to get the best possible marks in her exams. He had seen how it had grated on her when she had acquired so much knowledge, after years of study, but not the actual certification. People had condescended to her, as if she had been a silly young woman imagining herself on an equal footing, and at the same intellectual level, with men. She had been thirty-nine when she started her studies, so it followed she was over forty now. He was twenty-seven. A boy, to her. But he did not think of himself that way at all.

"Isn't it your job to help them, if you can?" he asked. "The police, that is."

Eve gave a short bark of laughter. "If they ask, which they seldom do." She looked straight at Miriam. "You don't know this yet, but this is the second one."

The last crust of her sandwich slid out of Miriam's hand and fell onto the piece of paper she was using as a plate. "What did you say?"

Eve's face was blank, almost shadowless in the white light. "I said that she is the second one like this." She did not turn to glance at the corpse under the sheet, but they both knew what she meant.

"How . . . *like this*?" Daniel asked.

"As far as I can see, exactly like it," Eve answered, meeting his eyes. "The first victim came in six days ago."

Miriam froze. "You didn't tell me!" she protested, as if denying the connection could somehow make it untrue.

"My dear, you've just arrived! So I'm saying it now," Eve replied. "The first was a young woman, Sandrine Bernard. She was wounded exactly like this. Not certain yet if it was the same kind of blade, but I think so. This woman seems to have been stabbed with a curved knife, very sharp indeed. Perhaps using the same instrument as before. Stabbed more than once, but the first wound deep enough to prove fatal. Nevertheless, they were both slashed afterward, and it seems it might have been done simply to vent emotion. Completely pointless. The first wound killed them. It's like . . ." She paused for a moment. "Either it was a cruel and deliberate signature, or he was out of control."

There was a moment's silence before Miriam spoke. "Left to right? Right to left?" She leaned forward a little over the table. "I mean, was it a right-handed person who attacked from the front?"

"Left to right, both of them," Eve replied.

"So . . ." Miriam moved her right hand in a slashing arc, right to left. "It would have been like this—a right-handed person standing in front of her, or a left-handed person standing behind her."

"Probably," Eve agreed.

"So, someone she was not afraid of," Daniel observed.

"Exactly. If the attacker was in front," Eve agreed.

"So," he asked, "did the attack come from behind, or was it from the front? Can you tell?"

"Not definitively," Eve replied. "It poses some interesting questions. And it was also raining like Noah's flood the night the first victim was found."

Without thinking, Daniel glanced back at the door he had come in through. It had not been raining all that hard, not much more than a drizzle.

"Not here," Eve observed. "Where she was found, poor little soul! We've had showers here, but torrential rain further east."

"Does that have any importance?" Daniel asked.

"I don't know. Might be just a coincidence." Eve lifted her shoulders a little. "If you go out in weather like that, what do you wear? What do you see? Who else is out? And what are they wearing?"

Daniel thought for a moment. "Raincoats," he began. "The longer, the better. Collar turned up. A wide-brimmed hat—"

"To protect yourself as much as possible," Eve concluded. "From getting soaked . . . or being recognized."

"A disguise," Miriam said slowly, realization dawning. "Behind a broad brim, or even a sou'wester, if you've got one. Maybe a thick scarf or an umbrella. You look like everybody else, and no one suspects you of anything, except trying to stay dry." She looked at Eve. "Do you think that was intentional, or just the way it happened?"

"Don't know," Eve admitted. "The first killing, of Sandrine Bernard, was four wounds, as I described them. She was killed between seven in the evening and midnight just off Chalk Farm Road, less than half a mile from the Chalk Farm Railway Station."

"Who was she?" Miriam asked. "What do we know about her?"

Eve bit her lip ruefully. "A twenty-eight-year-old. Pretty, dark hair, slender. Half French, apparently. Came over here from Paris to visit her grandparents. Been here a month. Differing accounts. Some say she was smart, independent-minded, plainspoken. Others say opinionated, too free with her comments—and with her favors to gentlemen of uncertain reputation."

"She sounds rather nice," Daniel said, with a wince of pain.

"Poor girl. Even if she was a little liberal with her affections, she didn't deserve to end up like this!"

Eve looked at him curiously. Then, with a sad, almost bitter smile, she went on. "This second victim was found on College Road, a few blocks away, and actually closer to the Chalk Farm Station." The fleeting expression on her face was both sad and angry.

"Any witnesses?" Daniel asked, turning to Eve. "I suppose everyone was hurrying, looking only in the direction of where they were going and trying to avoid stepping in deep puddles."

"No one of any use," Eve replied. "Everybody had their heads down. The people they passed were little more than shrouded figures in the early darkness. And in such driving rain, they couldn't see a thing!"

Daniel felt a sort of hopelessness overwhelm him. It all sounded so forlorn, and yet so rational. Figures bent and shrouded, soaking wet, looking only where they were going, seeing nothing. Outwardly, the street appeared as usual. Only this time, one of those hurrying shadows was carrying a knife of some sort. And killing with it. Leaving behind a dead body and blood, much of it washed away by the rain. Death, blood . . . and fear.

"Is he selecting his victims? Killing women he knows?" he asked. "Or just anyone in the street? Is there any purpose in looking for a connection?"

"I don't know," Eve said honestly. "We can't hide the murder of this poor creature. But when the newspapers get hold of it, which of course they will, some people will panic. And who can blame them?"

"I suppose it is a man killing them, not a woman killing other women?" he asked.

"It's possible," Eve said grimly. "Not likely. Women are more disposed to kill a husband or lover. They don't stalk people in the streets. And they usually use poison rather than knives. But there's always a first . . ."

Daniel said nothing, but he sensed that there was something he was not being told. He looked from Miriam to Eve, and then back to Miriam, hoping to find something revealing in her face. Finally, he said, "Miriam?"

She pressed her lips together, as if wishing to hold back the words.

Daniel glanced at Dr. Eve, who was giving him a narrow-eyed look.

"It's the finger," she explained.

When Daniel seemed confused, she crossed to the table and pulled back a bit of the sheet covering the victim. She pointed to the hand. Daniel leaned closer. Where there had once been an index finger, there was now only a bloody stump.

"Both women are missing part of the index finger," Eve explained. "And no," she added quickly, "it is not a coincidence. These fingers were severed at the time of death."

Daniel turned to Miriam. "Why would you rather I not know this?"

The look of determination on her face did not soften. "Some things must not be known by the public," she said. "If the newspapers learn of this, it will explode in the press."

"And you think I would reveal this fact?" he asked, a challenge in his voice.

"We can't take the chance," Eve intervened. "Let the public know and we'll have mass panic."

Daniel nodded. There was nothing he could say to argue that point. "You have my word," he told her.

Dr. Eve nodded abruptly, and then gave Miriam a little smile. "We can now proceed," she said.

Daniel saw profound relief cross Miriam's face.

As the two women worked, Daniel looked from one to the other. Two women, very much alone. If this was done by a madman, then who was safe? He himself had no wish to go out into the darkness alone.

He turned to Miriam. "Can I take you home?"

"We haven't really finished here," she replied.

"Do as you're told," Eve said sharply. "Go now! I'll stay here. There's a place to sleep upstairs."

"I can wait a little longer," Daniel offered.

Eve gave him a hard yet strangely sweet smile. "And you will do as you are told as well! Take her home."

Daniel did not argue. Eve would work long enough to tidy everything, put all the notes away. He knew that Miriam felt as if she should not leave until everything was finished—whatever the hour—but what Miriam wanted did not matter to him. Her safety did. He stood up. "Come on," he said, making it very nearly an order.

Miriam looked at him steadily, without blinking, then smiled. "Thank you."

Staying close together, they walked out of the morgue and along the footpath in the dark toward the main crossroads, where the lights were brighter. After a few minutes, they found a horse-drawn taxi. They jumped across the deepening puddles, climbed in, and rode off through the increasingly heavy rain.

He wanted to say something about how pleased he was to see her, but it seemed out of place now. In truth, he was more than pleased, but he was not yet ready to tell her that. The violence and tragedy of the bodies on the table, and the horror that had brought them there, made polite trivialities more than absurd. They were like an evasion, a denial of what he had seen in the morgue. And he did not dare reach across and take her hand. It could be misunderstood.

They stopped first at Miriam's family home, where Daniel saw her to the door. When she was safely inside, he went back to the taxi and directed the driver to take him to his lodgings. As the taxi navigated the increasing downpour, he could not shake the thought of the woman's hand . . . with her index finger missing.

IT WAS HORRIBLY early, even before delivery of the morning mail, when there was a knock on Daniel's office door. "Come in," he answered, assuming it was Impney. Who else would call at this hour?

Impney came in, looking apologetic. "There is a police inspector here, sir. He says he knows you. In fact, he said he is a longtime friend. His name is Ian Frobisher. Shall I let him in, sir? And would you like a tray of tea?"

Daniel was startled, then immediately realized that he should not have been. It was nearly a year since he had last seen Ian, but he had known him for as long as he could easily remember. "Yes. Thank you, Impney, that would be excellent."

"Certainly, sir." Impney withdrew.

A moment later, Ian Frobisher came in.

Ian and Daniel were both in their late twenties now, filled out a little from the schoolboys they had once been, but easily recognizable to each other. Ian was an inch taller than Daniel, still on the lean side. His fair hair dropped forward, as it had so long ago, and covered his brow.

"Sorry," said Ian, advancing into the room. "I apologize for sending Wolford to you," he said, looking contrite, "but you are probably the only decent lawyer who'll have the patience to work with him. He's in serious trouble." He frowned. "He really hit that fellow Tolliver a wallop. Broke his nose. And several of his teeth. At least the nose will mend . . . probably."

"Fortunately, I am not saving a beautiful woman's reputation, or prosecuting some dastardly thief," Daniel replied lightly.

If Ian chose to be lighthearted, even flippant about it, Daniel would do the same. He knew to let Ian set the tone. It was only a year since his wife had died, leaving him with an infant daughter and an overwhelming legacy of grief. They could both take it for granted that Daniel cared how Ian was doing. If he asked, his friend would reply that he was fine. It did not need to be put into words. Daniel would always care, and Ian would never be fine.

"He's guilty, of course," Ian said, sitting in the chair on the other side of the desk, crossing his long legs a little awkwardly. "It's really a matter of saving what you can out of the situation. The best thing would be if you could get the fool to apologize, without dragging it into a courtroom. And with all the best intentions in the world, he won't keep his temper for long. One word out of place and he will erupt like a damn volcano. You'll be picking up the debris for a week."

"He's not guilty of plagiarism, even unintentionally, I suppose?" Daniel asked.

"Good God, no!" Ian looked startled. "He's not being charged with it. They quoted from the same sources, so of course they used the same words, and the publisher was a little careless about attribution, that's all. An hour's research would have told any competent researcher that it was a mistake—and not Wolford's."

"Then why mention it at all?" Daniel asked.

"Academic rivalry, I suppose. New young writer trying to draw attention to himself. Seeking a bit of publicity, perhaps?"

"And Wolford, like an idiot, hit him," Daniel concluded.

"Not quite as simple as that, but close," Ian agreed.

"Honestly, how serious were the injuries? Who struck first?"

"That depends on who you listen to. According to Tolliver, he called Wolford something offensive. General opinion seems to be that he called him a liar and a plagiarist, and an intellectual hack."

Daniel winced. "I assume he was looking to provoke a fight?"

"Looks like that to me," Ian agreed. "Then he swung his arm, but nowhere near making contact. Actually, I think it was likely he overbalanced."

"And fell onto Wolford's outstretched fist?" Daniel tried to hide his smile and failed.

"You'll have to work hard to make anyone believe that," Ian said, giving a sharp laugh. "Perhaps you could say that Wolford overbalanced, pitching forward, at the same time? With his fist outstretched. Frankly, I think you'd do a lot better being honest and repeating what Tolliver called him. Hopefully, he'll accept the apology and not make more of an ass of himself than necessary."

There was a knock on the door, and Impney came in with a tray. On it were a silver teapot and porcelain cups with matching saucers.

Daniel thanked him and murmured something appropriate. Impney nodded and withdrew discreetly.

"I am duly impressed," Ian observed. "Not like the stewed tea at the police station, served up in an old enamel mug!"

"Yes, Inspector," Daniel called Ian by his title. It was in gentle fun, indicating both friendly teasing and professional respect. "Any more ideas as to how I should conduct this case?"

"Not at the moment," Ian replied, watching as Daniel poured the tea. "But I'm always available, if you wish."

"So, Wolford . . . he struck me as difficult . . . yes?"

Ian shrugged. "Sorry," he said again, and then shifted his attention to the tray. "Are those ginger biscuits?"

"Of course," said Daniel with a smile. "Help yourself."

Three

Mᴵᴿᴵᴬᴹ ʜᴬᴰ ʙᴇᴇɴ home a few days now. She had gone to work almost immediately, and the responsibility was both exciting and frightening. The work itself, however, was familiar, and she was more than qualified.

She closed the front door and walked across the parquet-floored hall. The drawing-room door was not quite closed, and there was a beam of yellow light shining through. She smiled, walked over, and pushed it open. "Good evening, Father," she said. "How was your day?"

She entered the room, closing the door behind her. The warm, slightly aromatic air wrapped around her. She knew immediately that the fire was burning applewood again.

At first, Miriam had believed she would miss her fellow students, who were able to talk interestingly about the finer details of the day's study. Instead, she found that after a day's work with real victims—the newly dead, people who only yesterday she might have seen, or even spoken with—the last thing she wanted was to relive any of it.

The aroma of burning applewood was a fragrant contrast to the antiseptic smell of lye and carbolic—and, of course, Eve's cigar smoke that permeated the air in the morgue.

Her father, Marcus fford Croft, was looking at her intently. "Well?" he asked, trying to hide his concern. "You look tired."

"Thank you," she said, smiling a little ruefully. It was kind, but hardly flattering.

"Feeling touchy?" His white eyebrows rose.

She tried to smile. "Sorry. It's different when it's a real case, rather than an old one that's wheeled out to be learned from." She saw his face crease with anxiety and she knew she had made a mistake. She should not have told him the truth, but it was too late to take it back.

He had been there all her life, from her very first memories to seeing her off to Amsterdam. She had been able to slip certain things past him—or she thought she had—but there were others that, try as she might, she could not hide. And he had read her like an open book, even if he did not say so.

Miriam forced herself to smile. "It is *real*, Father, and that's what my work is about. Not an exercise, but real murder, with real victims on the table. What would be a tragedy is if it didn't upset me—then it would be the time to walk away."

He nodded slowly and his smile was very gentle. "I'm proud of you," he said softly, his eyes bright, his voice a little husky. "Have you seen Daniel yet?"

Suddenly, she was self-conscious. "He came by the morgue today." She smiled, feeling her cheeks warm a little. "It was nice to see him, even if it was over a sandwich dinner on a table for cadavers."

"But you enjoyed it?"

It sounded to her half a question, half an assumption. She knew what he wanted her to say. "Of course I did." And it was the truth.

He thought for a moment or two, took a deep breath, then let it out again. Without saying anything, he leaned forward and put another log on the fire.

That was something she would address one day; this weight of silence could not sit indefinitely between them. Her father had suffered a serious heart attack in early summer. One of his concerns now was that his only child should be able to earn her own living, no matter what happened to him. Well, she had always been able to do that. But there was something more. He wanted to know that someone would look after her in the ways that mattered; someone who believed in her abilities, that what she did was important—not only to others, but most of all to her. He wanted her to be with someone who would look at her and see the reality: acknowledge her failures as well as her successes, understand how hard it was for her to deal with death, taking responsibility for other people's grief or fear. He wanted someone to love her. Which also meant curbing her, now and then, but gently.

Miriam knew all of this, but she was not ready to face it just now. She must speak of something else, so the silence did not have time to become an obvious evasion. "It is quite different when it's a current case," she went on, setting herself firmly back in the laboratory again. "I think I know things, I can see what we have in front of us, but Dr. Eve always sees something more in the evidence. She sees deeper meanings. I don't think she's ever said anything boring in her life."

"Would you wish to be like her?" he asked, his face puckered very slightly, as if he were not certain if he wanted an answer.

But he had asked. An evasion would be a sort of lie, and there had never been that between them. With every second, the answer grew more important. There was no sound in the room except the flickering of the flames. Her father reached for the fresh applewood. There was silence outside. It must have stopped raining.

"Yes, and no," she said at last. "I would like to be as diligent, which is up to me. And as brave. I've never seen her flinch from anything. And hardworking. That is up to me also." She was watching his face. He was listening, but she could not read his emotion. "Whether or not I have it in me to be as brilliant," she went on, "I don't know. But I will certainly try."

She gave a rueful little smile. She knew that what she was about to say was what he was waiting for. "But I don't think I wish to be as eccentric. And I either will be, because I can't help it, or I won't be, because I'm just not so highly individual as she is. To do eccentric things just to be noticed is absurd, and quite sad. Dr. Eve is entirely honest. I would like to be that, too, but I have no idea what that will mean . . . yet." She looked at him steadily, with a candid smile.

She knew what his question would be, if he asked it. Did she intend to follow her career to the exclusion of all else? Would she marry, if she received an acceptable proposal? She was past forty. What chance was there? She would marry only if she found someone she could love, who loved her as she was: a woman with a career and a passion, with a mind that had to be used to its fullest extent, in the endless pursuit of knowledge and justice.

A thought rushed into her head: she might not marry.

So, the answer to her father's question was probably *No, I would not*. But could she love anyone? Perhaps Daniel Pitt? She could not imagine it. She banished the thought, pushing it away, mocking herself for even allowing it to enter her mind. "I don't even know what tomorrow will bring," she said aloud. "Ask me again in a year. Now, what would you like for supper?"

He accepted this dismissal of the subject. Perhaps it was more painful, and closer to the surface, than either of them had assumed.

"I think there's some hot mutton stew with white turnips," he answered. "Cook mentioned something like that. And rosemary leaves fresh from the garden. Always gives it that extra flavor."

Miriam smiled. "Excellent, it's just what I would like."

That, at least, was true.

THE NEXT DAY started early. Miriam had expected to be in the lab before Eve, but she arrived at 8:30 to find her mentor in white overalls and busy at the sink, washing her hands as if she had just finished a job.

"Good morning," Eve said gravely.

Miriam did not reply. Instead, she asked a question. "Have you been here all night?"

"No," Eve replied, returning her stare. "I was in bed for most of it. Now, have you brought anything to eat? Because if you haven't, don't bother taking your coat off. Make yourself useful and get me some decent coffee and a couple of bacon sandwiches."

Miriam knew better than to argue, and so she turned and walked back into the street.

There was a considerable queue at the restaurant and she had to wait to be served. The boy behind the counter would have given her preference, but she would rather take her turn. She had eaten breakfast at home, but the bacon sandwiches smelled so good that she bought one for herself as well.

It was an overcast day, yet the wind was dry, and there was no edge to it. In fact, it was quite warm for February, often the harshest of months.

She walked quickly along the pavement, energy in her step, and arrived back in the morgue with the sandwiches still warm and the flask filled with scalding coffee.

Eve gave her a nod and a sudden, charming smile. "You'll get used to it," she promised.

Miriam wondered what she was talking about, exactly.

"Working real cases," Eve explained, as if Miriam had spoken her thoughts aloud. "With nobody watching over your shoulder to see if you're doing it properly. Nobody here to pick up your mistakes. So . . . you just don't make them. Lonely, isn't it?"

"You will check for them," Miriam replied, but suddenly there was a tremor of uncertainty in her voice.

"Sometimes," Eve said, still smiling. "But you won't know whether I'm going to or not. So don't rely on me. The whole purpose of your education has been to ensure you don't make mistakes. Although, of course, you will! For a while."

Miriam had no answer to that, so she ate the bacon sandwich. It was one of her favorite things. She had missed them while in Amsterdam, despite all the Dutch delicacies she had found there. This food was not only comfortingly familiar, it was very satisfying.

"What do you make of our slasher?" Eve said suddenly.

Miriam was taken by surprise. "Are you sure it was the same person?"

"Do you doubt it?" Before Miriam could answer, Eve said, "And don't you feed me my own words!" Her voice was tart. "Answer me honestly. I'm not testing you; I damn well want to know what you think."

Miriam sat up more sharply. Eve wanted her opinion! One glance at the woman's face and she saw that she was concerned. There was no light in her eyes, and certainly no glimmer of humor. "The wounds were made by some sort of blade, one with a serrated edge," she said thoughtfully. "The stabs were deep, and probably— at least the first one—made from behind. Whoever did it seems to have been between five-ten and six feet tall, pretty strong, and right-handed. But that's all very rough, and not a lot of use. It doesn't tell me what we're looking for. There are half a million people in London who would fit the right description. It's probably a man, but not necessarily. It could be a tall woman."

Eve nodded slowly. "What else?"

Miriam looked away. She did not want to say what she could see.

Eve was staring at her. "For heaven's sake, go on. This is no time to be squeamish."

"At least she died quickly, poor—" She stopped and took a deep breath. "Both victims fitted the same age description: between twenty and thirty. But one was dark, and one fair. Both were slender, of average height. The attacker might have known them, or he might not."

"And the finger?" Eve asked.

"Oh . . . yes," Miriam had been avoiding that piece of information; it was a peculiarly personal piece of mutilation. She found herself clenching her own hands protectively. "The left index finger of one woman was severed. On the other woman, it was the right index finger."

"What does that tell you?"

"A keepsake for the killer? The police didn't find the fingers. That's . . . disquieting. We're dealing with a madman."

"I suppose there's some point in stating the obvious," Eve said grudgingly. "At least it keeps it in mind. But why?"

"Why what?"

"Why an index finger, for heaven's sake?" Eve persisted. "Why not a thumb, or a little finger? Why not a ring finger?"

"I don't know! Perhaps it's because . . ." She paused for a moment—she knew Eve was going to say "Then find out!"—before continuing. "We'll point it out to the police, when they come to see us. They may have an idea, but I doubt it. One thing we can say, it was cut off after death. The poor girl didn't fight. She had no chance."

"Quite," Eve agreed, her voice surprisingly husky.

Miriam knew that, even after all these years, some deaths reached deep into Evelyn Hall's emotions. They exposed, if only for a moment, a pity she could not hide, no matter how extensive her procedural knowledge and professionalism.

Maybe Miriam never would be able to crush these emotions either. She wanted to—she certainly needed to—and yet she also knew it would never become simply a job, the kind where one got used to the sense of loss.

Miriam stared at the young woman and could not let go of the questions rushing through her mind. Why would the killer take the time to remove the victim's gloves and cut off a finger? Didn't this mean a greater risk of being caught? Had he taken the severed digit with him? Or had he simply left it, and the rain had washed it into the gutter, where it would eventually end up in the sewers and be eaten by rats? If he had not taken it as a keepsake, then perhaps it was a message? To whom? And why the left hand of one victim and the right of the other?

Then a thought occurred to her: Was one of the victims left-handed and the other right-handed? There was not much evidence to go on, but she was compelled to take a look at the bodies again. If she studied them closely, could she tell from the musculature of the arms which had been the dominant hand? And if the killer had taken the finger from the dominant hand, did that mean he had known his victims well? How else would he know which hand they favored?

Miriam thought about the people she knew and realized that, with perhaps half of them, she had no idea whether they were left- or right-handed.

IT WAS LATE morning when Ian Frobisher arrived at the morgue. At his last visit, Dr. Eve had been alone, and Miriam had not yet returned from Amsterdam. Now, only eight days later, she had a new woman working with her—and a new corpse.

"Inspector Frobisher," Eve said, looking him up and down. Today, he was very serious, and he looked tired, even this early in the day.

"Dr. Hall," he greeted her, with easy familiarity. Perhaps empathy came quickly when working on a case like this. Both victims were barely a year or two older than him.

Miriam watched him. He was around Daniel's age, twenty-seven. She wondered if he suspected that these women were the victims of the same killer.

Eve introduced Miriam. "Inspector, this is Dr. fford Croft. Just

qualified in forensic medicine, but very good. Taught her myself . . . at least, the last year or so. To be a pathologist takes a lot
longer than that."

Miriam smiled at him. She did not offer him her gloved hand,
still wet with carbolic. "How do you do, Inspector Frobisher?"

"How do you do, Dr. fford Croft?" He smiled back at her warmly,
easily.

He did not look or sound like a regular policeman. Too young
for the high rank, and too easy in his manner. He had an accent
very similar to Daniel's. Could he possibly be a Cambridge gradu-
ate also? If he was, what was he doing in the police? Had he studied
law, and possibly dropped out for some reason? That was none of
her business.

"I have information for you," Eve said quietly.

The inspector said nothing, his face impassive as he waited.

Eve turned to Miriam, as if to indicate that her student was prepared to deliver the promised information.

"Inspector," said Miriam. "Dr. Hall and I have judged that these
women were murdered by the same person."

Frobisher took one step closer to the body on the table and
looked at it, then back at her. "Are you . . . sure?" he asked.

"Yes," Eve confirmed. "We might have a madman loose. Definitely a man, I think. Or a very strong woman, but not likely. Can't
tell you much that's useful. Long, serrated blade, unusual shape.
Curved at the end."

"More curved than is usual?" he asked.

Miriam wondered why Eve wasn't mentioning the finger, but
said nothing.

"Most knives are curved only on one side, the cutting edge," Eve
replied. "With this one, the whole thing is curved. And used with
some skill." She made a cutting motion in the air, harsh and vicious, as if scooping something out, like the insides of a pumpkin.

Frobisher winced. "Anything else you can tell me about him?"

Miriam saw little hope in his eyes, and she felt sorry for him.

"His height, but only roughly," Eve replied. "But you can work that out for yourself. And his strength." She fell silent, but the angle of her head and the way she regarded Frobisher showed expectancy, as if she had something more to say.

He must have seen it, too. "And . . . ?" he asked.

"It was more violent than the first time," she answered. "More damage done with the knife."

He let out his breath slowly. "And the finger?"

"Ah, yes." Eve shook her head slightly. "The finger. That's where it gets interesting."

Miriam took this as her opportunity to share their ideas with the young policeman. They had not yet determined if the women were right- or left-handed, but this young man might find their suspicions interesting. "Dr. Hall and I believe that—"

Eve Hall cut her off with a quick shake of the head.

"What?" Frobisher asked curiously.

"Too early," said the older woman, her jaw tightly clenched.

Miriam nearly stepped back. Why had Eve interceded? Whatever the reason, she would ask her the moment the young man left the morgue.

"What I can tell you"—Eve continued as if there had been no pause—"is that the fingers of both women were cut off cleanly, and after death. The heart had stopped. Not a lot of bleeding, as there would have been had they been alive when the fingers were severed."

"So, it wasn't done as . . . punishment," he said. "Then what was it? Did he take it with him? Or was he trying to send us a message? We can't read it, if he was."

"It's possible the finger was washed down the gutter with the rain," Eve answered, throwing a quick glance toward Miriam. "Don't look for sanity, Inspector." She was very pale now, white around the lips.

"Not sanity, Dr. Hall, but I do look for a reason. Many lunatics have some reason in their minds, even if it seems insane to you or me."

Dr. Eve did not answer, which was unusual for her. Miriam knew that, even if the policeman did not.

"We'll let you know if we find anything else, Inspector," Miriam told him. "Do we have your police station telephone number?"

"I believe Dr. Hall has it," he said. "And thank you. We haven't much to go on at the moment. The killings were in the Chalk Farm area and Kentish Town. Sandrine Bernard, the first victim, was French—or at least she lived in France, in Paris—but she'd lived here for a while and was back to visit her grandparents. The second victim . . . we don't know much about her yet." He gave a quick glance at the woman on the table. "Her name is Lena Madden, and we think she lived locally, but she has no family in London. She was two years older than Miss Bernard, nearly thirty. No connection that we can find so far."

Miriam waited for Eve to respond. When the woman said nothing, Miriam asked, "Do you think he's a madman looking for opportunity, preying on someone who's vulnerable?" She hoped this was not true, because everyone was vulnerable, in one way or another. She needed to remain focused and professional and use her reason. Why, she wondered, did reason make things seem less frightening? Perhaps it gave the comforting illusion that they could deal with it or, at the very least, stop it from happening again?

"I'm sorry to say that we don't know yet," Frobisher replied. "If you do see anything, please let us know."

"But you are looking for a connection between the two women?" Miriam asked.

"It would help, yes. Beyond their age and physical resemblance, which we can see. But if there are other, less obvious, connections . . ."

She nodded.

Inspector Frobisher took his leave, and Miriam turned to Evelyn, who was still standing by one of the benches. She looked drained of all color.

"Eve, are you all right?" Miriam asked anxiously.

"Yes, of course I am!" she replied tartly. "Just a headache. Don't fuss!"

It was the first time Eve had mentioned a headache in all the hours, days, even months Miriam had worked with her. The younger woman did not bother to ask for reassurance; the tension in Eve's posture and the challenge in her eyes warned her into silence.

She turned back to continue the work she had been doing before Ian Frobisher arrived.

Four

"I DON'T KNOW," IAN Frobisher admitted. It was hard to say, because it had been more than a week since they had been called to the sodden Prince of Wales Road, with its overflowing gutters, to look at the body of Sandrine Bernard, the first victim. And now, only two days ago, a second body had been found, mutilated in exactly the same way.

"Well, you'd better think of something!" his sergeant replied.

Billy Bremner was the opposite of Ian in almost every outward way. He was shorter and sturdier, his hair verging on auburn—or, less glamorously, dark ginger—whereas Ian was tall, slender, and fair-haired. And there was Ian's voice, his choice of words, the easy way he wore his well-cut clothes; these also differentiated him from Bremner.

Bremner was from the industrial northeast, shipping and coal mining country. A wild coast with historic castles, some of them half submerged beneath the high tides of the North Sea, leaving only dark towers above the water. Bremner's grandfather had been a miner, his father a junior manager in one of the great northern steel mills that provided the metal for the shipyards of the area's industry. Billy's voice had the lilt of the north in it—and, at times, the highly individual vocabulary. He was a scholarship boy, both proud and ashamed of it at the same time. Proud because nobody had given him anything—he had earned it all—and ashamed because his grandmother could not even write her own name, although she could cook a meal fit for a king, and do so out of very little. He had described her to Ian as a plain, comfortable woman, indistinguishable in a crowd, except by those who loved her. Her smile was imprinted on Bremner's memory, although he rarely spoke of her.

And his boss, Ian Frobisher? He was from the soft south and Cambridge educated. He dressed and spoke like a gentleman. It was not an affectation; these things were as much his history as the north was Bremner's.

Ian broke the silence. "We followed every lead I can think of and looked at the bodies again, and as far as I have seen, we still have nothing. We've searched the rooms where Sandrine Bernard stayed and looked through the few books and letters she had." Frustration was evident in his face. "We've spoken to the landlady, and she can't tell us anything useful. She says that Sandrine was a charming, pretty, and very well-dressed young woman who paid her bills on time and was always polite. She was on an extended holiday from her home in Paris. She had no visitors, but went out quite often, and received several letters."

They had examined her belongings, one of the jobs Ian liked least of all. It seemed both sad and intrusive, but it was a necessary part of the job.

Now they had also looked at the apartment rented by the second victim, Lena Madden, searched her belongings, questioned most of her friends. So far, nothing was useful or offered any other avenues to follow, as far as they could see.

Both of the women were well educated. In fact, both had graduated from Cambridge University, a couple of years apart. They had studied at different colleges, and despite extensive questioning of people at the university, the police could find no indication yet that they had known each other.

"Then we aren't looking at it right," Bremner replied at last. "Even if the killer is barking mad, in his mind there's some connection here." He gave a shrug. "Unless, of course, they haven't been killed by the same flaming lunatic."

It was exactly what Ian had been thinking, but it still jarred to hear it said. He had been preparing himself for it, but he knew he would never be ready. "A much better choice," he said unhappily. "We've got two madmen on the loose, and they both suddenly appeared here, this winter. Right! They opened all the asylums, and forgot to tell us! Maybe they thought we'd figure it out for ourselves—eventually." He smiled to rob the remark of its sting.

"Did your fancy university freeze your brain?" said Bremner. "What about copycats?"

"How? The details weren't in the newspapers," Ian said reasonably. "You don't need a university degree to know enough to keep some details back. And don't tell me anybody here leaked the information. It would cost them more than their job's worth."

"You wish!" Bremner said with a bleak smile. "You wouldn't get away with that, anyhow."

"The threat of public disgrace would scare the hell out of them, though," Ian replied. For an instant, he relished the idea.

Bremner grinned, as if wisely resisting the temptation to answer.

"Copycats," Ian repeated. "I don't think so. There were things—" He winced. "Like . . . what was done to . . ."

"Last joint of the right index finger cut off," Bremner answered.

Ian froze. "That's it!" he said jerkily, excitement in his voice. "You've just done it! You're brilliant!" He hesitated, lowering his voice. "At least, you might be."

"Have you any idea what you're talking about?" Bremner looked confused, but there was a flicker of hope in his eyes. "Because if you have, please tell me."

"Damn it," insisted Ian. "Don't you see? On Lena Madden it was the index finger on the left hand!"

"Oh! Then perhaps he didn't care which hand it was," Bremner suggested.

"Can you write?" Ian asked.

"Of course I can damn well write," Bremner said sharply. "Better than you, actually. And I can even read my handwriting! Yours looks like you squashed a centipede on the page. Sometimes you can't even read it yourself."

"Because I'm in a hurry," Ian said, brushing this subject aside. "So, show me, how do you hold a pen?" He fished in his pocket, brought out a pencil, and handed it to Bremner.

Bremner took it and held it between his thumb and index finger, steadying it with his middle finger. "Just like anybody else holds it."

Ian raised an eyebrow. "Even if you're left-handed?"

Bremner passed the pencil to his other hand. Suddenly, his face filled with understanding. "You're saying she was left-handed? Does that mean something? Does it help? How?"

"Of course it does. Of all the people you know, how many are left-handed?"

Bremner shook his head. "I'm not sure. One or . . . maybe five or six. One in twenty? Actually, I have no idea. There are quite a lot of them. What . . . oh!" A sudden light dawned.

"Exactly," Ian said. "I don't know either. That's the point. If Lena Madden was left-handed, and Sandrine Bernard was right-handed, then the killer knew that."

Bremner stared at him and could not suppress a shudder, his thoughts clear in his face, but he said nothing.

"If they were attacked at random, because they saw something, or they reminded him of something, he wouldn't know if they were left- or right-handed," Ian continued. "But he did know . . . and how? Because he knew them! Not just a chance meeting. He knew them well enough to know which hand they wrote with."

"If that's what he was doing it for . . ."

"Have you a better idea?"

"No," Bremner admitted. "So, now we have to see what they had in common. We already tried that and came up with very little."

"Which only means we didn't find it. It's there," Ian said.

"We're looking into the past? And that's another problem," Bremner pointed out.

"What's that?" Ian asked.

"Why now?" Bremner replied. "If he's known them for some time, years maybe, then why kill them now? And slash them? That's vicious." He winced, as if seeing the injuries again in his mind's eye. "He could have stopped after the first fatal wound, but he carried on stabbing them. What made him flip his lid now?"

"God knows," Ian said bleakly. "We've got almost nothing to work with. And as you say, the victims don't appear to have anything in common, except they were both around thirty, and both women. One was English, one French. They both studied in Cambridge, but not the same subject or at the same time. Something must connect them in his mind, but I'm damned if I can see what."

"And that's going to be the first thing Petheridge asks you," Bremner pointed out, referring to their superintendent. "There must be something they both knew, both saw or heard. If it wasn't in the past, perhaps it's in the future? Something they were going to do?"

"Well, they can't do it now," Ian said bitterly. There were several moments of silence, then he spoke again. "Why does he go out in this downpour, anyway? Nobody goes out in this—not if he doesn't have to."

"Maybe he does have to?" Bremner suggested. "Which means his victims have to as well. Maybe it's the only time he can catch them alone."

"Then are they random choices?" Ian turned over in his mind all the possibilities he could think of. "People who work and have to go home alone? People who wouldn't be alone at any other time of the day?"

"And who would go home, whether it was raining or not," Bremner added.

Ian thought about it, imagined it: the cold, the drenching rain getting into everything, stinging your eyes, streaming down the back of your neck. You had to watch where you were stepping or find yourself splashing through a puddle or some gutter, your shoes soaked by the run-off. "You would look where you were going," he said aloud. "Not at the people around you. They wouldn't notice anyone else. You don't stop for a chat, even with someone you know well. You just call out something and keep going. That's why we can't find a witness who could identify anybody."

"And they're wearing hats to keep off the water, scarves up to their chin," Bremner added. "Damn it, I hate this weather!"

"I thought you'd be used to it, coming from the frozen north," said Ian, but it wasn't a real dig. He knew that Bremner missed the wide-open country he came from. That he loved the great mass of the mountainsides, wind-scoured, and the huge skies, the villages huddled against the earth, houses shoulder to shoulder. Mining villages where men had dug coal for generations, faced its hardships and tragedies, where families knew their neighbors. Most of them had never even been to a big city, let alone lived in one—or ever wanted to. Bremner seldom said so, but Ian knew that there was a part of his sergeant that missed the open skies, the exposed, bare hills, the familiar, harsh beauty of it. He once said it was like seeing the bones of the land heaved up to the sky.

Ian came from the flatter, gentler south, and he missed the fields and woodlands, the green slopes, the wild flowers of summer. Even so, he did not want to be a country policeman. He wanted to face what he considered the real enemy: the crimes committed in big cities, by people crammed too tightly together, the violent, the greedy. In truth, the only time he considered changing his life, returning to the country, was when he thought of Hannah, his little girl, living with Ian's parents. She was already a year old, a free-spirited and happy toddler. Ian sometimes wondered if she missed her mother, but then he reminded himself that Mary had died in childbirth—that the two people he loved most in the world had never had a chance to meet.

He pushed these thoughts away and pulled his focus back to Bremner. "So, are the victims chosen at random, or not?"

Bremner had worked with Ian long enough to know that his superior was thinking aloud, rather than expecting a reply.

"And does the rain set him off? Or is he just waiting for it, so he can catch them more easily?"

Bremner was sitting with his elbows on his knees. He looked up at Ian and gave an involuntary shudder.

The door opened and a constable put his head round the corner. "Superintendent Petheridge wants to see you," he said to Ian. "He looks . . . he looks like a rat that somebody absentmindedly kicked, sir."

"Right," Ian answered reluctantly.

He had been expecting this. He had hoped that he or Bremner would have come up with a new lead to follow, but his mind was tired and empty. Nevertheless, he must answer the summons. Petheridge would want a report, and he was entitled to one.

PETHERIDGE LOOKED UP when Ian entered the office. It was warm from the fire burning slowly in the grate, settling as the coal was consumed. If more fuel was not added soon, it would die. For Ian, this symbolized the whole case.

"Sit down." Petheridge waved an elegant hand toward the chair opposite him. That was a bad sign. If he expected Ian to be there long enough to sit, he obviously had a lot to say.

"Yes, sir." The chair's legs caught on the thin rug, and Ian had to lift it to pull it out from the desk.

Petheridge looked at him steadily, his smooth face almost without expression. He was a naturally elegant man, very pale, with light blue eyes and fair, almost white hair. He had a sensitive mouth, a rather long nose, fastidious. He frequently wore gray, never black, and his clothes were always well tailored, effortlessly graceful. He had accepted this promotion as his due, and had earned it, but now he made it known that he disliked the amount of paperwork it forced him to do. Ian watched Petheridge push police files away from him. Ian felt the same way.

"You're supposed to be the brains of the outfit, Frobisher," Petheridge said quietly. He seldom raised his voice, even when circumstances warranted it. "God knows, you've studied this case enough. Every time I see you, you're poring over more interviews. And now this second body! What have you got? Do you know any damn thing at all about this . . . this *rainy-day slasher*, other than the obvious? If you tell me one more thing any idiot could have worked out, I'll put you back on the beat. And don't tell me you wouldn't mind. You'd hate it like hell, because your family who put you through the best schools in the country didn't spend all that money to have you become Constable Plod!"

That was true, but Ian could not afford to answer back in kind. He ignored the insults; they were only expressing his own sense of futility. Ian could understand them, in a way: he had been privileged, and he was certainly aware of that. At the same time, he felt the burden of having to justify it. He felt as if he should have done better.

"Yes, sir," he answered. "I think so. That is, I have learned more. Both of these victims suffered the same mutilation: each one had a part of the index finger cut off."

"I know that!" Petheridge said sharply. "Don't tell me you just noticed it!"

"No, sir," Ian said, keeping his voice level. "But I have just realized what it might mean." He ignored the look on Petheridge's face. "On one of the victims, it was the right index finger, but on the other it was the left."

"And you just noticed?" Petheridge repeated, his voice incredulous and almost taunting.

"I don't know if there's a way the pathologist can tell if a dead person was right- or left-handed, but if they can, it will confirm my theory."

There was a sudden spark of interest in Petheridge's face.

"I think the killer cut off the index finger so the person would never use it again. Never write, for example," Ian explained. "Never play a musical instrument again, and never be able to point it at someone."

"Has it not occurred to him that killing them would accomplish that, without having to do anything else?" Petheridge's voice had become soft, very carefully controlled, as if he had suddenly seen a spark of hope he dare not fully realize.

"Yes, sir. But this man hates them. It's symbolic, sir. His way of saying that it was their sin that caused his rage." He leaned forward a little, just a few inches. "What I'm saying is, he knew them, sir."

Petheridge raised his hand, pointing a finger at Ian, and then they both stared at the finger, his right finger. Clearly, he was right-handed.

Petheridge took a slow breath and let it out. "Good. Yes, that makes sense. He knew both of them. So, find out what they had in common. What set him off? Why in the rain? We've got to find this bastard and stop him before he kills again. What are you going to do next?"

"Try to find the common thread, sir. Millions of people use their fingers for something special. What was it about these women that made them different? And the rain? Not sure, but I do believe he knows where to find his victims. I'll keep looking into their circle of friends, business acquaintances, and of course their pasts. See where their paths crossed and what, if anything at all, they still have in common."

Petheridge was listening closely, nodding. "At least we know now, if you're right about the fingers, that they do have something in common. More than the random misfortune of having attracted this madman's attention."

"Yes, sir."

"Then get on with it, Frobisher!"

Ian rose and stood to attention for a moment, then left the room.

IAN AND BREMNER walked to the local chippy and treated themselves to hot, freshly fried fish and chips prepared in the traditional style: straight out of the fryer, wrapped in a layer of greaseproof paper and then newspaper.

"I sometimes think that's all they're good for," Bremner said with a scowl, indicating the newspaper. "Got to have something to wrap your fish and chips in."

"Or roll them up and they're good for lighting the fire," Ian added, before stepping out into the street. "Looks like the rain has stopped for a while. What is it you called it—a February fill-dike? I thought a dike was a wall the Dutch build to hold the sea back."

"Never been to Holland," Bremner said, unwrapping one end of his fish and chips. He pulled out a hot chip and put it carefully into his mouth, causing him to draw in his breath sharply.

"Go ahead and burn yourself," Ian said jokingly, and then his voice became serious. "I've got to speak to the pathologists again. We need to know, if possible, whether the victims were left- or right-handed. If it doesn't equate with the mutilation, it leads nowhere."

Bremner took another chip and ate it more carefully. "This is one thing you people in the south do right: that's a really good chippy." He gestured toward the shop they had just left. "And a dyke is also a deep ditch, often between fields. A sort of run-off for extra water. You can drown in one," he said cheerfully.

Ian realized how much Bremner annoyed him at times. He did it on purpose, he knew that. And yet he also knew that it was a form of acceptance. For all their differences, they worked well together; much of the time they complemented each other, whether they wished to or not.

"Now, let's head for the morgue," said the sergeant, between mouthfuls. "When I've finished my lunch . . ."

Ian looked up and smiled.

THEY REACHED THE door to the morgue and stopped. Ian glanced at Bremner and saw his set jaw and steady eyes. He knew that his officer was afraid, not of anything in the room that awaited them, but of what would remain forever seared in his imagination. Bremner pretended to be a hardheaded, practical northerner, but the legends of the past, the heroes of myth and folklore, they were as real to him as great-grandparents, just beyond reach and one step past memory: a wordless poetry in the blood.

They glanced at each other, then Ian opened the door and stepped inside, Bremner following closely.

Ian had been here many times before, and it was always the same: bare, aggressively clean, as if nothing lived here, not even insects or germs. He could sense Bremner on his heels, so close that he would bump into Ian if he stopped suddenly.

A man in a white coat met them. They identified themselves, but the attendant knew them anyway, just as they knew him.

"Thank you, Joe," Ian said, then took a deep breath and walked into the hard, white light of a room with glass cases along the wall, each one filled with bottles and jars. There were steel tables and the soft sound of trickling water. It seemed to him like a monument to death, as if something were actually washing away blood and taking the memory of life with it.

Dr. Hall was standing by one of the tables. Dr. fford Croft was also there, both women wearing white coats that concealed and protected their clothing.

Ian noticed the burnished red of the younger woman's thick, curling hair, and how it was pushed inside a net to keep every whisper of it from getting in her way.

Dr. Hall spoke to Ian, her voice brusque. "Well, don't just stand there, young man! What do you want?"

"The women killed in the rain—" he began.

"Ah, yes, the *rainy-day slasher*," she responded with distaste. "What more do you want to know? Yes, they were both killed by the same person. No, I cannot tell you anything more about him than I have already. I say 'him' because it is unlikely the murders were committed by a woman, but not actually impossible. I have already told you his height—five-ten, within an inch or two— which I conclude from the depth, angle, and strength of the injuries. And the regions where the victims were struck, according to their height—"

"Is he left- or right-handed?" he interrupted.

"Right," she answered. "Not very helpful. Most people are right-handed. Some are ambidextrous. He could be one of them, but so far there is nothing to suggest it. It's hardly helpful."

"And the victims?" he asked.

"I beg your pardon?" Her eyebrows rose slightly, as if the question itself were dubious.

"The victims," he repeated. "Were they left- or right-handed? Do you have any way to tell?"

She took his point immediately. "Ah! The mutilation. You think it has a meaning? One left index finger, one right?"

He was surprised she was so quick to grasp his point. "Yes."

"And it will help you to know if they are left- or right-handed. Surely, they have friends, family, associates who would know for certain. What did they do? Don't you know that?"

"Only that they have no known acquaintances in common," he answered. "At least, none that we can find. We didn't ask if they were left- or right-handed; it only just occurred to me."

"Why does it matter?" Her face took on a look of sudden, fierce interest. "Do you know what the mutilation means? You have an idea!" She did not need to add that she had seen it in his face.

"Yes," he told her. "It's not what they do that's important; it's that whoever killed them knew whether they were left- or right-handed. Which means he knew them personally, and well enough to have noticed that. I don't know the dominant hand of most people I've known for years. Do you?"

"Ah." She let out a sigh, a peculiarly satisfied sound. "He knew them well enough to know that. How do you notice such a thing, usually? If you are looking for it . . . because you see which hand they write with, or paint with, or sew with. But writing is the most obvious. That is something you do in public, as it were."

"Yes," Ian said. "I hadn't thought of painting, but neither of them was a painter, as far as we know. But he knew them, I'm quite sure of that."

"Any other thing that ties them together?" This time it was Miriam who spoke. "Relatives? Interests? I presume you have tried occupations?"

"Yes, and there's nothing that we can find," Ian answered, addressing both of them. "They lived nowhere near each other. In fact, Sandrine Bernard was French, and she lived part of the time in Paris. She came over to London fairly often and spoke English extremely well—that is, good colloquial English. Lena Madden was from Gloucestershire."

Dr. Eve thought for several moments. "But they were both killed in London. Do you know where they lived? You must, by now. And no doubt you've spoken to their neighbors."

"Near Chalk Farm, not far from Kentish Town. Northeast from here," he answered.

"I know where Kentish Town is," she said tartly.

"Is there any connection you can suggest?" he asked. "We've looked into everything, spoken to neighbors, asked in local shops. People knew Lena, but were no help. They didn't know Sandrine, but she was only a visitor. Which suggests either the killer was waiting for her, and her arrival triggered the crimes, or the timing was random."

Dr. Eve seemed to be mulling this over for a moment. "I know there must be something; I just don't know what it is."

Miriam spoke again. "Hobbies?" she suggested. "They can bring the oddest people together, who care intensely about the subject; they have success there which they don't have anywhere else. Perhaps they both collected Roman coins, or butterflies, or listened to Beethoven concerts. People can sometimes get very jealous of each other. Such rivalries may seem petty, but if your hobby is your pride—the thing you devote your time to, where you excel—then your belief in yourself is threatened. It may be absurdly trivial to someone else. But to you, it is your identity—" She stopped suddenly, as if they had criticized her.

Dr. Eve turned to Ian, to see if he understood.

"You have to fit into the killer's world," Miriam finished. Her voice suggested that she spoke self-consciously.

Ian understood her. Perhaps he had been looking for what made sense to him, rather than exploring how the killer thought. If he used his own values as a gauge, he'd get nowhere.

The younger woman with the bright hair had opened a door in his mind and showed him a small, lonely world where perspectives shifted and things assumed utterly different shapes. Reasons formed where there had previously been none. And then they dissolved into smoke, obscuring the sense of other things, leaving a dark confusion so that nothing was recognizable anymore.

Was that what madness was like? Or was reason simply an illusion, whispered by the human mind with its need to form patterns, to see cause and result, holding on to the delusion of being in control, because that was the only way one's assumptions could be comfortable? He thought of religion, and how many people built their lives on the belief that a given action would promise a given reward.

"Thank you," he said to both women. "I appreciate your time. If you should come up with anything else, please let me know." He fished a card out of his pocket and handed it to Dr. Hall. And then, with a smile, he turned and left, Bremner following close behind.

"I suppose you know what you're talking about?" Bremner said when they were out in the clean, unsanitized air of the street, with the noise of traffic, movement, and living people.

"I think so," Ian replied.

"Good," said Bremner. "Because that one, Hall, she scares the hell out of me. Why does anybody, let alone a woman, choose to pick apart dead bodies? And that place . . . it smells of death . . . and cigar smoke." He looked at Ian. "Is that possible?"

Ian shook his head. He had no idea.

Five

Miriam watched with interest as the two young policemen left the laboratory. She had been home less than a week and was still new to working on current cases, as opposed to studying ones long finished. Everything mattered, as it always had. But the reality of a case where the bodies were fresh, where she studied people who had died violently and yet had been alive only hours earlier, was quite different from the corpses she had studied before.

She had grown used to an academic approach, knowing that the main purpose of the exercise before becoming certified was to discover what she knew, how accurate she was, and how skilled. At university, it was she who was being examined and judged. And she had passed with very high marks. Along the way, she had learned so much. One of those important lessons was that the presence of grief, humor, or pity had no part to play in the evidence given.

That felt so wrong to her. How could she not grieve over the pain, the terror that must have overwhelmed the victim now laid out on the slab in front of her, even if only for a moment? She had thought she would be good at remaining detached, sufficiently well trained to stick to the facts. And she was. But she also had to learn that feeling pity was all right. In fact, anyone who did not feel pity had no place in this work.

Miriam had also learned that a quiet, silent pity was one thing, while expressing fear was quite another—and that no matter what she felt, she could not express ambition. Her role was to uncover and relay the facts that science could deduce through the most rigorous testing, and to stick firmly to the subject, with no room for conjecture or supposition.

The subject here was not her feelings, but the tragic deaths of two women who had been living people, with passions and purpose, laughter and grief. Miriam did not matter: no one was watching to see that she got it right, or how quickly, or how precisely she did her job. What mattered was that she learned everything the corpses could reveal about the crime that had taken their lives. And then, of course, she must determine how it had happened, where, and by what means. All of this she must do by exercising her intelligence, relying on the knowledge she had gained during her studies, and gathering facts that could be testified to in court. There must be no ambiguity and, above all, no error.

Miriam had worked hard to be acknowledged in a field that, in England, was for men only. Evelyn Hall had broken through, but only because the men had not perceived her to be a serious rival; some had even regarded her presence in their field as an amusing novelty. She had proved her brilliance before they were able to look more clearly at who she was. It was her belief in Miriam, and her patience and influence in finding Miriam a place to study in Holland, that had made Miriam's qualifications possible. All of her professional dreams, her status as Dr. fford Croft, she owed to Evelyn Hall. She must not fail.

She looked across the table at Eve, who appeared tired. She never gave in to it, but over these intense couple of years, Miriam had come to know her too well not to recognize the signs. It was not the weight of work, because this work was mostly routine, merely a matter of confirming the cause of death when most of the facts were known. But this case was different. It hung over all of London. Even the young policemen who had just left were distressed by it. They all sensed an unreasoning violence and the anger that lay behind it, which seemed to be growing more intense.

Miriam asked the question that was at the front of her mind. She guessed it was at the front of Eve's as well. "Do you think it is one person responsible for both murders, in spite of there being no connection that we can find?"

Eve raised an eyebrow. "Perhaps we'll find a whole string of killers? Like Jack the Ripper and friends, striking again and again?"

Miriam was used to Eve's sharp tongue, and she seldom was cut by it. In fact, she normally gave as good as she got. "Then, if it *is* one person, there must be a connection. We just haven't found it yet."

Eve looked at her quizzically, that eyebrow raised yet again. "Any forensic ideas?"

"No, not yet," Miriam admitted. "I'm not even sure what to look for. But if the killer is the same person, the violence must have something in common. These women were killed in different places, at different times of the day, but both murders were committed after dark and in the heavy rain."

"That's easily understood," Eve responded. "He doesn't want to get caught! In the dark, and pelting with rain like the Great Flood, everyone is muffled up. I wouldn't know my own mother in those conditions."

"Then did he kill these women knowing who they were? Or if he didn't know them and killed at random," Miriam pointed out, "then he didn't care who died!"

Eve was tight-lipped as she shook her head. She reached for one of her cigars, which Miriam considered vile, clipped the end, then lit it. She drew in her breath and blew out the pungent-smelling smoke.

"Balderdash," she said vehemently. "Of course it's one person. What can we deduce from these victims? They have nothing in common that we've thought of. What have we not thought of? Religion. Politics. Some society that pursues a forbidden purpose, or at least one they prefer to keep private." A look of distaste crossed her face. "Some sexual aberration? Let's hope not!"

"There was nothing apparently sexual about the killings."

Eve remained absolutely still. "A very small blessing," she said. "But the hate is there, the passion, the violence." She stared directly at Miriam. "And it's increasing. Just in small ways. Our second victim suffered deeper cuts, wider. Studying them, I'd judge these wounds to be less directed. They may be deeper, but there's less cutting and more slashing. He's getting practiced at it. No hesitation now."

Again, Miriam voiced what she knew they were both thinking. "He isn't finished, is he?" But it was not a question.

"No," Eve agreed, "I'm afraid he isn't. But I have no idea what kind of person the next victim will be. If we're expecting him to hold to present form, it will probably be another young woman."

The women stood together in contemplative silence for a long moment.

"We do know something about these two victims," Eve finally said. "And if we are right in our deductions, then this mutilation has meaning. It isn't casual, or done by chance. He knows these people. He isn't hurting them so they can't do . . . whatever it is he imagines No, I'd say he's punishing them for something they've already done."

"We should look at their hands again," Miriam said. "The dominant finger is gone, but there might be something on the other fingers. Calluses, stains, anything that could tell us something about them."

"A hobby? A political belief?" Eve suggested.

"And what does the killer's passion come from?" Miriam continued, speaking her thoughts as they came to her. "What did these people do to him? Or what does he believe they did? Perhaps they broke something, or took something from him, made a fool of him . . . cost him something he cared about intensely."

Eve nodded. "So, let's look at the bodies again."

Miriam swallowed hard, as if there was something stuck in her throat. "Yes," she agreed. "There's nothing else waiting for us. Nothing urgent, that is."

It was a deeply unpleasant job. The bodies were still in storage because they were unsolved murders and, as such, they could not yet be buried.

The first corpse they inspected was that of Sandrine Bernard. She was brought in on a stretcher and moved to the autopsy table.

Eve lit an even more pungent cigar than the previous one. She lowered the sheet and surveyed the body, her scientist's face showing barely any emotion.

Nevertheless, Miriam knew what Eve was feeling. She had seen that expression many times before. And the way Eve's back became straight as a ramrod, her shoulders low and tight, as if she were preparing to withstand some immense pressure. In a sense, she was. Being a pathologist brought with it the powerful weight of responsibility, and Miriam knew that Eve felt it keenly.

But there was something else in Eve's response, and Miriam had seen this before as well. It was a depth of grief, perhaps remembered from some other time. Maybe, one day, Miriam would know its source, maybe not.

Miriam looked at the body of Sandrine Bernard again, bleached of all color now. The flesh appeared shriveled, like something that should have been on a butcher's block. The woman's face was drained of expression, her eyes closed. There was no one in that empty shell, nor had there been since they first saw the body, after the blood had been washed away.

Miriam looked more closely. The slash marks were bloodless, and the skin no longer looked like flesh. The woman seemed smaller than the five-four written on her chart.

Miriam and Eve stood on either side of the table and stared down at this lifeless entity who had once been a living, breathing young woman. Sandrine Bernard.

Miriam picked up the cadaver's mutilated hand and examined it again. The time she had first done this came back vividly to her mind. The body had arrived before she had returned from Holland. Eve had shown it to her as an outstanding case. Then, it had felt as if Sandrine had only just left: the fear and the pain were so easily imaginable. Now it seemed as if she'd been dead so long that she herself would not have regarded this cold flesh as her own. The finger had been hacked off at the second joint.

Miriam felt quite certain that Sandrine had bled to death quickly, in only minutes. Apart from the wound that had killed her and the post-mortem slashes, there were no other injuries. She and Eve had re-examined her closely, looking for anything that might later prove of interest, but they had found nothing that Eve had not seen the first time. That is, no injury of note, no broken bones, no surgery.

Sandrine Bernard had a scar on her leg that appeared to be a recent cut, probably from a fall. And there was a slight scar above her left eyebrow, almost invisible. There were corns on the little toes of both feet. Miriam felt for her, knowing only too well the pinch of fashionable shoes that were always a fraction too tight, which is why she had given up wearing them. No woman was glamorous when wincing with pain at every step.

She felt a sudden prick of tears. It was as if, for an instant, she had changed places with this woman. She blinked the tears away impatiently. Mourning her was not Miriam's job. Finding out what happened, and who had done this to her, was.

She looked up and found Eve staring at her. She gave her mentor a tight little smile and bent to focus on her work again.

How many other people had they done this with? Miriam knew that you could learn only so much from books, diagnoses, organs preserved in jars. You had to see an actual body that had belonged to a living person only hours ago, see how it all fitted together to form a pulsing, breathing human being with emotions, ideas, and people who loved them. Miriam's job was to stop feeling . . . and to think.

Eve had taught her that, and sometimes Miriam had needed great patience to get past the empathy. Even so, now and then there were those rare times when she had seen Eve's own rage and pity overwhelm her, and she had watched the woman retreat into her own imagination. Or was it memory?

It had taken several months of them working together in Holland before Miriam realized that the death of young women, especially those between the ages of eighteen and twenty-five, affected her mentor the most. Instinct had warned Miriam not to ask, not even to let Eve know she had observed it.

Eve's voice interrupted her thoughts now. "I don't see anything that we didn't see before."

They put Sandrine Bernard back into the ice chamber and took out the second body, that of Lena Madden, who had been found only a few days ago.

Miriam felt a sudden wave of defeat, as if they really should have prevented this. The look of faint surprise had left the victim's face. The spirit had long departed, and the body that lay on the slab, white and empty, no longer held anything but the memory of who she had once been. But even washed and impersonally covered in a white sheet, as soon as they began to re-examine her, they were struck again by the savagery of her wounds.

"What did he imagine she had done to him?" Eve said quietly. "The wounds to the two bodies are pretty much the same, and the hand is similarly mutilated. What did she do with that hand?" She turned over the right hand and looked at it more closely. The second finger had a very faint indentation. "Pen?" she asked, looking up at Miriam. "Did she hold a pen between these two fingers? Or was it a paintbrush?"

"We didn't find any paint marks on the women's clothes," Miriam replied. "If they were both artists, surely at least one of them would have had a spot of paint somewhere? And if they used oil paints, a splash of turpentine? Even the smell of it?"

"Perhaps they drew in charcoal, or soft pencil," Eve suggested. "Or sepia? And with watercolors, there would be no oil or turpentine. If she wore a smock, nothing would get on her clothes. I've been thinking about musicians. A pianist might not have any marks on her body we could recognize but would perhaps lose a brilliant career without a finger. Or what about a violinist? Could you hold a bow with a finger missing?"

"To cripple a violinist," said Miriam, "he would maim the left hand, the one that makes the notes, presses on the strings. In fact, it would make it nearly impossible to play any stringed instrument, or brass, or woodwind. God! What would we do without our hands? What a hideous thing to do, to deliberately cripple—" She closed her eyes and did not finish. It was not necessary. "Eve, we've got to find this monster. I'll tell that young policeman what we've determined. What's his name again?"

"Frobisher."

"Yes, Frobisher. I'll tell him he's right about the killer knowing his victims. That he's not attacking strangers. The police might be able to find out what these two women had in common, and figure out who else is on this lunatic's list! Every time we have a rainstorm now, I dread the sound of the telephone."

Eve seemed to grow smaller. She had forgotten to put out her cigar, and it lay on the counter smoldering, giving off a rank, offensive odor. "Put her back in the ice room," she said quietly. "We'll close this up. Won't take long. Then I'll drive you home. And don't waste your breath or my temper by arguing."

"It's not raining," Miriam pointed out.

Eve glared at her. "Not yet. Want to risk your life on the chance that it won't? You'll do as I tell you. I'm not wasting more than a year of my life, not to mention my skill, teaching you your job, just to have you throw it away because you think you're invincible! You aren't. You are flesh and blood, like the rest of us. Like these poor souls in the ice room!"

"Yes, Dr. Hall," Miriam said, feeling a wave of relief.

As soon as she got home, Miriam sought out her father.

Marcus fford Croft was the head of the prestigious legal firm that bore his name, and had experienced more than his share of cases involving murder. He was seated by the fire and looked up from the newspaper he was reading. "You're late," he said. "Not another murder by this creature in the rain?"

"No, Father." She gave him a quick peck on the cheek. "Nothing new. We keep looking at the evidence." She did not say *bodies*. "We learned a few things, but I'll tell you if it turns into anything. I'm going out to dinner this evening."

"You didn't mention it!" There was a note of challenge in his voice.

She had, she was quite sure of it, but it was not worth arguing about. Proving him wrong, questioning his memory, would not make either of them feel better. "Sorry, I thought I had. I'm joining Daniel at his parents' home."

"Oh!" he replied, although his expression was unreadable. "Well, enjoy yourself. And . . ."

She waited, but he did not continue. "And what?" she said at last. Then she wished she had not; getting drawn into a conversation with her father would make her late. "I must go and change into something fresh, something that doesn't smell like the dead!"

He called after her, but she did not want to answer—whatever it was.

She went to her bedroom, stripped down to her underwear, and then walked into the bathroom to wash. She wanted to be rid of the

taste and smell of corpses, even the memory of them and the imagination of what they must have suffered.

What should she wear? She'd had no time to think of it earlier.
No, that was not really the truth. She had thought, but reached no
conclusion, and so had banished it from her mind. Now she must
make a decision. Red, slim dress, but too low-cut, perhaps? No, the
color clashed with her hair. Or maybe it exaggerated her bright
auburn coloring too much. It had looked different in the shop, not
so outstanding on its hanger.

The black one was safer. Black was always safe, unless it did not
fit well. But this one made her feel predictable. From what Daniel
had said about his mother, the one thing she was not was predictable. Charlotte Pitt had never played anything for safety! From
refusing her parents' choice of a husband for her, to expressing her
opinions when they were socially unacceptable. After all, young
ladies were not supposed to hold opinions of their own! And, of
course, her major disobedience had been when she married socially
and financially far beneath her. Unlike her younger sister, Emily—
who had married extremely well, wedded to the wealthy Lord
George Ashworth—Charlotte had married a man who worked for
the police. From what Daniel had told her, Charlotte had been
poor for quite a long time, but she had never, ever been bored, with
either Pitt himself or her own life. And while Emily had suffered
the death of her husband, Lord Ashworth, and was now happily
remarried as plain Mrs. Radley, Charlotte was now Lady Pitt!

And what was Miriam? She was Dr. fford Croft. Always interested, always busy doing something she believed in passionately.
Did she want more than that? This was something she was not
prepared to consider—at least she would not give it a place at the
front of her mind, anyway.

She pushed aside thoughts of dressing safely, predictably. That
was surrender! She was too old to wear pastels; they would make
her look as if she were pretending to be something she was not.
No, she would wear the red dress, and to blazes with what anyone

thought! Besides, she had met the Pitts a year earlier and they seemed to be people who did not judge hastily.

The red dress fitted perfectly. Perhaps a little too perfectly. Without looking at her reflection yet again, she bade her father goodnight, went to the front door, and had the butler call her a taxi. She was an excellent driver and had a very dashing motorcar, but this was not the sort of event to which one drove oneself.

Miriam arrived at Keppel Street twenty minutes later and alighted from the taxi, grateful that there was a break between showers. She paid the taxi driver and walked up the path to the front door, ready to ring the bell. That was unnecessary. The door opened before she reached it and the bright, warm light shone across the step. It was Daniel himself who stood just inside.

Miriam had been introduced to Daniel by her father, the head of the legal firm for which Daniel worked, and had done for the last three years. He had come straight to them after graduating from Cambridge with an excellent degree, but of course no practical experience. Marcus had taken him on as a favor to Daniel's father, Sir Thomas Pitt, and had been well rewarded for that decision. Daniel was turning into an excellent lawyer. He still made mistakes. He probably always would, because he took on awkward cases, sometimes giving in to his emotions or convictions rather than using his mind. But he was learning. And he made new mistakes, not repeating old ones . . . mostly. He and Miriam had become friends, sometimes working together on a case.

She felt a wave of relief that it was Daniel who greeted her now: she would not have to explain herself to a servant.

"Come in," Daniel said, holding the door wider and stepping back.

As soon as she was inside, he closed the door, shutting out the night, the damp air, and the rising wind. He took her cape, and she suddenly wished she had played it safe and worn the black dress. The red was too striking, and certainly immodest. She felt like a splash of red paint in the middle of a watercolor of discreet and delicate shades. It made too much of her throat and décolletage, her white skin.

Daniel smiled. "You look lovely. So much alive, and I know you've been working hard all day. Are you happy?" It was a serious question and his look required an answer.

"With the work? Yes, I am," she said sincerely. "But, like you, I deal with things when they have gone wrong, sometimes very tragically wrong. But somebody has to sort it out. And so, yes, thank you for asking, I feel as if there is a long road of this ahead, leading to a place where I belong." She took a deep breath. "A place that matters."

He smiled. For a moment, it was as if they had not spent more than a year apart. It felt like those few days on the tiny island of Alderney, when they had worked together to solve a case. Although the situation had ended violently, with the deaths of good people, in her mind that time stood out like a pillar of brilliant sunshine in the middle of a storm.

As if Daniel had suddenly realized they were standing in the hall, and that surely his parents must have heard the door and would be waiting for them to go inside, he walked ahead of Miriam and opened the withdrawing-room door, stepping aside as she went in ahead of him.

It was a large room, and it was evident that it had originally been two rooms, now turned into one. There was only a slight trace of where the dividing wall had once been. There were bay windows opening onto the front garden, now closed off by drawn curtains. The back wall was broken by French doors that led outside to the rear garden. These doors were nearly hidden by floor-to-ceiling curtains of dark blue velvet.

Miriam welcomed the fire burning in the hearth and warming the large space. Above the simple carved mantel was a seascape, painted in soft shades of grays and blues, with splashes of luminescence in the seawater where ships rode at their anchors, the softer outlines of buildings nearly obscured by the dusk. Miriam stared at it. She had never seen anything so filled with peace.

Charlotte spoke, but Miriam did not hear her words. She was caught off guard, like a schoolgirl who did not know how to behave.

"I'm glad you like the painting," Charlotte repeated smoothly. "It has that effect on me, too. I brought it with me when I married Thomas. It was my parents who let me take it, and I've always been grateful. It's Dutch. I don't know whether it's an original or a copy, and I don't care." She smiled as she said it, and it was perfectly clear that she meant it.

Charlotte Pitt was quite a tall woman, an inch or two taller than Miriam, with thick wavy hair of a rich, dark brown hue, with auburn lights in it. Now it was also sprinkled with gray at the temples. Miriam could see where Daniel got his coloring from, and even a certain cast of his features.

"I wouldn't care either," she said aloud, speaking for the first time. "I'm so pleased it is loved." Immediately, she thought this a ridiculous thing to say, but it was exactly what she meant, and she saw Charlotte smile.

Miriam turned to Thomas Pitt, who was standing nearby. He was also tall, several inches taller than her own father. In fact, they were nothing alike at all. Marcus was a meticulous dresser who loved his cravats and velvet waistcoats of all shades. Pitt was very plainly dressed in clothes that, though probably tailored for him, still looked as if he wore them for comfort and not style. Daniel had told her it had taken Charlotte over twenty years to teach him not to stuff his pockets full of all sorts of odds and ends he would probably never need.

"Would you like a drink before dinner, Dr. fford Croft?" Sir Thomas asked, with a smile.

She found herself wavering a little. It seemed so odd that a man about whom she knew so much from Daniel should address her as *doctor*. But would it be too familiar if she asked him to call her by her Christian name? "No, thank you," she answered, then thought that sounded a little cursory. "I feel warm and comfortable enough just to be here."

Charlotte gave a little laugh of pleasure. "You are exactly as Daniel described you before we first met," she said to Miriam. "And congratulations on your victory over the establishment. They will have to take you seriously now." She looked at Miriam earnestly. "You have changed a little since we last saw you, though, ages ago. You have an air of gravity about you. You have learned how much you can accomplish, I think. Was Holland interesting? I've never been there, and I would love to hear about it. Come, sit down, and please tell us what it was like for you. Was it very different from London? Were your lodgings acceptable? I imagine you had to work very hard to fit so much into what you already know and identify what was different. Do they all speak English? Or is a lot of medical terminology a language of its own, similar enough in Dutch and English?"

"Mother!" Daniel protested, but with a smile. "Only five questions at a time!"

Charlotte shrugged gracefully and laughed. She looked at Miriam. "One at a time," she said meekly.

It struck Miriam that Charlotte was not simply being polite. Her face was alive with interest.

"A lot of the scientific language is more or less similar," Miriam replied. "But I did learn quite a lot of Dutch, just to make friends, and to talk of other things. They are very cosmopolitan, and English is an easy and fluent second language for so many people there."

The conversation moved easily from one subject to another. Charlotte seemed genuinely interested, and Pitt was also drawn in. They were making Miriam feel very welcome in their home.

Daniel sat to one side and spoke little. But every time Miriam looked toward him, as if she would draw him into the conversation, she found he was already looking at her. She wanted to know what he was thinking. Maybe he would greatly have preferred her to wear a less conspicuous dress? She almost looked as if she had dressed for a romantic affair, rather than for a friendship . . . or dinner with his parents! And there was the issue of being fifteen years older than Daniel, practically a different generation. She hoped desperately that Charlotte did not imagine . . . She could feel the blood burn up her face at the idea.

The maid came to say that dinner was served. Miriam assumed that Charlotte had not cooked it herself, as she would have done when she and Pitt were first married. Daniel had told Miriam tales of the years before he was born, as recounted to him by his mother, and of the maid they had had then. These were memories that warmed him, made them all seem so much closer, made Miriam laugh and occasionally cry. She felt as if she knew the family, but she must be careful not to say anything that would let them know that Daniel had shared such things. He would be mortified. Worse than that, he would never trust her again.

The meal was served and Miriam ate with pleasure. First, a very light vegetable soup, then roast lamb with mint sauce and winter vegetables. The conversation continued, and sometimes it was quite funny. She laughed easily with them.

"Now you are working with Dr. Hall?" Pitt asked her.

"Yes," she said quickly. "There is still so much for me to learn, and no one knows more than she does. Not only about medicine and forensic procedures, but about jurors and, in many cases, lawyers." She smiled across at Daniel and saw the quick amusement in his eyes. He knew how profoundly she admired Evelyn Hall, not only for her skills and the speed and agility of her mind, but for the courage she summoned to support her through all the battles. And for her honesty in the search for truth, which obliged her to acknowledge her mistakes and then go back over things, again and again, until the answer was undeniable. Dr. Eve had rescued more than one case for Daniel, pulling facts together, lining up the many elements of evidence, and making lucid, unarguable sense out of them.

During dinner, Daniel teased Miriam, although gently and over little things, and she found herself laughing. She teased him back, but only a little, stopping short of appearing too familiar, perhaps revealing how much he had spoken of his parents—especially his father—often without realizing it.

She felt Charlotte look at her and knew she understood. It was as if she had seen the same thing: the admiration and the pushing back a little, in case he revealed too much of himself. She felt the warmth creep up her face again. It was an acceptance, a kind of belonging she both wanted and feared. Was she somehow following a path Charlotte herself had walked? She pushed the thought away. It was absurd. She was allowing this to be too comfortable.

They returned to the sitting room and Miriam told them more about Holland and, inadvertently, how she was glad to be back in London, in spite of the rain. It rained in Holland, too, she observed, and probably all over northern Europe at this time of the year, but it wasn't London.

She was relieved that no one mentioned the killer the newspapers had dubbed the "Rainy-day Slasher." It did not need to be said that he had no place in this warm room, with its fire burning low in the hearth and its slightly mismatched furniture that was so comfortable to sit in. And, of course, the seascapes glowing on the walls, with the curtains drawn against the night.

They laughed together at the things they all understood.

Miriam had long known that Daniel was striving to be like his father, to have his rare, quiet authority and his ease of assurance. Thomas Pitt had made mistakes, and he had conquered them. He had earned the respect of his peers and the loyalty of his juniors. Naturally, Daniel wanted to be like him—and yet, at the same time, not mimic him. Miriam recognized this in him: when Pitt made a remark about the prime minister, Daniel drew in his breath, as if to agree, but then seemed about to make a rather pointed remark from a different point of view. Pitt opened his mouth as if to argue, then closed it again.

The moment passed.

Miriam understood perfectly. She did not meet Daniel's eyes, although she knew he was looking at her. She understood more than she wished him to know. She knew Daniel adored his mother, but she realized how much she herself did not want to be seen in the same light. She had no idea where she wanted to belong, and she was afraid of causing offense. Daniel's parents had welcomed her into the warm embrace of the family, and to reject the implied intimacy would embarrass him and hurt unbearably.

Charlotte turned to her and was saying something.

Miriam, lost in her thoughts, had not heard her. "I beg your pardon," she said.

Charlotte smiled. "Dr. Hall is a remarkable woman, so Daniel says," she repeated. "And from what I observed in court a year or two ago, she is both brave and extremely clever. I'm glad you have had such a mentor. Clearly, she believes in you."

Miriam felt herself blush. "Yes, it seems that she does, and I owe her my professional existence. It is an impressive reputation to live up to." That sounded arrogant in a way she had not intended. "I'm sorry, I meant to say that I will do my best to live up to her expectations, not that I will ever be likely to match her achievements."

Pitt smiled. His expression was charming and so natural that she found herself smiling back.

"I used to feel that way about Lord Narraway, when he was head of Special Branch," he told her. "But I could never be like him. I push hard to be the best I can be, in myself."

"I would like to be like Dr. Hall, but . . ." She was at a loss for words, uncertain how she had meant to finish the thought.

"But less eccentric," Daniel said for her. "At least, please don't smoke those god-awful cigars!"

"She smokes them for the smell!" Miriam explained. "It's because—"

He was laughing.

Charlotte frowned, looking puzzled.

"The smell of dead bodies, Mother," Daniel explained. "Self-defense, that's what it is. The older the corpse, the more pungent the smoke."

"Oh." Understanding flooded Charlotte's face, and then revulsion.

Miriam was about to chide him for such a reference, but she saw he was waiting for that, smiling at her. Suddenly, she cared about what they thought of her far more than she wanted to. She stood up, not quite certain what she was going to say, and saw with amazement that the clock on the mantelpiece showed a quarter to eleven.

Daniel stood up, too, although reluctantly. "You have an early morning? I'm sorry." He looked at his father. "May I take the car to see Miriam home? She can't take a taxi at this time of night."

"Of course I can—" she started to say, looking at Pitt. She nearly asked Daniel if he could drive now, because he had not been able to before she went to Holland, but she bit back the question. It would sound so patronizing. She was a very good driver herself, and he knew it.

"Of course you may," Pitt replied. "But I would rather like to take her home myself. I could drop in on Marcus. I haven't seen him lately." He turned to Miriam. "I won't keep him up late. Just to say hello. It's a good excuse, not to look as if I'm fussing over him."

Miriam had forgotten how close her father had been to Thomas Pitt only a few years ago. It was not by chance that Daniel had begun his legal career at fford Croft and Gibson.

There was only one answer to give. "Thank you," she accepted. Actually, she was pleased. She had enjoyed herself all evening, but now she wanted to retreat into polite, unemotional conversation. She turned to Charlotte to thank her for the evening, then finally to Daniel. There was nothing more to say, just "thank you" again, but she meant it more than ever before.

The evening had been a total pleasure, easy and comfortable, yet she still felt a tide of emotion shifting underneath. Not like the waves of the sea, but a deep, relentless current that moves far below the surface.

Six

DANIEL HAD EXPECTED to find Nicholas Wolford difficult, and he was not surprised to find him unhelpful as well. He could see why Wolford had lost his temper. His publisher had been careless in omitting a reference in his book. How else could a reader be certain that an account was consistent with how others recalled events?

Linus Tolliver, who had brought assault charges against Wolford, was making an issue of something that was not entirely Wolford's fault. It seemed to Daniel that the younger man had been spoiling for a fight, and in all likelihood was hoping to get publicity out of both the assault and the plagiarism accusations. Nevertheless, Wolford was extremely foolish to have allowed it to come to physical blows.

Daniel read over his notes. It did seem likely that Tolliver had lunged first, but the attempted blow had not actually struck Wolford. According to three different accounts, however, Wolford's blow had been both accurate and strong. The injuries had been more serious than Wolford had conveyed to Daniel. Not only was Tolliver's nose broken, but also his jaw and several teeth.

Daniel could not possibly advise Wolford to plead innocent. He considered arguing self-defense on his client's behalf, but that would be difficult to prove. The very best he could get away with was to urge his client to apologize, and to say he had not meant to strike so hard. Daniel might be able to argue—if the medical evidence did not make it impossible—that some of the damage from the blow was due to the fact that Tolliver was lunging forward to strike, adding all of his own weight to the impact of Wolford's blow.

But Wolford would still probably pay some financial damages. Tolliver was hurt badly enough to warrant that, and the fact that he had been temporarily disfigured would carry weight in his favor.

Wolford, on the other hand, was not hurt at all. A bruised knuckle was the worst of it.

Daniel decided to go confront Wolford with the weight of this evidence and offer the best advice he could give. He was not looking forward to it, so the sooner he got it over with, the better.

WOLFORD WAS AT home, as Daniel had expected. It was one of those miserable February days, with a gray light, fine drizzle, and wind gusting around street corners. No one would go out in it if they did not have to.

"Come in, come in!" Wolford said, opening the door wide.

Daniel stepped in gratefully and closed the door behind him. The house was dark, the hall paneled in wood, the sitting room lined with books, a fire burning in the grate. The air smelled of leather, paper, and wood smoke; he was grateful for the room's warmth.

"Well?" Wolford demanded, pointing to an armchair for Daniel before settling into another at the far side of the fire. "What have you got for me?"

Daniel was not looking forward to this. But at the very least, Wolford—as any other client—deserved his trust.

"You were unhurt, Professor. Tolliver did not even touch you. Except, according to all the witnesses, he lashed out first."

"Certainly. I told you that," Wolford said sharply.

"Indeed. But we will have to present an account of what happened. That is, other than your description of the events."

"Do you think I lie?" Wolford demanded

"No, I don't. But I know you and trust your word, whereas I don't know Tolliver. The judge hearing the matter won't know either of you."

Wolford conceded the point rather ungraciously. "So?"

"On the other hand, Tolliver was injured, and rather more seriously than you indicated to me."

"I broke his nose. Noses break quite easily."

"And his jaw. Plus he has had to have considerable dental reconstruction work done."

"Oh . . ." Wolford look temporarily disconcerted. "Are you sure that was because of me? It was weeks ago! Anything could have happened between then and now."

"Yes, I am sure," Daniel said patiently. "And so were the doctor and the dentist who attended him."

A shadow of anxiety crossed Wolford's face. "Was it very expensive?"

"Not for the work the dentist had to do. Tolliver will need to have three false teeth on a plate. The nose will heal by itself."

"That'll put him off accusing anyone else of plagiarism," said Wolford. "He tried to ruin my reputation! He wanted to get me thrown out of the university." His voice was rising in outrage, and there was a sharp note of fear in it.

"Yes, it certainly looks like it," Daniel agreed.

"Are you questioning me?" Wolford was now really angry. His eyes were blazing and his shoulders were hunched, as if preparing to fight. He made as if to rise from his chair.

Daniel was startled, then realized he should not have been. He already knew that Wolford had an unruly temper, and now here was the proof, threatening to lunge at him. "No," he answered, "I'm not. But do you plan on hitting me, too?"

Wolford crumpled, his body slumping back into the chair. "No, of course not. What do we do?"

"We have to argue injuries and reparations," Daniel said, measuring his words. "From the witness responses I have seen, at least half the force of your blow can be explained by the fact that Tolliver was lunging toward you. Had he not been, I think his teeth might well not have been broken."

"Can you argue that in court?" Wolford said eagerly.

"Not really," Daniel replied. "If we can get away with a sincere apology for breaking his nose, and for contributing to the breaking of his teeth, I think that will be the best we can do."

"But he accused me! He—"

"Professor!" Daniel said sharply.

Wolford froze.

"You need this settled, with as little publicity as possible. Cambridge will not like this. We need to make it disappear, and as quickly as we can; the last thing we want is a long, drawn-out court case. You need—and believe me, I use the word intentionally—you *need* to act with as much dignity and grace as you can. If you quarrel, or refuse to accept any blame, it could still ruin you. Take my advice and don't be tempted to go out in a blaze of glory. You'll leave behind a heap of ashes containing the embers of a truly unique career. I still remember your classes that I attended. You gave me a love of history that I will follow up one of these days, when I'm not fighting in court. Don't throw that away. You're cleverer than that."

Wolford stared at him.

"If you have academic rivals," Daniel continued, "they'll use your temper to crucify you. Don't play into their hands."

Wolford sat quietly for a few moments, then reluctantly nodded his head. "Yes," he said slowly, as if trying out new and complex words. "Yes, I see . . ."

DANIEL TOOK A chance that Ian Frobisher might be at the police station, and he was lucky.

Ian looked up from his desk and the pile of papers scattered across it. "What?" he asked with a very slight smile. "You fed up with Wolford? He's not that bad, Daniel. He's just—awkward. He tends to misunderstand."

Daniel pulled out the chair opposite Ian and sat down. "No, he's being quite reasonable. Honestly, I think it was at least as much Tolliver's fault. He threw the first punch and missed. According to the witnesses, his momentum propelled him forward, right into the path of Wolford's fist."

Ian looked surprised. "Really?"

"Wolford says he'll apologize and pay something toward the dental bill."

Ian smiled. "Thanks. Now, would you like to solve this one, too?" He tapped one finger on the pile of papers in front of him.

"What is it?" Daniel asked.

"Some lunatic is killing and slashing women, leaving them to die in the street, in the rain," Ian replied.

"I . . . I saw one of the bodies," Daniel said quietly. "I dropped by to see my friend Miriam fford Croft. She's working on these cases with Dr. Hall." He looked at Ian a little more closely. "But perhaps you know that?"

"Indeed I do. But there's very little to work with except for the mutilation of the hands. Index finger cut off at the second joint. One right, one left." Ian was tense, his face lined with thought and a mixture of grief and frustration. "What does that mean? Who cuts off fingers? Is that a fetish of his own?"

"Do you think these women represented someone who had offended him somehow?" suggested Daniel. "We say *him*," he quickly added, "but does it have to be a man?"

Ian thought for a moment. "The odds are pretty heavy that it is. Most violent personal attacks are committed by men. What are you thinking? Rivalry? Revenge?"

"I wasn't really thinking," Daniel admitted, "just feeling the horror. And wondering how Miriam could deal with it. Having seen one of the women's bodies, I still feel an overwhelming pity. One minute they are alive, full of thoughts, ideas, emotions. The next it's just an instant of alarm, unbelievable pain, and then nothing."

"You have too much imagination," Ian said. "Always did have!" He smiled suddenly. "You haven't changed. I'm glad you took Wolford's case. Thanks."

"I might not win, but I think he has a good chance," Daniel replied. "If he manages to keep that temper of his in check." He meant it, and he knew better than to promise anything.

"I wish I could be as optimistic about my case," said Ian, the smile vanishing from his face. "I dread hearing that there's been another killing. I suspect the victims are connected, not chosen at random. But is he attacking individuals he knows? Or is he choosing them because they fit a certain type?"

"About the fingers," Daniel said. "What does it mean? If you knew that, you might have the answer. Or at least some idea of the next step."

Ian gave a bleak smile. "I know," he replied. "If only . . ."

Seven

"I HAVE PUT IT together the best I can, sir," the constable said to Ian apologetically. "The purse was pretty soaked."

"Thank you." Ian took the now dry piece of paper from the young man.

It was backed with another piece of heavier card, which was clearly holding it together. It had been sodden for some time, but the heading was printed and still legible, even though the body of it was nothing but blobs and smears of ink.

"St. Wilfrid's Church, Adelaide Road, Chalk Farm," Ian read aloud. He looked up at the constable. "This was in Lena Madden's purse?"

"Yes, sir. At first it looked like nothing much. Don't know if it'll be any use." He looked hopeful.

"It could be," Ian said, with a lift of the spirits. "The congregation might know her. In fact, she might even have confided in the vicar, if she was aware of any kind of threat. We're struggling to

find any connection between the two victims, and this might be it."
The voice of reason moderated his hope a little. "It's worth trying.
Thank you, good work."

He left the police station half an hour later and walked along
the street briskly, eyeing the clouds moving across the river from
the east. So far, they had not dulled the day. He was heading for the
underground railway station to get the train to Chalk Farm, only a
few blocks from the vicarage on Adelaide Road.

Lena Madden might have made a chance visit to the church, but
possibly not. With any luck, the vicar knew her. People often attended a service far from home, where they would not run into
people who knew them, perhaps seeking a little comfort without
facing intrusive questions. The police had searched her flat in Is-
lington and had found nothing of help. There was no Bible among
her books, or anything else to indicate her beliefs. Who had she
been? What had mattered to her? The search through her belongings, including her address book, had revealed very little about her.
And the few personal notes she had kept, in neat copperplate handwriting, were testaments to her education but were not in any way
contentious. She seemed to be well thought of by those who knew
her.

He went down the steps and caught the next rattling, roaring
train that wound its way through the endless web of tunnels under
London. He found himself smiling for no reason. Perhaps it was
this feat of engineering that always astounded him, in both its arti-
ficial light and its unnatural warmth, as the train raced from one
station to the next, before he finally ascended into the fresh air,
miles away from where he had started. Chalk Farm was one of the
nicer outer suburbs of London, and the station was quite close to
his destination. In fact, he could already spot the spire of the church
nearly two hundred yards in the distance.

He turned in to Adelaide Road, a wide curving street with handsome houses on both sides. They had neat winter gardens cut back,
showing the occasional holly bush or laurel, still green, and lots of

well-turned earth ready for spring planting. The church was very easy to find because of not only its soaring spire but also the dark ring of yew trees around it. There was a large, handsome grave-yard, very old and filled with gravestones, a few of them carved with names dating back centuries. Marble angels graced the area, their white wings shadowed by the dark towering trees.

Ian turned in at the path leading to the vicarage's front door. He knocked and was about to knock a second time when it opened, and a very handsome woman stood in the entrance. He judged her to be somewhere in her thirties. Her face was strong and intelligent, with remarkable hazel-green eyes. Her hair had a heavy natural curl and was so soft it was falling out of its pins.

She looked Ian up and down curiously. He was not in uniform, so there was no visible sign that he was a policeman.

"Good morning, ma'am," he said. "My name is Ian Frobisher, inspector of police, and I'm looking for some help." He smiled apologetically. "We have reason to believe that a young woman, possibly in some distress, may have come to your church recently." He saw her face change and immediately fill with pity. "We know very little about her. Anything you can tell me would help." When the woman did not respond, he added, "I'm sorry, but she was re-cently murdered."

"Oh dear. How dreadful. But what makes you believe we can help?"

"She had an order of service for St. Wilfrid's Church. We won-dered if you had noticed her? Or even if she had sought out the vicar for help or advice."

Without speaking, she pulled the door wider open and stepped back.

"Thank you." He followed her into the wide hallway filled with coat stands, hat racks, and a handsome mirror above a table littered with newspapers and unopened mail and flyers for various events. He was briefly aware of the pictures on the walls, only some of which seemed to be church related. No angels, no saintly-looking past bishops or notable martyrs. He found himself immediately feeling more at ease.

The woman closed the door against the bitter cold outside, then offered him her hand. "I'm Apollonia Rhodes, but everyone calls me Polly. You'll be here to see my husband, no doubt. But short of confession and the like, I may be of help to you." She saw his confusion. "Richard is blind," she added. Then she smiled slightly. "He hears things most people don't, shades of emotion in a voice, hesitations and things like that. And he isn't swayed by all the small visible things that affect most of us: a pretty face, a warm smile. They don't mislead him. Voices can tell so much, you know." She smiled and glanced at her own skirt. "One's choice of clothes can also reveal a great deal, not only about tastes, but other things as well, especially to another woman." She smiled again, as if to rob the words of any arrogance.

He decided at once to accept her offer to speak. He could always ask the vicar to speak to him alone—if indeed they knew Lena Madden. Were they already aware of her death? More likely she had not even spoken to them, just slipped into one of the back pews, finding the familiar comfort of the church. Each church was in some way unique, but they all held a sense of peace, an expression of timelessness, the essence of hope and grief, earnest prayer for a hundred things. At their heart was the same need for comfort, the belief that there is a higher power, something that endures after we've gone.

Polly Rhodes gave a sharp rap of her knuckles on the drawing-room door and then opened it. "Richard, there's a young policeman here who is investigating the murder of . . ." She glanced at Ian.

"Lena Madden," he supplied.

"Lena Madden," she repeated. "She had an order of service from our church. They know very little about her and thought we might be able to help."

Richard Rhodes was a big man. Sitting down, he did not look as if he would be particularly tall, but he was generously built, and his face had strong but gentle features beneath a mass of wild black hair that was just beginning to show some gray at the temples. He did not wear glasses, and to look at him quickly, there was no way of knowing that the large blue-gray eyes were blind. Certainly, there was no sign of injury. The only thing that gave him away was that, when he looked in Ian's general direction, he did not meet his gaze.

A black and white dog of no particular breed, except perhaps a trace of border collie, stood up and wandered over to inspect Ian.

He offered the back of his hand for the dog to sniff. She seemed satisfied and returned to her place at her master's feet, beside the fire.

"Excuse Dido," Richard said. "She's come back to me, so you must have passed inspection. Police, Polly said?"

Polly indicated the other chair near the fire, opposite her husband, and Ian accepted it with a nod of thanks.

"Inspector Ian Frobisher, sir." He sat down. The chair was firm and extremely comfortable. He would imagine years of parishioners coming here for advice, comfort, forgiveness, or simply a short break from the burdens of day-to-day life.

"Well, Inspector, what can I help you with?" Rhodes asked.

Polly sat down a little behind them, so as not to be in Ian's direct line of sight.

"Lena Madden, sir." Ian was about to give a brief description of her, then stopped himself in time. "Other than knowing she was in her late twenties, we don't have much information about her." That sounded very bare, but all he knew for certain was what he could see. He had no idea what her voice was like, whether it was loud or soft, or if she had any regional accent. Some people were so skilled at such recognition that they could place a person within a few miles of their hometown.

"I remember her," Rhodes said thoughtfully.

He had a beautiful, rich voice, and Ian could imagine it filling the church with comfort and authority. It would be such a disappointment if he had nothing of any significance to say, but he could probably make even the most familiar phrases sound important.

The vicar turned toward his wife. "She is the young woman who came in for tea a couple of weeks ago. She only stayed about half an hour, but she was very memorable. Frightened. What did she look like? I didn't ask at the time, because it seemed unimportant. But Inspector Frobisher might like to confirm that it was her."

"Of course," Polly agreed. "Average height and build. Typical English sort of fair hair, more or less mousy, but thick and a nice wave to it. Very soft. And perfect skin. Fair, blemish free, and with a faint color in her cheeks. Nice hands. Very ordinarily dressed. Looked as if it all took no effort. I had the idea that she might be studious, clever. I don't know whether that's true or not."

Ian remembered the body vividly. The white, blemish-free skin was indelible in his memory. When he spoke, his voice was choked. "That sounds like her." He looked back at Rhodes. "Can you tell me anything about her, sir? I don't know how long the confidence lasts between minister and congregant after a person is dead. But if we don't find out who killed her, he may go on to kill again. I'm afraid she was not the first, and her death was even more violent, so there may soon be another victim."

He watched Rhodes's face become pinched with grief, and he regretted being so direct. But what the vicar had to say might make a difference of several weeks in their investigation and determine how quickly they caught the man. Perhaps even whether they caught him or not.

Rhodes turned to his wife. "Did you know that, Polly? That there had been two murders like this? Was the other victim a young woman also?"

"Yes," she said quietly. "I'm afraid so. But we didn't know the other girl. The newspaper said she was French, from Paris. That she only came here to visit friends. At least, that's what they reported."

Rhodes shook his head. He turned back to Ian, as if he could see him. "Polly will make us a cup of tea. I expect you're cold. You're not from the local station, are you?" It was not really a question, more of an observation.

"No," Ian agreed. "A little more central, a couple of stops away on the underground. And thank you, I'd love a decent cup of tea." He smiled at Polly. "The stuff at the police station is drinkable, but barely."

"Of course," she said, as if understanding that her husband's offer gave him time to be alone with Ian, perhaps confide something this situation made necessary—something that he would rather his wife not hear.

As soon as she closed the door, Rhodes turned to Ian. "She was a very serious young woman, Inspector," he said quietly. "And she was definitely troubled by something that had reminded her of a situation a few years back, for which she still felt a sense of guilt. She did not tell me what it was, except that she was young and uncertain of herself, going with the crowd because she wanted to belong. Not an unnatural thing, at any age, but especially when you have not learned to know yourself yet, and very much want to be liked." He smiled a little ruefully. "You want to be exceptional, never mistaken for anyone else, and yet, at the same moment, you want to be like everyone else. You want individuality and anonymity at the same time, and do not realize that you cannot have both. At least, not at once. You end up, of course, just the same as most of your contemporaries, all trying to be different in the same way."

Ian could remember that, with embarrassment. He had studied modern history without any particular career in mind. It had disgusted his professor at the time, Nicholas Wolford, who had thought him capable of far more. In fact, Wolford had told Ian that he had an obligation, with his fine mind, to make the best of it and carve out a career that could end in government, as a member of parliament, eventually with even higher office. "If we do not get the best people in leadership, there is no hope for us," Wolford had lectured him. "Intelligence and the opportunity for a fine education are not gifts without obligation, Frobisher," he had insisted. "Remember the parable of the talents! God, or fate, or natural justice—whatever you like to call it—will demand to know what you have done with what was given to you, and not to many others!"

Ian realized that Rhodes was speaking quietly, his voice rising only slightly above the comfortable sounds of the crackling fire and the gentle snoring of the dog, who had fallen asleep so close to the fire as to be in danger of singeing her fur.

"She was troubled by how she had behaved," Rhodes went on. "I think acknowledging it helped. You see, the person she had wronged was no longer alive. I pressed her on that, because I felt that it was the key to her distress. I was right. Her friend, the poor soul, had been in deep trouble, and instead of support, the people she thought to be her friends had accused her of some sin. Lena did not tell me what. It hurt her too much, and I feared if I pushed her, she would stop talking to me altogether." His face was full of doubt, as if he now thought he might have been wrong.

"Did you ever find out what happened?" Ian asked. "And why she would come to you now, if this happened some years ago?"

The vicar turned his face slightly away, as if aware that Ian might read his expression too clearly. "I asked her, and she wouldn't tell me. But there was a young woman who died in terrible circumstances. Very—" He shook his head and his face showed signs of deep distress. "May she rest in peace." The last was more of a prayer than anything directed to Ian.

Ian was startled. He drew in his breath to speak, but Rhodes cut in.

"No," the vicar insisted. "It is not some criminal case from the past, unfinished business for the police. Just the casual cruelty that people can so easily sink to. Fear, ignorance. The need to belong. At least, that is what I gathered. Lena seemed to feel better for having acknowledged it. Guilt is often like that." He gave a gentle, bleak smile. "That is part of any pastor's job, Inspector. To help people face guilt and deal with it. To stop lying to themselves. It gets rid of all the increasingly tortuous excuses as to why it was not your fault. It hurts less than you think it will to say, 'Yes, I was wrong.' Confession gets rid of the lies and allows you to say, 'I'm sorry.'" He gave a slight shrug of his shoulders. It was a gesture full of regret. "Then you can put your burden of guilt down. It doesn't change anything, at least not for a while, but it does get rid of lying to yourself. It's surprising how hard that work is. The lies inside you send out tendrils that wrap themselves around other things and stifle them, too. And all the while you still hate yourself, because inside you know they are lies."

Ian's mind went back to his school days and their chaplain. He had not liked the man, but he had respected him. "Still, it doesn't get you out of paying the price," he pointed out. "If there is still a reckoning, something that needs to be cleared up."

"If there is, then you are fortunate," Rhodes answered. "Because so often by the time you acknowledge it, it's too late to pay."

"Is that what Lena Madden felt?"

"Undoubtedly, since her friend was dead. I don't know that Lena did anything to cause that, but she certainly did not prevent it."

"Did you say she was frightened?"

"It was an impression," Rhodes corrected. "She did not say so. And I cannot tell you what she feared, if indeed she did. It may have been facing the others involved, or one of them specifically. She didn't tell me. Perhaps it required confessing to someone else, someone whose opinion she valued. That is always difficult. Some people are more forgiving than we expect, and some a great deal less."

Sadness was clear in his face, and Ian could not help wondering if he was thinking of someone, or some instance in particular.

"It's like lancing a boil," Rhodes added, smiling with a downward curve of his generous mouth. "The day comes when it has to be done. I think Lena had come to that day. And before you ask, I have no idea why."

There was a light tap on the door, and before Ian could jump up to answer it, the door swung open. He saw Polly pick up a tea tray from the table in the hall, then bring it into the room.

"All right, Dido," Polly said, as the dog heard her and sat up. And, probably more importantly, smelled the faint, delicious aroma of ginger cake.

Polly set the tray down, smiling at Ian. "Sorry, but she thinks she's going to be included in anything to eat, or any errand that involves going for a—" She stopped abruptly, avoiding the word that was guaranteed to excite Dido. "You can guess," she finished, with a rueful expression.

"Of course," Ian replied, relaxing completely at last. "And I presume she's right?"

"Naturally. Do you take milk?"

"Yes, please, but no sugar, thank you."

"And ginger cake?" Her eyes were bright. She knew what his answer would be as well as she knew the dog's.

"Yes, please," he repeated, looking not at Polly but at the dog, who had come from her place by the fire and approached the tray. She sat down obediently, as if she had been told to.

Polly cut a slice, a thin one, and put it on a plate, and then set the plate on the floor for the dog. The second slice, thicker, was offered to Ian, and the third to Richard, placed on the corner of the table nearest him. His hand went to it immediately, and Ian presumed it was always put in the same place.

The tea was hot, fresh, and fragrant. The ginger cake was delicious, perfectly moist, probably baked yesterday.

It was all reassuringly comfortable. Had Lena Madden sat here, maybe in this room, just days before her death? Had she unburdened herself to this amiable vicar, and then left and walked away to meet her fate? And was she less anxious after her visit when, in fact, she should have been very much more afraid?

Eight

ONE DAY LATER, sitting in Marcus's office with the papers before him on the desk, Daniel was finding it hard to keep his mind on the assault case of Nicholas Wolford. He was reporting to Marcus as head of chambers, but he was anxious to get back to work.

Ian Frobisher had told him about the knifings in the rain, and the newspapers were referring to the culprit as the "Rainy-day Slasher." Daniel wished he could be of help to Ian, but even more so to Miriam. It was a terrible case for her to begin her professional life with.

As for the charge against Wolford, there did not seem to be much to decide. It was a matter of Wolford's self-esteem. Daniel was seated across from Marcus and informing him of the situation, but only because it was a matter of professional courtesy. He expected Marcus to advise him, and he wasn't disappointed.

"You must be careful," Marcus warned. "Don't take it too lightly." He gave a small gesture of distaste, then sighed. "It looks like time wasted, but it still needs handling with care. There could be things about the relationship between Wolford and this man Tolliver that you do not know. Be prepared for Tolliver's people to dig up something more powerful at the last moment. Something grubby or dishonest. They'll maintain they've just discovered it, even if you can prove they knew it all the time. And they'll be prepared to rebut your claim, so all the justification in the world will do you no good. Wolford has a good reputation for scholarship, and he can fall back on that, but so has Tolliver. Or, to be more accurate, nothing seems to be known to the discredit of either party. I can say this because I've made appropriate inquiries . . ." Marcus hesitated. His face registered that he was uncertain whether to make light of these suggested legal maneuvers, or to warn Daniel more specifically of the traps he might not see in time.

Daniel was caught off guard by the disclosure that Marcus knew about Wolford. "You've heard of him?" he asked in surprise. "I didn't think . . ." He had been about to say that he didn't think Marcus was interested in modern European history, particularly the outbreak of the revolution in France, followed by uprisings all over Europe. The political upheaval of 1848 was before Marcus was born, but Daniel calculated that his parents would have seen the devastation. "I didn't think it interested you," he finished.

"Doesn't, in historical terms," Marcus replied. "Only as a fascinating study of human nature, and how the protesters ultimately became the very oppressors they rose up against."

"Is that what Wolford concludes?" Daniel asked, trying to remember back to his university days. At the same time, he avoided glancing at the clock, a reminder that the day was rushing by and he had much to prepare for this case.

Marcus shook his head. "When you get up in court to ask a question, you have to think of everything. There are twelve jurors to convince, not to mention opposing counsel to outwit. What's your man like? What's the court going to see when they look at him, eh?"

Daniel thought about this for a few moments. He visualized

Wolford's face, his demeanor, the very precise way he spoke. How he habitually searched for just the right words. "They're going to see a man who takes his writing very seriously," he replied. "A man who has never before been accused of plagiarizing anyone else's work, and whose thoughts have been considered original until now. Wolford's opinions are consistent, although I will have to work hard to demonstrate that, and do so without being boring, or seeming to patronize the jurors. I don't want to make them feel as if he comes from a different world, and is in no way like them. Of course, he had no right to hit Tolliver, but Tolliver had threatened his honor, even his career, which depends so much on reputation."

And wasn't that what this case was really about? Not a fist to the jaw, but a black stain on a man's hard won reputation. Daniel needed to make it sound like a threat anyone could understand.

"When I show the court how this man's career is threatened by being accused of stealing someone else's ideas, they'll understand why he reacted as he did. The jury also will learn that both Wolford and Tolliver had the same source material, available to anyone, and they drew the same conclusions from it, independently of each other." He shrugged very slightly. "Of course, that explains Wolford's outrage, but convincing the jury that an assault was justified is a different matter. They both lashed out, but only Wolford connected. That was lucky for Tolliver—though, of course, he came off worse physically. In any case, a fine levied against Wolford should be enough to settle the case. Partly as a penalty for disorderly conduct, and partly as a contribution to cover dental costs. Don't you think that should be sufficient?"

"Do I?" said Marcus, his eyebrows rising. "That's a lot for twelve men to observe on their own. But if you point it out to them, do it subtly. Don't talk down to them." His tone was amiable, his voice quite gentle, but his eyes were sharp. "Don't expect too much of them, Daniel. You aren't hoping to pick your twelve good men and true from Cambridge graduates, are you? Pity Kitteridge is on leave. He could have been helpful."

Daniel held his tongue with difficulty. He did not need Toby Kitteridge's advice, either as his friend or immediate superior, but he knew that Marcus was meaning to be supportive. "I want them to see an alarmed and confused man blamed for something he did not do," he stated roundly. "Threatened with the loss of his good name because of a false charge. Everything he owns, everything he is, depends on my being able to do that."

"Better," Marcus said approvingly. "You've got to get them to understand it's a battle between two men with one idea. Be careful, Daniel. Don't overreach yourself and lose the jury's sympathy. And above all, don't say your man was justified in breaking the other fellow's face. It's overly aggressive, and you know it! It makes Wolford seem violent."

"Yes, sir, I know it does," Daniel admitted. "I'll watch out!"

DANIEL WENT OVER his notes one more time and was even more certain that no one could prove Wolford's guilt as a plagiarist. The assault was another matter.

Then he put all the papers in his case and took a taxi to his client's house.

Wolford opened the door the moment Daniel knocked, as if he had been waiting in the hall.

"Good morning, Professor Wolford," he said, with a slight smile. "Thank you for making the time to see me." He stepped inside the dark, austerely decorated hallway and followed Wolford through to his study.

The room was comfortably warm, every wall lined with books. To some it would have been oppressive. Daniel found it exactly right. He settled himself in a chair opposite Wolford and opened his briefcase to pull out the notes he'd made earlier.

"I'd like to go over all this at least once more . . . to be sure I've covered everything. You've given me the source material for your conclusions, and I've been over your notes and your book—

fascinating and frightening. I've also studied Mr. Tolliver's work, which he claims you copied. That is important, because it explains why you were so angry with him that a fight could arise."

"Thank you," Wolford said.

Daniel looked up, surprised. "It's my job."

"For finding my work interesting," Wolford corrected. "And perceiving that Tolliver is lying."

"It would be better if we did not say that," Daniel advised him.

Wolford fixed him with a glare, his face dark, eyes accusatory. "It's true!"

"Professor Wolford, if the truth were enough, there would be no need for most trials," Daniel replied. "There are tactics to apply, and some skill is required to present your case well. It's a matter of persuading people, recognizing their beliefs, what they can understand from within their own lives, then using those beliefs and fears to our advantage." He knew he was lecturing, and he could see the flash of understanding in Wolford's eyes. He drew in his breath. "You can't beat the jurors over the head with facts, your sense of outrage, or injured pride, however justified it is. Remember, they don't have to explain their decision. What you want is to make them see your point of view, maybe even come to like you."

"I'm looking for justice, not emotional comprehension—" Wolford stopped. He looked astounded and then unhappy.

Daniel realized he was speaking from his own conviction as a barrister, and not addressing Wolford's needs as the defendant. "Sorry," he apologized. "A lot of evidence will be presented. There are arguments to be made on both sides. It depends upon who the jurors believe, and that will not be a matter of cold, hard facts. They will believe what and who they want to; what they can understand that makes them comfortable. And most of them don't understand the idea of plagiarism, anyway. It doesn't touch the lives of the ordinary man. It's no use to us that they see you as clever. Maybe they don't like clever people, or they are afraid of them." He sat back a little in his chair. It was warm and comfortable in this oddly familiar room. It reminded him of university: the companionship, the hunger to explore ideas.

"I can't stand there and make them like me!" Wolford protested. "I'm a professor, a teacher, not a damn politician!" There was a defensive quality in his voice, audible on a rising note.

"Of course, you can't," Daniel said gently. "That's why you have a lawyer. It's my job to make them see you as the victim here, the man who was robbed of something of great value, and who momentarily lost his temper, for a very justifiable reason. That is another issue—and Tolliver struck first, anyway, albeit ineffectually. But your reputation is a different and far more serious matter. It encompasses the regard of your fellow man. Indeed, it is your livelihood. Any man can understand that, whether it's his reputation as a teacher, a writer, an honest shopkeeper, an accurate bookkeeper, a skilled butcher, or whatever it is he does." He leaned forward a little. "The jurors will be with you on that. They are not judging between two academics. They are judging between a decent, honest man they can identify with, and the sharp-edged young man who is trying to steal his work and profit wrongfully from it."

Wolford dropped his head into his hands, running his fingers through the thick hair till it stood on end. Daniel could see that he was forcing himself to concentrate.

Daniel had been in this position several times, working with clients on a case. He could understand the need to protest one's innocence, and how insecure everything could suddenly feel, as if it were slipping through one's fingers. "Listen to me," he said calmly. "If you claim injustice and blame Tolliver, you sound angry and self-pitying, albeit justifiably. But it also shows you to be unlikeable. You want to come across as a strong, dignified man who has been robbed of the rewards of his work. A man who has been wronged. At the same time, if you do prove to the jurors that you are a respected and admired academic, and have always been cleverer than Tolliver, they might feel sorry for him. And believe me, his lawyer will have thought of all this. If you testify, he will try to make you seem angry, boastful, and far cleverer than his client—and, incidentally, than all the jurors put together. That would make them feel insulted and defensive and, above all, create sympathy for Tolliver, not you!"

Wolford looked up and stared at him. "Clever," he said quietly. "I'm glad I'm innocent. If you thought I were guilty, would you still defend me so assiduously?" He gave a brief, twisted, and unreadable smile.

"Probably not," Daniel answered with candor. "But not only do I believe you, I also think that all the evidence is on your side. What I need to do is persuade the jury to look at it fairly. That isn't as easy as it sounds, because unless one of them is a writer, the whole concept of academic honesty—the idea of researching, studying, forming a conclusion—will be unfamiliar to them. And if the opposing barrister is any good, he'll make sure the jury is comprised of ordinary men—who can read and write, but not as authors do, and certainly not as historians. They won't be Cambridge professors, you could lay money on that!"

Wolford bit his lip in an unconscious sign of anxiety. "So, what are you going to do?"

Daniel struggled to think of an honest answer that would take the desolate look off Wolford's face. When the jury looked at him, they would see fear, and to them, fear would mean guilt. No one wanted to believe innocent people were convicted; that opened up an abyss of horror that jurors preferred not to peer into. They could so easily be swayed by the prosecution to believe that an innocent man would trust them to find him so, and therefore have no fear. He would tell Wolford that, closer to the time. He knew how much the man had to lose, and he was truly sorry for him. "You are innocent," he said steadily. "Trust them. And please trust me!" He smiled bleakly. "If you don't trust me, the jury won't cither, and then it will be an uphill climb."

Wolford smiled. "I do trust you, insomuch as I can trust anyone. It's not easy."

"No, it isn't, but you must try, this is so important." Daniel could see Wolford's point of view. The longer he practiced as a barrister, standing up in court and passionately putting forward an argument, the more difficult it was to allow anyone else to speak for him. And so it was with Wolford. He was used to lecturing students, to speaking rather than listening, and never having anyone speak for him. It was Daniel's job to see that Wolford did not prejudice his chance of victory, even lose the case unwittingly, by trying to take over his own defense.

Daniel saw how Wolford stared at him. It was clear in his eyes, in the tension in every sinew of his body, that he wanted to argue. "You are in the right," Daniel said firmly, denying Wolford the chance to speak without openly cutting across him. "You are the victim! It's not your job to fight, it's mine. And if you rob me of that, you could lose, all because the jury won't like you. So, stop thinking of this as a mathematical exercise, balancing one side of an equation against the other, and realize that it is a drama! Make them feel, and they will be in a mood to look for your vindication."

"But . . ." Wolford began. "For God's sake, Pitt, we are civilized people! Appeal to reason! Reason is on my side. I am innocent!"

"The jury is not made up of students, Professor. They are the representatives of the ordinary man in the street—and I do mean man . . . no women allowed. And there's no point in speaking to their reason until you have their understanding and their sympathy, to feel what your loss will mean to you. That is when . . ." He stopped. Wolford was staring at him with mounting impatience. "Words are my business, too," Daniel continued. "Words that inform, but also that engage the emotions, move the jurors. Now give me the weapons that I can use."

Wolford nodded silently, as if the annoyance had seeped out of him.

"Tell me about Tolliver and your relationship with him," Daniel instructed.

Of course, he had already researched the matter both personally and professionally. He knew of the hostility and rivalry between the two men. He knew the facts, but he needed to understand the emotions. Why had Tolliver chosen to accuse Wolford of such an ugly crime? For that matter, did he really believe it? Above all, what evidence might the opposing team have that Daniel had not foreseen? The counsel for Tolliver was a middle-aged man named Cobden, who had won far more cases than he had lost.

"Professor!" Daniel said sharply, pulling them both back into the conversation.

Wolford met his eyes, and Daniel saw in his expression a strange mixture of confidence, anger, and real fear. He was overwhelmed with a rush of pity for the man. His instinct was to reach out and touch him, which was ridiculous: Daniel was a professional, a lawyer who had been hired to defend this man in court. At the same time, he understood Wolford's fear. If they lost this case, the legal punishment would be no more than a fine, one that might impose some hardship. It would not be prison. But there were worse things than prison for a man like Wolford. It could result in the ruin of a reputation that he had spent a lifetime building.

Daniel understood that Wolford would not be a cooperative client, but the man's attitude in court would matter greatly.

"Pay attention!" he said grimly, in exactly the same tone he remembered Wolford using with him when he had sat spellbound, listening to the historian recount the events of the uprisings, describing vividly the almost unbelievable characters of the French Revolution. Wolford had brought them all to vivid, passionate life for the students who had sat in front of him, transfixed by his words.

Daniel saw the flare of recognition in Wolford's face. Was he seeing the same past in his mind? Daniel had felt so small then, discovering that his excellent mind for school dissolved in the presence of the best young minds in Britain. What was excellent before was only average in Cambridge. He had been overwhelmed by a wave of excitement, self-doubt, fears that seemed huge and ridiculous, and the belief that to be given an entrée to that vast world of knowledge and passion was worth any price that was demanded of him.

This university life had been only a few years before, but it felt like a different lifetime. Daniel Pitt was a boy then, a man now. Big dreams had become rock-hard realities. Nothing was theoretical, with another chance to get it right. Now it was all real: real people, real tragedies, real guilt, loss, and failure. And in some cases, real death.

He began again to take Wolford through every phase of his work, all the points he had made, all the references, the sources he had drawn on. As they talked, memories of university friends came back to him, and he used them to make Wolford smile.

"Oh, he went to America," Wolford said in answer to one name. "He's teaching and loving it. I had a letter from him only a month ago." His face relaxed at the mention of a student who had kept in touch.

Daniel saw the light in his face and made a mental note to use that in the trial.

He did not expect it to take up more than one day, as there was only a single line of questioning to answer: If Wolford and Tolliver had reached the same conclusion on historical incidents, was it because they had read the same facts and deduced their shared stance from the same source? Or had one copied the other? Tolliver claimed that he had written it out first, whereas Wolford claimed that he had. Daniel could not understand why Tolliver had even brought the accusation, except to gain some notoriety, since Wolford's source was clearly stated in footnotes in his manuscript.

Daniel would point out to the jury that Wolford had used his own wording, sprung from his earlier work, and that the reasoning was also similar to his past work. It was impossible to prove that he had even seen Tolliver's work—though it was also impossible to prove that he had not. Cheating, copying, these were difficult to prove, but not so difficult to believe; they happened far too often.

"What about this?" Daniel asked, picking up a paper written by Tolliver a couple of years earlier. He passed it to Wolford. It was contentious and argumentative, but he wanted to provoke Wolford and see how he reacted. From his days at Cambridge, he could remember Wolford's temper: sudden, at times almost violent.

He was seeing it now, as a flash of contempt crossed Wolford's face. "Irresponsible. A stupid man," he said sharply. "His reasoning is flawed; he has delusions of infallibility. It's obvious! The man's a total incompetent—" His voice was rising, as was the color in his face.

"That's what I mean!" Daniel interrupted him. "Don't do that—don't shout people down. Don't be aggressive and make them feel foolish, inferior to you."

Wolford looked startled into silence.

"For heaven's sake, use your brain!" Daniel said briskly. "I can't win this case if you get in the way."

Wolford remained silent.

Daniel relaxed for a moment, then drew a deep breath and squared his shoulders. He continued to guide his client through how to answer all the questions he might face. He was beginning to seriously wonder whether Wolford wanted to win this case or not.

Nine

Eight days after the murder of Lena Madden, Ian Frobisher was dozing after dinner.

His landlady, Mrs. Jones, approached his door. She still had the lilt of Welsh in her voice and regarded the mountains of Wales as her home, although she had not lived there in forty years. There were two other lodgers in the house, both of them older men, but Ian was her favorite, and she did not hide it.

He was more asleep than awake when he felt his shoulder shaken gently.

"I'm sorry, Mr. Frobisher, sir," said Mrs. Jones, her voice full of apology. "But there's a gentleman here wishes to speak with you."

Ian forced his attention back to the present. He knew by the formal way she addressed him that this was not a casual, friendly visitor. He had a few of them, mostly old college friends, or even older ones from his school days and sports teams. He had been good at sports, especially cricket, and those friendships lasted.

He sat up straight, just as his sergeant, Billy Bremner, entered the room. Bremner's hair was wet at the front and streaked across his forehead. Otherwise he appeared to be dry, until Ian glanced at the man's legs and saw that his trousers were sodden at the bottom, his boots drenched. He knew that the man's raincoat and his sou'wester would be hanging in the hall. He also knew that Bremner should have been off duty.

"Thank you, Mrs. Jones," Ian said, with a tight smile. "What is it?" he asked, directing the question at Bremner, although there was a tight knot forming in his stomach. He already knew. "Another?" he said under his breath.

"Sorry, sir," Bremner said miserably.

Ian stood up. "Everything else the same? No chance it's a copycat killing?" He did not really believe it was, but he clutched at any thread.

Bremner glanced at Mrs. Jones, who was standing a few feet away, perhaps waiting to see if Ian was going out. "No, sir, none at all," Bremner replied. "At least, I don't think so." He moved his weight from one foot to the other.

Ian understood. The longer Bremner stood in this warm room, the harder it would be to brave the drenching cold again. "Right. Thank you, Mrs. Jones. Looks like I have to go out. Don't wait up for me, it could be all night."

Mrs. Jones said something under her breath that Ian did not understand, even though the sentiment was unmistakable. Presumably it was in Welsh. He turned to her. "That sounds very satisfying, Mrs. Jones. You'll have to teach it to me, one of these days." He smiled at her and saw the humor in her face.

"Oh, Mr. Frobisher, I couldn't do that! It's . . . it's . . . miner's talk. I learned it from . . ." She shook her head, her cheeks pink. "Never mind. I'll just see you to the door and lock it behind you.

Be sure you've got your key, just in case you're back before I get up to light the fires."

"Thank you, Mrs. Jones. I've always got it. And don't keep breakfast. I may not be home in time."

"I don't know what the world's coming to," she said, with foreboding. "I suppose you won't be wanting a cup of tea before you go?" She looked from Ian to Bremner, eyebrows raised.

"Love one," Bremner said, smiling back. "But no time, sorry."

"Then take a piece of fruit cake with you?" she suggested.

"Yes, please," both men replied eagerly, and in one voice.

It took her no longer than the time they needed to get into their heavy raincoats and boots and wrap thick scarves around their necks. She handed each of them a large wedge of cake wrapped in greaseproof paper and slipped into brown paper bags. "Keeps 'em dry," she observed.

"Thank you," Ian said, putting the bag in his inside coat pocket. Then he opened the front door and went out into the wind and driving rain. Bremner was a step behind him, his precious slice of cake similarly protected.

They got into the police car waiting at the curb and Bremner drove. Ian did not need to ask where they were going. Bremner had mentioned Ferdinand Street, off Chalk Farm Road, and Ian knew the way.

It was nine o'clock on a dark, rain-soaked winter evening, when shops and businesses were all closed and gutters were like mountain streams washing torrents of foaming water out into the streets. No one was about. And those few who had been caught on the rain-slicked pavements were rushing to find any doorway or the shelter of some corner out of the wind.

"What about the victim?" Ian asked. "What the hell kind of person is out walking on a night like this?"

Bremner did not bother to answer.

The car drew up in a side street where a couple of constables were standing in the rain, collars high and hats pulled down low, their brims dripping water. As the car stopped, one of them leaned forward to open the door.

They were close to a streetlight and, in its arc, the rain slanted in the driving wind, bouncing back off the stones in luminous rods and into the gutter. Another arc of light shone from the next streetlight several yards along, illuminating a short tunnel of lashing rain. A dirty, indeterminate huddle of what looked like old clothes was lying on the narrow pavement.

Ian climbed out of the car and thanked the man holding the door for him. He was aware of Bremner climbing out of the other side. There was no traffic in the street to be aware of. He heard the door slam shut. "What have we got?" he asked.

"Man, about forty-five, I'd guess," said the constable. "Slashed all over. Haven't looked close. Didn't want to disturb him in case any of it meant something to you, sir. It being as you got the other cases the same."

"You sure it's the same?" Ian asked. "How?"

"Please God there ain't two like it," the constable said, with intense feeling. "Stab wounds all over the body. But mainly because the tip of his right index finger is missing. And that ain't known, sir. At least, it ain't been in the newspapers."

"What do you mean?" Ian pressed. "How did you know about the other fingers missing?"

"Just talk. Whispers, like."

"Who's whispering?"

"Er . . . I . . ."

"You mean police?" Ian pulled his collar up as the icy rain slid down his neck. "Come on, man, I'm not going to jump on anyone. We need to catch this bastard before he kills again. We haven't got any leads at all. It's no time to be protecting anyone. If you do, you could be protecting the killer as well. Is that what you want?"

"No! No, sir. Just one copper to another." He shook his head fiercely. "That's how I heard it. It was one of the men who found the second victim, sir. I'd rather not—"

"No," Ian cut him off. "I understand that. Warn him, from me, that he'd better not let his tongue slip again or he'll regret it, and so will his sergeant. Understand?"

"Yes, sir."

Perhaps Ian was being too strict, but he wanted cooperation from the constable on the beat, not fear—and, above all, no secrets. "Have you sent for the police surgeon?"

"Yes, sir. He should be here any moment. I expect you'll be wanting to take him to the morgue"—indicating the huddled corpse—"to look at him in the light." No one could do anything much out here in the dark and the driving rain. The gutters were already overflowing across the road.

Ian nodded. "I see you've got the street roped off. Not sure how much we'll find in the dark. Rain probably washed away a lot of the blood, anyhow."

"Protected what we could, sir, but I don't know how long he were laying here before we found him. His clothes is fair soaked. I put my raincoat over him, to save anything we could."

Ian noticed for the first time that the constable was in his regular jacket and was also soaked through, probably to the skin. The man must be frozen. But there was no indoor task Ian could give him now. "Good man," he said, meeting the man's eyes. "We're lucky to have anything. Did you find anyone who will admit to seeing him before you discovered him?"

"Just one, sir. I expect if anyone passed this way, they would've thought he was a drunk, or . . . or else they didn't want to look." He hunched his shoulders in a protective gesture. "People are scared, sir. Don't want to see anything. More than that, they don't want to stand here in the rain and wait for the police."

"Not surprising," said Ian. "How did you know he was here?"

"Woman screamed, sir. Constable round the corner in Malden Crescent, leads into Prince of Wales Road. Heard her and came to find us."

"Where is she?"

"Constable took her to the café round the corner to sit down. Says she was all of a heap, if you understand me."

"I do." Ian looked up. "Bremner!" he called out. "There's a café round the corner where a constable is sitting with the woman who found the body. Go and see what she says, before she forgets."

"Don't you want to do that, sir?" Bremner asked.

"I do, but you're going to do it for me."

"But, sir . . ." Bremner started.

"Get on with it," Ian snapped. "We're all going to be freezing and soaked to the skin before the night's out." He knew Bremner hated questioning a distraught witness, as did everyone, but there were no pleasant jobs on a scene like this. No matter how annoyed Bremner was, he would be civil. He pretended he had no patience, especially with women, but Ian believed he actually had too much pity; it was in his nature to want to protect them.

His sergeant went off to the café and Ian went to look at the corpse, shining his torch across the man's face. This was the part he hated most, the first look at a person who only a short while ago had been alive, and terrified, possibly in almost unbearable pain. He told himself he was stupid to imagine it. It helped nobody! But it did make the person real, as if some essence of him were still palpable.

"Do you know his name?" Ian asked.

"Yes, sir," said the constable. "Wallet, and a couple of letters in his pocket. Roger Haviland. Lives in Park Road, just off Haverstock Hill, according to the address on the envelope the police have. And . . ." His voice trailed off.

"What?" Ian probed.

"He's married, sir. One of the envelopes is addressed to Mr. and Mrs. Haviland. We ain't sent anyone to tell her yet."

"We'll do that," Ian replied, immediately revising his opinion about the worst part of his work.

He moved the torch slowly across the dead man's face. He was pleasant-looking, good features, strong, with a full head of dark, wavy hair. Ian could tell at a glance that his shirt was a very good fabric and cut. He would not be surprised if it was from Jermyn Street, off Savile Row, where the best shirtmakers in the world were situated. He had had a shirt from Jermyn Street once, as a Christmas present. He wore it only for special occasions, and it was still like new. His mother had given it to him.

Who had given Roger Haviland his shirt? Or had he bought it himself?

His suit was of good quality, but not personally tailored for him—at least, not according to the label. But then, it had been so violently slashed that it was impossible to tell much.

There was nothing else he could discern in the dark and the wind. The torchlight made the rain look like silver daggers, the blood on the stones smeared. He wondered how pathologists like Dr. Hall and Dr. fford Croft could deal with what had been a living, breathing human being. This victim would have had both good and bad in him, like anyone else, along with hopes and fears. Please heaven, the terror had been short, the pain quickly lost in oblivion.

He stood up. "Thank you, Constable. Would you shine your torch down and see if you notice anything else?"

The man obeyed and together they searched the blocks of pavement, the edge of the curb, moving the beam of the torch to the wall that ran the length of the street, all the way to the next block. They went into the road, but the gutters were full to overflowing, their murky contents swirling out to meet the black tar of the road. Everything seemed to be in motion, water spilling sideways across the dark surface of the roadway and carrying with it odd pieces of debris. And, perhaps, evidence.

"What do we know about Mr. Haviland?" Ian asked. "What was he doing here? Have you found anyone who knows him? Passed him coming from somewhere?"

"No, sir. We can ask around the local shops, offices, people who come this way regularly. But we'll be lucky to find anyone."

"Well, push. If they don't admit to having seen him, ask them where they were earlier this evening, and if they usually pass this way. People work in offices around here, and in the shops, too. Ask what they've sold in the last hour or so. Who works here? Which way do they go home? Let them know that if they lie, that means they've got something to hide."

"Probably just don't want to be involved, sir."

"I know that!" Ian shot back. "But they *are* involved if they passed this way tonight. Depending on the time, this poor devil was here, or he wasn't. Either they saw somebody else, or they didn't. If they usually come this way, but tonight they didn't, why not? If they left work at a different time from usual, why? If the reason is innocent, they have nothing to fear. If it isn't, as long as it has nothing to do with Haviland's death, we can probably leave it alone. But a lie, any lie, is suspicious, right?"

"Yes, sir, right."

"Good," said Ian. "As soon as the mortuary van comes with the police surgeon, we'll get started. Expect to take this poor beggar to the Home Office pathologist, like the others."

"Yes, sir. And that'll be Dr. Hall?"

The response surprised Ian. "You know her?"

The constable gave a lopsided smile. "Got told off by her once. Never forgot it. Thought she'd have my head to put on the wall . . . till she smiled. But I won't never give her lip no more."

Ian smiled back at him. "I'll bet you won't. I wouldn't try it with Dr. fford Croft either."

"Who's he, then?"

"She," Ian corrected. "She's the next one coming up, behind Dr. Hall."

"Didn't think women could do this sort of thing. Still, I suppose Dr. Hall's a woman, sort of."

Ten minutes later, the mortuary van arrived. A stocky figure climbed out and came through the heavy rain to stand at the street-light and look down at the corpse.

"Speak of the devil!" the constable said under his breath.

"I heard that!" Dr. Hall snapped. She looked at Ian. "Another one?"

"Yes, ma'am. Seems to be."

She looked down at the corpse. "Poor devil," she said very quietly. "All right," she announced. "Get out of my way!"

Ian and the constable stood nearby. Bremner came through the curtains of rain, acknowledged Dr. Hall, then turned to Ian. "I got the woman's name and address," he said, referring to the possible witness. "Nothing that looks like being much help. She comes this way most evenings, on the way home, and she's passed our victim a few times, but has never spoken to him. So, he comes here regular." He did not say aloud the possible meaning. They both understood it.

"What does she do?" Ian asked.

"Works in a milliner's shop fifty yards up the street."

"Who the devil goes out buying a hat, for heaven's sake, on a night like this?"

"No one," said Bremner. "That's why they shut up shop on the early side."

"Don't know why they opened at all."

"Winter hats," Bremner explained. "Some of the fur ones are pretty fancy." He gave a quick, amused smile.

Ian shrugged. His feet were wet from stepping off the curb into the overflowing gutters. If anything, the rain was getting harder. It was keeping everyone inside who was not compelled to go out. And if they were, they moved swiftly, heads down, collars up, looking only where they were going, to avoid the worst puddles.

The officers continued the search, speaking to a few shopkeepers and a couple of clerks from offices close by. Two or three of them recalled seeing shadowy figures, but no more than outlines in the rain.

"There's no point!" Bremner complained. "One man on a pavement trying to keep dry looks exactly like another. I wouldn't recognize my own father in this weather. Not that he'd be outside unless he had to be. We're wasting our time." He lifted his face to look at Ian. "You're only putting off telling the poor sod's wife that she's a widow. She's probably already beginning to worry that he's late, so get it over with. We're not learning anything here. Everybody is cold, wet, angry, and frightened."

Ian's eyes widened. He wasn't accustomed to being spoken to like this, and especially not by his sergeant. They were all under intense pressure, and this downpour was not helping. "We've got to talk to the people around here before they go home and we lose them," he said, more tartly than he had intended. "I'm surprised you need to be told that." The minute the words were out of his mouth, he thought how unfair they were. And yet, considering Bremner's tone with him, he knew it sounded like retaliation. His feet were wet and so cold he could hardly feel them. He was being childish, and he knew it.

"A lot of good that's going to do us," Bremner retorted. "If we learned a single thing of use, it must have been you who learned it, and you forgot to tell me."

Ian needed to get this under control. He took a deep breath. "We've got to try," he said, doing his best to keep the anger from his voice. "It could be that somebody saw something."

"Sheets of rain, that's what they saw. And other people hurrying by with their heads down. What the hell use is that? I could've told you without asking them." Bremner hunched his shoulders against a blast of wind coming down the alley. "Let's go and ruin the poor woman's life, and get it over with."

Ian began to say something and changed his mind. Lashing out wasn't going to make anything better. He was feeling guilty because he had not a single new or useful idea, and this was the third murder that appeared to be following a now familiar pattern. The major difference was that this one was a man, and the attack appeared to be even more savage.

Ian was plagued with the realization that they had worked hard ever since the first murder, yet they knew nothing more about who the killer was than they had known at the beginning. Or, for that matter, who might be the next victim. This Roger Haviland seemed to have nothing in common with Lena Madden or Sandrine Bernard.

It took him a moment, but then he knew what was wrong with Bremner: the man was frightened. He, too, felt the case slipping out of their control, so perhaps he was right to be. He pretended to be a tough northerner, growing up in a hard climate, but inside he was as soft as butter! Once, he had spent all night looking for a lost dog. When he came in the next morning, half asleep, Ian had pretended not to notice. They had never referred to it.

Ian put his head down and rushed into the blast of wind that was being funneled along the narrow street, then walked around the corner and onto the main thoroughfare. Bremner was close behind him.

The car was waiting for them beside the curb. Ian gave the driver Haviland's home address from the envelope they had found in the man's jacket.

Looking out of the window at the teeming rain and the deserted streets, Ian realized his night was about to get even worse. He was on his way to someone's home to tell a devoted and unsuspecting wife that the man she loved would not be back. Not ever.

Ten

IT WAS A half-hour drive, and neither Ian nor Bremner spoke. Ian wondered if perhaps Bremner was thinking of what they would say, how they could break this news and have it sound less terrible than it was. The only sounds were the hum of the engine, the swish of the rain, and the soft squeak of the windscreen wiper whenever the driver rotated the handle from inside the car.

"Here you are, sir," the driver said, breaking the silence. "I'll wait here."

Ian thanked him and got out. He was hit immediately by the torrential rain. After the relative warmth of the car, it felt like ice on his skin; it probably would be, before morning. The only thing worse than rain was hard, pelting sleet.

With Bremner following a step behind him, he walked up the garden path in the dim light from the porch. Even though they were between streetlamps, the rain obscured nearly everything.

Ian fumbled for the bell and pulled it.

The silence seemed endless, but it was little more than a full minute before he heard footsteps and the click of the latch, then saw the door swing wide. A brown-haired woman stood just inside. She was tall, handsome, with fair skin and dark eyes. Her face registered shock. Clearly, she'd been expecting someone else: her husband, whom she would never see again.

"Mrs. Haviland?" Ian asked.

She looked guarded. "Yes. Do I know you?"

"No, ma'am. My name is Inspector Ian Frobisher, and this is Sergeant Bremner." He showed her his badge. "May we come in?"

"My husband's not at home," she began. Then doubt flickered across her face, as if uncertain whether she should have admitted that she was alone.

Ian felt his throat tighten. This was the worst job any policeman faced, and he could never think of a way of making it any easier. At least he had never had to tell a woman that her child was dead. No doubt, that would happen one day.

Mrs. Haviland stepped back into the hallway. Ian followed her in, Bremner on his heels.

She stopped in the foyer, and they stood there for a moment before Ian spoke.

"I'm sorry, Mrs. Haviland, but I have to tell you that your husband was attacked in the street this evening, and he was killed." It sounded so short, delivering the end of her world in one sentence. He held out his arm in case she should collapse. Sometimes, people did.

She stared at him. "Roger . . . killed?"

"Let's go inside, ma'am, and sit down." He extended his arm further to offer support. Even in the warm light of the hall, the color had drained from her face, giving her a deathlike pallor.

Bremner closed the door behind them, shutting out the rain. Suddenly, the hall seemed almost airless. Mrs. Haviland's hand was heavy on Ian's arm as she began to lean on him.

Bremner moved ahead of them and through a door leading to a sitting room, then turned back to help the woman to the couch.

Ian was looking at her, watching for the telltale signs of shock. He barely had time to notice the bookshelves filled with volumes, the small fire in the grate, and what looked like family photographs on the walls and in upright frames on the shelves.

"What . . . what happened?" she asked, perched on the couch, her weight still on Ian's arm. "He didn't have anything worth robbing! It doesn't make any sense!" She was still fighting a sense of disbelief; it was etched strongly in her face.

"No, ma'am, it doesn't," Ian agreed. "It looks as if this might be the same person who killed the two women found recently. You may have read the newspaper reports . . ." He did not want to use the word *slashed*. "I know this is no comfort."

She jerked up her head. "Why can't you catch him? Are you just going to let him go on and on, killing decent people and . . . ?" Her face twisted with the distress she could no longer struggle against.

They were unfair, these accusations, and she probably knew that, but Ian was stung by her blame nevertheless. Yes, he could understand it, and arguing with her would only make her feel worse. But if he responded, at least it would feel like he was doing something. He had to remind himself that anger hurt less than grief.

"We're still trying to identify him . . ." he started.

"Still?" she demanded. "He's killed all these people, and you don't know anything about him? What are you doing?" she demanded. "Sitting around, waiting for him to kill again . . . and again? You are—"

"Did your husband play a musical instrument?" he interrupted.

"What?" Her voice was harsh, her expression incredulous.

"Was his index finger used for something special, a skill of some sort?"

"What on earth does that have to do with . . . ?" Her voice trailed off as the last bit of color vanished from her face. She looked as if she were going to crumple.

Ian felt clumsy, stupid, and insensitive.

"Why?" she demanded, pulling herself together with a concerted effort. "Why do you want to know that?" Her voice was rising, as if she were seizing on this question as something she could fight. Perhaps if she could prove this was nonsense, then the whole nightmare would go away.

Ian decided not to try to calm her down. In a way, it was like trying to deny her grief. "Mrs. Haviland, all the victims had part of their index finger removed. It means something to the person who did this. It tells us there could be a connection between them."

"That wasn't in the newspapers!" she said, as if clinging to any argument she could, anything that could change the nightmarish reality in which she found herself.

Bremner rose to his feet and wandered soundlessly around the room. Ian knew he was looking for little things that might tell them more about the victim, little mementos of his life.

"You think his death was intended, not just . . . ?" She struggled to go on. "Some random lunatic, some madman . . ."

"Yes, I do," Ian replied, his voice now softer.

"No." She shook her head sharply. "He didn't do anything with his hands. He was a thinker, a writer," she said defensively, as if this would somehow mean it was not his own fault.

"A writer?" Ian asked.

"Yes, and he was good."

"Was your husband right-handed?"

"Yes. But what does that matter?"

"It might not," he said. "We are just trying to find anything that the victims have in common."

Something changed in her face. When she spoke, her voice was little more than a whisper. "Are you saying they knew each other? That Roger knew the killer? That they might have been friends?"

Ian did not respond.

"That he could have been talking to Roger, just as you and I are talking, and suddenly he realized that he was with a monster? My God, he would have been terrified."

"I know," said Ian. "I'm sorry." He meant it, and it tore at him. "But we must explore any avenues that might help us find whoever is doing this."

She closed her eyes. "What a hideous thought. It could be anyone. The gentlest, the kindest . . . a priest, or a doctor, or a friend's husband. But if we could look into their minds, we would see death." She bent her head and covered her face with her hands. Her fingers were long and slender. "No one is safe."

"Almost everyone is safe," he said firmly. "You haven't been attacked, and neither have I. And, please God, we never will be. Most people go all through their lives without such trauma. But a killer is on the loose and we have to find him. If he knew your husband, then almost certainly your husband knew him."

She looked up. "The doorway to hell has opened and . . . its darkness is in my street, my garden . . . even in my house."

Ian sat with her and quietly answered her questions. He explained that her husband had died near his office, on a fairly busy street. It had to be someone he didn't suspect, someone he knew. And if Ian was right, the other victims knew him, too. "Now, think very hard, please," he said, working to keep the urgency from his voice. "Sandrine Bernard. Lena Madden. Do these names mean anything to you?"

She shook her head slowly, looking bewildered, furrowed brows drawn together.

"Think, please." Again, he tried to keep his voice level. She was so wounded, so vulnerable.

"Sandrine, that's an unusual name." She blinked slowly. "Was she French?"

"Half, I believe. But yes, she spoke French." He must not push her. It was so tempting, but it would invalidate anything she came up with if he put thoughts into her mind, words into her mouth.

She wanted so much to help. He could feel it, see it in her eager face, her gripped hands.

"This Sandrine, was she a writer, too?" she asked.

"I don't know," he admitted, again resisting the temptation to prompt her.

"Roger knew a girl called Sandrine something, when he was up at Cambridge. That's a long time ago." She shook her head. "But not as long as you might think, because he went back to do some special course a few years ago. I forget how many. Could that help?"

Ian felt excitement stir inside. "It might," he answered. "I'll certainly follow it up." He swallowed hard, trying not to grasp too tightly to this piece of information. He went on asking her questions, some of them useful, some just talking for the sake of it. It seemed to soothe her. "Can we call anyone for you?" he asked. "Have you any relations close by? Or a good friend who could stay with you?"

She shook her head sharply. "No, no one close. And I don't feel like talking just now."

"Do you go to church?" Ian asked. Perhaps it was an intrusive question, but it was all he could think of.

"Yes, sometimes."

"Can we contact your minister?"

"He's blind," she said, stumbling over the words. "He can't come out at night like this."

"Would that be the Reverend Rhodes?"

"Yes!" she answered. "How did you . . . ? I think I would like to speak with him." She fought to get her words under control. "Do you think he'd . . . no, I can't ask him on a night like this. I couldn't." Slowly, that momentary light of hope faded from her face.

Speaking gently, he extracted a promise that, should someone from a newspaper wish to interview her, she would say nothing about the mutilation. And then he promised to take a message to Rhodes. "I know him, and he has a car."

"I told you," said the woman, "he's blind."

"Yes, but Mrs. Rhodes drives." Ian stood up. "I'll ask him. You shouldn't be alone. It's too much."

It was a promise, and he had no choice but to keep it.

THEY WERE HEADED toward the Rhodes house when Bremner said, "You're as soft as butter, you are!" But his voice was warm, and he smiled as he looked out of the window, as if concerned that his expression might give away too much.

Ian didn't answer. He knew that this was his sergeant's sideways apology for his anger earlier on. He felt a slight easing of the hard misery inside him.

It was a wretched night and it took longer than usual to drive through the windblown sheets of rain to the vicarage. They both got out of the car and went to knock on the door, getting soaked again by the time Polly Rhodes opened it to them.

"Good heavens! Come in before you drown," she said, opening the door wide and then closing it immediately behind them. "You're drenched! Both of you. It must be one devil of an emergency to bring you here." Her face was filled with pity for the disaster she already knew was coming. "Take your shoes off."

Bremner looked down to where his oilskins were shedding water onto the floor, and his boots were clearly soaked through. Ian was no better.

"Come on!" she ordered. "Before you tell me what's wrong, I'll put your shoes in the oven and get you some dry socks. Take them off, and go talk with Richard. Somebody's dead, no doubt." She looked at them through stray strands of soft hair that had escaped most of the hairpins securing her curls.

They obeyed and followed her through to the sitting room where Richard was reading a book, his fingers running over the raised dot patterns of Braille, Dido lying on the rug beside him. Master and dog both heard Ian's and Bremner's footsteps. They looked up, and Dido came forward, wagging her tail. No doubt she remembered the tiny piece of ginger cake Ian had given her.

"Richard," Polly said. "Ian Frobisher and his sergeant are here. They've come with bad news."

"Oh dear," Richard said, closing his book and turning his head toward them.

"I'm sorry, sir," said Ian. "There's been another murder . . . the same pattern as the others."

"I take it it's someone we know?" he said quietly.

"It's a Mr. Roger Haviland, sir. We've just come from Mrs. Haviland. She has no family anywhere near, and she says she knows you."

"Handsome woman," Bremner replied, then blushed as he remembered Richard Rhodes was blind.

"I know her," Polly put in quickly, looking at Bremner, not Richard, as if it were perhaps his feelings she was looking to save. "She sings. A nice voice, rich and full. She doesn't come to services all that often, but she does join the choir on occasion. And she's done one or two solos. She will need someone." She turned to her husband. "I'll take you now."

"It's raining like hell," Richard objected.

"Nonsense," she said, already preparing to leave. "It doesn't rain like this in hell! If it did, it would put out all the fires!"

Richard started to say something, then stopped.

Polly rushed out of the room and returned moments later with dry socks for the policemen. As they pulled them on, she crossed to the cabinet at the opposite side of the room and poured two glasses half-full of whisky.

Ian started to speak, about to say something about being on duty, but she held out one of the glasses to him and met his eyes with a steady stare. She had marvelous eyes, an arresting shade of hazel green, with long lashes. The argument died on his tongue and he accepted the glass. "Take it," Ian ordered Bremner. Not that Bremner was listening to him.

A long night lay ahead of them. They finished their drinks, thanked Mrs. Rhodes and the reverend, then removed their shoes from the oven, put them on, and went out into the rain again.

"At least we know Mrs. Haviland will be looked after," Ian said as he got back into the police car.

Bremner nodded. "But damn little help to find the slasher," he said sourly. "Nice people, even if they don't live in the real world."

The remark caught Ian on a raw edge; he could not alleviate the sense of failure that they had been unable to prevent a third murder. He felt overwhelmed. "I think their world is a damn sight more real than ours," he returned. "We went to tell Mrs. Haviland that her husband had been murdered, and then we left. They're going to deal with her grief, the day-to-day reality of waking up every morning to an empty side of the bed, getting up with no one to cook breakfast for or share dinner with each night. No one to talk to, never mind no one to earn the money, pay the rent, the grocer, the coal merchant, or anybody else!" He glanced at Bremner. "We brought her the bad news; now they have to help her believe in something that will enable her to carry on."

"Lots of people live alone," Bremner replied. "Or as good as. And lots of women have husbands who drink, or beat them, or gamble, or are just cold and don't talk to them. Lots of men have women who—"

"All right!" Ian snapped. "The reverend probably has all that to deal with, too. Tonight, and tomorrow, and the next day, and the next. And now he's got to think of something to say that helps this poor woman hold herself together and get on with living, one grief-filled day at a time. It would help her if we could find the bastard who's doing this."

"Do you think she'll care?" Bremner asked. It was not meant as a criticism, merely a question born of blind frustration. "It won't bring him back. Is it worse than being walked out on? I wonder."

"Oh, for God's sake—" Ian began, then stopped. Quarreling with Bremner wouldn't assuage the helplessness he felt. He had lost his wife. He understood how that hurt, a loneliness that would not go away. He took a deep breath. "We ought to be able to learn something from this. What did Haviland have in common with the others? And now we know there's a link with Sandrine. And we know that Lena Madden regretted something she still felt guilty about. Let's think!"

Bremner turned sideways and glared at Ian. He could see little of his boss's face except when the car was briefly illuminated by a streetlamp. The sergeant was angry but curiously vulnerable, as if conscious of being no help at a time when he desperately wanted to be.

"There's a pattern," Ian said, filling in the silence. He could not let it stand. "Tip of the index finger cut off. It's the thing that joins these people together. But how? Writing is one occupation, something that all ages can do."

"Anonymous letters?" Bremner suggested. "Could they all have . . . no, that doesn't make sense." The car was now inching forward with extra caution as the rain increased.

"No, it doesn't," Ian agreed. "But they could all have written something. Perhaps they wrote on the same subject. Mrs. Haviland said her husband went back to Cambridge to do a special course—presumably related to finance or banking in some way?—so it's unlikely his studies crossed over with Lena Madden's and Sandrine Bernard's, even if their time there overlapped." He sighed heavily. "They are different ages. What could they possibly have had in common? There's nearly a twenty-year difference between the oldest and the youngest."

"So, then, other things," said Bremner. "If not their studies, a club or society of some sort?"

"Could be," Ian agreed. "Or a letter to the newspaper on some subject?"

Bremner was doubtful. "Do you kill someone over a letter to the papers? No," he brushed that away. "That's crazy!"

"Yes, but this killer *is* crazy. And what sane reason could there be for stalking someone in a rainstorm and stabbing him—or her—to death?" Ian asked. "And then cutting off part of a finger?"

"Point taken," Bremner agreed. "We're looking for a lunatic. A very, very nasty one. Driven by rage. But in weather like this, I could pass an elephant in the street and not notice it."

"I'll keep an eye open for elephants, then," Ian told him.

Eleven

IAN FROBISHER WOKE in daylight. It must have been time to get up if the sun was already above the horizon. He had been late to bed, and he was exhausted. His dreams had been filled with dark streets and gutters where water had turned to blood.

Even though he ached and his muscles were stiff, he was glad to get up. He and Bremner had done everything they could in pursuit of this elusive killer. It was the tenth day since Dr. Evelyn Hall had told them that the murder of Lena Madden was committed by the same man who had killed Sandrine Bernard. And now, Roger Haviland. This third murder broke the pattern in only one way: the victim was a man.

The newspapers were screaming at the police for their inability to catch someone who was clearly a madman. Ian could not blame them, but it was far harder to identify the killer than they appreciated. He probably looked like anybody else, except when the fury overtook him and he became—what, a raving lunatic? Perhaps he

was a quiet man who chatted like any other, until something provoked him and rage replaced calm. Not a gradually rising tide, but
a monstrous rogue wave that comes out of nowhere.

Ian was up, washing and dressing automatically. These were everyday habits that needed no thought. They made him consider
how sudden changes in behavior do not come out of nowhere. They
come out of something that often has not been recognized—or has
been only when it is too late. Anger, rage, some emotion that might
have lain dormant for years. They can transform someone who has
been perceived as rational, at least on the outside, into a madman
capable of killing violently and then escaping without being seen.
So what provoked this killer?

He went downstairs, already late for breakfast, and found Mrs.
Jones at work in the kitchen. It seemed that, upon hearing his footsteps in the hall, she had put the frying pan back on the stove. Two
eggs and several strips of bacon were on a separate plate, ready to
cook.

"How did you sleep?" she asked.

"Quite well, thank you," Ian said, hoping he was convincing.
How could he sleep, with this killer on the loose?

"Well, go and sit down at the table," she said. "I'll bring you
your breakfast when it's cooked."

He obeyed, gratefully.

A few minutes later, she came through and placed a hot breakfast
before him. He thanked her and ate it mechanically; his mind was
still wrestling with the problem that had spoiled what little sleep
he'd enjoyed. He was so lost in his thoughts that he did not even
notice her bringing fresh toast or topping up his teapot with boil-
ing water.

Perhaps his reasoning was flawed? Maybe the killer did not
change into a monster suddenly but thought things through, was
both careful and clever. Maybe he went out only on rainy nights,
when the weather disguised him and everybody was hurrying, head
down, collar turned up, sheltering where they could, speaking to

no one. He attacked and then disappeared back to wherever he lived. By morning he looked just as he usually did. Could manic episodes come and go like that? He was certain they were missing something. But what?

"START AGAIN FROM the beginning," Ian said to Bremner as soon as he walked into his office and had shed his raincoat and hat. "Are we sure that all three victims were killed by the same person?"

"Dr. Hall is," Bremner replied. "Do you think she's wrong?" His face had its usual twist of humor, but he wasn't smiling. His reddish hair was wet at the front, and he had obviously not combed it but rather run his fingers through it impatiently. There was an empty enamel mug on the desk beside him. He had already had the first cup of tea of the day.

That was not the answer Ian wanted, and it clearly troubled him. Could Dr. Hall be wrong? As for his sergeant's humor, he understood that it concealed a whisper of fear. "No, I don't think she's wrong," he answered. "But I suppose it's possible." He sat down in his chair. He kept forgetting to get a new cushion for it. He really should remember.

"She gave us reasons," Bremner reminded him. "Are you thinking of three different killers, each one copying the last? Surely the similarities couldn't be coincidental?" There was barely a trace of sarcasm in his voice when he said this, and his face was perfectly innocent.

"No! Of course not," Ian said sharply. "Not three times. But if we find what they have in common—even if there's one accidental mistake—it could put us on the right track."

Bremner bit his lip. "I get your point. But here's another way of thinking. If we look at them all, one victim might stand out as being different." He sat up a little straighter, looking at Ian. "And maybe that's the one, the victim that the killer has a reason to hate and fear. Maybe that one person was the actual target."

"And there was no real reason for killing the others," Ian added. "Then if his true target is dead, the killings will stop?" He thought, *Please, God, make that the case.* "What a callous bastard. To kill two other people casually, only to hide the real reason for killing his intended victim." His memory flashed backward to other cases. "Everyone's story has an element of tragedy behind it, something we can hardly understand. We all have certain things . . ." He thought of one woman who was frequently beaten by her husband. Finally, unable to take another assault, she had turned on him when he was asleep, putting a butcher's knife to his throat. It was wrong, yes, but he had seen her plight as tragic rather than wicked. What about all the people who had known what she endured? Who had known, and yet chose to ignore it because it would have obliged them to do something?

But this was different. This might be a case of one intended murder, with the other two committed cold-bloodedly to disguise the killer's true intent. Could that be what they were dealing with?

"Maybe all of the victims were witnesses to something," he wondered aloud. "Have we established if all of them were in the same place at any one time?"

"We know that Sandrine Bernard was a journalist in Paris," Bremner observed. "Mainly non-political stuff for fashion magazines and the like. We read some of her work, but she didn't express any unique opinions—at least, not as far as we could find. We've spoken to her friends, asked the Paris police, but they haven't got back to us with anything."

"And Lena Madden, she worked for a charity, an adoption society that places orphans and foundlings with good families," Ian added. His team had spoken to everyone who had worked with her, asked about her friends and whether she was courting. They had run down the leads they were given, but they had led nowhere. "Roger Haviland was a banker," said Ian. "Quite senior. Nothing in common with the others, except for the Cambridge connection— which I suspect will turn out to be a red herring."

Bremner chewed his lip. "It doesn't make any sense, does it! The Cambridge connection was years ago. As far as I can tell, not one of them had any reason to meet the others in recent weeks."

"But they must have," Ian insisted. "We just haven't found the link yet. It doesn't seem to be connected with their work. They had no religion in common, no political views, no social—" He stopped abruptly. "But Lena Madden went to St. Wilfrid's in Adelaide Road, and Mrs. Haviland knew the minister there, Richard Rhodes. That's where she went for comfort."

"Religion?" Bremner said incredulously. "It's Church of England, for heaven's sake. It's as bland as can be! It's like accusing someone of going raving mad on a cup of lukewarm milk."

"I hate lukewarm milk," Ian said, although his mind was racing. "I like it hot, or really cold. Tepid, it makes me gag."

"What?" Bremner said, perfectly seriously. "What are you thinking? Not the Reverend Rhodes? He's blind."

"I know. How well do you know him?"

"I've met him a few times. Work, like. I'd hardly know him socially." Bremner gave a slight shrug. "But he's a good sort."

"And Mrs. Rhodes?" Ian asked. He had no idea where he was going with this train of thought, but something caught in the back of his mind: the image of a dark figure in the rain, a person no one would suspect, such as a minister's wife going about doing good deeds for her blind husband. It was absurd. He forced it out of his mind. "Sorry," he said quickly, before Bremner could consider it.

"That's weird, sir," Bremner said quietly. "Really weird."

"Yes, I know. Forget I said it," Ian replied.

But Bremner was not looking at Ian. His eyes were glazed, as if he were gazing at something in the distance, or within his own imagination.

"Bremner!" Ian said sharply. "I said to forget it; it's absurd!"

"Yes, sir," Bremner answered, but automatically, as if from obedience rather than agreement.

"Do you know something about Mrs. Rhodes that I don't?" Ian asked.

"What?" Bremner shook his head. "No, sir. It was just such a horrible idea that I couldn't get rid of it. Blind minister's wife going out in the rain to bring comfort to scared or lonely parishioners, with a serrated dagger in her pocket."

"For God's sake, man, get a grip!" Ian said sharply. The idea was repellent, a violation of everything that was decent. "What the hell's the matter with you?"

"Sorry, sir."

Ian was about to go on about self-control, but he could see that Bremner was badly rattled. Perhaps they both were. This was a bad case, violent and bloody, no sense to it that they could see. The days were dark and cold, most of them with driving rain. Both men were tired. And as much as Ian did not want to admit it, they were also afraid. The bodies were mounting up, and they had made no progress. None at all.

"No," he said, more quietly. "Any idea's worth looking at, whatever it is. Even a minister's wife. We have no reason to suspect her at the moment; but I really hope it's not Polly Rhodes. I like her. The whole vicarage, even the dog—in fact, especially the dog—it all seems like an island of sanity; warm and dry in a cold, wet world. I don't want to let go of that image."

"It's probably just what it looks like, sir," Bremner replied. "That is, the vicarage and everything it represents. But something . . . somebody out there is clever enough that we haven't found him by now."

Ian ran his hand through his hair, in unconscious imitation of Bremner. "We'll start again. It has to be something recent. Don't forget that the first murder was only weeks ago. What happened then that started him off? It may not look like much to us—in fact, it must seem like a minor event, or we'd have found it already—but to him it was major."

"A failure of some kind," Bremner suggested. "Or a rejection. That's about the hardest thing to take—" He stopped, a shadow over his face.

Ian wondered what he was thinking of, or perhaps remembering. Sometimes, very small things hurt more than expected, a pinprick that feels so deep that it aches long afterward. Moments of pain came back to him with sudden sharpness, like his wife's death. At first, he had refused to accept the enormity of it. How could she have been alive one hour and dead the next? And how could she leave behind their daughter, Hannah, a tiny, perfect baby, to live without a mother? And Ian, a helplessly bereaved father? That baby was now turning into a little girl who could run so quickly, eluding his grasp and laughing. And starting to talk—saying "Dada" all the time. He could not think of Hannah without smiling and, at the same time, wanting to weep.

Bremner had been talking and Ian had not heard him. "What?" he said abruptly.

"I said, it could be a love affair that didn't work out," Bremner repeated. "But there's a twenty-year age difference, near enough, between Haviland and the female victims, so I doubt romance is at the core of this. So, is it money? An investment of some sort that went bad?"

"Let's look in more detail at Haviland," Ian suggested, searching his own memory. "He was a banker, so perhaps there's a connection. I'll do that. You see if any of the others suffered a financial loss recently. Or invested in anything that went sour. If you need permission to do that, ask Petheridge."

"Yes, sir," Bremner said. "Keeping Haviland for yourself?"

"I am," Ian admitted. "My mathematics are better than yours." He said this with a smile.

Bremner eyed his boss for a moment. "It's because I didn't go to Cambridge, right?"

"I went there, but not to study maths," Ian returned.

"What did you study?" his sergeant asked.

Ian expected his response to evoke a dramatic reaction. "If you must know, modern history."

"Well, that explains a lot!" Bremner shook his head. "We're supposed to be solving current cases, not historical ones."

Ian did not bother to reply. They had entertained this subject before. Bremner knew very well what Ian Frobisher had studied. There was a sort of comfort in this give-and-take, like the words of a familiar rhyme.

BEFORE LOOKING INTO Roger Haviland's career at the bank, Ian examined the man's academic history. He had studied both business and modern history at Cambridge, having graduated with a first-class degree, and then almost immediately had gone into banking. Would Professor Wolford remember Haviland from the modern history classes? Almost certainly he would. The man's memory was remarkable. It always had been. Could there be something about Haviland that Wolford might recall? Something relevant? A flaw in his personality? Greed, or dishonesty, or a weakness that an enemy could exploit? But knowing about the man's frailties was no help, unless they suggested a link to the other victims.

Ian debated going to see Haviland's widow, but he doubted she was sufficiently over the initial shock and grief to be of use to them. And the sight of him would bring back the appalling reality of her tragically changed circumstances. The details of his own beloved Mary's death were as unlike Haviland's as possible—Mary had died in childbirth, while Roger Haviland's death had been terrible and apparently senseless—but perhaps the love of a loyal spouse, the sudden nightmare of bereavement, were the same?

What was it about the man that had brought him to such a violent end? Could it be something as innocent as knowledge accidentally obtained that was dangerous, even fatal, to somebody? Did all the victims share this deadly knowledge?

It was a place to start. He would go to see Mrs. Haviland later, if he had to. Meanwhile, Bremner's absurd suggestion about the minister's wife still haunted the edges of his mind; it occurred to him that Mrs. Haviland might still be at the vicarage, wounded in heart and mind, seeking what solace they could give her.

IAN WAS OUTSIDE the bank when they opened the main door to the public at ten o'clock. It was a bleak February day, with clear skies and an ice-tipped wind that crept its way through even the warmest clothing.

"Good day, sir, may I help you?" a dapper young clerk asked, with a smile.

"Yes, please," Ian replied. "I would like to see the manager." He produced his card and passed it over. "Inspector Frobisher, in regard to the late Mr. Roger Haviland," he added.

The young man paled. "Yes, sir. I'll inform Mr. Weller. If you would be so good as to wait." He disappeared through a doorway, his step quickening as he walked.

The clerk was not gone five minutes before he reappeared and asked Ian to follow him upstairs. They walked along a handsome corridor, where the young man knocked on a large, wood-paneled door—mahogany, judging by the rich tone of it.

Weller turned out to be a dark-haired man of perhaps fifty. Ian knew that Haviland had been an area manager, so presumably Weller was manager of this branch.

They exchanged somber introductions and then sat down in the leather-padded chairs, Weller behind the desk, Ian in front of it.

"What may I do for you, Inspector?" Weller asked gravely.

Ian decided not to waste time on explanations. They were unnecessary, and he was quite certain that Weller understood the situation.

"I'm in charge of the investigation into the murders committed by the man the newspapers are calling the 'Rainy-day Slasher.'"

Ian disliked using the name the press had given, but it meant that Weller would understand him and not waste precious time. "I'm afraid it seems unarguable that Mr. Haviland was the killer's latest victim. As you may imagine, we're trying to see if there was any link between the three. It's not something obvious, or it would have been spotted by now."

"Yes, of course," Weller agreed. "Very tragic business. I can't imagine what Mr. Haviland had to do with it, other than being in the wrong place at the wrong time." He looked both guarded and confused. "There is obviously a maniac on the loose. I don't know where to begin." He shook his head. Ian saw it not as an outward show of emotion, but an unconscious expression of his complete confusion.

"I understand that, sir," Ian agreed. "I'm afraid we feel the same. There's nothing we can readily see to connect the victims. And yet there must be something." He shifted his weight. The chair was polished and very hard. "All the victims were well-educated people, and all were employed in some respectable job. If they did anything on the side, as it were, we haven't been able to discover it."

He saw a change in Weller's face and interpreted it as denial. "Mind you," he quickly added, "we are not looking for such a thing, but we have to preclude it. The other victims, both young women, were in their twenties. But now there's Haviland, an older man. None of them appears to have any debt, and none is known to gamble, which is one of the obvious things we looked for. They did not drink to excess. Nor, for that matter, did they use opium or any other addictive substance."

Weller winced.

Ian smiled bleakly. "We have to look into all these things. We're certain there is some connection. And yet, they had different jobs, different social connections, no religious persuasions or political affiliations that are obvious. There are other possibilities that they shared something in common—we're currently investigating some leads." He wanted to see Weller's response to this.

Weller blinked. "Could the killings be coincidental?" He did not sound as if he believed that himself.

"Are you suggesting that the killer felt the mood coming upon him, and so he went out with a knife and waited until someone came by, alone and vulnerable?"

"It does sound very appalling," Weller responded. "Are you saying this lunatic looks just like any of us during the day, and when night comes on, or it rains, he turns into a monster and . . . ?" His voice trailed off and he looked miserably confounded by the idea.

"I will ask Mrs. Haviland about any personal acquaintances, hobbies, or interests her husband had," Ian went on. "She will know a different side to him, perhaps. This will be most painful for her . . ." He left the rest of the sentence unsaid, but saw understanding in Weller's face.

"Of course," Weller agreed. "Poor woman." He closed his eyes for a moment, as if remembering some bereavement of his own. Then he met Ian's gaze directly. "What can I tell you? Haviland worked here four or five days a week. He traveled occasionally, but it was on instructions from the head office. His duties were highly confidential." He smiled apologetically. "I inquired once, to see if I could be of assistance, but I was politely told it was not my concern."

Ian was interested but not hopeful. Haviland's expertise was almost certainly financial, perhaps to do with big loans, bad debts, international currency movements. Certainly, it had no imaginable connection with a young charity worker or a non-political journalist. But he should still look into it. "It may help," he said, without optimism, "if you would show me any papers that have to do with his clients, his movements, documents from the office . . . whether you know what they relate to or not. There might be something that cross-references to the other victims. So far, we have little else."

"Yes, of course," Weller agreed. "Do you know banking, sir?" It was asked politely, but his eyes indicated that he already knew the answer—in the negative.

Ian spent the next four hours in Haviland's office reading, or at least glancing at, the papers Weller had given him, and struggling to understand exactly what Haviland's job had been. The unavoidable conclusion was that it was exactly what he had supposed it to be, and he was good at it. Haviland had made fairly frequent trips to Europe, principally to German-speaking Austria and parts of Switzerland, and to Germany itself. They were all banking countries, especially Switzerland, so that was easily understood. He also noted the dates of his travel and his destinations. He did a quick search of the desk drawers and shelves but found nothing of interest.

When he had completed his study of the documents, he asked Weller to explain some of the journeys that had occurred most frequently or at regular intervals, pointing to the documentation. Weller could easily explain each of them in banking terms.

"And these?" he asked, indicating a final few.

"Not certain," Weller replied. "Haviland was multilingual. He spoke French very well. And, of course, German."

Ian wondered if these trips could have been in pursuit of financial business beyond the skill of Weller's knowledge as a bank manager, or perhaps too confidential for him to be included. Could they possibly have anything to do with other victims? He felt foolish even asking, but he had little else left to pursue.

"I'm afraid I don't have access to that information," Weller answered. "Let me put in a telephone call to the head office."

"Would you like me to wait outside?" Ian asked, beginning to rise to his feet.

"Not at all," Weller replied. "They may wish to speak to you."

Weller placed the call and was finally put through to the appropriate authority. He explained who Ian Frobisher was and why he was inquiring. Suddenly, his face clouded. "Mr. Haviland was murdered, Sir William. This is an ongoing case. He was the most recent of three victims, apparently the same killer in each case—" He stopped and it was clear that the man on the other end had cut him off. Weller waited and then spoke. "Sir, the police inspector in charge is in my office and is prepared to speak with you—" He stopped again. A flush of color rose to his cheeks. "He has already spoken to the widow, sir. I—" Again, he was cut off.

Ian began to feel thoroughly uncomfortable. He regretted having put Weller at some disadvantage with his superiors. Having an occasionally sarcastic boss himself, Ian identified with the embarrassment of being condescended to in front of others. But the more he heard Weller being cut off, the more he felt that there was indeed something to hide.

"Yes, sir," Weller replied, then drew breath to continue.

Even from where he sat, Ian could tell that the line was dead. So, this Sir William, whoever he was, had hung up?

"I'm sorry," Weller said unhappily. "Apparently, it all concerns confidential information."

Ian did not know if it could be relevant to Haviland's death or not. "You did everything you could," he replied to Weller. "Maybe I should have my chief superintendent ask Sir William . . . what's his surname?"

A bleak smile touched Weller's lips, even reaching his eyes. "Neilson, sir. They call him Willy Nilly." He licked his lips quickly, his eyes anxious. "But I didn't say so."

"I assume you said that as an *aide-memoire*," Ian replied, with a faint smile. "So I should not forget the name."

"Of course," Weller agreed. He stood up. "I hope you catch this lunatic. Haviland was a decent man. But even if he hadn't been, no one—not even an animal—should die like that." He reached across the desk and shook Ian's hand, holding it hard for an instant longer than necessary.

It felt like an apology.

Twelve

I AN SPENT THE early afternoon making further inquiries about
Roger Haviland. He learned nothing he thought to be of use.
When he went back to the station, he was told that Petheridge
wished to see him immediately.

"Yes, sir?" he asked, as soon as Petheridge told him to enter his
office.

Petheridge looked uneasy and confused, as if the cold February
afternoon had settled inside him, chilling him to the bone. "What
the hell have you been getting into, Frobisher?" he asked. "I've had
calls from the Home Office about Haviland. He is dead! Let the
man rest in peace, and have some respect for the feelings of his
widow."

"Sir?" Ian was startled. "I haven't suggested there was anything
to his discredit. I'm only trying to find some connection with the
other victims. Do you really think that he was an accidental choice?
That a killer just happened to be in a filthy temper, so he put on his

wet-weather clothing and went out on a spree? He happened to find himself on an isolated street with Haviland, so he took the opportunity?"

Petheridge's face was pale, his long nose a little pinched, as though the room were cold.

"Don't be impertinent, Frobisher. You're becoming desperate because this is a sad case, and as far as I can see, you are getting nowhere. People are frightened. This is out of control. Nobody expects you to solve every case you're assigned to, and—"

"Just this one," Ian interrupted him, something in normal times he would not have dared to do. "I can't solve this if you tie my hands, sir. I need to find out why he chose these people, and why now. What else do you suggest?"

Petheridge's face paled still further, and all the muscles tightened in his neck and jaw. "I realize you're in a difficult situation. So am I. I've been told from the Home Office to leave Haviland's reputation alone. He was a good man, unable now to defend himself or his poor wife." His jaw tightened. "That was their polite way of saying to leave her out of it, or they'll demand that I put somebody in your place who can understand orders and damn well obey them." He took a deep breath and let it out slowly. "And if it comes to it, they'll put someone in my place as well. Go find your slasher, God help us, but do it some other way. Haviland's affairs are not to be excavated." He looked embarrassed. "Do you understand me?"

Ian bit back the protest that was on the edge of his tongue. He knew the chain of command went far beyond either of them, and however inscrutable it was, they were bound by it. "Yes, sir," he said, although his thoughts were racing. What kind of special privilege had Haviland possessed that his reputation must be so protected?

"Good," Petheridge replied. "Now go home and eat something, then start again tomorrow."

IAN DID NOT go home. This case was getting out of control. He felt as if his mind were going round in ever-decreasing circles: he began by following all the rules of logic and deliberation, sooner or later ending back where he had started, with nothing resolved.

He decided to go and consult the most lucid thinker he knew, a man who had no connection to this matter, but to whom he had lately been able to extend some help.

He arrived cold, wet, and tired on the doorstep of Nicholas Wolford's home. He knocked and waited, standing in the cold, wind-driven fog. He could see light through the curtains and knew it was coming from the sitting room. He knocked again and then rang the bell.

The door flew open and Wolford stood there, glaring at his former student.

"Professor Wolford?" Ian said. He was not questioning his identity, but only asking if he might be invited in.

Wolford shook his head sharply, as if the cold air had awakened him. "Frobisher? For heaven's sake, don't stand there, man, it's an ice house outside!" Ian walked through the door, and Wolford quickly closed it behind him. "By the way, that Pitt that you recommended? Good fellow. Every bit as sharp as he was in his student days. Are you all right? No, you aren't. Sorry for such a fool question. You look like hell!"

Ian smiled. In fact, it was an almost luminous grin of relief. "Thank you, sir." He shed his raincoat on the mat so as not to drip water all over the polished wooden floor.

Ian recalled that Wolford lived in this house on and off, taking only temporary lodgings in Cambridge during the term. This had always been his retreat.

"Come in, come in," Wolford repeated, looking Ian up and down. "Yes, you really do look like hell. What's the matter? Have you eaten? How about a cold lamb sandwich and a glass of wine?"

Ian had not even thought of dinner but now realized he was very hungry indeed. "I didn't mean to . . ." he began. He hadn't come with the intent to be fed. What he needed was to sort out his thoughts with the help of someone whose mind was cool and logical and would not dissemble or retreat from uncomfortable facts.

"Incidentally," Wolford smiled, a surprisingly gentle expression for him, "what did you come for?"

Ian decided to be totally frank. Wolford despised excuses. *Waffling around*, as he had called it. "I came to get my thoughts in order, with someone who won't be swayed by pretense or emotion, and who thinks that honesty is the only way to make sense of a complex problem."

Wolford's dark eyebrows went up. "Indeed? You compliment me."

Ian felt himself falling into old habits, the years since college having slipped away. In those days, it had all been ideas and arguments: defining "argument" not as a quarrel, but as a line of reasoning toward reaching a conclusion. No real situations, griefs or horrors, cluttered the pure train of thought. Argument could be a retreat from reality. It was also a step away from emotional tangles. "What I need is your cool head and logical mind," he explained.

Wolford smiled. "Then you oblige me to live up to your estimation of me."

Ian followed him into the sitting room, where the fire was burning and filling the air with warmth and the faint odor of aromatic wood. It awoke in him a rush of old memories, when study was hard, exercise of the mind vigorous, even exhausting, but also thrilling. They had dealt with theories, ideas, dreams, and occasional nightmares, but in those days, Ian had not yet fully determined what he wanted to do. He was faced with no grieving families, no loss of his wife, no bloody corpses in the rain or hours spent outside in a cold so intense that it ate into your bones.

Ian sat in front of the fire while Wolford went into the kitchen. He returned five minutes later with a tray holding thick slices of fresh bread, roast lamb, a dish of butter, and a little mint sauce. And, of course, two glasses and a bottle of red wine.

The men sat together in the quiet of this room. For Ian, time flew backward, and the world felt comfortable again. Reality had disappeared behind the curtain of rain, growing steadily heavier, and gusts of wind blowing against the glass. All sense of time vanished.

"So, what's the problem?" Wolford asked, after he had finished the last mouthful and Ian had put the dishes on the tray and taken it through to the kitchen, where he left it on the bench by the sink, as Wolford had instructed him.

Ian settled back in his chair again, beside the fire.

"Facts only," Wolford pressed. "We'll get to opinions later." He leaned back, crossed his legs at the knees, elbows bent and resting on the arms of the chair, hands locked together. He looked extraordinarily comfortable, but Ian saw that he was listening intently.

"I'm in charge of what the papers are calling the 'Rainy-day Slasher' case," he began, looking into Wolford's face. "I know all sorts of things about each of the victims, but nothing that's common to all of them. They're different ages, different occupations, one man and two women." He caught a flicker in Wolford's eyes. "What?" he quickly asked. He recalled this look: it meant his former professor had an idea. He stopped, waiting for the man to explain.

Wolford gazed at him steadily. "Do you suppose they were killed for an obvious resemblance? Something all these people share?"

Ian shook his head. "No, we've looked into this."

"It does seem unlikely," Wolford agreed. "More probably it was external, a circumstance common to them all. By chance, rather than something rooted in their lives? Or perhaps more likely still, harder to find or recognize but more interesting, a quality of character they shared. Have you considered that?" He smiled very slightly, as if amused by an idea inside his head.

Ian considered it for several moments. "Quality of character? You mean that they acted together . . ."

"Not necessarily," Wolford said thoughtfully. "If they all possessed one character flaw, one quality that was . . ." He shrugged.

"Something that made them act in a certain way, and that finally caught up with them. More to the point, look for something quite apart from their professions . . . try looking into their interests more closely."

"Well, I've hit a wall there," Ian admitted. "Somebody high in the government has shut one door in my face. Apparently, the last victim was someone important."

Wolford gave a twisted little smile. "*Important*. Interesting word. A matter of values. Important to whom? Perhaps there's a secret that's very much in their interest to hide? Did you say there were three victims so far? Have you considered that perhaps one of them is the real target, and the others were killed simply to conceal that fact?"

Ian was shaken. That had occurred to him, yet to hear it voiced was chilling. It was a horrifying idea. "So, you're saying that two of them were totally random, killed to hide the one that mattered?"

Wolford's eyebrows rose. "You've already considered that and it horrified you?" He nodded slightly. "Good, it should. Are there crimes, injuries to innocent bystanders, random wrongs, that don't horrify you?" There was something close to disgust in his face.

Ian did not need to consider his reply. "No, but most crimes are thoughtless. They are often the result of rage that the perpetrator can't or won't control, fear for their own safety. Greed, or some other appetite run wild. Eventually, selfishness, a sense that *my life is everything and yours doesn't matter*."

Wolford sat forward a little. "What about self-defense? Or a kind of natural justice for crimes the law does not recognize? Injury . . . without recourse."

"You think individuals should be allowed to decide that?" Ian was startled. "I wouldn't like to contradict you, sir, but consider your own situation: someone has accused you of a crime and has sought the law to get reparation when, in fact, he is the one to cause the injury in the first place. The law is meant to deal with this. Isn't that how civilized people behave, or how they should behave? It's the purpose of having a jury. The strong protect the weak, and the community chooses representatives to hear the argument and then decide. Going back to Saxon times, before the Norman Conquest, they used to do it by armed combat, literally. We've progressed to verbal argument and reason winning."

Wolford smiled. It was a little derisive, but the humor came through. "Bravo! I see you really were listening. And you, who sent me a good barrister, a civilized champion, if you like, to argue for me. I thank you again for that." He stared hard at Ian with what seemed like anger in his eyes. "Now, why the hell didn't you go in for law yourself? You have the brains, at least as much as young Pitt has. Why are you trudging around in the damn rain, looking for you have no idea who? Instead, you could be sitting in your warm office puzzling over the law and defending the weak." He pointed and leaned a fraction further forward. "Or attacking those you believe to have broken the rules, seeking always principle, compassion, and reason! There was no limit to the heights you could have reached. Now, what can you do, at best? Become a superintendent, telling other people what to do?"

"You make it sound like directing traffic," Ian said, surprised how deeply he resented the belittlement of his job. "But somebody has to direct the traffic. Imagine the chaos if no one did."

When Wolford spoke, his voice was filled with disgust. "You can teach any fool to do that. One day, we'll have machines that will do it for us!" he snapped. "You have a first-class mind. Or, if you want to quibble, a good second-class one. You're not a genius, but they are rare, and damn difficult to deal with. You might have done far more than this!" He spread his arms out, fingers stretched as if to catch the invisible. "Instead, you are morally a street sweeper! Taking the few solid or dangerous bits of rubbish and putting them in the bin. Is that enough for you, Frobisher? Does it stretch your intellect, satisfy your soul? Does it make good use of your imagination, your wit, your discipline of the mind? Is that your contribution to mankind?"

Ian scrambled for an answer. For a moment, the questions stung with a pain that amazed him. And he knew without doubt that Wolford meant it. His words were not designed to sting, or to hurt, but to make him think, make him doubt his path, perhaps enough to change it.

He tried to frame an answer. Not to satisfy Wolford, but to satisfy himself. "Police work is society's first defense against chaos," he said.

"Don't be melodramatic," Wolford answered coldly.

"Chaos doesn't begin with worlds crashing into each other," Ian argued, jerking his hands sharply to suggest a colliding motion. "It happens when small things are out of place, little tears not mended, small offenses becoming habit. And when these things are tolerated, they become bigger, and they frighten people into defeat or give opportunists the chance to become more dangerous. Petty thefts unchecked become embezzlement, the systematic erosion of property, grand theft. Injustice is ignored when it becomes habit, and there's no recourse for the weak, the frightened. Domestic violence becomes habitual abuse. Drunken brawls become open fights, and—"

"You make your point," Wolford interrupted, nodding grudgingly. "But it doesn't take brains like yours to deal with such chaos."

"Not to be a foot soldier," Ian agreed. "But to be a general, yes, it does. And you don't go in as a general. You start at the bottom and work your way up. A good commander first learns how to obey."

"Who told you that?" Wolford demanded. "It certainly wasn't me!"

"You taught me the theory," Ian pointed out. "Or, more importantly, you taught me how to learn."

Wolford drew in his breath, then let it out again without speaking. It was an old argument he had used many times himself.

"The best commanders are the ones who have learned how to do the job from the bottom up," Ian went on. "Who learn how to deal with people, real victims, real witnesses who are terrified, bereaved, injured, who know what it's like because it has happened to them. Then you know the right questions to ask. You know what it feels like, what to ask and what you don't have to put into words, because you've been there, and they know that."

"All right!" Wolford said sharply, nostrils pinched. "You've made your point. And you imagine you will get to the top? Or anywhere near it?"

"If I don't, then I don't deserve to."

"Oh, don't be so bloody ridiculous!" Wolford shot back. "Do you think every man gets what he deserves? If you do, you're beyond naïve; you're stupid."

"Of course I don't," Ian said, keeping his temper in check with difficulty. "I'm not the only man with brains and ambition. But I'll do the best I can every day, and it'll be hard. I may get to the top, and I may not, but I'll clear a lot of rubbish along the way. Some of your students may make it to the top, but certainly not all of them, and yet we will be better than we would have been without your teaching. You taught us well, but you don't decide for us what we should do with everything we have learned."

For a second or two, Wolford sat motionless, his face unreadable; then he moved suddenly, startling Ian so that he flinched. "Have some more wine?" he offered.

"Thank you, sir," Ian accepted. He did not really want it, but he knew that refusing would be a tacit refusal of Wolford himself, rebuffing his proffered concession, and that was a breach of the professor's hospitality he did not wish to make.

Outside, the wind was blowing rain against the windows, and against the slates on the roof, causing them to rattle. There would soon be sleet. It was going to be a long, miserable journey home.

Thirteen

THE NEWSPAPERS WERE relentless, splashed with headlines about the "Rainy-day Slasher." The papers were obsessed. Probably everyone in London was. Daniel tried to force it out of his mind. He knew about the murders, including this latest one of a respected banker, but there was nothing he could do about it. And he needed to focus all his attention on the assault case against Wolford.

He had read Wolford's manuscript twice. He had studied it carefully but had also been carried away by the sweep of history and the detail of the extraordinary characters involved. It was a fascinating book; Wolford was an eminently readable raconteur. It was history, but it was far more than that. Daniel found it to be drama of Shakespearean complexity. The terror of revolution, the execution of kings, these were subjects of timeless interest. Wolford had concentrated on the individual people but had drawn from his research the truth of how revolution eventually consumes itself, often leaving behind it an upheaval even more drastic, more violent, and more extreme than the original insurrection.

He was deep in thought when Impney knocked on his door. "Yes?" he answered, a little impatiently. He had just reached the final scene, ready to topple Robespierre and bring an end to the High Terror.

Impney entered the room and stood in front of Daniel's desk, his face grave. "I am sorry to interrupt you, sir, but I have just been speaking with Mr. fford Croft. He is concerned about this third, terrible murder."

There was a folded newspaper in the chief clerk's hand, instead of the tea tray Daniel would have preferred. It was still early, but he had been hard at work.

"I'm sorry, sir," Impney repeated gravely. His normally benign face was creased with concern, and there was an unusually somber tone to his voice. "I thought you should see the newspaper this morning."

"Something more about the German navy?" Daniel sounded flippant, but he was only half joking. There was always some sort of tension in Europe, and alarmists were making more of it than it was.

"No, sir, not so far as I know. This is not *The Times*, sir. It is one of the less responsible newspapers."

"So why did you bring it?"

"Because it leads with the news, sir, of this new murder in the rain." Impney opened the newspaper for Daniel to see, while not actually handing it to him. "There are certain facts not included, sir, but unfortunately, this victim was attacked in exactly the same manner as the two young women and has ended up as Miss Miriam's responsibility, sir."

"I'm truly sorry, Impney. I'm aware of this new victim, but it isn't our case. There's nothing we, here in chambers, can do to help anyone. Does the paper suggest that the police have an idea who did it? Or is the victim someone we know?" He asked the last question slowly, the ice of fear settling in the pit of his stomach. It was not so very long ago that he had been called out to identify a dead colleague.

Impney winced. "Miss Miriam is dealing with these bodies, sir. Mr. fford Croft is concerned for her, but he doesn't like to meddle, in case she isn't up to it, if you understand me, Mr. Pitt."

"I know," Daniel said quietly. He had been trying not to think of it.

"He doesn't want to ask and have her think he is worried about her," Impney said, his voice filled with anxiety. It was only a matter of months ago that Marcus fford Croft had suffered a heart attack and spent some time in hospital. That was not an experience his daughter was likely to forget—nor would she want to be the cause of any additional stress.

"I took him a pot of tea, sir, and a very small nip of brandy, just to keep him warm. But it might not be a bad idea, Mr. Pitt, if you were to call in and see if he's all right. I took the liberty of serving your tea there, sir."

Daniel drew in his breath, then let it out. "Thank you." That seemed all there was to say. Impney had manipulated him neatly, deftly, as usual. He stared at the man a moment longer, trying to read in his eyes if he were particularly concerned.

Impney merely smiled, gave a little nod, and left.

Daniel went straight along to Marcus's office and knocked on the door. It was answered immediately, with an instruction to enter.

Marcus fford Croft was not a big man, average in height, probably a little less, and he was definitely rotund, but he had immense presence. His thick hair, which had once been the same shade of red as Miriam's, was now snow white. His clear skin glowed against the reflected color of his signature velvet waistcoat. Today's was a rich plum, a stylish contrast to his violet cravat. These articles of clothing and their color combinations were usually more successful than Daniel expected. He would have felt absurd wearing them; on Marcus, the look was rather splendid.

"Good morning, sir," he said, regarding the waistcoat and cravat without comment. Instead, he smiled.

Marcus must have seen his amusement, because he had a slightly puzzled look on his face. "Tea?" he asked.

Daniel sat down. "Yes, please," he accepted.

"Then pour it, dear boy. What else did you come for?"

Daniel obeyed and passed Marcus a cup. He poured his own and sipped it gingerly. It was very hot.

"Did something happen?" Marcus asked, sitting totally still.

"Just the continuation of these *slasher* murders."

Marcus muttered something under his breath that sounded uncharacteristically like blasphemy.

Daniel looked at him and decided to change the subject. "I'm more or less up-to-date on the Wolford case, sir, and—"

"How is it going?" Marcus interrupted. "He's a bit eccentric, but he knows his subject. Still, a difficult man. Moody. Takes offense where it isn't meant. But like him or not, I don't believe he'd copy anyone's work. For a start, he wouldn't think anyone was better than he was. So, there would be nobody worth copying!"

It had not occurred to Daniel that Marcus was quite that familiar with Wolford's work. But then, thinking about it, he should have considered that. Marcus's subject was obviously law, but he was a naturally curious man. He had kept up with many of his university fellows. Friendships formed at a time when they were changing from boys to men, and many men fondly recalled those shared adventures and new horizons.

Marcus smiled and settled more comfortably into his chair. "Wolford was long after my time, of course, closer to Miriam's age. But I do keep up with the old friends, you know." He smiled at some memory. "I hear what's going on. Who's doing what. Never had a son, but if I had, I would have sent him to Cambridge, whatever he studied." He smiled rather mischievously. "You know, they don't like women in forensic medicine." His smile broadened. "But they wouldn't refuse a man, if he was halfway fit." He glanced at a photograph on a shelf that was crammed with the books he referred to most often. It was of Miriam, around the age of seventeen, looking so young and, at that particular angle, so reminiscent of her mother. Daniel had never met Marcus's wife—the man had been a widower for many years—but he had seen a painting of her in the fford Croft home.

"Would you like me to go and make sure Miriam's all right?" Daniel offered. "It wouldn't seem so obvious that someone was checking on her—at least, not as obvious as if you went."

Marcus nodded. "She won't listen to me. She says I'm fussing. Just make sure that dragon isn't working her too hard, will you? No sleep. No food. You know, she's . . ." He could not find the word he wanted, or else he changed his mind about using it.

Daniel understood the urge to protect. "Yes, sir, I will."

"Thank you." Marcus hesitated for a moment, then continued discussing the Wolford case, as if they had never strayed from the subject.

On leaving Marcus's office, Daniel passed Impney in the corridor and gave him a nod and a smile. Impney understood a great deal without the need for words.

"Will you be back this afternoon, sir, in case anyone should be asking for you?"

"I'm not sure," said Daniel. "I may go and see Mr. Wolford. There are still some small points I need to clear up. And I might call in and see how Miss Miriam is."

"Very good, sir."

Daniel realized with momentary surprise that Impney had probably known Miriam since her birth. He had seen the family through happiness and grief, joy and bereavement, success and danger. Perhaps the fford Crofts were the only family he had? If he were an orphan, the chambers might be the one place where he felt he belonged.

"Impney," said Daniel.

The clerk stopped and turned round, eyebrows raised inquiringly. "Yes, sir?"

"Thank you."

"You're welcome, sir." There was a slight flush in his cheeks, as if he had read quite clearly what was in Daniel's mind—except he could not possibly have.

Outside in the street, Daniel considered taking a taxi, but it had stopped raining sometime before dawn. The rainfall had been so heavy that the street looked freshly scrubbed. The air sparkled with sharp, cold winter sunlight, and the wind was brisk.

It was a beautiful day to walk to the underground railway station, so he set off.

WHEN THE TRAIN arrived at his destination, he climbed the stairs up to the street and continued briskly, his step light.

He arrived at the laboratory about fifteen minutes later. The attendant let him in, and he found Miriam, apparently alone, bent over her work. At first, she did not even glance at him, as if he had been an assistant bringing or removing something she required. When she looked up, her face suddenly lit with pleasure.

"Daniel!" She put down the instrument in her hands and came toward him. As she moved closer, he could see the fine lines of weariness around her eyes and the tightness in her neck and shoulders. "Are you here to check on me for Father?" She tried to smile, but there were dark shadows beneath her eyes.

"He wants to know how you are, of course," he replied. "He worries about you. Just as you worry about him. But no, he didn't send me." He looked at her steadily. "I came for both of us, and for Impney. I imagine you've known him all your life."

She relaxed a little. "Yes. Father being an only child, Impney is the only 'uncle' I have. He doesn't say much, but he never forgets my birthday. Not for as far back as I can remember." She looked away from him for a long moment.

"Miriam?" he asked.

"Daniel, it was the same man," she said quietly. "But this attack was even more savage than the last one."

The newspapers had said that, but he assumed they had exaggerated, as they did with so many things. Hearing it from Miriam was different. It was frightening, and his first thought was of how she must feel. She had seen the victim and touched the stab wounds, and she knew how quickly or slowly the man had died. She must have been able to sense his horror and pain, his realization, even if it was for only a few seconds, that he was dying alone, his killer standing over him, in the rain, on the pavement, in the dark.

Did Miriam have any defense against that? He wanted to say something that would ease the horror, but the moment he opened his mouth he knew his words might convey only his lack of understanding. To protect her would be to deny the reality of her job; she was a woman of courage and intelligence who should not be sheltered from reality when it became too ugly. And if he was honest, to concentrate on protecting her was an escape for him from that reality. It was much easier to think of her than of Roger Haviland— or the man's widow.

He smiled bleakly. "I came to find out how you are, and to see for myself, so I could go back to Marcus and Impney and tell them you're all right. And perhaps to get you food or hot tea, even though I know they're not going to solve anything. You still have to look the tragedy in the face, take it apart, and see if you can tell the police anything to help them find this . . . this madman. He is mad, isn't he?"

She pushed her hair back and tightened the net holding it in place. "I don't know. But I can tell you he was in the grip of some uncontrollable fury when he did this. And the tip of the index finger was gone, like the others. I can't help feeling that it has great meaning to the man who cut it off. It was symbolic of something moving like poison through his mind."

"Can you tell anything about the latest victim from his body?" he asked.

She thought for a moment. "He wasn't weak or incapacitated in any way, but he wore glasses quite often," she began. "You can see the ridge on his nose where they sat, although we didn't find them. Or, rather, the police didn't. And if you look carefully at his hand, the mutilated one, you can see the slightly misshapen middle finger, just an indentation and a slight staining of ink, as if he wrote a lot. It is, at least in part, a guess. I'll tell Inspector Frobisher when he comes, but I'm not sure it will help. It's not solid proof of anything, and it may not be significant." She looked down. "I wish I had more, but stretching a point to give it disproportionate importance would be misleading." She bit her lip and then took a breath. "I'm afraid the newspapers will magnify this latest killing, raking over the details, until some weak-minded person, or someone driven out of their senses, will try to copy it, leading to yet another murder."

He wished he could think of some answer that would comfort her, but there was no honest response he could give, and she did not deserve anything less than honesty from him.

Dr. Eve came out from the back room where she had been working, unseen. She was wearing her usual white coat, stained in places. Her hair was too short to need a hairnet or pins. She looked Daniel up and down. "Have you come for any useful purpose?" she asked, a trifle acidly. "Miriam doesn't need looking after. And if she does, I'll do it. Once she's here to work—well, she's perfectly capable of doing so, or I wouldn't allow her in my lab." She looked at Daniel with a cold eye, waiting for him to blush and retreat.

Instead, he met her gaze unblinkingly. "And how are you, Dr. Hall? Would you like a fresh cup of coffee from the shop down the road? I can fetch you one with pleasure. That is, without interrupting your work, so you don't have to get it yourself. And I do know that Dr. fford Croft is all right. She is always all right. But her father tends to worry, so I will telephone him and tell him she's fine. That is, before I get your coffee, and then go to question my client about a matter that is pending."

Dr. Eve's eyebrows rose. "Oh, and is your client connected to this miserable business in any way? A bereaved relative, perhaps?"

"No connection at all, except that he knows Inspector Frobisher. But then, so do I. I knew him at university."

Eve smiled. Something seemed to amuse her. "Indeed. And is this another one of your dramatic court appearances?" she asked.

"Not at all. Our client in this case is clearly not guilty, and it is going to be fairly simple to prove. Unfortunately, he punched the man who made an accusation against him, which will prejudice the case a bit, but not seriously."

"Sure of yourself, aren't you?" she said, still looking directly at him. "Pride cometh before a fall."

"It doesn't take a clever lawyer to prove this one—" he replied.

"So, not very exciting for you," Eve concluded. "Which explains why you have come here to see what we are doing."

"Since nobody has been charged with any of the murders, or looks like they will be soon, there's nothing for me to do here," he replied. "And I would hate to defend whoever is responsible. It will be best if he is so obviously insane that there is no need for a full trial."

"No opportunity for brilliant tactics?" Her eyebrows rose. She was still needling him, and they both knew it. "How tedious."

Daniel smiled. It was a compliment, in an oblique way, indicating that she thought he was worth the attention. Or was she testing him to see if he was worthy of Miriam's time? He raised his eyebrow just a fraction, as if he were not sure that question should even be addressed. "Even if I were senior enough to pick and choose my cases, and then only take the complicated ones, I don't think I would. Some apparently simple cases may be deeper than they look at first. They can change with a single piece of evidence, a single lie discovered."

Eve was not quite finished. "Is that all?"

"No. It would be boring to see in advance where a case was going. Grubby to take what you think are going to be the most career-enhancing cases," he answered. "A bit self-serving. And in the end, not a good idea."

Eve nodded slowly and then announced, "Go and fetch the hot coffee." She stepped back a pace. "If you expect to be welcome here, you'd better earn your keep. We're going to be a long time on this one."

"This one is worse than the others?" Daniel asked, glancing at Miriam, then at Eve, although her face told him the answer before she responded.

Her voice was gentler. "Yes, it is. Now . . . go."

He walked briskly in the sharp, frosty air, but it was dry, and everything still sparkled with that unmistakable newly washed look. The proprietor at the coffee shop smiled and wrapped up shortbread slices without being asked. When Daniel said it was for Dr. Eve and Dr. fford Croft, the man replied, "For the docs?" He would not allow Daniel to pay.

He arrived back at the lab and was let straight in, where he took the jug full of hot coffee and divided it between three mugs. Both Eve and Miriam stopped working, scrubbed their hands, and came up to the bench. They did not take off their protective overalls.

Daniel looked around the laboratory. Every shelf was crammed with bottles and jars, all carefully labeled with letters and numbers, barely a quarter of which he understood. There were various machines, all silent at the moment, and a cluster of glass jars holding specimens he preferred not to look at, as well as instruments whose purposes he could only guess.

He watched Miriam as she drank her coffee. She seemed different from before her stay in Holland; a tension within her had eased. She was tired, certainly, and even at this hour of the morning her hair looked hastily pinned up.

Was this what she really wanted, he wondered, now that it was real? To deal with death, often violent, the remains of human bodies after the horror of an accident or a murder or the ravages of disease? Why? When most of her friends were dealing with marriage and motherhood, what had compelled Miriam to reject convention?

Miriam must have realized he was gazing at her because she stared back, as if daring him to speak.

Evelyn Hall was watching them both.

He must either evade the question or voice his thoughts. He would have to do this sometime, anyway. "It's a rotten case to come back to, but there aren't ever going to be nice ones," he said.

Eve maintained her silence, now watching Daniel rather than Miriam.

"Is there any such thing as a nice crime?" Miriam asked. "And aren't quite a few of your own clients guilty? Or are the jurors mistaken half the time?" There was both a challenge and a certain amusement in her eyes.

So, she was going to meet him and not evade the question. He felt a little shiver of satisfaction. Over the time she had been away, he had nearly forgotten how pleasing she was, how direct. And how much he enjoyed talking to her. It was never about nothing.

"Nice crimes?" he repeated. "No, of course not. For me, the satisfaction is in untangling the truth from the lies and the errors, and then finding some sort of justice. Or mercy. Quite often, it's learning to understand what happened and how I can, at the least, mitigate its consequences."

Miriam's face lit with what Daniel saw as profound satisfaction. "I couldn't have put it better myself," she said. "The crime cannot be undone. The dead cannot be brought back to life. But what hap-

pened can be understood. What was accidental, what was on purpose. How it might be prevented in the future. And all of this with
at least some possibility of learning the lessons and dispensing as
much justice as possible."

For an instant, Daniel wondered if she had deliberately led him
into this. Then he realized he had thrown down the challenge, and
she had picked it up. He gave her a wide smile. "When it works,"
he added. "And accepting the outcome with a little humility when
it doesn't. At least I get to pick and choose most of my clients. You
have to take them all. I'm sorry about this. It's hard."

Miriam's smile said more than words could. It was sudden,
bright, and blazingly honest. Then it was gone, and she turned
back to her work.

Daniel hesitated only a moment, said goodbye to Miriam and
Dr. Eve, and went out into the still, bright morning.

HE RETURNED TO fford Croft and Gibson and reported to Marcus,
but only that Miriam was well, if tired, and that she was dedicated
to her work with a pride and a conviction she had not been able to
find before.

"She's changed, hasn't she?" Marcus said, seated behind his desk,
leaning back in his chair a little. He was smiling slightly and looking up at Daniel, clearly trying to read in Daniel's face the emotion
he was feeling, whether it was happiness with the change in Miriam
or a certain uneasiness. Had she drifted away from Daniel? From
the person she had been, even to Marcus?

"Yes," Daniel agreed. "But she's in a group she always wanted to
belong to, instead of being on the outside, standing alone. I don't
mean it will be easy. Dr. Hall is accepted because only a fool would
deny her superb skills. Miriam has yet to prove herself as good as
that."

"She may never be able to do that," Marcus said. "But if she does . . ." His face lost its confidence, his eyes direct yet troubled. "Will she turn into a future Dr. Eve? Are you sure she won't change so much?" It was a heartfelt question.

Daniel knew what he meant but was not saying. Would Miriam become as isolated as Eve? Feared and admired by her colleagues, almost worshipped by her students, but always essentially alone, because she was a woman in a man's world? She was not only equal to the men but superior to most of them.

Daniel thought painfully for several moments before he answered. "Evelyn Hall is unique. She had to fight even harder—and without another female role model to inspire her, as Miriam has. But Miriam won't be like that. She won't be like anybody. I can't see what's ahead for her, but I can't choose for her, and neither can you. If you try, she won't trust you anymore. And if she gives this career up for anyone, in the end she'll hate them for persuading her to abandon her skills and the chance to belong to something that deeply matters to her."

"Will she?" Marcus asked. "I mean, will she belong, really?" His brow puckered. "She never has, you know. Even as a child, she was always different. She never had dolls, just stuffed animals. But she treated them as if they were human." He smiled at the memory.

Daniel could believe this without any difficulty at all. He had regarded animals as his friends when he was young, particularly cats and dogs.

Had Miriam been as lonely as that made her sound? One day, perhaps, he would find out. "Don't worry about her work," he said aloud. "Just know that she'll succeed, and that's something we don't all do."

"I get your point," Marcus responded. "I won't interfere. So, how's your case going with Wolford?"

"I don't think the prosecution has a leg to stand on. I was going to see Wolford today, but I think I'll go up to Cambridge instead. I should be there by late afternoon, if I catch the next train. See if I can trace some of Tolliver's background and when he first started researching the subjects of these essays. Wolford says their paths never crossed, but it could be something he doesn't remember or didn't even know of."

"Sounds reasonable." Marcus nodded. "But didn't you already do that?"

"I've looked into Tolliver's career as a published author, but if I'm able to find a few people who knew him, or knew them both, I might get a better understanding."

"Are you worried about the case?" Marcus asked, with surprise.

"Not worried, but I don't want to get ambushed by something I should have known—or could have, if I'd done my homework properly."

Marcus nodded slowly. "Good. Diligence and background. Sometimes it's the cases you thought were already won that catch you by surprise. Drake always knew that." A shadow passed over his face, and he smiled bleakly. He was referring to the best lawyer the chambers had ever had, with the possible exception of Marcus himself. Drake had met a violent death the previous year. They did not refer to it often, but none of them had forgotten it.

"Yes, sir," Daniel agreed. There was no need to add more words. He bade Marcus goodbye and went back to his office.

DANIEL ARRIVED IN Cambridge in the late afternoon and started looking up old friends among the professors who had taught him. It was strange, walking the familiar streets, seeing the college buildings in the twilight, the quiet green where they had played cricket with such energy and passion, as if the result of the smallest match carried the weight of national pride. He recalled how they had talked about the brilliant boundary strokes, the missed catches, the tactics, as if these were the marks of history. In some ways they were. The friendships, the supreme effort for something that was only sportsmanship, playing for the team, doing your best for something that did not matter at all. Someone hit a ball or missed

it. Tomorrow, it would be nothing, a few matches one way or another. Nothing was changed.

The green was still the same, the wind in the trees, the last of the
sunlight coming and going as the clouds passed overhead, the silence except for the vivid remarks of the umpire, a shout of ap-
plause.

He took in the view. In some way, this epitomized everything. A
verse of Sir Henry Newbolt's poem "Vitaï Lampada" came to mind.

> There's a breathless hush in the close to-night—
> Ten to make and the match to win—
> A bumping pitch and a blinding light,
> An hour to play and the last man in.
> And it's not for the sake of a ribboned coat,
> Or the selfish hope of a season's fame,
> But his Captain's hand on his shoulder smote
> "Play up! play up! and play the game!"

Emotion overwhelmed him for a moment. The sense of belonging was intense, like a joy surging through his blood. Then he
shook himself and returned to the present.

He continued his walk across the green to the pavement and
over to the office of the first man he wished to speak with. The
lights were still on. There was somebody there.

DANIEL RETURNED ON the last train, getting in close to midnight,
but he had seen everyone he wished to. He was tired, but London
was the last stop on the line, so he could not get carried beyond the
terminus. He fought sleep at first, rehearsing in his mind what he
had learned. It was all familiar territory but seen from a different
view. It was only five years since he had left university, but since
then he had seen violent death, defended the guilty and innocent,
made great strides forward in his knowledge and dedication—and

a few slips backward as he gained knowledge of his own ignorance. Or perhaps, when viewed differently, those were also steps forward. He was far more urgently aware of how much he did not know.

He had spoken to six different people who knew both Wolford and Tolliver. They had added texture and dimension to the picture he had of the two men, offered proof of the incidents he knew of, and mentioned a few he did not. Tolliver came across in all their accounts as an honest man, deeply convinced of the originality of his observations as published in his essays, papers, and other works. Most particularly, they mentioned the book that was the object of his lawsuit, a book containing passages that he believed Wolford had copied because Wolford had given no references. Daniel knew that this was not true.

All the people Daniel spoke to could see Tolliver's reasoning but also his error. Some sympathized with him, but most agreed that Wolford had always come by his opinions independently. No one was prepared to give evidence of any plagiarism on either man's part.

Daniel had all the evidence he needed to defend Wolford, and yet he was bothered by a certain disquiet that he could not put into words. This indefinable sense that things were not quite right niggled at his brain and made him uneasy. Was it just that this was all too simple? Was Tolliver bringing this suit, continuing with it, because he did not know how to withdraw gracefully? Withdrawing with an apology might be the best way forward not only for Tolliver but for Wolford as well. Should Daniel explore that?

A settlement out of court could be the best answer, for both parties. It was worth considering.

Fourteen

MIRIAM WAS WORKING hard in the morgue laboratory. Dr. Eve had come in late that morning, which was most unlike her. Miriam thought for a moment to ask her if she was all right, but a glance at Eve's face made her decide against it.

The first job was to examine the body of a very stout man who had apparently died of a stroke. Miriam had already looked at him and made preliminary notes, with the help of their laboratory assistant, Joe. He was a young man with the strength to move and lift bodies when necessary as well as the dedication to do whatever was asked of him, no matter how busy he was or how curt the instruction.

Miriam and Eve set to work, the room silent except for the words necessary to do to their jobs.

"Heart attack," Miriam said at last.

Eve looked at her inquiringly.

"It's just a matter of confirming it," Miriam insisted.

"Or not!" Eve said tersely. "What did they tell us about him?"

Miriam recited the notes from the doctors who had been in attendance.

"So, what do they expect from us?" Eve asked. "Are they afraid it's something else, but they don't know what? Who is he, anyway?" She looked at the corpse with distaste. "How long do you intend to stand and stare at him?"

Miriam was about to respond, but she saw the pallor of Eve's face and picked up the scalpel. She regarded the corpse for a moment and began to cut.

The silence continued, apart from her comments to Joe, who made notes while Miriam worked. For half an hour, Miriam examined, weighed, and measured, speaking only when describing what she was seeing.

Eve watched, but she did not speak.

Miriam turned her attention to examining the organs. The liver was enlarged, damaged, but she had expected that. There was nothing remarkable about it.

"Why would the doctors want this done?" Miriam asked finally, referring to the autopsy.

"Just to make sure they didn't miss anything," Eve replied, "even if they presumed the cause of death is a heart attack. Did you test for poison?"

"What?"

"I asked if you tested for poison."

"No, I—"

"Good," Eve interrupted. "It would be a waste of time. Perfectly natural causes, as you said. Now, let's get on to something useful."

"Cup of tea?" Joe suggested.

"No!" Eve snapped, and then changed her mind. "Yes," she said brusquely, then turned and walked out of the laboratory and into one of the storerooms.

Miriam glanced at Joe and followed Eve into the storeroom, where she found her leaning over the bench, her head low. Miriam felt a twinge of real fear. Her instinct was to protect, to comfort, but she knew Eve would not accept it. The scientist could not afford to be vulnerable, least of all in her own estimation. What was the right thing to say? What did she need?

Miriam had always thought of Eve Hall as not only unbeatable but indestructible. Sympathy might come across as pity. She finally had to ask. "What hurts?" She was standing close to Eve but not touching her, reminding herself that she was still the pupil. But then, probably, she would always be.

Eve did not answer.

Miriam took the plunge. "What are you afraid of?" Her voice was soft, caring.

Eve turned slowly. For a moment there was anger in her face and then, with obvious effort, she overcame it. "I've got a cracking headache, that's all. I've taken aspirin. It will have its effect soon. Don't fuss!"

Miriam stared at her, remembering the last few days here, trying to assess the truth of what she said. Would it pass soon? She was flushed, the color in her face bright and patchy, flaming in her cheeks and white around the eyes and across her brow. "Then sit down and have a cup of tea," she replied, not so much in a soothing tone as a commanding one.

"You're getting bossy," Eve said, but she gave a faint smile and stood a little straighter.

They returned to the lab, where Joe brought them a pot of tea and poured it. Drinking enough liquid was one of Eve's golden rules. Golden, perhaps, but administered with an iron hand. She could not now argue against it. Or was she feeling too ill to do more than comply? Miriam knew that, even if Eve was sick, she felt compelled by her conscience to be here. Or worse than that, perhaps she did not think that Miriam was able to take the responsibility alone. Miriam had the knowledge—she had proved that in her exams, which she had passed brilliantly—but now she had to apply it in the laboratory.

And it was so different when it was this brilliant woman awaiting her thoughts, rather than an exam paper awaiting a textbook response. In an exam, no one's fate depended on someone identifying a sign of contagious disease, or spotting a clue to murder in a death that was assumed to be the result of natural causes. Mistakes could be seen and understood, prevented in the future. But in reality, misunderstandings, lies, ignorance—all of these only served to create further grief.

Miriam occasionally wondered if she could trust herself when dealing with real people and not the hypothetical cases in an exam. She knew what to do and how to do it. But was she making mistakes—and perhaps did not even realize it?

What had happened to her confidence? Perhaps it was fatigue. They were working hard, but that was the case more often than not. Deaths did not occur at regular intervals, and violent murders almost always paralyzed people with horror. People demanded answers more fiercely because they were afraid.

For Miriam, those answers were found in her knowledge of pathology. But even the most brilliant understanding did not always provide the vital clue that helped reach the desired conclusion. Forensic scientists could determine exactly what had happened, what kind of weapon was used, whether it was wielded by the left hand or the right, the attack coming from behind or being launched from the front, face-to-face. But sometimes knowing all of this was no help in determining who had committed the crime.

To date, neither Miriam nor Dr. Eve could tell the police anything that would help them find this *Rainy-day Slasher*. She brusquely pushed the moniker away. People were dead. Brutally killed. Some journalist-created nickname for a vicious killer felt shabby, as if diminishing the horror.

She sipped at her hot tea and turned back to thoughts of these three victims. She had discussed them with Dr. Eve at length, but they could identify nothing these people shared in common—at least, that they could see—and it was something that sat heavily on her mind. When she had worked with Daniel some time ago, before she went to Holland, she had been able to be of great help. Now it seemed as if there was nothing she could do, even with Eve's assistance.

Why did she feel this drag of disappointment? Perhaps it was because she had enjoyed working with Daniel. It had been both exciting and comfortable. She'd missed that when she was in Holland, but she was too busy trying to learn in one year all that she needed to know to pass her pathology exam—and do so with flying colors. An average grade would not be good enough to get what she craved, which was acceptance as a woman scientist in what had long been exclusively a man's world.

Had Eve ever felt that weight of responsibility? She must have. She pretended that she knew everything and had no anxieties, but she was far too intelligent and self-aware to imagine that was true. Did she have someone who could correct her, who would catch her error, if she ever made one? If she did not, it was no surprise that she occasionally buckled under the demands of the job. She must be tired, lonely, beaten down by the endless presence of death. Eve had no one, but Miriam had Eve. It was time she took some of that weight off Eve's shoulders. Judging by her pallor, Eve needed a rest.

They drank the last of their tea in silence, then stood. "I'll finish up," Miriam offered.

Eve looked at her sharply. And then, to Miriam's surprise, she agreed.

Miriam continued taking tissue samples from the corpse's organs. She agreed with Eve that his death was due to a general neglect of his health. The tests were not difficult, but they had to be done properly. She felt Eve watching her, but neither of them spoke. Half an hour went by, and Eve resumed working with Miriam. They went on steadily with the task at hand and completed the autopsy together.

Before they could relax, a new body was brought in: a man who looked as if he were merely asleep. They saw no obvious cause of death. He had not been in the care of a doctor, so they had nothing to indicate how he had died. He appeared to be in his late sixties.

While they began their methodical examination, Joe went out and brought back some fresh tea and sandwiches for lunch. Usually, Eve ate heartily, but today she seemed uninterested. When Miriam tried to persuade her to eat more, she turned and scowled. "Oh, stop fussing!" Her voice was curt, with a hard edge to it.

Miriam thought there was more than temper in her voice: it sounded like fear.

They were soon back at work, concentrating on the steps required to discover why this man had died.

Eve was holding a scalpel, about to make an incision, when she suddenly let the blade fall to the floor. Then she doubled over. Before Miriam or Joe could grab her, she slid awkwardly to the ground.

Miriam froze with horror. For a moment, she was paralyzed.

It was Joe who threw aside the notepad and pencil and dropped to the floor. Miriam came to life, bending down and feeling for a pulse. When she felt it, strong and regular, her clinical mind went into action. "Let's straighten her out," she said to Joe. They did so with no resistance from Eve, who was unconscious. "Bring a rolled-up blanket."

Joe stared at her for a moment, naked fear in his eyes.

"To make her comfortable," she explained. "She's only fainted."

"Are you sure?" Joe did not move.

She forced her own fears down and responded more gently. "Yes, I'm sure. Now, the blanket."

Joe had known Evelyn Hall longer than Miriam had. Perhaps she was even more important to him. Eve had never told Miriam how she had come to employ him. Maybe there was a story around that, too. She reached out and touched his arm. "She's probably worked herself into exhaustion," she said softly. "You can order your body to do things for just so long, then it will do what it needs to."

He stared at her for a moment or two and must have seen reassurance in her face, because his body seemed to relax. Miriam realized that, unconsciously, she had copied Eve's tone of authority, certain that she was right. Was Eve, at heart, sometimes as unsure as Miriam?

Joe left to fetch a blanket, and he came back with two. "We can use one as a pillow," he said, "and the other to keep her warm."

"Good thinking," Miriam told him. It was very cold in the morgue. Just standing still one could quickly become chilled, never mind lying on the stone floor. She tucked the blanket around Eve's motionless body, then gently lifted one of her eyelids.

"What the hell are you doing?" Eve demanded, becoming alert with a start.

"Seeing if you were in there!" Miriam replied, with a wave of relief.

"Of course I am," Eve snapped. "Who did you expect?"

"Possibly no one."

"Don't be so damn silly!" Eve replied. She took a deep breath. "And what the hell am I doing on the floor!"

Miriam thought Eve was about to try to stand up, so she placed her hands on the woman's shoulders. She pushed back. "No," Miriam insisted. "You're going home and you will stay there. Joe and I will take you. You will see the doctor, and if you need to be taken to the hospital—then you shall be."

"No!" Eve declared, but there was no resistance in her voice. She was arguing without really meaning it. "You can't—"

"Oh, but I can!" Miriam cut across her. "You taught me, remember? Now lie down and stop being a nuisance. I've got more important things to do than sit on top of you!"

Eve smiled, but it was only tinged with amusement, a wry humor at the absurdity of the situation. Still, she had not the strength to push Miriam away.

It took a little time for a doctor to come. The thought that frightened Miriam most was that Eve would not accept what she was told.

They moved her to a sofa that was tucked in the corner of the lab. The doctor examined her and announced that she was suffering from exhaustion. What was more, she had a slight fever, and he thought it best that she be taken to the hospital.

Eve made a token argument but gave up when she realized that these three people were going to overrule her. "It's all for nothing," she insisted, but her voice lacked its normal argumentative tone.

"Perhaps," Miriam agreed. "But that's where you're going, so don't be such a damn nuisance!"

Joe and Miriam locked up the morgue. The doctor hailed a taxi and they all went with Eve to the hospital; Miriam stayed only long enough to be assured that her friend and mentor was in receipt of good care. She would have stayed longer, but Eve would hear nothing of that.

"Go and do your damn job!" she said, when the doctor had gone and Miriam was alone with her. "And don't make any stupid mistakes because I'm not there to stop you. You wanted this work, and you nearly broke your back to get the job. They said you couldn't do it and I said you could, and you would. Don't make a liar out of me."

Miriam felt her throat tighten and a prickle of tears in her eyes. She would not weep. It was not about her, her fears or doubts, or her pride. She told herself that this was about doing the job, and only that, but she knew it was more. She cared deeply about Eve Hall. "Then lie here and get better," she said tartly. "And do as you're told!" She leaned forward and kissed Eve on the cheek. While her composure was still tight, she went out of the room.

MIRIAM AND JOE worked for the rest of the afternoon. They tidied up, sterilized all the instruments, and brought the notes on each case up-to-date. They were just about to leave when Daniel came into the laboratory. He must have noticed immediately that Eve was not there, because his face became serious. He also saw that they were ready to leave. Some of the lights were already off, and Miriam had the keys in her hand.

"What's wrong?" he asked, meeting her eyes.

It was a moment before she could marshal her thoughts. She wanted to be in control, steady. She wanted to be the person Daniel thought she was. "Eve was taken ill," she replied. "She's in the hospital. I think it's only exhaustion—that's what the doctor said, too—but she won't slow down."

"I'm sorry," he said quietly. "But I suppose the same qualities that make us admire her are the ones that also infuriate us." He gave a slight smile. "I'm sure you'll be the same one day—if you aren't already."

Was that a compliment? Evelyn Hall was admired, intensely. And feared. Did Miriam want that, particularly from Daniel? One would not dare to be overly familiar with Eve Hall.

"I might be . . . eventually. Perhaps," she conceded. Why did that hurt? She knew the answer even as the question formed in her mind. She had a fear of being separate from other people, admired but not understood or included. Her instinct was to make the separation herself, before someone else could do it and she had no choice.

She studied Daniel's face. He looked so young. And why not? He was fifteen years younger than she was, and his mother only fifteen years older—and Charlotte Pitt had grandchildren!

Before he could ask, she said, "If you've come to see whether we've found out anything further about this 'slasher' case, I'm afraid the answer is no."

"I haven't," he replied. "I came to see how you are—more or less."

"What do you mean, more or less?" she asked, not sure if she should be angry or flattered. "Did you know that Eve was ill?"

"No, I'm sorry, I didn't. I really just came to see you. You were away in Holland a long time. I . . . I missed you."

Miriam recognized that expression: he was feeling self-conscious. Daniel was a man, not a boy, and yet she so easily could imagine the child he had been. He had that thick, wavy hair that flopped forward, and he was always pushing it back. The bones in his face were strong, and she thought it could be years before he aged at all.

She looked away. "Thank you, Daniel. That's very nice of you. I can't remember whether we had lunch or not."

"We?" Confusion was evident in his expression.

"Joe and I. Joe is . . ." She looked around and realized that he had already left. She couldn't actually remember saying goodnight to him. Had she remembered to thank him? He deserved it.

"Gone for the day," Daniel concluded. He looked at the keys in her hand. "You were about to leave. Were you going home?"

"I suppose so. It's been a long day." That was the simple truth: long and difficult. She had not meant to admit it; it sounded like complaining, as if she could not cope. Of course she could. This is what she had wanted for as long as she could remember, but the responsibility was bigger, heavier than she had imagined. This work required so much more than technical skills.

"Let's go and have dinner," Daniel suggested.

"Yes, I'd like that. Something other than sandwiches," she urged. "But I need to call in at the hospital and see how Eve is doing."

"Of course," he agreed. "Nothing will taste good, or have any taste at all, if we don't."

They drove to the hospital in Miriam's small red car with its sleek lines. When they arrived, Miriam walked in ahead of him, her head held high, her back rigidly straight. Watching her, Daniel realized how frightened she was. She had pretended to be calm, but he could see that she was afraid the problem with Eve was serious.

Upstairs they met a hospital matron in stiff uniform and white apron.

Miriam introduced herself with her full title and managed to hold on to her authoritative manner toward the matron. With only the slightest tremor, she asked how Dr. Hall was doing.

The matron replied, "She needs rest, Dr. fford Croft. She's asleep. Please don't disturb her, unless it's absolutely necessary. Can't the dead wait?"

Daniel saw Miriam's shoulders relax.

"Oh, yes, indeed," Miriam replied, her voice overwhelmed with relief. "Please, just tell her that I came by."

DINNER WAS EASIER than Miriam had thought. They went to a simple restaurant and ordered steak and kidney pudding. It was hot and delicious, and the suet crust was as light as the best sponge cake.

For a little while, Miriam forgot her worries about Eve. Her concerns about the rain, the cold, even the lunatic slasher who was killing people in the street, could be put away for the evening.

In the course of their dinner, Daniel asked her what it was like, working at something she had wanted since childhood. "Is it much as you imagined?" he asked with interest.

She sensed that he was not simply making conversation: he wanted to know. "Yes and no," she answered. She was not waffling but trying to frame an honest answer. "It's exciting to be faced with a challenge and know that I have the help and guidance I need, and the responsibility. I don't have to ask anyone's permission, and I have access to all the latest equipment. But with that, of course, comes the responsibility for whatever answer I give, or fail to give." She looked down at her plate. She had eaten everything without even thinking about it. She looked back up and met his eyes. "I like that. And I admit that I've got the best of both worlds. I have the freedom to do as I please, as I think best, but then I have Eve to stop me from making mistakes. At least until today. It . . ." She gave a brief smile. "It is very different, even with her in hospital for half a day."

"It's like standing up in court when you're the one the defendant is relying on for his freedom, his reputation, even perhaps his life," Daniel said.

She searched his face, saw the empathy in his eyes, and knew that he was putting himself in her own place, and he understood more than simply her words. She smiled. "This afternoon was appalling. I was so frightened for her. She looked dreadful. Tomorrow will be better, but right now I feel as if I'm drowning. Which is absurd, because we haven't got a backlog of cases. It's just . . ." She gave up looking for the words to describe her feelings.

"It's the unknown," he said, supplying the words. "What you cannot prepare for, because you have no idea what it is, and you can't arrange plans, not knowing what those plans entail. It's having the ability to inspire everyone else with confidence, when you don't feel it yourself." He smiled. "You have to make them believe you know something they don't."

She thought him both funny and gentle. She was about to laugh, when she suddenly realized that there was a good deal of truth in what he said. She found herself telling him about the last case of the day. It was not serious, and it gave every indication of having been a natural death, albeit sudden. It was only a family quarrel that gave it any attention at all.

"It's expected at the end of a serious illness," she told him. "But in this case, there are grieving relatives who have made our opinion important."

"Some things require tact rather than skill," he observed.

Miriam thought that her trouble was being able to concentrate on it at all. "When Joe and I were finishing with the examination, the only thing I could see in my mind was Eve's white face and her uneven breathing."

"Were you afraid?" Daniel asked.

"For Eve, yes. And I don't welcome the prospect of working without her. Everything seems so easy, until one thing goes really wrong. When I came back to work, I kept second-guessing myself. And it showed. Joe didn't say anything, but I know he saw it."

"Tomorrow will be better," he said with assurance.

Did he mean it, or was he treating her gently because he was afraid she would fail? Mentally, she shook herself. She could do better than this. She must. "Of course it will," she agreed. "I just never thought of Eve being ill. She's such a force of nature. Like the wind, or the tide! It's time I grew up, isn't it?"

He smiled, and she saw softness as well as amusement. "Yes," he agreed.

For a moment she was extremely comfortable and nearly said as much. Then she realized she was making too much of it. He was expressing his understanding because he, too, had thought himself qualified—even gifted—in theory, then suddenly found himself in chambers, not following but leading, and often alone.

"Be careful," he warned, his voice grave again.

"Do you mean about making assumptions and mistakes? I am!"

"No," he said, shaking his head vigorously. "Be careful of trying to do everything yourself. Eve has been driving herself into the ground. Don't you do that, too. If you do, who's going to pick up the pieces? Part of doing the job well is pacing yourself, not driving yourself to the point of exhaustion. It's also your job to attend to what you can, and assess your abilities realistically. To be there tomorrow, and the day after—"

"I understand," she cut him off. "Don't talk to me as if I were an emotional amateur."

"Miriam, being an amateur doesn't strictly mean that you don't know what you're doing. It means that you do it for the love of it. From the Latin *amare*, to love."

She was obliged to smile. She *was* behaving like an amateur, or at least thinking like one. "I understand." And she did, acutely. "You're saying that part of the job means not believing myself to be indestructible, or worrying that everything is going to fall to pieces if I can't perform all the steps myself."

She thought about that for a few moments. He was right: she was feeling anxious for Eve, and the thought of this powerful woman falling sick was overwhelming. She was nowhere near ready to take on Eve's level of responsibility, but circumstances did not always wait on your convenience. A lot of the time, you weren't ready for what you faced: plague, bereavement, war. She could not anticipate what the future would bring. She could imagine, with horror, the pressure of too many things to do at once. Yes, she had worked in situations of great emergency, and yet nothing could prepare her for the reality: the conflicting emotions of exhilaration and fear, and the hollow feeling in the pit of her stomach.

Miriam wondered if she would rise to the occasion, because she had been taught well. And hadn't she reacted the right way so many times in the course of her studies? But this was real. Other people were now relying on her—just as they, and she herself, had relied on Eve Hall. She was confident that she would get most things right, from habit. She might make mistakes, but she knew how to correct most of them. Never panic, no matter what. Isn't that what Eve had taught her? Panic made everything worse. More often than not, that was when the real mistakes were made.

She took a deep breath and let it out slowly. "This is the challenge I have always wanted," she admitted, with a disarming smile. "Just not so soon!"

Daniel smiled back, and for a moment she was filled with happiness.

He picked up the wine bottle. "It's not particularly good, but would you like another glass?"

"Yes," she answered with certainty. "Yes, I would, please."

Fifteen

Daniel had enjoyed the evening with Miriam as much as he had expected, possibly even more. He had not known anybody in whose company he felt so comfortable, and at the same time so disturbed. More than anything, he wanted to encourage her, understanding so well how deeply she wished to succeed. He also realized that this need to succeed was even more important to her than his career success was to him. Perhaps that was because his had come to him relatively easily. Of course, he had worked hard, certainly from the end of the first year at university onward. How could he not? He had felt very keenly the need to justify his parents' sacrifice to pay for his highly privileged education, as well as their faith in him. As it happened, the more he learned, the more he worked hard for his own sake.

But Miriam's dreams were different. At first, early on, they had been impossible to fulfill. He had to remind himself that all of established society—both personal and professional—was stacked against her. Too many people in positions of authority felt that, for the good of all society, women should fulfill the destiny for which they were designed, and that was to marry, settle down, support their husband's needs and goals, and bear his children. Of course, not all could do so, either by nature or by choice, but that was irrelevant to the general good.

Miriam had had to fight uphill all the way, in order to pursue a career in which she was as good as any man, and even better than many. But Daniel knew that she had achieved this success at a considerable cost to herself. At over forty, and viewed by society as middle-aged, she had finally reached the top of that steep mountain she had struggled so diligently to climb. Her father was justifiably proud of her, and Daniel understood why.

He was proud of her, too, because he had known her for more than two years and had been by her side through some of the hardest battles she had been forced to fight . . . and win. That thought made him realize, with something of a jolt, that he had no right to feel as if he were even the smallest part of her victory. She had achieved this on her own. But he could certainly support her now, and he intended to do just that: to be there as a friend, as someone who believed in her and would always do so, through both the successes and the failures. And to tell her the truth. If there were moments of uncertainty, he would be there to help her fight her way through them, and then guide her gently back to believing in herself once again.

Was he on the verge of making a fool of himself? Possibly. He should put such disturbing thoughts out of his mind. He did not want to spoil a friendship, a valuable one, by asking questions. She would find that embarrassing and absurd.

He bent his attention to the rather tedious legal argument he was preparing. He had done as much as he could with Nicholas Wolford's case. He was as confident as he ever dared to be. He felt certain that Tolliver's allegation was not so much frivolous or damaging as it was bearing on an unfortunate collision of ideas and the coincidence of two men addressing the same subject at the same time. With a little goodwill, it could be settled, possibly to the advantage of both men. The only real hurdle would be persuading them of that.

But there was still the assault charge to confront.

He tried to focus on the Wolford case, but he found his mind wandering. It had been nearly a week since the autopsy on the third body had confirmed Miriam and Dr. Eve's assertion that they were all killed by the same person. And the fear that Daniel sensed everywhere was not subsiding. People he spoke to—the newspaper vendors, the street hawkers, drivers of hansom cabs—were tense, making small talk to their customers and avoiding the subject so purposefully it became obvious that they were all waiting for the next attack.

IT WAS LATE afternoon and the light was beginning to fade when Impney knocked on Daniel's door and, knowing he was alone, opened it.

Daniel looked up. "Yes?" He was hoping for a cup of tea but paused to notice the spatter of sleet rattling against the windows. Spring seemed a long way ahead.

"There is a Mr. Frobisher here to see you, sir. He looks cold. And rather miserable. Would you like a pot of tea, and possibly a crumpet or two?"

"Yes, I would!" Daniel said, with total conviction. "And even if I wouldn't, it's the barest civility one can offer a guest."

"Yes, sir, I thought you might say that," Impney replied, with the slightest of smiles. It was all in his eyes.

Two minutes later, Ian came into Daniel's office, already relieved of his heavy outer coat. His hair was blown across his face and damp, pushed back roughly by his hands. His cheeks were flushed from the ice and the wind. Impney was right; he looked profoundly miserable and was no longer attempting to hide it.

Ian sat down. "Good man, that." He was clearly referring to Impney.

"The best," Daniel agreed. "He'll be back in a moment with fresh tea and crumpets. You look bad. Has something worse happened?" There was no purpose to be served by pretending.

"Yes," Ian said. "The last victim, Roger Haviland."

"What about him?" Daniel sat forward. "Ian, have you found a connection between all the victims?"

"No, not yet, but there must be one, however fragile. There's no link that any of us can find." He shivered and moved his chair closer to the fire. "It's worse than that. Naturally, we have to look into the lives of all the victims, and— "

"I know that," Daniel said, interrupting him. "So, what is it that's new?"

"Haviland's a banker," Ian replied. "Ordinary enough, even at his senior level. But here's the thing: the government is clamping down on all information about him." He gave a tiny shrug of his shoulders. "Everything. I've been tactfully warned not to dig into anything concerning Haviland." He looked cold and defeated. "But why? Why are they protecting him? He can't be guilty: the poor devil was slashed so badly he bled to death." His voice was strained, and his face creased as if in concentration. "What could he have seen, or known, that they are protecting him? Has he done something wrong? Does he have some hold over somebody important? I can't find out anything about him; he seems to have been so ordinary that he sounds like a pleasant enough man, but a crashing bore." He stopped, staring at Daniel as if he was aware of saying more than he meant to.

"Then there must be something major about him that you don't—"

Ian cut him off, his voice rising sharply. "I know that! But what? And why do they feel it's more important to keep that secret than it is to catch his killer? It's as if he was related to someone with power. I could even believe that he might be the slasher, except he certainly didn't do that to himself."

Daniel was surprised by this government edict to keep a distance, and he was also confused. There was something profoundly important here, but he could not even guess the shape of it. But it was real, he was certain of that. He stared back at Ian. "I wish I had something that made sense so that I could argue with you, but I don't."

"What can I do?" Ian asked, anger and hopelessness evident in the lines of his face and in the rigid angles of his body. "Who the hell is more important than all the people this man has killed?" Then his eyes widened. "Daniel, nobody could do that to himself, but what if . . . ?" He stopped.

Daniel finished the thought for him. "What if someone knew that Haviland was the killer, and someone murdered him to save his family from the stain to their reputation? Killed him in the manner of the slasher . . ." He saw in Ian's eyes that he understood the rest of the thought, and he fell silent.

"That's one place I never thought to look," Ian admitted. "So, are we dealing with a cold-blooded killer prepared to murder other people . . . in order to hide the one he really wants? Or," he added, going back to Daniel's premise, "did someone know Haviland was the killer and so murdered him in 'slasher' fashion to cover his guilt?"

Daniel leaned back in his chair. "God knows," he said quietly. "They both make a kind of horrible sense, as theories. But I don't know if I believe either of them. What kind of a lunatic kills two people randomly, in order to hide a third who is the real object of their crime? Or, even more bizarre, the true killer? And if the first two killings were random, could the killer be acting from hatred? Fear? Or even, I suppose, greed? Apart from being unbearably cold-blooded, it's an idiotic risk. If he's doing this to get to one person, isn't he running the risk of being caught before he gets to that one victim who really matters?"

They were interrupted briefly by Impney's return with a tray of tea and crumpets. He set it down on the end of the table, accepted their thanks with a slight nod, and left them.

"If that's the case, he got away with it," Ian resumed. "And he's just as clever as he thought," he went on. "Perhaps we'd better stop looking for connections between all the victims—not that we're getting anywhere with that—and try looking for a powerful connection to just one? I don't think I'll tell Petheridge. He'll take me off the case and put me on traffic detail!" He gave a rueful, downward-curving smile. "I could always tell him you suggested it, but then he'll tell me what an idiot I am to discuss it with you at all, and he might forbid me to do it again. And then he'll say I'm not fit to direct traffic and I'll end up directing half of it into the river."

"I'd avoid telling him anything, if you can," Daniel answered. There was another idea in his mind, but he did not want to mention it to Ian. At least, not yet. He would do what little he could by himself. Besides, there was nothing Ian could do about it, and if he were wrong, he would get Ian into more trouble than he was in already. "Try the families of the earlier victims," he suggested, finally pouring the tea and handing Ian his. "If Haviland was murdered by a copycat slasher because he actually was the killer, you might dig up that link."

"Trying to keep me from making a fool of myself?" Ian asked, with a smile. "Or just from tipping off the slasher, whoever he is, and having him come after me?"

Daniel was lost for an immediate answer. He knew that Ian could read him like an open book. He had always been good at it—or perhaps Daniel was just more obvious than he realized?—but his friend's suggestions were too near the truth to admit to him. They drank their tea in near silence and ate all the crumpets before they had time to get cold.

Finally, Ian stood up. "Never mind. And thanks. You've given me several new lines to follow. At least, I'll look as if I'm doing something. It all feels so—" He did not say *hopeless*, but it hung in the air between them.

"What you're looking for will probably emerge when you least expect it," Daniel told him, trying to be encouraging.

"Well, it damn well isn't jumping out at me," Ian answered. "But thanks for the tea and crumpets. Very civilized."

Daniel shrugged off the appreciation. For a few moments, it felt exactly as it had been years ago, when they had little more than an idea for an essay to discuss. It was all so much more complicated now.

When Ian had gone out into the cold, drizzling day, Daniel put on his coat and hat, grabbed a large woolen scarf, and ventured outside. He walked briskly to the main crossroads, where he could usually get a taxi quite easily. That was among the several things he liked about living in London. His thoughts turned to his family: his parents were always interested in what he had to say, and he knew exactly what he was going to tell his father.

By the time Daniel got to his parents' address in Keppel Street, he was expecting to find his father at home. And if he was not there, he would wait until he arrived. He was quite prepared to discuss everything with his mother in the meantime, having long ago learned that she had good ideas about many things, crimes of violence among them. She needed no protection from ugly truths— and wanted none. Daniel had discovered over the years the role she had played in helping to solve murders, including those involving members of society's higher ranks. Along the way, she had developed into a very clever detective. Her husband, now head of Special Branch, would not argue that point. It was from his mother, and his father's reaction to her, that Daniel had learned about the intelligence—and, all too often, the overlooked importance—of women.

Daniel paid the taxi, then walked up the short pathway to the house and rang the doorbell. It was answered within moments by the maid he had known for years, Minnie Maude.

"Mr. Daniel!" she said, with a broad smile. "Come in, come in! It's a rotten night, but February won't last forever." She pulled the door open and stepped back to allow him space to enter.

When Minnie Maude had moved into the house in Keppel Street several years ago, she had settled in as if she had been made to fit the position, with only one exception. She kept rescuing stray, lost, and injured animals, making beds for them and keeping them in the cellar, feeding them on leftovers—until they were discovered. That was when Charlotte stepped in to aid and abet her, insisting that the animals live in the kitchen where it was warm and light and there was almost always someone to talk to them.

Cook, who was a more recent addition, had learned to put up with these strays. She grumbled a lot, but let anyone threaten to put the animal out, and they soon learned the difference between grumbling and anger.

The warmth of familiarity closed around Daniel like a cocoon. Yes, *cocoon* was the right word. He could easily creep back into the protection of it and forget that it was meant as a place of safety for only a short while, until it was time for him to fly.

He found his father at home, seated by the fire, an open book on his knee. When Pitt saw his son, he put the book aside, as if it no longer interested him, and rose.

"How are you?" he asked, searching Daniel's face.

Daniel knew he could hide little from his father's astute gaze, and he did not bother to try. "Like everyone else, I wish they could find this wretched man who is knifing people in the streets."

Pitt sat back in his chair and looked at Daniel expectantly.

Daniel hesitated. He had thought he knew what he was going to say, but now that he was faced with the reality, it was more difficult than he had expected.

Charlotte must have heard the front door, because she entered the room. She was wearing a very ordinary dress in a warm shade of deep pink. Daniel liked it immediately; she often wore rich colors, and it brought back memories, good ones. He rose to his feet and went to hug her, harder than he had intended.

She pulled away from him and looked at his face carefully. "What brings you here?"

"Dinner," he replied.

"Nonsense," she said. "Do you want to speak to your father alone?"

That was Charlotte, always reading him too well. He hesitated.

"And you are staying for dinner?" she asked. "Minnie Maude has already told Cook you are here. And by now, the extra place has been set at the table."

"Then I had better," Daniel replied immediately, smiling at her. "And yes, please, I would like a few words." If he did not say anything now, it would hang over the dinner table, intruding into their comfortable evening as a family.

She nodded, glanced at Pitt, and then, giving Daniel a quick kiss on the cheek, she went out of the room, closing the door softly behind her.

Pitt sat quietly, waiting for his son to speak. They both knew that Daniel did not come by unannounced, especially at this time in the evening, without an urgent reason.

Daniel sat down and began. "Ian Frobisher came to see me this evening. He's pretty stuck, looking into these murders. And, naturally, he's looking into all the victims and trying to find something in common. Anything at all that would help to identify their enemies . . . anybody or any interest that connects them."

He stopped but realized that his father was waiting for him to continue.

"The higher authorities have stepped in," he went on. "Don't ask me who, because I don't know. But they spoke to Ian's superiors and made it very clear that he's to drop any further investigation into Haviland. That includes inquiries into his family, friends, and specifically, his job. He was a banker, quite high up in the ranks, but Ian has been ordered not to probe at all. Do you know why this is, or could you make an educated guess? Because it's raising all sorts of questions."

"What kind of questions?" Pitt asked.

"Such as, is he connected with something secret? Too secret even to tell the police? Was he the slasher's real target, and were the others only killed to confuse the issue? Because if he were the intended victim, then we might get to the killer more quickly." He nearly added this newest thought—that Haviland was the slasher and was killed to protect his family's name and his legacy—but decided against it.

Pitt raised his hand slightly, in a discreet gesture of interruption.

Daniel sat motionless. "You know him?" It was barely a question, more a request for information.

"Not personally," Pitt replied. "But I know what he does."

"Special Branch is protecting him," Daniel said, more as a confirmation than a suggestion, and with a touch of accusation in his tone.

"Protecting what he was doing," Pitt countered. "Clearly, they failed in that."

Daniel met his father's eyes but refused to comment. It was suddenly a time for the utmost seriousness. "Is that why he was killed, Father? Was he the only intended victim? Did someone really kill two other people first, to—"

"I don't know!" Pitt said sharply. "Perhaps he had some connection with the other victims that we don't know about. I'm sorry, Daniel. I can look further into it, and if there is anything linking him to the other victims, I can tell Frobisher."

"But why is Special Branch stopping the police from investigating him, even if he's the key to . . ." Daniel stopped, not sure where to go with this.

Pitt took a deep breath and let it out slowly. "Tell him to leave it alone, Daniel. I will look into it. If there is anything at all to be learned from Haviland's death, I will inform the police. But don't go digging into Haviland's life. Don't even give the appearance of having done so. I mean that very seriously." He looked at Daniel, without a flicker of emotion.

Daniel felt a chill run through him, a cold touch of reality beneath the everyday surface. "Yes," he agreed. He nearly called him *sir*; but it might be taken as sarcasm, rather than respect. "I'll tell Ian to back off."

"If Haviland was the intended victim all along, and not just in the wrong place at the wrong time, I would say it had a bearing on some other part of his life, outside the bank. Perhaps he learned something, or was a witness to something, that meant he had to be got rid of. But you have to find out some other way. I'm sorry."

"You mean Ian has to . . ." Daniel was reminding himself, more than correcting his father.

"No, I mean you must leave it alone also," Pitt replied. "As hard as that is, I'm afraid the investigation can't take precedence over whatever Haviland was doing. I'm not going to explain it any more than that, and you are not going to explain it to Frobisher at all. I'm sorry. Blame privilege—the old boys' network—whatever you like; it's the best choice out of a poor selection." He looked as if he would have liked to say more, but he apparently was satisfied that Daniel would understand. There was no possibility of misreading his face.

"I'll tell him," Daniel conceded. He was about to add something, then changed his mind.

The silence was broken by Charlotte coming in. She glanced at Pitt's face, then at Daniel, and closed the door behind her. She walked over, signaling Daniel to remain where he was, in what was usually her chair, and sat on the couch instead. "How is Miriam enjoying working in the real morgue, fully qualified?" Charlotte asked. "Marcus must be terribly proud of her." She looked truly interested, not as if she were making polite conversation to break the silence.

Daniel was pleased to tell her. In fact, he found that he really wanted to. "It's difficult," he started. "I think it's a much heavier responsibility than when it's your exam marks at stake. This is real, a dead person whose cause of death is going to be based on your decision; the living are going to be affected by it. And if there's no one living who cares, that's even worse. It's not easy knowing you're that person's last connection with life, so to speak." It was a harsh and lonely thought. His immediate concern was Miriam. Had she felt that way? "Eve Hall is ill," he added suddenly. Outwardly, it did not follow from what they had been talking about. But in his mind, it was intimately connected.

"Ill? How ill?" Charlotte asked with concern. "Is she home? In hospital? Did Miriam tell you? Who's helping Miriam?"

He smiled, because the flood of questions was so characteristic of his mother, and he felt a sudden rush of emotion. There was such a stark contrast between ethics, professional standards, ambitions, and the human feelings that drove all of them; they were the dominant force, those feelings, and all you had in the end. That was so like his mother, focusing immediately on her concerns for others. This was the woman who had taught him about compassion.

"She fainted in the laboratory," he answered. "Miriam and Joe were there and got her to the hospital. I don't know exactly what happened. They say it wasn't her heart. So far, they expect her to recover, but not immediately. It leaves Miriam working alone, as the only forensic pathologist. At least, for now."

"She has the training, and the spirit, to do it," Pitt said with certainty.

"Of course she has, Thomas," Charlotte said. "That won't be the issue. But could you cut up dead bodies alone?"

"Certainly not," Pitt said, his face screwed up in surprise, and showing a sense of revulsion. "It's not my skill." He was totally serious. "But I can shoot a man, when I have to, and when there is no other way to stop him from killing others."

"That's different," said Charlotte. "I know she's got the qualifications, and certainly the skill, but other people don't believe it. She's going to have to prove herself with every case."

Pitt put his hand out and touched her gently on the arm. "Has your memory wiped it out so completely that you don't remember the days when I was sent to the servants' entrance to question people about murder? What they thought was, here's a man from a working-class background who can't possibly understand any of our ways, our views or values, our elevated position in society. And, in some ways, they were right. But I learned, and so can Miriam. Not immediately—it takes time—and not at all, if she lets them stop her from trying."

Charlotte bit her lip. "I forgot." She gave a little smile. "I don't know what they say about you behind your back, but they are far too afraid of you to say it to your face. And whatever it is, they dare not say it in front of me! Or perhaps they say nothing, because you know their weaknesses. After all, it's your job to know."

Daniel suddenly remembered when, as quite a small boy, he had seen some well-heeled gentleman in the street disregard Pitt, as he would a peddler or a workman, and he recalled the shadow of anger in his mother's face. He had not understood it then. And now things were so very different. Was it like that for Miriam: the change now, when they knew who she was?

He smiled again. "And it's Miriam's job to know how marvelous and how fragile our bodies are," he said. "And to discover what actually happened to the deceased, from the injuries that she has been trained to detect."

"You are worried for her," Charlotte said softly, as if seeing through him. "I'd think less of you if you weren't."

Pitt shook his head. "You've known Ian Frobisher since you were at prep school, and I know you're concerned for him as well. But keep him out of this . . . if you can. I mean it, Daniel! I'll look into it myself and tell you what I can." He stared levelly at his son, as if waiting for him to answer.

It was not lost on Daniel that his father had abruptly changed the subject. He would do so only if he was concerned. Or afraid.

"I'll try," said Daniel. As he spoke, he heard how this fell short of a promise.

Sixteen

"D<small>O YOU UNDERSTAND</small> me, Frobisher?" Petheridge asked quietly. His expression was grave, his eyes searching Ian's face as the man sat behind his desk, its surface piled with papers.

Ian heard this not as a demand or an order, but as a question that required an answer. A request for the truth, rather than obedience. He hesitated, thinking that Petheridge meant more by his carefully worded question than anything else he was saying. The truth was in what he did not say, what he had skirted around. The unspoken words, Ian was quite sure, held the real meaning.

It was also Ian's judgment that the evasion was not because Petheridge was afraid of declaring himself, but because he wanted to obfuscate his meaning to the point where Ian could take from it whatever instruction he wished to, and still be credible.

"Frobisher!"

"Yes, sir," he replied, stiffening slightly. "I understand. I'll be very careful not to make inquiries, other than superficially, about

Mr. Haviland. Not to ask any questions at all would draw attention to him. But, sir . . ."

"What?" Petheridge asked suspiciously.

"Won't it be highly suspicious if we look into the other two victims' lives, histories, relationships, and so on, and don't do the same with Haviland? If someone was being protected—because he's got powerful relatives or knows something about somebody or is part of Special Branch—that's how the powers that be would react in the event of his death. That would make Haviland stand out like a black frog on a white ceiling."

"You ever seen a black frog on your ceiling, Frobisher?" Petheridge inquired politely. His manners were flawless.

"No, sir," Ian replied, straight-faced. "But on the floor, it would be less conspicuous. I could—"

"Get out, Frobisher."

"Yes, sir." Ian rose to his feet and stood to attention for a moment, then turned on his heel and left.

He was grateful to escape. The last thing he wanted was to argue with Petheridge, which meant obliging his superior to define exactly what his orders were. Petheridge had been instructed by someone far higher up not to investigate Haviland any more closely. Now he was again passing on those orders to Ian, but with the tacit understanding that Ian was to catch the killer . . . and achieve this while taking as little notice as possible of Haviland. Petheridge had done as he was ordered but had deliberately phrased it so his demand could be misunderstood. That was all the permission Ian needed.

He went immediately back to his own office, where he knew Bremner would be waiting for him. He glanced at Bremner's expectant face and closed the door behind him. "We can," he said.

Bremner's eyebrows shot up. "Can . . . what?"

"Petheridge told me to leave Haviland alone. Orders from above."

"But you just said—" Bremner began.

"I know what I said," Ian interrupted, with a tight smile. "And I know what Petheridge said—and what he didn't say."

Bremner's eyebrows rose. "Am I supposed to understand that?"

"Yes," said Ian, "when I explain." He sat down comfortably in his own chair, allowing Bremner to do the same. "As I told Petheridge, if Haviland really is Special Branch, then if we treat him differently than the other victims, with kid gloves, we'll only draw more attention to him. And believe me, that would be a perfect way to betray him." He was about to go on when he saw understanding dawn in Bremner's face. "Right?" he asked.

"Of course," Bremner said, with a grin. "He's just like anybody else. We treat his widow politely, and all his friends and contacts, but nothing special. Very good, sir. And by the way," he added, "do you think he really is Special Branch?"

"As opposed to what?" Ian asked. "Somebody's friend—and that somebody owes him money?" He paused for a moment, and then became more serious. "Yes, on balance, I think he has something to do with the government. It doesn't have to be Special Branch, not specifically, but we've got a long way to go before we can afford to exclude anything. And if he was as important as they say, we'd be badly in the wrong if we broke his cover."

"Unless, of course, he was the actual intended victim," Bremner argued. "Do you think he was?" His face shadowed. "God! That's cold. Murder two innocent people in order to disguise the one you really want?"

They had discussed this possibility several times, and it continued to rise to the top of the list of potential explanations.

"I suppose if it's spying, and all that, they're playing for higher stakes than one or two bodies sacrificed along the way."

Bremner's eyebrows shot up. "You mean . . . war?"

Ian shrugged. "I hope not. But it's not impossible. If you're a general going to war, you expect to lose a few men."

"Yes, but I don't deliberately kill two of my own, slash them to pieces in the rain, and then run away," Bremner said hotly. "Or a couple of women, at that! Isn't that what you're suggesting?"

"I suppose so." Ian sighed. "But war in regiments, uniform and all that, is a different world from the sort of secret war I'm talking about. Just don't decide what it is before you actually know."

"Do you think we ever will?" Bremner's face was tight, his jaw muscles hard. "I know that's not the solution I'm prepared to accept. Sacrifice of soldiers in war is one thing; allowing civilian women who don't know anything about it to be murdered in the street is another. That's what we're up against . . . isn't it?"

"Yes," Ian agreed. "But we don't get to choose. Let's think clearly. We know the occupations of each one of them, and—"

"Haviland was a banker," Bremner repeated. "But we suspect he might have been something else, or they wouldn't be warning us off. What if they all were, one way or another?"

Ian was startled. "You mean all working for some sort of secret service? Two women in their twenties? Then why didn't they warn us about all of them? Or simply take over the case?"

"Perhaps they did, and that's why we've been getting damn little help," Bremner suggested.

"We're only getting warned off Haviland. They don't appear to care in the least about the women," Ian pointed out.

"Anyway, wasn't the first victim French? She didn't even live here," Bremner added.

Ian shook his head. "They've got something in common, but it's not that they were all working in some area that required security. If it were, the government would have handled it differently."

"You mean they'd have solved it themselves, instead of leaving it to us?" Bremner said sarcastically.

"Well, at least they'd know what it's all about!" Ian exclaimed in irritation. "Or are you suggesting they've got so many agents that when three of them get hacked to death in the streets of London, it takes them weeks to notice it?" There was bitterness in his voice.

"Come on!" he added. "The security services are discreet, but not invisible, if you know what to look for."

Bremner drew in a deep breath. "There are times, sir, when you are extremely difficult to work with. If you'd think like a cop, and not a professor of comparative politics or whatever it is you studied, we might get further along!"

The comment was fair, and it stung. "All right, then, you're a cop from the top of your orange head to the soles of your polished boots. What are your ideas?" Ian asked.

Bremner looked at him, grim-faced. "What you're saying is, we should go back and look yet again at what all the victims had in common." He said this slowly, as if measuring his words. "And if Haviland was Special Branch, do they know anything they'll share with us? Or," he added, "is there some element of this that we haven't even thought of?"

Ian was silent for several moments, as a new thought occurred to him.

"Unless . . ." he finally answered, "is it possible that Haviland's a double agent? And Special Branch found out and got rid of him in this way?"

Bremner drew in his breath sharply, his eyes wide. "Do you really—?"

"No," Ian said, his voice soft. "Probably not. But it's possible. Maybe they didn't start this, but they could be taking advantage of it."

"The devious bastards!" Bremner breathed out slowly. "This means that we should only look at what's common to the two women, and exclude Haviland? But we've got to look at everything, or we give ourselves away."

"Yes," Ian agreed. "But we move with care, when it comes to Haviland." After a long pause, he said, "This is a worse case than I thought. And anything we do, we must do it when investigating all three victims."

"Starting with?"

"We'll take a fresh look at everything we know: what the victims might have had in common, as well as the differences. There's got to be a pattern. And yes," he added quickly, "I do know that we've already looked, but we haven't found it yet. It's there for the finding, I'm certain of it. I need paper," he said, looking around him. "I think it's best done on paper. At least, that way I can see what we have."

"Excellent," Bremner agreed, aware of his boss's habits. "But I'll write it all down."

"I can't read your writing," Ian complained.

"No, but I can," Bremner replied. "And no one can read yours, including you!"

It was true. The more exciting Ian found the thought, the less legible his writing. He conceded the point.

Bremner wrote the names of the victims across the top of a large sheet of paper and subject headings down the side.

Ian watched him. "We need the places where the bodies were found and when. Also, the presumed time of death, as close as possible. Leave the injuries for the moment."

"But they are important," Bremner protested. "I want to go back to the pathologist. That is, when we've given it more consideration and know what to ask."

Ian nearly responded to that but let it go. "We've looked at all the usual things, so what's left? Political interests, religious affiliations? And what about finances? Debts, for example. There's got to be a common factor."

"Unless they just happened to be someone who got in the way when the slasher was in the road," Bremner suggested. "Do you suppose that could be it . . . and nothing more than that? Or perhaps they were all a witness to something that we don't know about yet?"

"Then we have to learn everything we can about all the victims,"

Ian answered. "And, please God, find something. A time, a place, an interest in common, and then pray they were all killed by the same person."

Bremner closed his eyes and swore under his breath.

The words were, no doubt, colorful—although incomprehensible to Ian because they were in the broad dialect of the northeast. He also sensed that they were immensely satisfying.

IAN ARRIVED AT the morgue by late morning and found Dr. fford Croft working alone at one of the tables. On it, a dead body lay, most of it decently covered while she worked on the open chest cavity.

She did not hear him come in, and Ian watched her for a moment. She was a small figure, slender even, under the shapeless white lab coat.

He knew who she was only because of the knot of bright red hair that poked out of the net holding it back. "Dr. fford Croft?" he said quietly.

Miriam turned around quickly, holding both hands up, fully gloved. There was a scalpel in one hand, smeared with blood. "Inspector Frobisher?" she said, with slight surprise. "What can I do for you?"

"Good morning, Doctor. I'm sorry for interrupting you, but I need your help. Please? Perhaps I could speak to Dr. Hall, if you're busy?"

She smiled. It was charming, with a rueful humor to it. "Of course. As long as you're not in a hurry." There was both weariness and amusement in her face.

He waited.

"I'm afraid Dr. Hall is in hospital," she explained. "She's getting better, but I'm hoping they keep her in a little longer. As soon as she's returned home, she'll come back here, and there's nothing I can do to stop her from working."

"I'm sorry," he said, feeling momentarily awkward. "I—"

"She'll be fine," Miriam repeated. "So, how can I help you?" She didn't wait for his response. "I didn't examine the first body because I was still in Holland. But I've read the reports, and I can look at them again, if that will help. Do you know what you're looking for? Or are you looking at everything again, in general?"

Several answers flashed through his mind, but she was so candid, her gaze so direct, he found himself telling her the truth. "We're desperate. We're going back to the beginning, hoping to find anything that all of these victims had in common and would tie them together in someone's mind. Allowing, of course," he added, "that this someone might be barking mad." He winced at his own words. "Sorry, but this case is stretching all of us to the limit. If they were all killed by the same person, there has to be a connection."

"At least in someone's mind," she agreed.

"There's another possibility," Ian continued. "And that is that only one of them was the target, and the others were killed to hide who the intended victim actually was. If we knew the answer to that, then we might see the motive quite easily. And that would lead us directly to the killer." He watched to see her reaction.

She hesitated only a moment. "Or there could be a third possibility. What if we've made a mistake?" she suggested. "And they were not all killed by the same person? Then this effort to connect them would be a waste of time."

"Yes, that's another possibility," he replied, his voice conveying a small thread of doubt.

Miriam nodded and then said, "So, you'd like me to check to make doubly sure there is nothing different about any of them. Nothing we might have overlooked before." Her smile was a little weary.

"Yes, please, and—" Should he tell her? It might matter. She was looking at him, waiting for him to continue. "And pay particular attention to Haviland," he added. "We've been told to leave him out of it altogether, not to inquire more than superficially into his occupation, private life, anything at all. If we do, we'll be putting other people at risk—" He stopped, aware that he was breaching a code of police confidentiality. And, in this case, perhaps national security as well. He nearly asked her to guarantee discretion, but he sensed this would not be necessary. Miriam fford Croft struck him as a highly professional and trustworthy woman.

Miriam frowned slightly. "Won't that make him stand out? Or is that the purpose of it? Is he—and I'm aware this will sound macabre—some kind of . . . bait?"

"Yes," he said bluntly. "That occurs to me as well. But—"

"Then I had better take the victims in order of their deaths. There are patterns that make sense only if the proper chronology is observed. Do you wish to remain, or shall I send you a report?"

"May I remain?" He hoped she would say no, or even show some reluctance. In truth, he did not want to see any of the victims again, and still less to see so closely the damage the killer had done to them. Perhaps that was an evasion of the full responsibility he owed them? If this woman could do it every day, what was wrong with him that he found it so difficult? "Please?" he added, although he had to force the word out of a tight throat.

"Of course," she replied.

Ian was sure she knew exactly how he felt, and he thought her tactful not to laugh at him, even gently.

IT SEEMED LIKE a very long day, although it was only a matter of five or six hours that they worked together. Miriam had given Ian an apron to make sure nothing marked his clothes. As a further precaution, she told him to stand back. That was a suggestion he needed to hear only once; he was perfectly happy to observe from as far away as possible.

One by one, Miriam examined the corpses of the victims.

The first was Sandrine Bernard. She looked almost as if she were made of hard rubber. She was the perfect model of a woman, had she been crafted from something synthetic. At the same time, she had been neatly stitched back together with lengths of heavy, coarse thread. There was no blood to see, and her flesh was spongy, not as if it had ever been warm and alive. Oddly, her hair was still beautiful, and her left hand was delicately boned, white, with perfectly formed nails.

Ian felt a wave of horror as he watched Dr. fford Croft's small, strong hands go over the body. Was his emotion based on fear? Yes, and he knew it only too well. Looking at the lovely body that no longer held even the ghost of the woman she had once been, he said nothing. There was nothing to say that was adequate.

Before going on to the next victim, Miriam suggested that they stop for a cup of tea. She had sandwiches, which she shared with him, accepting no argument. After eating, they resumed their work on the second body, that of Lena Madden.

"These cuts are deeper," she said, shifting her gaze from the cadaver to Ian. "Do you see here . . . and here?" she pointed out. "More random than we saw on Sandrine Bernard."

"Can you tell the order in which the slashes were made?" he asked.

"I think I can," she replied.

"I'm sure you've considered this," he said, and then winced at the thought of the savage attack. "If he wanted his victims to suffer, or to know who was attacking them, he wouldn't worry about being recognized. But would he want it done quickly? If so, wouldn't he strike first at the jugular? Or at least an artery?"

She stared at him, as if appreciating how he was thinking this through. "Yes, I would say he wanted it done quickly. It's quite apparent that the first blow was fatal, and then he went in for the mutilation." She leaned closer to the body. "You see here? Shallower cuts, painful, but not lethal. But first this," she added, pointing to the deep, ugly abdominal wound. "This is revenge. Either that, or he is a complete madman all the time. But if this were so, surely you would have found him? He would have betrayed himself by other extreme behavior. However, if the attacks were random, there must have been easier victims to find than these people. They were all reasonably well-to-do, at the least well educated, with good jobs. Weren't they?" Her question was urgent. "Weren't they?" she repeated.

"Yes," he said quietly. "Haviland, the last one, was a senior banker. Not just the manager in a local branch, but higher than that." Should he tell her more, or had he said enough? But then, how could she help fully if he gave her only some of the facts? Daniel trusted her, he reminded himself.

He knew that Miriam was waiting for him to finish what he was saying. "This is very confidential, so nothing I'm about to tell you can be repeated." He waited for her to respond. She nodded. He was not only breaking his own code of ethics; he was breaking his word to Daniel, and he was painfully aware of it. And yet, the sight of these bodies was driving him to do everything possible to prevent there being another like them.

Miriam was waiting, as if giving him time to order his thoughts.

Ian took a deep breath and forged ahead. "We've been told by Special Branch not to inquire into Haviland too deeply," he continued. "It seems he was more than a well-educated banker, financially comfortable. He was part of their world. So, was his a random killing, or did the stalker have a reason? Was he the main victim, which means that the others were merely incidental? If that was so, maybe he's the last?"

"Is he?" she asked. "That is, is he the last?"

"Yes, so far, but you know that."

"I don't," she contradicted him. "I don't know that there hasn't been another that we haven't identified, or whose death didn't occur around London. So, I can't say there won't be more, can you?"

"Oh God!" He breathed out slowly and then shut his eyes for a moment. He was being irrational, he knew, but only because he hoped so fiercely that there would be no more. "Yes, of course there could be more," he said very quietly. "Maybe there will be, if we don't catch the bastard."

"Let me review all we know," she said quietly. "We may find something. But I can tell you now, Inspector, that it's conceivable one of them was killed by somebody else, who took the opportunity to hide his intended kill among the other random attacks." She waved her hand, as if dismissing this idea. "But it's so unlikely that we'll be wasting our time even considering it."

"Why do you think so?" Ian asked, hoping to get some new insight into this tragedy, and also relieved to think they needed to find only one murderer and not two.

Miriam studied his face for a moment. "Because there are details we have not released, which is standard practice."

Ian waited, hoping she would reveal something that would assist him, something he had not already seen for himself. "Other than the severed finger—"

"The use of the blade," she interrupted. "It was wielded by both the right and left hands. And details about the wounds themselves. The chances of someone else inflicting them in exactly the same way are extraordinarily low," she replied.

Ian looked at her intensely serious face. It struck him that this was like a nightmare. He was standing in an antiseptic room designed for examining the dead, and nearby was an attractive woman talking calmly, rationally, about insane killings.

"Another possibility," she went on, "and it's slight, is that someone killed all of them, but only one mattered, and someone paid him to do it."

"That's—" he began.

"Possible," she finished for him. "But highly unlikely. And one other thing, I believe . . ."

"What?"

"In two of our victims, the right index finger was cut off, and in one it was the left."

"We've thought about that," Ian acknowledged. "Tell me why you think this is important; I'm interested to know."

"From looking at the size and musculature of the arms and wrists," she replied, "I'm quite sure that, in each case, the finger was severed from the dominant hand. This means that the victims were not random at all. Our killer knew them, and well enough to know whether they were left- or right-handed."

Ian waited for her to say more, suddenly aware of the penetrating cold in the room.

"Do you know if your friends are left- or right-handed?" she asked. "I don't, not for most of them."

"Nor do I," he said. "But I agree with you, and it certainly lays out a line of thought that we're already pursuing. And now, with your observations, we'll do so with even more attention." As if experiencing yet again the full horror of the situation, a chill ran up his back. "He had to have known them quite well, including Haviland."

"If I'm right," she said grimly.

"All the more reason why I have to know if Haviland's death was incidental or not; if the connection was something personal, having nothing to do with his job." He thought about this for a moment. "Whatever his job really was." After a moment, he added, "So, it's up to me to find out if Haviland was connected to the rest of them. And if he was the real victim, and the others were killed to hide that fact. It's looking a bit less likely, don't you think?"

Miriam nodded. "Seems that way, but we can't be sure. I suppose whoever did this is not only cold-blooded but also methodical. These attacks were done with rage, but also with logic. And if that's true, it's important for us to remember. Also, the rage is increasing with each succeeding attack. If I were to show you the slicing pattern—"

"No, thank you," he interrupted. "I believe you. Still, I need to pursue the unlikely possibility that the first two were killed by a lunatic, and someone else might have copied this pattern when killing Haviland, hoping to hide that he was the intended victim all along. I agree it's unlikely, but I'm obliged to give every possibility its due."

"I suppose two killers are possible," she replied, as if choosing her words carefully. "But I'm not sure how you can find out. There's no forensic proof, at least not yet. If Haviland's attacker was, in fact, a different person, someone clever enough to copy the pattern identically, both in the act and in the escalation, then you're going to have to be very clever to find him. He might not do it again."

"I think he will," Ian replied. "That is, if he needs to cover the fact that Haviland was the target. One more killing might achieve that."

Miriam thought about it for a long moment. "And then he will disappear as easily and as quickly as he appeared."

Ian swore and then apologized.

She smiled. "I'd say the same, only I didn't have to. I'll ride on your coattails."

"Anything to be of service," he replied dryly. "What's most important is that you've pretty much confirmed that, as far as any forensic evidence is concerned, they were all killed by the same person and by the same weapon. And with increasing rage." When she nodded, he said, "Thank you, Doctor."

The thought crossed his mind that he was certain Daniel was in love with this woman, whether his idiot friend realized it or not. When she smiled, he added, "I appreciate your taking the time, when weighed down with Dr. Hall's work, as well as your own."

"It's a slow day," she replied. "Or I couldn't have. Good luck, Inspector."

He inclined his head slightly. "Let's hope that luck is with me. I think I'm going to need it."

Seventeen

D ANIEL WAS FINISHING up his work at fford Croft and Gibson when Impney knocked on his door.

"Inspector Frobisher to see you, sir. He says it will only take up a short amount of your time."

"Of course," Daniel said. He felt a sense of pleasure that surprised him. Was it good news? Had they caught the "Rainy-day Slasher"? In any case, it was bound to be more interesting than the very dry papers, written in tortuous legalese, that he had been reading before handing them over to Impney to put in the post.

Ian entered, thanked Impney, and sat down.

Daniel knew even before Ian spoke that he had not come to announce any success. "What can I do for you?" he asked. "Not another victim, surely?" A chill ran through him as he thought of it. There had been nothing in the newspapers, or Impney certainly would have told him.

"No," Ian said wearily. "We are very little further forward. We've got to get this bastard before he kills anyone else."

"How can I help?" Daniel took it for granted that he could, or else Ian would not have come to see him. Unless, of course, it was to ask how the Wolford case was coming along, but he could have done that on the telephone.

Ian looked uncomfortable. Daniel sensed that there was something he needed to say, but he was finding it difficult. It brought back a flood of memories, going as far back as school days, even before Cambridge. Ian had been a prefect, responsible for several younger boys when it came to certain matters of discipline. Ian had carried the heavy weight of his responsibility, with his ready sympathy for how other people felt. Daniel saw that same heavy burden in his face today. "Is something wrong with Wolford?" Daniel asked.

Ian looked surprised. "No, not that I know of. He's a contrary bastard, to be sure, always has been, but, no," he went on quickly, perhaps glad to be forced to come to the point. "I've not come about Wolford. It's about Haviland, the last victim."

"You mean the most recent?" Daniel grimaced. "Please God, he is the last. What is it about Haviland?"

Ian hesitated.

Daniel felt a chill of anxiety, like icy fingers touching him.

"We can't find the pattern," Ian replied at last. "I think Haviland is the key. But as you know, all useful information about him has been shut off."

"With Special Branch involved, your hands are tied." He immediately thought about his last meeting with his father and being warned that he should walk away from this one—and be very careful.

"No matter what the authorities say—and that means my superiors—we need to know." A shadow of urgency crossed his face. "Daniel, what I'm saying is that *I* need to know. How else can I do my job?"

The two men said nothing for a long moment, each of them lost in their own thoughts. When Ian finally spoke, his voice was more forceful. More authoritative.

"So, if Haviland worked for Special Branch, is that what these murders are all about? Or did some lunatic wielding a knife kill him by chance?" There was disbelief in his voice. "Or does his death have anything to do with spying, sabotage, the kind of thing we associate with Special Branch? If so, that means the other victims were casual slaughter, killed only to hide the fact that Haviland was the intended victim . . ." He paused and then leaned forward. "What if they were Special Branch, too? Which seems highly unlikely." He stared at Daniel. "Well?"

"For God's sake, Ian, do you think I'd know?" Daniel exclaimed incredulously.

"No, but I do think you might be able to find out . . . if you ask the right person."

Daniel felt the anger rise inside him. Or was it fear that Ian could be right, and that, in spite of his father's implicit denial, Thomas Pitt knew more than he had admitted about this? Or even worse, that he knew the identity of the killer, but for some reason he believed it was necessary to keep silent? Even to withhold it from his son? The idea was sickening. Could anyone balance one murder against another, or in some way allow it to happen? He could never believe this of his father. But then, he did not know what other factors there were. Perhaps all of this was tied to the prospect of some far greater atrocity. It could even be the threat of war: that was not impossible.

Daniel knew that Ian was waiting for a response from him. "You mean, if I ask my father, will he tell me what's at stake? And what Haviland was doing? Who is going to live, or die, if we find the answer to certain questions?" He heard the anger in his voice. He knew it was emotion speaking rather than reason, yet he could not control it.

The color rose up Ian's face. "I wouldn't phrase it like that," he said hotly.

"But isn't that what it amounts to?" Daniel shot back. He had no intention of telling Ian that he had already asked his father and been told, decisively, to leave it alone.

"I don't know," Ian admitted, with a tight little movement of his shoulders. "Perhaps Haviland was killed for a reason that had nothing to do with Special Branch. But if it does have to do with state secrets, I need to know. Three people are dead, Daniel. And horribly murdered at that."

"I know!" Daniel said. "I saw one of their bodies at the morgue. I saw in raw detail what he did to them. And if I knew anything, I'd tell you."

"They were all killed by the same person," Ian said, with steady conviction. "I went to see Dr. fford Croft today and asked if she was sure of that, and she was."

Mention of Miriam's name made Daniel suddenly aware of how unfair he was being. He felt his muscles knotting as, with difficulty, he got both his anger and defensiveness under control. He met Ian's eyes. "I don't know. All sorts of things are possible. But I'm not going to be your advocate and ask favors on your behalf. It's unfair for you to ask me to do that."

"I am not asking you to!" Ian responded. "What I am asking is that you get me in to see your father without having to go through Petheridge and the whole line of officials I need to deal with before I get to him. By then, we could have even more bodies." His voice rose in pitch. "For heaven's sake, Daniel, there are living, breathing people with families, jobs, dreams. They could all be at risk!"

"I know that!" said Daniel, feeling his frustration rise. At the same time, he understood Ian's emotion, even shared it. He, too, was angry with a situation he could not address, much less control. "I'll ask my father."

"When?" Ian asked immediately.

"Now!" Daniel snapped. "Is that soon enough for you?"

Ian breathed in and out slowly and gave a half smile, little more than an easing of his face. "Yes, thank you."

Daniel picked up the telephone and placed the call, the two of them sitting in prickly silence until the telephone rang back. "Daniel Pitt," he answered.

Five minutes later, Ian quietly said, "Thank you." Then, bidding Daniel goodbye, he went out into the gathering shadows of early evening.

IT WAS COMPLETELY dark, and the wind had driven the clouds away by the time Ian arrived at the Pitts' doorstep in Keppel Street and the maid let him in. He waited in the entry hall, with its shining polished wood and gentle landscape paintings, while she went into the sitting room to announce his presence.

She returned a few moments later. "Sir Thomas will see you, sir. If it's a matter of business, perhaps you'd like to come to the study?" she offered. "And I'll put some more coal on the fire."

"Thank you," Ian accepted, and followed her to a large room, which in another house might well have been the morning room. It was smaller than most sitting rooms, and more formal. There were many shelves filled with books and a large oak desk with drawers and pigeonholes. There were comfortable chairs: not armchairs, but what were known as "captain's chairs" with back and arms of carved wood, with rails and padded arms. They looked most inviting, but out of respect Ian remained standing.

The maid was quite right: there were hot embers still in the fireplace. When she put a shovelful of coal on top of them, they immediately began to reignite, and flames soon licked more vigorously. She smiled at him and went out straightaway, just as Thomas Pitt was entering the room.

"Sit down, please." Pitt waved at one of the chairs and sat in one of the others. "What may I do for you, Inspector Frobisher?"

He smiled, but it was not an idle question. Ian knew he would require a prompt reply. "I remember you from both school and university, but I presume you are here on official business of a different sort?"

Ian felt uncomfortable. This was not a matter of friendship. And by using his surname and title, Pitt was making it clear that the boundaries had been gently, but very firmly, set. "Yes, Sir Thomas, I'm afraid I am in charge of what the papers are calling the 'Rainy-day Slasher' case."

Pitt nodded very slightly. "Daniel told me."

"Perhaps he also told you that we—the police—have been warned not to dig into anything to do with the third victim, Mr. Haviland. Not his life or his profession, his relationships, or anything else about him." Ian took a deep breath. He was aware of Pitt watching him, no expression on his face but polite attention. It made Ian nervous. He cleared his throat and continued. "Sir, I need to know if Mr. Haviland was the intended victim, and the two women were killed in order to conceal that fact."

Pitt did not move beyond blinking. His expression of interested attention did not alter.

"But whether or not Haviland was one of three specifically targeted victims, we need to treat him exactly the same as the others. If not, we draw attention to him." Ian stopped and waited for Pitt to respond.

"Of course," Pitt said slowly. "Nothing must stand out in any way that puts the attention on him. I imagine you would be able to handle this situation far more effectively if you knew what to avoid. You could then investigate everything else, no matter how closely, with the appearance of giving his death equal treatment."

Ian took a breath and let it out slowly. "Yes, sir," he said, relieved to know that his dilemma was perfectly understood.

A faint smile flickered on Pitt's face. "I will tell you as much as I know and anything I think may be of use to you. It seems I have more to lose by not telling you."

Ian leaned closer, in anticipation that he would finally get the answers he had been seeking.

"It is possible that Haviland was the intended target," Pitt said. "But it seems to me an inefficient way of dealing with the matter. And our enemies are not inefficient. If they wished to get rid of Haviland—and remember, this came off as violent murder—they would not choose to draw attention to him. Were I in their place, I would have made it appear like an accident, a misfortune that was unconnected with his position."

Ian could see the reasoning in that. Why had the official who had spoken to Petheridge not seen that also? Lack of imagination? "Yes, sir. So, do you think it's possible the victims were chosen at random?"

"Do you think so?" Pitt countered, with interest.

"No, sir. I think there is a common link, although we can't find it. But it was certainly not coincidence."

"And it seems the others were not aware of being in immediate danger, or they would not have been walking alone in the rain after dark," Pitt observed.

Ian's mind raced forward. "Maybe we are not so stupid, not finding the connection, when the victims didn't know it themselves. Or else, as you say, they would not have taken the risk of being caught alone in the rain. We don't know so very much about them, but we know, at the least, that Haviland was highly intelligent. And if he was Special Branch, he would have known enough to be careful. Not conspicuously so, but always on guard. I wonder—"

"You wonder what?" Pitt cut across him. "If Haviland recognized his killer? For what it's worth, I don't think Haviland would have known him. Did the pathologist say there were different wounds on any of the victims? Slashes on the arms, for instance? Hands? Other than the index finger, which we presume was done after death. Was it a trophy? A particular type of vengeance—for the killer, or for someone else?"

"You mean like a paid assassin?" Ian asked.

"Or someone trying to please somebody else, or wanting to impress?" Pitt shook his head slowly. "Might be, but I think this man is following his own agenda, not somebody else's. Don't you?"

"Yes, sir, I do. There's so much violence in it. So much hatred. And it's getting worse with each killing." Should he mention what Miriam had said about the index finger in each case being from the dominant hand? Before he could decide, Pitt spoke.

"Do you think Haviland is the last, or is the killer not yet finished?" Pitt was speaking to himself, rather than to Ian. Then he looked Ian in the eye. "I presume you are following the paths of each of the victims, to find where they cross?"

"Yes, sir, except for Haviland's . . ." He held his breath for a moment before letting it out. "Movements," he said finally. He watched Pitt's face, every line and shadow of it, every movement of his eyes. It was a strong face, gentle, despite the deep lines etched by age and experience.

Pitt spoke at last, after what seemed like a long silence, but in fact was less than a minute. "Then we had better do that tonight," he said. "Have you eaten?"

"Eaten?"

"If we're going to follow Haviland back to the cradle, we'll do it better on a full stomach. I'll have some sandwiches and a pot of tea brought here. Our cook always obliges. She's been with us for years." A quick, sheepish smile crossed his face.

"Thank you, sir. And no, I haven't eaten," Ian replied, trying to quell the excitement building in him.

THEY WORKED UNTIL past midnight. Pitt had no compunction whatever about calling various people on the telephone and asking questions, always without giving his reasons for wanting to know. Judging from what Ian could hear on Pitt's end of the conversation, no one made any complaints about the call. Ian was impressed. That, he realized, was real power. There were not many people who could call someone at midnight, whether it was an ambassador or the retired dean of a university, mention his name, and receive a civil answer.

By two o'clock in the morning, they had all the pieces to the puzzle. Pitt laid them out. There were a few blank spaces, but he knew what fitted into them, even if he was unwilling to share some of that knowledge with Ian.

"We knew he was at Cambridge," Ian said, "but so were the others, although they weren't all undergraduates at the same time. And they did not study the same subjects. Hell! There are thousands of people at Cambridge in any given term. They might never have even met."

"You were at Cambridge at the same time as Daniel," Pitt said slowly.

"Yes, and with thousands of others."

"Where else did you and Daniel meet? Other than in lectures and so on?"

"Sports, especially cricket," Ian answered. "But women didn't play, and two of our victims are women."

"Something else," Pitt insisted. "Amateur dramatics? Musical groups? Collecting butterflies? Political debate? Philosophy? Think. Trace it back. There is a connection. It may not be Cambridge, but so far that is the only link common to all of them."

"But sir, they are all different ages!"

"I know, but try it." He piled together the notes they had made and passed them to Ian. "Anyway, these are your main points, without verification, but it's a good start. And I can't help but think that Cambridge might be the key."

"I'm very grateful indeed." Ian was conscious of the debt he owed Pitt, but now it was up to him to take the pieces of the jigsaw and make them fit together. Heaven alone knew what the final picture would reveal.

Pitt smiled, but he said nothing more.

Eighteen

THE FOLLOWING MORNING, Ian Frobisher came early to the police station, almost on the heels of the night shift.

"Good morning, sir," the desk sergeant said with a little surprise in his voice. "Sir, nothing bad happened overnight, I hope?" He said it with a note of anxiety in his voice. These days, he was used to disaster.

"No, not at all," Ian replied, giving as much of a smile as he could on a wet morning, after only a few hours of sleep.

Despite the fatigue, he was still feeling excited. Pitt had given him permission to pursue Haviland's past as much as he could, but to do it discreetly. Whatever business Haviland had been pursuing— and Pitt apparently was not able to tell him what that was—it might be important. He knew how sensitive the case was because Pitt had made a point of warning Ian that any unusual steps might jeopardize the lives of those still working on it.

"How about a cup of tea?" Ian said to the desk sergeant. "And a bun or something. I didn't have time for breakfast." He did not explain to the puzzled man that he was not only early but exhausted. And hungry. And then he told himself, *This is ridiculous.* No one from the station had called him, and the sergeant would know that nothing had happened.

And yet everything had happened. He reminded himself again that Sir Thomas Pitt—*the* Sir Thomas Pitt—had given him Special Branch's permission to investigate Haviland, and that permission was unhampered by anything but a cautious reminder of discretion—which, in view of Haviland's position, he would have used anyway.

He went into his own office and began to make notes. Several minutes later, the sergeant brought him a big enamel mug of piping-hot tea, freshly brewed. The man also offered him a large bun, still warm from the oven, prepared with butter and cheese. Ian suspected that this might be the sergeant's own breakfast. He would remember that and repay the man sometime. Now was not the time to embarrass him by making a fuss over it.

He thanked him and went back to his notes. They were in his own handwriting, with plenty of abbreviations. It was not intended that anyone else, by either chance or design, should be able to read them. There were lists of what they knew about Haviland, facts he assumed should be checked out and confirmed, and other things to find out, now that he had permission. Although Pitt had said that it must be done discreetly, he knew that his efforts would most likely not go unnoticed by Special Branch. So any inquiries he made had to be explainable by the fact that Haviland was apparently the third victim of a very dangerous man who was on a killing spree, his mind perhaps unraveling and slipping beyond control.

He must avoid making a splash during this investigation of Haviland. What Ian needed to know, if it was in any way possible to determine, was whether this crime had something to do with Haviland's personal life. Perhaps an enemy he had made privately, an unpaid debt or a romantic affair? Also, was it in any way connected to the other deaths, even though the other two victims were both young women in their twenties? They were both well educated but had not risen to prominence in any particular field. Haviland was another story. He had been in his mid-forties, a well-to-do and very senior banker. These were the realities Ian could explore, but nothing that could be linked to his work with Special Branch. It was a tightrope he needed to walk, and with great caution.

Ian stared at his notes. So much of what was written there was available to anyone taking the time to collate information. What was not available in any of the biographical information, unless someone had been extremely careless, was that the man had worked for Special Branch. It was a department of the government that was not quite the police, not quite military, but a well-oiled and highly professional group of men and women responsible for combating threats to the country, such as domestic terrorism, as well as threats to the safety and stability of the government. The organization had been originally created to battle against the Irish Fenian acts of terror in England, which had brought with them arson, bombings, and other attacks. Now, however, it had spread its presence far wider, dealing with terrorism and national threats of nearly every sort.

Ian ran through more of his notes. He absolutely had to know if Haviland's death was in any way connected with his clandestine work. Was some enemy of the state riding on the coattails of this so-called "slasher" and hoping that this murder would be credited to the man who had killed the two women?

But there was another possibility, a classic "on the other hand" situation. Perhaps Haviland had a connection that even Special Branch did not know about? A connection with both Sandrine Bernard and Lena Madden. If that was so, how could Ian prove it? To date, no one had found the connection between the two women, if one existed.

Bremner came in around a half hour later and was quite openly surprised to see Ian sitting at a desk already scattered with papers, an empty mug among them. "Good morning, sir. You been here all night?"

"It feels like it," Ian answered. "But no, I haven't. Only about an hour, if that." He gestured to the chair facing him, across his desk. "Sit down and get ready to pay attention." He put his pen down and started to explain, even before Bremner had time to hang his coat up on the hook. "I went to see Sir Thomas Pitt yesterday evening."

Bremner looked surprised. "You . . . what?"

Ian leaned forward a bit. "Pay attention, Bremner, I'm not going to say everything twice. And nothing I say goes beyond this room." When Bremner gave a slight nod, he continued. "You don't need to know the entire conversation, but the short version is that we have his permission, not to be quoted, but to do anything we can to find out who killed Haviland. What he wants us to supply is informa-tion about whether or not he was killed for his job. Or if his death had nothing to do with it, and he was a genuine victim of the slasher."

"Makes sense," Bremner said reluctantly. He moved his chair a bit closer to the desk. "If there is somebody else trying to hide their kill by making it look like our chap, very clever, eh? So clever that not even Special Branch will figure out it's someone else. Cold bas-tard. But, as I said, clever."

"Yes," Ian agreed. "But Haviland might actually be a genuine victim of the slasher, and he might not have known anything about either of the women, except what was printed in the newspapers. That's why it's so important to know which it is. Are we after one man, or are we looking for one lunatic and one clever imitator? And is there anything we know that hasn't been mentioned in the news, or some distinctive element that anyone curious enough could rea-sonably deduce? Or, I suppose," he added, "some difference dic-tated by circumstances." He wanted to explain more clearly, but even he wasn't sure exactly what he meant!

"In other words, look for signs of a second killer."

"Yes," Ian said, with a firm nod. "I suppose that is what I mean.

To get anything settled would be a step further. At the moment, we're splashing around like pigs in muck, and achieving nothing!"

Bremner leaned forward, and rested his forearms on the large desk. "I don't like your farmyard picture, and I believe pigs like muck, but I suppose it's close enough. What else?"

Ian thought about this for a long moment before responding. Unlike so many homicide cases he had worked, nothing was clear in this one, nothing that he could grab hold of and run with. He was more than frustrated; he was fighting that insecurity that came with holding a high position, the feeling that too many people just a rung below him wanted his job. If he botched this case, they'd be after him like hyenas going in for the kill. "There's the possibility that it has nothing to do with Haviland's life or work," he said finally. "And it might not even be the slasher. But that means someone else is cashing in on the general panic." When Bremner didn't respond, he added, "But that's not very likely. I'll start with Dr. fford Croft. I hate to bother the poor woman again, but we have to be as sure as we can be about this. I've been studying everything Sir Thomas gave me. Haviland was an undergraduate at Cambridge as well, but many years before the two women. According to his wife, however, he went back to do some further studies in recent years. But his subject was mathematics and finance, which had nothing to do with their areas."

"What were their subjects?" Bremner asked. "I mean, what do women study at a university like Cambridge? They'd have to be pretty bright even to get in, wouldn't they?"

"Definitely, yes."

"Then they were all bright," Bremner said, with a touch of awe in his voice. "That is, far more than just ordinary bright—brilliant in practical ways—and they could prove it."

Ian stared at the man. "What's your point, Bremner?"

"It would help to know what they studied. Literature? History? And did they get a degree?"

Ian thought of what Daniel had told him about Miriam fford

Croft. "I'd guess probably not. There doesn't seem to be a connection there. But suppose it had to do with geography?"

Bremner's face expressed confusion.

"Suppose," Ian went on, "it's because they lived among and were acquainted with the same groups of people? We know that both Lena Madden and Haviland knew the Reverend Richard Rhodes, and possibly his wife as well."

"Church of England," Bremner said with a nod. "But aren't we pushing it a bit? Lena only went to the vicarage on Adelaide Road once that we know of. That's what it sounded like, at least from what Mrs. Rhodes told us. As for Mrs. Haviland, Rhodes went to her because she needed someone to comfort her immediately after hearing of her husband's murder. A lot of people want some sort of religion in cases like that."

"But it is a connection," Ian insisted.

"Good luck," Bremner said dryly.

"Mrs. Haviland herself," Ian went on. "She might feel strong enough to talk to us now, or have remembered something. If we ask carefully, not to suggest any blame attached to his past."

"Blame?" Bremner said with a shake of his head. "Blame for what?"

"We want to avoid suggesting an affair with another woman," Ian explained. "Or a debt he couldn't, or wouldn't, pay? Or something he knew about somebody, and that person felt threatened? Or something he believed? There are a lot of reasons why people get killed, and not all of those victims are without guilt."

They sat together in silence for a long moment, staring at the desk covered with papers, before Ian continued.

"For a start, Haviland may have known a secret about someone who was sensitive, or proud, or ashamed, and needed it to be kept hidden. That seems a fairly obvious possibility. We see enough of those, right?"

Bremner's eyebrows shot up. "And you think that he'd have told his wife about that?"

Ian's derision was obvious. "No, of course not! And especially if it had anything to do with Special Branch. But wives hear things. They can add two and two together and come up with some very astute answers. At the time, it might have made no sense, but now . . ." He saw comprehension, perhaps even agreement, in Bremner's eyes. "We'll also need to see the people at the bank," he went on. "And to be clear, I'm talking this out with you because there are so many lines to follow, and we need to think of them all."

"What do you expect to find at the bank?"

"He was there for years," said Ian. "He has a whole history there, one that includes rivals, even people he advised against lending money to. There might have been possible money scams, or funds moved suspiciously, even embezzlement. Things he knew, secrets he harbored. Was he discreet, or did he lord this information over people whose lives and careers could be destroyed? Not everyone loves bank managers. And I'll bet a few of them know some dangerous secrets. There are lots of leads to follow, now that we've been cleared to follow them . . ." He paused, and then asked, "Do you like your bank manager?"

Bremner was accustomed to his boss's shifts in conversation. "Don't know him," he said with a smile. "And I aim on keeping it that way!"

"That I can understand," Ian agreed. "But apart from the bank, there's still a lot we can do, and plenty to explore. We need to pay close attention, in case either of the two women's names crop up anywhere at all. Sandrine Bernard lived in Paris after she finished university, so I doubt you'll find anything there. But study Haviland's history of travel as well as you can. See where he went in Europe. And, more to the point, when. Focus specifically on Paris. If he worked for Special Branch, he could have traveled all over the place. We need a full timeline of his travels, and a calendar going back several years for Sandrine Bernard. That might tell us if and when their paths crossed."

"And Lena Madden?" Bremner asked.

"You can put somebody on to a search into her past actions. Places she went, and with whom. Did she have any romances? There's bound to have been. Any debts? Oh, and find out where both women banked! Get somebody thorough, Bremner, no one who cuts corners." He pushed his chair away from the desk. "Come on! We've got a lot to do."

"Yes, sir," Bremner replied, giving a halfhearted salute. "Where do you want me to start?"

"Begin with Haviland's travels. And then see if they connect with that of either woman. And if he did go to Paris, look for anything that could be interesting. Then look into Mrs. Haviland."

"Is that it?" Bremner asked, with slight sarcasm. "Nothing else?"

Ian smiled. "You also have Reverend and Mrs. Rhodes! Let me know by the end of the day how you're doing, just in case there's anything we should share. I'll be here until nine or ten o'clock. Oh, and Bremner," he added, almost with nonchalance, "not a word about Special Branch . . . to anyone. Even if the mention might turn up information we need. Trust me," he said, his face turning very serious. "One word and we'll both lose our jobs."

Bremner's face darkened, as if a cloud were passing overhead. "Yes, sir. Are you going to the bank as well?"

"I am, but let's compare notes before then. I don't expect them to be particularly helpful, but it's important to have as much information as we can get our hands on before I show up and start asking them questions about Haviland. Wouldn't want to look like an idiot."

Bremner gave a lopsided smile and declined to make any comment. That sentiment was something he understood very well.

IAN BEGAN WITH Mrs. Haviland, who had been staying with the vicar and his wife since her bereavement. It was perhaps a little too early to call on her. But when he had met Mrs. Rhodes, he sensed that, in her capacity as the reverend's wife, she was most likely an early riser. Not so unusual, he reasoned, considering that she was not only his wife, but his eyesight as well. He had no objection if Mrs. Polly Rhodes chose to sit in on his interview. Indeed, it might be helpful.

One thing Ian distinctly recalled from his first meeting with Polly Rhodes was that he had immediately liked her. There was a warmth to her that he found comfortable, as well as comforting. It might have been part of her vocation as a minister's wife, but she exuded that warmth with what felt like a natural ease. He realized that it was expected of her, and that this warmth was often needed by congregants. Nevertheless, he felt it was real. Perhaps she had chosen the vocation as much as she had chosen the man.

The vicarage was easy to find. Ian took the underground train to Chalk Farm, exited the station, and turned right. And then he turned left and along the pavement leading toward the church spire, visible high above the trees. In minutes, he arrived at the vicarage. He turned up the path and knocked on the door. It was opened by a pale-faced maid who looked as if she was barely holding on to her composure.

"Yes?" she asked, without fully opening the door.

Ian wondered if she was perhaps afraid. After all, murder and mayhem were all about them at the moment. "Good morning," he said. He made a point of not smiling. A smile seemed clumsily inappropriate. "My name is Frobisher. I'm sorry to disturb you, but I'm afraid I need to speak to Mrs. Haviland again. I believe she is still staying here."

"She's not very well, sir. She's just been horribly bereaved. Could you call back at another time? Maybe in a few weeks?"

"Yes, I know. It is about this that I'm calling on her. And I'm afraid it can't wait. I'm from the police."

"Oh!" she declared, pulling the door open a bit wider.

Ian realized that, in first introducing himself, he had failed to use his official title or show his credentials. He made a note to himself that he must be more careful. "Will you ask her to spare me a little while, please? It really is important."

"Oh, yes, sir, of course," she said meekly. "Will you come in?"

Ian entered and was led into the sitting room, expecting to see Mrs. Haviland arrive shortly. However, it was another twenty minutes before she appeared, alone and apparently well in control of herself.

He stood up immediately. When he looked at her, he tried not to show alarm. Mrs. Haviland was ashen, her hair dull and scraped back off her face with no attempt at finesse. It was clear that she had ceased to care about the outside world, and perhaps the inside one as well. He tried to understand how she was feeling, but he quickly realized that he had no idea. After his wife Mary's death, everything else had seemed so unimportant. Loss, especially compounded by grief, altered everything. It was only their tiny daughter left behind, a newborn without a mother, that had forced him to eat, to stop hiding, to demand that he not drown in grief, but pick up that baby, so small and vulnerable, and depending on him. How bitter would be Mary's disappointment in him if he failed her, failed them both! And, controlling the agony that he knew was etched on his face, he had held the baby, talked to her. And he had promised that he would love her and take care of her forever. And then his mother had stepped in, and he'd seen that she loved his baby as fiercely as she had always loved her son. That was when he knew they would be all right.

"I'm sorry to trouble you again, Mrs. Haviland," Ian said quietly, pushing away these poignant memories. "I do have some idea how you feel."

"Do you?" She was too deeply mired in grief to bother hiding her anger. "Have you lost a wife, then? Murdered by a lunatic that the police can't find?" She glared at him.

"No," he said quietly. "My wife died in childbirth. There was no villain."

The last vestige of color drained from her face. He thought she was going to faint. "Oh. I'm . . ." She took a deep breath. "I'm so sorry." She hesitated a moment, started to speak, and then fell silent again.

"The baby is fine," he told her, offering a little reassuring smile. "A little girl, and she's talking now. I even understand quite a bit of what she says."

"I was afraid to ask," she admitted, her eyes wide and full of a terrible pity.

He smiled. "I would have been, too, if I were in your place. But," he added, his voice shifting to a more professional tone, "this is important business. Mrs. Haviland, we need to find this man. We don't think he's a lunatic, attacking people at random. It looks much more like he was picking specific people."

She drew in a quick breath, almost choking on it. Her body stiffened. "Are you saying that Roger somehow . . . did something to deserve this?"

"No, not at all," Ian responded quickly. "Please, sit down." He indicated the chair closest to her, and then sat down himself. "We think it's more likely your husband knew something that would lead us to this man," he went on. "That, for some reason, he had to be silenced. Or that he knew something, perhaps not realizing its importance, and the killer feared he would one day realize its significance, and remember something criminal, immoral, or unethical he had done." That was not exactly the truth. Was that sparing her feelings, or simply good practice at gaining information?

She frowned. "You mean it was someone he knew? He was a banker, Mr. . . . Inspector . . ."

"Frobisher," he replied. "And we're looking for something that all the victims had in common. And since the other two were young women, it's not likely to be a social connection." He shifted in his chair and leaned forward a little. "More probably a business connection, or some circumstance where they were all witnesses to the same thing. Mr. Haviland traveled on business quite a lot, I believe.

Perhaps you have notes of when he left and when he came back. Also, he probably contacted you, or left you the address of which hotel, or where he could be reached, if you needed to contact him. All of this is valuable information for us." He watched her face carefully. There was a fraction more color in it now. "And he might have mentioned how he traveled. I mean, was it by train or boat? Anything you can remember him telling you about his trips might be valuable information."

"Do you really think that could help?" She seemed dubious. "Surely, it wasn't someone from abroad who did this? And to the others? The first woman, too?"

"There is some connection, and we think it more likely an incidental one, rather than a relationship."

Her face was pinched with distaste, and for a moment he thought she was going to protest, then she made what he sensed was, again, a very deliberate decision to control her feelings. "Yes, of course," she conceded. "I'll tell you anything I can remember. I've brought my diary with me from home—it's upstairs in my bedroom—just to read."

"I understand," he said.

"It's for last year, and it will have dates of when he was traveling, and possibly where he was going." She rose from her chair.

"Thank you very much. It could provide the clue that gets us started on the right path."

When Mrs. Haviland returned from upstairs with the diary, he noticed that she had also taken time to brush her hair and pin it up more gracefully.

"As it happens, I've found diaries for the past two years," she said, placing them on the table in front of Ian.

He took out his little notebook and a pen. Together, they went through them, with Mrs. Haviland commenting on several entries. At first, her voice was a little wobbly, as one memory after another shook her. Ian did not interrupt, nor did he offer to help. He was very aware of her grief, having experienced much of his own, but he forced himself not to show it. And certainly not to dwell on it within himself. He listened, interrupting only when there seemed a question to ask, something to clarify.

As they worked together, there emerged the picture of a dedicated, rather humorless man who devoted much time and attention to his work. Perhaps he would have liked to share it with his wife, but Ian knew he could not.

Mrs. Haviland also began to sense that her husband might have been engaged in work that he kept from her. Ian was watching her face and thought she perhaps not only sensed this, but regretted it as well. From one entry to another, there were so many questions she could not answer. She had noted what train her husband was taking, or which boat. There was a ferry to Calais, and a steamer to some port unnamed. There was a train to Edinburgh. There were notations of which hotel he would stay in, but other trips where she wasn't told. She said that her husband had explained that sometimes he didn't know in advance. He had told her about the cities he had visited all over Europe, but he did not describe them, or the business he conducted.

"I wish he would have," she said, looking not at Ian but into the distance, toward something beyond the warm, comfortable room in which they sat. "I sometimes think he barely noticed the cities," she said, "and only recalled the banks." She blinked several times. "Or perhaps he didn't?" Her voice trailed off. "I sometimes looked at pictures of those places—in books, you know? They looked wonderful to me. All different. Berlin was so different from Paris, which bore no resemblance to anywhere in Italy. Rome looked fascinating. So much history, thousands of years, literally. And Florence, it seemed just breathtaking. I don't know why, because I'll never go there, but I so wanted to see them, imagine him there, gazing at all that history and beauty. Hearing different languages. I think he understood a lot of them, and really knew what was being said. I suppose you pick it up, if you are there often enough. He was very clever, you know."

Ian nodded. He wondered if Roger Haviland had really been so blind that he didn't see how observant his wife was. Or if he felt he was protecting her from even an accidental knowledge of what he really did. Was it the desire to protect that drove him, or was it habitual secrecy? And did he really not see the beauty of these places? Or was he focused only on the task for which he went, and the people he saw secretly?

Ian spent all morning at the vicarage, and accepted Polly Rhodes's invitation to stay for lunch. She seemed pleased to have someone to cook for.

While lunch was being prepared, they continued with the diaries. Ian developed a palpable sadness for the wife of this man. What a hideously lonely life she must have led, unable to share with the person closest to her, excluded from all the teeming emotions, the danger, the beauty, even the tragedy, he must have seen. What sort of people did Haviland know in those places? Bankers? Or perhaps not bankers at all. Was banking a doorway to other things, an effective cover for his real business?

For that matter, what sort of Special Branch business was conducted in so many different cities in Europe? Or even in half of them? Was it all legitimate, as far as Special Branch was concerned? There was only one person who could answer these questions, and Ian wasn't sure another visit with Sir Thomas was wise. Thinking through this, he argued with himself. Should he take the information from Mrs. Haviland's diaries to Thomas Pitt to verify it? Possibly. Might it shed any light on who had killed Haviland? "He studied at Cambridge, didn't he?" He said it aloud.

"Yes. Modern history and languages. He added business studies in his final year, by which time he knew he wanted to go into banking. He got a first," Mrs. Haviland added, with a smile and obvious pride. "And he took a course or two more recently. He was very good at what he did."

"He must have been," said Ian. He did not have to affect admiration, having studied modern history himself. He knew how fascinating, and at times how broad, it could be.

She looked at him earnestly, wanting something, some point of connection, perhaps.

"I did, too," he told her. "Cambridge and history, not the languages. It's never-ending, really interesting, but there's such a lot to remember, never mind to understand."

"Did you?" She was surprised. "And—" She stopped, as if aware of possibly being tactless.

He smiled easily. "Yes, I got a good pass, and my family was very shaken when I went into the police instead of politics. But after my wife died, they became very understanding and didn't push at all. And, to be honest, I never wanted to go into politics, and I didn't want to teach either. There are things about police work I hate, but things I like, too. And somebody has to attack the mess!" He was afraid he'd said too much, but her response was encouraging.

"I understand," she said quickly. "I've been trying to think what to do with my time, now that I have no one to look after." She gave a shaky smile. "We have two sons, but they both emigrated to Canada. I haven't written to them yet. I can't think what to say. I suppose that's cowardly, isn't it?"

"No." He shook his head quickly. "You need a little while to compose what to say to them." He lowered his voice a little. "You want to sound as if you are strong, brave, in control. And if you wait another few days, we may even know who was responsible. And they will be comforted to know that the reverend and Mrs. Rhodes are caring for you."

She nodded, tears in her eyes. "Mrs. Rhodes has been such a comfort. A remarkable woman. She has a degree in some subjects, other than just relying on her knowledge of the scriptures. If she were not a woman, she would have gone into the clergy."

"Did she have any helpful suggestions for you?" Ian asked.

"Oh, yes, several. In a little while, I'll think of them seriously.

There is such a lot to do, so much that can be done for others. And Mrs. Rhodes is always out there, somewhere, helping. Her husband is very wise, very gentle, but he's blind, you know? That limits where he can go. She goes in his place, at all hours, all kinds of weather."

"Yes, I've met the reverend," he agreed. "Did he study at Cambridge, too?"

"I think so. Why, does it matter?"

Ian saw confusion in her face. "It might," he said, speaking slowly, as the thoughts came to his mind. "It seems they all did—all the victims—but at different times. In addition to these recent post-graduate courses, did your husband ever go back there, to see old friends? Or attend guest lectures, or anything?"

"I don't know," she responded. "Oh, wait, yes." She sat up a little straighter. "Once, I remember he went to listen to the choir at King's College. I mean, in the chapel. It's very famous, you know."

"Yes, I do. And did he ever take you?"

"Twice, and it was marvelous." She was smiling, but there were tears in her eyes at the memory of something she would never do again.

"Did he meet old friends there?" He did not want to push it, but he was compelled to.

"Yes, several. Is that important?"

"I don't know, probably not. But you never know when one thing leads to another. And we could use anything at all to make a connection between the victims. So far, we can't see one." He waited for her to speak, aware that there was something she wanted to say and was clearly finding it difficult to put into words.

"Inspector," she finally said. "Is it possible that there was a second killer, someone copying the others? Or that they simply made a mistake when they killed Roger?" There was a lift of hope in her voice. "They thought he was someone else? What I'm saying is that, wrapped up against the weather, hat low, collar up, how do you know one man from another? If they were roughly of average height and build, head down, looking where they're putting their feet so as not to step in a deep puddle? One man looks like another. Could he have been taken for somebody else?" Her eyes filled with tears again, but she refused to look away.

Ian would not deny this as a possibility, nor could he completely rule it out. What did this mean, if it were so? That if the slasher had a particular person in mind, and had made a mistake with Roger Haviland, then whoever he had intended to kill was still in danger?

"Thank you, Mrs. Haviland," he said, gratitude in his voice. "I think I should have thought of that possibility a little earlier."

He could not tell her that her husband had been an agent of Special Branch. But perhaps it was not as important as they had assumed. "Thank you," he said again.

At that moment, Polly Rhodes came in quietly to say that lunch was ready.

Ian welcomed this. It was a hot lunch in a warm house, with the weather so cold and wet outside. These alone were excellent reasons to stay.

After lunch, Reverend Rhodes went into his study to prepare his sermon for the following Sunday. Mrs. Haviland excused herself to go up to her room and take a short rest. Mrs. Rhodes asked Ian if he would like a cup of tea by the fire before he had to leave.

He did not hesitate. Apart from the fact that it was raining again, and the wind was rising, it was a chance to speak to her alone, casually. She might know more than she was aware of. Mrs. Haviland had been here since the death of her husband, which was more than a week ago now, and Lena Madden had confided in Richard Rhodes. Surely there had to be some connection between the victims? Could she have noticed something without realizing its importance?

He glanced at the rain that was streaking the windows.

"Do you like your work, Inspector?" Polly asked.

It was a very layered question, and meeting her eyes, he could see that she meant it as such. Was that politeness to center the conversation on him? Or was she truly interested? Or did she have a darker intention: Was she trying to assess how much danger he might represent to her husband's parishioners, or perhaps even to her husband's calling?

Ian leaned back a little in the chair. It was extremely comfortable. The air was warm, and after assuring herself that Ian had no more pieces of biscuit to offer her, Dido was asleep at his feet. What could possibly be more comforting than the patter of rain on the window, the crackling of the wood fire, and the gentle snoring of a contented dog at one's feet?

"Do I like my work?" he repeated, thinking hard how best to answer this question. "It goes all the way from the immeasurably satisfying to the starkly tragic," he answered. "Often it is very uncomfortable, and sometimes it is frustrating, as this case is. There are times when it makes me happy. But it's always interesting, because it is to do with people, their triumphs and disasters. It's challenging, and important to get it right, because somebody's life will be changed, even damaged, if I get it wrong." He smiled. "And sometimes it's wonderfully comfortable, like this . . ." He looked very directly at her. She really did have beautiful eyes. "And it's a challenge of wits."

She smiled back at him, quite genuinely. "Like now, for example?" She did not mince words. "You look quite at ease, yet you are thinking about what information I might have, knowingly or not, that would further your investigation." It was a statement that reflected her intellect.

"And whether your husband's vow of silence regarding what he might have been told, might extend to you also, when you take his place, visiting parishioners in trouble," he added.

"A distinction without a genuine difference," she answered. "But no one has confessed to me about being this slasher. And I think I know Richard well enough—yes, he still surprises me sometimes, thank God, but not often. It would be terribly boring if one were completely predictable, don't you think?"

"Yes," he agreed. "And dangerous. You could take far too much for granted. So, you think you would know if such confidences had been shared with him, even though he would say nothing?"

"Yes." She brushed a stray wisp of hair off her brow. "I believe I would know. But I'm not sure. You didn't expect any better an answer than that, did you?"

"I thought you might be able to detect whether he knew the man, or not," he said truthfully. "And I was contemplating how much longer I could sit by the fire, instead of going out into the rain."

She laughed very gently. "Of course. I think he may have his suspicions, but I am almost sure he doesn't know with any certainty."

He met her eyes, searching for what she was feeling. "A very heavy calling," he said after a moment or two. "And if he did know? Would he then feel a terrible burden of guilt if there was another murder? Would he feel as if he could have prevented it?" It was a fearful question to ask, and yet he would be equally complicit if he did not.

It was several seconds, elapsing into a minute, then two, before she answered.

"Yes," she said at last. "And before you ask me if he is delaying facing the truth, making himself doubt when at heart he knows— and I am not protecting him—I genuinely don't know the answer. But if he has to face it, he will."

He sat forward. "Mrs. Rhodes, for heaven's sake, do protect him! If that person realizes he knows, or even confesses to him, he may be in danger himself!"

"Do you think I don't know that?" she said softly. "Believe me, Inspector Frobisher, that is in my mind all the time."

He looked at her gentle, enigmatic face, and could think of no answer at all.

Nineteen

Daniel put down the last page of Wolford's manuscript with a sigh. It was a beautifully written piece of work, and as far as he could see, everything was taken from reliable sources, some in English but mostly in French. Many incidents and descriptions were backed up by more than one source. He found it annoying to have to check at the back of the book for such accuracy. He would rather have read it only for pleasure, but this was now his remit. This was work.

He had made half a dozen notes to question some of the references, but his intention in going to see Wolford was actually to reassure him. The man had telephoned twice with nervous questions, the answers to which he already knew. Daniel did not blame him. His whole life's achievements were being questioned, and it seemed to Daniel as if the accusations were baseless. In fact, all of this was quite possibly intended to draw attention to Linus Tolliver's work, rather than being based on any legitimate cause.

He would go and see Wolford, talk with him, reassure him that his case was sound, and if he kept his temper, there was every chance his charge of assault could be settled at a reasonable financial cost, and nothing worse.

This was an excellent time for a visit. The air was sharp, but it was actually sunny, and looked likely to remain so all day.

"Just going to check a few last facts with Professor Wolford," he told Impney on his way out.

"Yes, sir," Impney said, with a polite smile.

The clerk had never expressed an opinion on Wolford. Daniel knew that he would not consider it proper to do so, unless asked, and even then, whatever he thought would be expressed with moderation. The only exception to that was if Impney sensed that some danger threatened a member of chambers, and that was certainly not the case with Wolford. The man was both overbearing and genuinely nervous, and sometimes he needed more reassurance than most. But he was extremely clever, and the two sometimes went hand in hand. "He needs something to put his mind to, sir," was all Impney said.

Daniel agreed. "Don't know if I'll be back today, or not. Depends upon how long it takes," he added.

"Yes, sir. I will inform Mr. fford Croft," Impney said. "Nice day for a walk, sir."

Daniel smiled, meeting Impney's eyes. "Indeed," he admitted, looking forward to it.

He took the underground railway again, with a couple of changes, eventually emerging into the fresh air at Kentish Town, and walking west. It gave him plenty of time to think. When he reached Wolford's house, he was feeling refreshed, and ready to sit down and talk.

Wolford answered the door looking untidy, his thick hair unbrushed and falling forward over his eyes, his jacket crumpled. "What is it?" he asked immediately. "What's happened?"

"Nothing's happened," Daniel replied. "May I come in?"

Wolford stepped back, blinking a little in the bright sunlight.

Daniel went in. He had not realized how cold the air was until the warmth wrapped itself around him. There was a good fire burning in the sitting-room grate, and the lamps were lit, as if Wolford had been reading. There was a pile of books beside his armchair.

"I'm sorry to disturb you," Daniel apologized. "Just a few things I want to be certain of."

"What things?" Wolford demanded. "It's all there. Tolliver was wrong to accuse me of plagiarism. I already told you that."

"Yes, you did," Daniel agreed. He had not been invited to take his coat off, or to sit down. He decided to behave as if he had. He put his coat over the arm of a chair and sat down, beside the fire, opposite where Wolford was now sitting.

"Well?"

Daniel heard in the man's voice that he required an explanation. "I need to be familiar with the characters you refer to in the book. I don't want the court to think I'm unaware of what provoked you to hit Tolliver," Daniel replied.

Wolford stared at him for a moment or two, then visibly relaxed. "I suppose you want a cup of tea?" he said, a little ungraciously, but it was a definite improvement on his greeting.

"Later," Daniel acknowledged. "Let's get the questions over first."

"Like . . . what?" Wolford looked suspicious, but he leaned back in the chair. "It's all there, in the endnotes. I made that decision ages ago, to list all the sources at the back of the book. It breaks the concentration to keep looking at the foot of the page. Haven't you any imagination, man? This was high drama! Life and death. The fate of one of civilization's great countries. It affected all Europe. Damn it, and even America. We all have revolutions, except the English, because we are too damned phlegmatic to go up in flames! Waterlogged! We turn around slowly, and not all at the same time!"

Daniel felt a little stung by that. It made the English sound dull, and he was English to the core, whatever that meant. "We've had our dramas," he said a little tartly. "Shakespeare managed to get a few stories out of English history. Civil wars, including between the king and parliament. The execution of a king. Several kings murdered, Richard II in a way I'll not even mention. An archbishop murdered at his own altar, by another king's man. And on and on. How about the rivalry between Elizabeth and Mary Queen of Scots, which also ended in a queen's head being cut off! We may not have had a guillotine, but we had a headsman, with an axe—"

Wolford held up his hand. "All right! So you were listening to my lectures, in your Cambridge days." He smiled. "You like the drama and sweep of history, don't you? You see it!"

Daniel smiled back at him, deliberately relaxing. "Yes. You brought it to life for me, and I thank you."

Wolford gave a bow, without rising to his feet.

Daniel relaxed a little. He got straight to the point. "Just a few things I need to know. Words, passages, and where to find them." He looked at his notes, and began with some of the easiest for Wolford to answer, which he did, calmly. And then he moved on to some of the more contentious issues, beginning with Danton. "Your reference to his trying to dig up the grave of his dead wife," Daniel began.

"What about it?" Wolford said sharply. "The man was crazed with grief. You want me to have the man standing there quietly weeping into his handkerchief?" His voice was heavy with sarcasm. "Stop pussyfooting about, damn it! He was a giant in every sense— physically, morally, emotionally. It would be a lie to paint him any other way. A damned lie. I won't do it, and I won't help anyone else do it!" His face was flushed and his eyes overly bright.

"Professor," Daniel said gently. "I only asked you, so that I don't look like a fool if they ask me. Where did you get the story from?"

"Gravediggers," Wolford replied. "No one asked their names— which are probably the French equivalent of John Smith, in any case."

Daniel left it. He asked a few questions that appeared to be less contentious. Then he referred back to Marat, and his famous murder in his bath, and then to Fouché. "Was Joseph Fouché really training for the priesthood?" he asked doubtfully. "The Butcher of Nantes? He did some appalling things. Really nightmare acts, which you didn't flinch from describing."

"Of course I described them!" Wolford snapped. "What do you want? Pretty little pictures? Euphemisms? No blood, no agony, no shame? He drowned people who were innocent of any crime. People who were slow to support the revolution, because they didn't understand it! Perhaps some of them were greedy, or stupid, or saw only what they wanted to. Aren't many of us guilty of that sometimes? He stripped them naked, then tied them together, face-to-face, man to woman. Children. Strangers, people you pass in the street: the butcher, your next-door neighbor. Naked, Pitt! Imagine being lashed together on the deck of a barge, trapdoors on the bottom open, and you sink in the river, the water comes up to your neck, then over the top of your head!" He was glaring at Daniel now, and he was shaking. "That was real! You want me to take the horror out of it? Sanitize it?"

"No!" Daniel said heatedly. "But how does it square with a man who came out of hiding when Robespierre was hunting him, in order to send him to the guillotine? He walked through the streets, behind the coffin of his dead child."

"I don't have to explain that!" Wolford was shouting now. "Stop trying to trip me up. Who asked you to do that? You've been listening to Tolliver!"

"Of course I've been listening to Tolliver!" Daniel said with surprise. "I need to know what he's going to throw at me! I need to be able to answer him if he comes up with something new. Any inconsistency he thinks—"

"Inconsistency?" Wolford interrupted, accusation in his voice. "I report history. I don't try to explain it, or justify it, or say when and if it will happen again. Who put you up to this?"

Daniel was startled. "Professor, nobody put me up to it. It's part of defending you, which you have hired me to do. He still believes you've copied what he's written . . ."

Wolford's face was white, all color drained from it, except for the two bright spots on his cheeks.

"Professor!" Daniel said urgently. "It's unjust, I know. So, tell me where you got the information and I can prove he's mistaken, or else he's just plain lying. But there's no point in saying that if I can't prove it, and I need you to help me do this."

Wolford stared at Daniel, his expression unreadable. He breathed in and out slowly. "I thought, for a moment, that you were against me, too."

"No, sir, I'm definitely on your side," Daniel said. "You give me the weapons and I'll use them. That's what I do. We'll win this together. But I've got to let them see that you are rational, that your work is based on facts and research, and that Tolliver lost his temper and lashed out at you because he was wrong—and he knows it. We need to show that he was so out of control that he lunged at you and missed, and then you defended yourself by hitting back, and you did not miss. That's why he was injured, and you were not."

Wolford dropped his head into his hands, hiding his face. "I'm sorry," he said. "I'm so tired of fighting them. I just want to teach history, to tell people about the past, and then perhaps we can all do better in the future. The very least we can do is learn from the mistakes of our forebears!" He looked up, staring intently at Daniel. "They were real people, Pitt, just as real as we are. Why in God's name can't we learn from them?"

"Because we don't learn from much," Daniel replied. "But you do more than anyone else I know to make me think. And I'll make sure you are completely vindicated. The charge is misbegotten, and I will prove that."

Wolford took a deep breath and let it out slowly. The fear seemed to have left him and he was in control again. "Thank you."

DANIEL WENT BACK to Lincoln's Inn and worked for the rest of the day, but he still finished earlier than had become his habit and, for once, it was not raining. In fact, it was a relatively mild evening. Spring was imaginable: new leaf buds, even early blossom. He excused himself without speaking to anyone except Impney, who needed to know where members of chambers were during office hours.

He caught a taxi to the morgue. It was not yet fully dark, but the winter months brought a chill by four o'clock, and the colors seeped out of the sky. He arrived just as the lamps were being lit along the streets, crisp and sharp in the frosty air. He trusted that Miriam would still be there. He knew her dedication to her work, and he greatly admired it. At the same time, he was troubled by its power to compel her devotion. He wondered what else there was in her life. And then he pushed the thought away. What he really wanted to know was if, in her life, there was room for him.

As the taxi made its way through the streets, he saw women with shopping bags rushing home before total darkness set in. With these murder cases unsolved, the city was on edge. If the population thought the killings were random, who was to say they wouldn't be next?

He pulled himself back to the burning question: What did he want for himself? Into his head slipped the image of a life with Miriam. This caught him by surprise. Yes, he cared about her, certainly, but . . . a life with her? Did he want that, with all it would mean? How would his life change, once he committed himself? That was a new thought. Was it possible to have something real with her, not just a dream that could be set aside, any time it was inconvenient or overwhelming? Perhaps it was simply a cozy picture in his imagination, where he was in control? That meant no risks, no disappointments. In other words, playing it safe.

His thoughts were interrupted when he realized that the taxi had arrived. He paid the driver and alighted, stepping onto the pavement. It was cold, which meant it would be icy in another hour. He went inside and followed the corridor straight through to the laboratory.

He saw her immediately. She was leaning against the edge of the table on which there was a body, covered to the neck with a white sheet. He felt as if he had intruded, because she had clearly given way to a moment of exhaustion, perhaps physical, but surely emotional as well. Her head was a little bent, her face half hidden.

He did not know whether to break the silence or not. Should he pretend he had not seen her like this, and then make a noise as if having just walked in? He didn't want to startle her, if she believed she was alone.

But it was too late. Miriam showed her awareness of someone else's presence by suddenly straightening up and turning round. When she saw Daniel, her face lit up with a smile.

Daniel was certain she had no idea how vulnerable she looked. He was touched by it, for a moment more deeply than he was ready to admit.

"Daniel! How are you?" she said.

"I'm fine," he answered, walking toward her, and smiling back as if he had noticed nothing. "I finished a little early, so I thought I'd call in to see how you are, and if you have any further news about Dr. Eve."

"She's recovering," Miriam replied, and he heard the relief in her voice. "But slowly. It took some time for the doctors to diagnose her illness." She pulled off the gloves she wore during examinations. "But now they're sure it's pneumonia."

"Thank heaven it wasn't a heart attack," Daniel said. "Or a stroke."

"Thank heaven indeed," she said. "The diagnosis was the easy part. The hard part is to keep this woman quiet and resting. And patient!"

They both smiled at the absurdity of that possibility. Dr. Eve was known for many positive traits, but patience was not one of them.

Daniel knew that, in the meantime, Miriam was working alone. Except, that is, for the assistance of Joe, a young man who was strong and reliable, but relatively unskilled.

As if reading Daniel's mind—something she seemed to do with ease—she said, "Joe's a big help. He's doing all the heavier physical work, the tidying up and keeping everything clean. Without him, I'd be overwhelmed."

"It's a big responsibility," Daniel observed. "Can the city hire someone to work alongside you, until Dr. Eve returns?" The moment he asked, he knew how unlikely that would be. Budgets were tight, red tape was a nightmare. By the time someone was hired—if hired at all—Dr. Eve would have been back for weeks, or longer.

"Are you finished for the day?" he asked, trying not to reveal how much he wanted her to be. He had nothing in particular he needed to talk about, but he looked forward to her company. How could he say that without revealing too much of his feelings?

It was at that moment that Daniel understood the meaning of *tongue-tied*. When was an attorney, much less the son of Thomas Pitt, ever at a loss for words?

"Finished? I'm never finished!" she said, smiling broadly.

"But . . . finished enough to have dinner with me?"

There was a long beat before she answered, causing Daniel to hold his breath. "Yes, just about," she replied. "There's nothing more to learn from this one," and she pointed to the corpse on the table. She gave a wry little smile. "Most pathology work is pretty predictable, but a slip of concentration might result in my missing the one anomaly that matters."

"May I help you put him in cold storage, or wherever he belongs?"

Miriam pulled the sheet over the man's face. "Thank you, but Joe is still here, in one of the back rooms. I'll ask him to take charge.

He's used to handling bodies. I just have to sign my notes, and then this autopsy is completed."

"Good, then we'll go to dinner. Somewhere a little smarter than the pub down the road, if you like." He had not intended to say that—the part about going somewhere a cut above the pub—but it seemed important. She looked so tired, and she deserved something more polished, certainly brighter than the local place, with its dark-paneled walls and curtained windows.

"Do I need to go home and change?" she asked.

Daniel was wearing one of his well-cut but discreet business suits that he kept for chambers. He had no idea what she was wearing under the white lab coat that protected her skin and clothing from the chemicals, as well as the bloodstains that often came with her job. Perhaps his offer was tactless, proposing something more than she wanted? He went to speak again, then realized he did not know what he was going to say.

"I'm not exactly dressed for the West End," she said, with a rather bleak smile.

The words came quickly to his tongue. "Then we'll sit in the darkest corner, away from the middle of the room. I could say that nobody would notice us, but everybody would notice your hair." Daniel saw how she blushed, and he thought he had made her uncomfortable. She, too, seemed to be at a loss for words. "Which is beautiful," he went on, aware now that he was being personal, and that he was making both of them self-conscious. "You can sit with your back to the room, if you like. Then everyone will wonder who you are. As for me, I shall face the room and exhibit a self-satisfied smile."

"Daniel! You're impossible," she exclaimed, turning sideways so she did not meet his eyes.

"So, will you come with me . . . to dinner?" he insisted.

"Yes," she said. "Of course I will." She took a step away and reached for her notes to check them one last time, and then she signed them. She walked to a doorway nearby and called Joe. He appeared from a back room, and she said something to him.

The young man approached Daniel, smiling and nodding. "Good evening, Mr. Pitt," he announced cheerfully. "You look after her, sir, and make sure she eats. If she collapses, I'll be really stuck."

"I'm not going to collapse, Joe!" Miriam told him firmly.

"That's right," he agreed, his voice mocking but friendly. "Just like Dr. Eve, you are."

"That's a compliment," she answered. "But I'm still not going to collapse!"

"You've Mr. Pitt to look after you," Joe said, as if it were the most obvious and most reasonable thing in the world. Then he set about moving the body from the table onto the trolley, and then out of the room.

Miriam looked down, her cheeks burning. "I'm sorry," she said, almost inaudibly.

"I think that was a compliment to me," he said. "Joe trusts me to look after you properly. See you eat something good, make sure you're not stressed, and refrain from asking too many questions. He's saying that I'm not selfish, that I won't keep you up too late. And that I think a bit more of your comfort than my own."

She shook her head, smiling. "Really, you got all of those messages?" Even while speaking, teasing him, she did not look up and meet his eyes.

THEY FOUND A very nice restaurant, tucked away on a little side street, and not far from Miriam's home. It was still early, and there were plenty of tables free. Daniel chose one in the corner, as he had said he would, and he offered her the chair with her back to the room. The waiter seemed surprised, but he made no comment. The customer was always right—even the most eccentric ones!

Daniel was happy to be able to sit quietly, with no telephones or messengers, no files stacked up on his desk for review. As much as he tried to push the thought away, what pleased him most was sitting here quietly . . . with Miriam.

Over the course of a leisurely meal, they talked of all sorts of things. The one subject they avoided, almost by tacit agreement, was work: there was no talk of death, investigations, suspects, and not a single mention of the Rainy-day Slasher. If either of them was thinking of the monster, nothing was said.

Instead, they spoke of events from childhood and university, vignettes that stoked their imagination. They described things they would like to do, and places they would like to visit. They delved into why these places held a fascination, and what there was to see. Even which famous or infamous people had lived there. It was easy, comfortable. For Daniel, it was the perfect evening.

When they finally left, laughing at something trivial and absurd—and yet, had they been asked, neither would have been able to put a finger on exactly what it was they found so amusing—Daniel was startled to find that it was long after eleven o'clock. In fact, it was closer to midnight. "I promised Joe I'd have you home early," he said, his eyes twinkling with humor.

Miriam smiled. "Mum's the word, Mr. Pitt!"

It took Daniel a moment to recognize the feeling rushing through him.

He was happy.

Looking sideways at Miriam, he believed she was, too. He might not have delivered her home early, but he had kept his word to Joe in one area: he was thinking of her and her well-being. Or was he too deeply immersed in his own happiness to think of anything else but that?

He tried to come up with something to say. As they climbed into the taxi, he ended by saying simply, "Thank you."

Twenty

I AN FROBISHER WAS not happy about having to investigate Polly Rhodes. He had liked her immediately upon meeting her. And yet he could see now that he must; it was inevitable. Both Lena Madden and Haviland's wife had known her. Had Haviland known her as well? There was nothing in Ian's notes that referred to her, nor had there been any mention of her from any other source. Even if Mrs. Haviland had confided anything to Polly's husband, that relationship between clergy and congregant carried with it the unshakeable assurance that these conversations would never go any further. If someone shared secrets about their sins or griefs, their dreams, perhaps even a crime, what could be more ideal than to whisper them in the ear of a vicar?

As for the vicar's blindness, in Ian's mind it only added to the man's reputation as someone who could be trusted.

Which raised the question he least wanted to examine: How much did Polly Rhodes also know? Presumably Mrs. Haviland

would not confide in her, as she might have done with Rhodes himself. She was not a minister of the Church.

So, what did she overhear? Or what had she been able to deduce
from the pieces she could not avoid knowing? Just how clever was
she? She was clearly well read, and with a trained academic mind
and a sharp observation of human nature. Otherwise, she would
never have survived the rigors of Cambridge.

There were also the prejudices and judgments people held that
might tend to exclude her from their calculations. For one thing,
she was past the first flush of youth and led a settled, domesticated
life. She was a loving wife, devoted to her husband's care and well-
being, in addition to the gentleness and concern she showed for
people, whether members of her husband's flock or not.

But he realized he had very little information about her. What
he did know was that she was a handsome woman, clever, and with
a rich sense of humor. He liked her, and he could not imagine her
doing anything as ugly as spying, much less killing anyone. The
idea was ludicrous.

But it was also the perfect mask behind which to conceal murder.

He set out for Adelaide Road again. As much as he wished to
avoid this, he could not put it off any longer. He made a conscious
decision not to take Bremner with him. There was plenty for his
sergeant to do with regard to Haviland. It was Bremner who was
working to match up the victim's trips with other events and, perhaps even more important, to ascertain when and where the travels
of the other victims, as well as their activities at Cambridge, might
have intersected.

It was a mild day for February, and he enjoyed the brisk walk to
the underground station, and then the journey to Chalk Farm.
There was no wind in his face as he walked past the heavy yew trees
in the graveyard, and up the path to the door of the vicarage.

The maid opened the door only moments after Ian knocked.
"Yes, sir?" she said inquiringly.

He wondered how long it had taken her to get used to the different sorts of people who, at all hours, came knocking on the door, some of them no doubt in a state of distress. She must be well trained to turn no one away, no matter how unwarranted their fears or intentions might be, or how distraught their manner.

He smiled at her. "Good morning, my name is Frobisher."

She nodded. "Yes, sir, I remember you." Not surprising, since it had been only the day before yesterday that he had last been here. "Come in, sir. I'll ask if the vicar is able to see you."

"Thank you." He stepped inside. It was warm, even in the hall. He wondered how many people had felt just as he did, with this welcome that induced physical ease, with the comfortable pictures of scenery, flowers, beautiful and harmless things; the carved-wood hall stand with its knobs for coats and hats, and under that the umbrella stand, with four or five black umbrellas in it of various sizes, and two walking sticks.

It raised a memory of the house in which he had grown up. Like his family home, this place had not changed since long before the turn of the century. All the other things were new and different: physical things like automobiles, ideas like the psychoanalytical theories of Sigmund Freud, and the art, which made the canvases of the Pre-Raphaelites look old-fashioned, laden with dreams, unlike modern reality. All of these changes made classic hallways like this one seem like islands in an increasingly rough sea.

He followed the maid to the morning room, where there was a fire already lit and burning well. Perhaps it was in this room where people spoke their fears and their griefs to a gently listening ear? Ian could not afford to be gentle.

It was a full five minutes before Richard Rhodes came into the room. Ian watched how easily he entered and crossed to his chair. It was as if he could see. He was a large man, and he walked slowly, but with grace, and no visible attempt to feel his way.

"Good morning, Inspector," he said easily, holding out his hand.

Ian rose to his feet and clasped Rhodes's hand in a firm shake.

"What can I do for you?" Rhodes gestured toward the chair where Ian had been sitting, and then he, too, sat down.

It struck Ian that Rhodes must do this a dozen or more times a week, meeting with people in need of a caring ear. And yet, Ian sensed that he had the man's full attention. Perhaps the vicar's sense told him that this conversation would be different than most.

"I'm sorry to be back again so soon, Reverend," he began. "But I believe you may be able to help me." He saw a shadow cross Rhodes's face. "I don't mean that you are aware of who is guilty, only that you know things about people that may help me understand who can be ruled out. And, possibly, what connects these victims to each other."

"If I knew that, Inspector, I would already have told you," Rhodes responded, a flicker of concern registering in his face.

Perhaps, unintentionally, Ian had been a trifle condescending. He had not meant to be. "I'm sure you would, if you were aware of it, sir. But I have to ask, because you seem to be the only person who knew two of the victims."

Rhodes looked astonished, and then suddenly his face changed and filled with something Ian thought could have been fear. He drew in a sharp breath, but silently. If it was fear, what was its source? Fear for himself, or for his wife? She could come and go, and he would not know anything but what she told him. Who would find a minister's wife suspicious if she visited parishioners in the early evening, when her husband was unable to? Certainly, there were times when she went out. If she stayed at home because of the weather, particularly when it was wet, then she would be home all of February. Or possibly January before it, and even well into March. Distress didn't wait for fine weather, nor did illness. And because Reverend Rhodes would find it hard to walk in the rain, unable to see puddles and curbs, as well as overflowing gutters, she might perform some of his functions, taking a good deal of the load from him, perhaps without even mentioning it.

Ian wondered if Rhodes knew how much his wife did for him.

Did she come and report to him each time she saw a parishioner? Ian tried to put himself in her place. He had assumed men took on most of the responsibility, as he imagined his father had. But since Mary's death, and his mother's decision to look after his newborn baby, he had begun to realize that many of the decisions he had believed were his father's were actually his mother's. She had done things quietly, and then informed her husband later. And Ian was quite sure that there were many times when she didn't inform him at all. She just did what was necessary. Not telling him was part of the gift.

He recalled one particular instance when there had been some sort of domestic problem. His mother had suggested a solution, but his father had dismissed it as impractical. The following day, when he suggested exactly the same solution to Ian's mother, she had praised his judgment with enthusiasm. Ian had opened his mouth to point out that it had been her idea, but she had shot him a sharp warning look. He was a bit confused, not yet having learned the balance of emotional and practical power beneath the surface of a successful marriage, but he had said nothing.

He pulled his attention back to the present, his body relaxing into the warmth of this quiet, softly furnished room. He wondered again if Polly Rhodes carried far more of the burden than her husband realized. Was his blindness an impairment to his calling? Perhaps his disability meant he had greater empathy for people's fears and shortcomings; greater patience, when they felt they were beyond the reach of decency and forgiveness.

Ian had no idea, but as much as he disliked probing into what might be very tender places, he needed to know more about the comings and goings at the vicarage. So far, the vicar and his wife were the only people who had any connection with at least two of the victims, and Ian might yet find a connection with Sandrine Bernard as well, however indirect.

"It gets dark so early this time of year, and this weather is so difficult," Ian said aloud. "It must restrict the amount of visiting Mrs. Rhodes can do on your behalf."

Rhodes stiffened almost imperceptibly. If Ian had not been looking at the vicar's hand resting on the arm of his chair, he would not have perceived how his fingers gripped it more tightly.

"Yes," Rhodes said very quietly. "But it is not an acceptable answer to someone in distress and fearful of spending the night alone. I can't tell them that I'm unable to help them because it is dark and wet outside. To explain this might be acceptable to them, but not to me. There are times when Polly goes in my place, but not often. And rarely at night. In fact, very few people call later than seven or eight in the evening. I've learned that it's mainly people who can afford to buy coal who will stay up later." He gave a tight little smile and leaned closer to the fireplace, as if aware of his own good fortune.

Ian liked him the better for this. He knew why people came here in times of trouble: the entire house exuded a warmth of spirit, aided by old pictures, comfortable and dated furniture, the faded golds and soft reds all about, and the bright curtains. Everything, put together, would make visitors feel as if they had been here before. Or, at the very least, there was a familiarity about this home that made them feel welcomed, even safe.

Ian realized that he needed to pull himself back fully into the present. He was wasting not only the vicar's time, but his own as well. "As I said, it seems that you know two of the victims . . . or their families. You are the only connection we can find."

"Really?" Rhodes was surprised. "Didn't you say that they all went to Cambridge?"

"Yes, but not at the same time, nor did they study the same subjects. Thousands of people have gone to one or other of the colleges in Cambridge without having any connection at all with each other. I graduated from Cambridge, and I know how difficult it was to develop friendships . . . or to sustain a lifelong connection."

"Polly and I met at Cambridge." Rhodes smiled. "Apollonia. She refused to answer to the name. I could see then, and she was so lovely to behold."

Ian found it impossible to tell how much of the emotion in the vicar's voice was pleasure, and how much was regret. Or was there fear as well? "And what about you? Did you know many people back then?" he asked. "I imagine that your work keeps you far too busy to meet up with classmates from those days. I keep meaning to, and then something comes up and I never get around to it."

Rhodes smiled, with a rueful downward turn of his mouth. "I'm afraid I wouldn't recognize them anyway, unless they spoke to me. And it might be uncomfortable for them."

"Of course," Ian agreed. "I'm just trying to . . ."

"Connect the threads?" Rhodes finished for him. "I have a duty to my parishioners, Inspector, and that includes meeting with any-one who asks. Believe me, if I knew anything of relevance that I could tell you, I would do so. And I give you my word that, at the moment, I know nothing that would help you."

Normally, when Ian was questioning someone, he looked into their eyes, where he believed he could judge the honesty of the answer. But with Rhodes, his blindness completely hid his thoughts. It marked not only his outward vision, but other people's percep-tion of him. "Did you know Sandrine Bernard when you were there?" Ian asked. He hated doing so. He wanted Rhodes to deny it.

"Polly knew her," he answered. "I didn't. Sandrine was very young. It was quite a while ago. She was French, you know, and I believe she went back home to Paris."

The room felt suddenly suffocating. Ian drew a deep breath, and yet he still felt as if his lungs were starved for air. Could that be it? Polly? The slasher was not a man at all, but a strong woman who carried herself with grace? And whose dignity made her look taller than she was? Possibly wearing boots that added another inch or two to her height?

It was not possible. He tried to shake away the thought. Not Polly Rhodes, certainly not. And yet now Ian knew with a flash of understanding that this was what Rhodes feared, this terrible suspicion at the edge of his mind that he was deliberately pushing as far away as possible. He suspected his wife!

Ian knew that one of them must say something. Before he could speak, however, Rhodes broke the deepening silence.

"Polly is out at the moment, seeing a parishioner in trouble. She did not tell me who. Or if she did, I have forgotten." His brow was creased. "So, I cannot tell you where to find her. There are so many people in trouble just now, I'm afraid. It is the time of year for colds, influenza, even pneumonia. Some people find winters very hard, with the long nights of darkness and the short, cold days, too often darker as well."

"I'm sure a visit from the vicar's wife makes a difference to them," Ian answered, but he felt as if he were speaking in a dream. He was sitting here spouting platitudes to the vicar, while trying to believe that they were both referring to visiting the sick, the troubled, or those who were merely lonely and faltering in their faith, rather than contemplating the possibility of crimes his wife might have committed, or wondering if she was out slashing someone to death. Ian hated it. He was sure that Rhodes knew what he was really asking.

"Yes," Rhodes said mechanically. "It is a bleak time, between Christmas and the beginning of spring, when illness strikes most often."

Ian was trying to think of something to say, when he heard the front door close and the sound of footsteps in the hall. He glanced at Rhodes and saw it in his face: the man knew it was Polly. He knew her footsteps, even if there were only three or four. His world was defined by sounds.

There were voices outside in the hall. Polly's and perhaps the maid's. Then the door handle turned and Polly came in. She had taken off her coat and was wearing a skirt and a thick sweater. The colors were dark, like a rich red wine. They suited her particularly well.

"Good afternoon, Inspector Frobisher," she said, almost as if she had expected him. But then the maid would have told her he was here. "Cup of tea? Late for elevenses and early for lunch, but tea and shortbread can be had."

"Thank you." Ian stood up as a matter of courtesy. He was prepared to yield her the chair by the fire.

She shook her head, touched her husband gently on the shoulder, then pulled the armchair closer to the fire and sat down. If she was aware of having interrupted anything, she gave no sign of it.

"Who did you go to see?" Rhodes asked. "Is there any new distress I need to know about?"

"Professor Wolford," she replied. "And no, nothing new. But his trial is about to start, and naturally he is anxious."

"Nicholas Wolford?" Ian asked, although of course he knew the answer.

Polly was looking at him. "Do you know him, Inspector?"

"He was my professor in Cambridge," he replied. "And a good friend of mine, Daniel Pitt, is defending him. But, of course, it's natural to worry. The trial must be quite soon now."

"In two days," she replied. "I just went to give him a show of support. He's a lonely man, in some ways. He makes people nervous because he's so obviously clever. And I regret to say, he can be impatient with people who don't think as quickly as he does. Which, according to his behavior, is most of us."

"Not you, my dear," Rhodes said quickly. "I think that is why he likes you. And you don't suffer fools gladly. Or perhaps I should say that you can endure difficult people better than anyone else I know—but not pretentious ones who think they are clever. Those, you will cut to pieces."

"Oh dear!" she said, with a patient smile. "Have I upset one of our parishioners again?"

"Of course," Richard replied, with an answering smile. "Don't tell me you didn't mean to."

"I did," she confessed. "I suppose that is worse, doing it intentionally. And I could say I was defending his wife, but it would not be true. I was just contradicting him because I thought he was wrong."

Ian looked at them, transferring his gaze from one to the other, confused.

"He was wrong," Richard agreed, then turned to Ian. "A difficult parishioner who communicates rather . . . badly."

Ian watched Rhodes for a moment, and the way he reacted to his wife. The man was turned toward her. Could he still see her amazement in his mind's eye? He was certain that he could hear it in her voice. But the dawning pain that had been there before she entered the room was still visible. Was he really afraid that she was somehow more deeply implicated in this horror than she had admitted? Or than he dared to imagine?

"I didn't know that Professor Wolford lived in this area," he said, filling the lengthening silence.

"Oh, yes, only a few hundred yards along the road," Polly replied. "I don't think he's a believer, by any means, but he likes the architecture and the music. We have a very good organist, and there are one or two people with excellent voices."

The maid came in with the tea and a plate of fresh, homemade shortbread.

"Just place the tray next to me, Elsie." Polly thanked her, began to pour the tea, and then passed it to Ian. She poured a cup for her husband and placed it on the side table near his elbow. After that, she put the shortbread where he could reach it, and close enough to Ian for him to help himself to it.

The conversation turned to Cambridge, and the various reasons why past students would return, renew old friendships, and perhaps listen to lectures on subjects that opened up new worlds to them, things they had not had time to study before.

Ian listened with interest, even enthusiasm. He was aware that he was almost certainly wasting time. Looking at Polly sitting in this warm, comfortable room as she made sure that both Ian and her husband had shortbread, that their tea was topped up, that the fire was freshly stoked; it seemed ridiculous to think that she was someone terrifyingly different underneath that smooth, warm veneer of domesticity.

He thought of the emerging field of psychoanalysis, and how some experts believed that one body could hold two entirely different personalities, so different that perhaps each was unaware of the other. Was that a definition of evil? Or a terrifying reality, because you had to lock up, or even execute, the bad one, while sacrificing the good one, who might not even be aware that the other existed within the same skin, the same mind?

Polly was looking at him now, saying something about an old tragedy, apparently one they all knew of. He had not been listening and forced himself to focus on her. She had said Sandrine's name, but only as a passing reference.

". . . and that was all very ugly indeed," she finished. "We were all distressed."

"Terrible," Richard agreed vehemently. His voice caught in his throat, as if the words were painful in themselves.

"Poor child," Polly said quietly. "Please, let us leave it in the past. She was young and unwise and paid an unspeakable price for it."

"It—" Rhodes began.

"It was a weakness," Polly overrode him, before he could go any further. "And please do not call it a sin. It was generous and misguided, a belief in love, where a wiser and more experienced person would have denied it. It was far too heavy a price to pay. And he, whoever he was, paid nothing. Unless, of course, his conscience wounded him? And I hope it did! But those who pointed the finger at her? That was pure and self-righteous spite."

Now Ian was listening, intrigued. The detective in him needed to know more. "What happened?" he asked, and then quickly realized that his words were far too blunt. He tried to moderate them. "I'm sorry, but what are you referring to? When was this? A long time ago? Perhaps the hurt has been healed by now."

Polly's expression was tense, even passionate, but Ian found her emotions difficult to read.

"Hardly," she responded, bitterness in her voice. "April died, poor creature. We tend to judge self-righteously, and with little or no understanding. I prefer to believe that God forgives when sin, great or small, is understood." She looked directly into Ian's eyes. "To understand is to repent, because you are able to see the ugliness of what you have done, and wish with all the strength of your soul that you will never do it again. That is the beginning of change. God wants change, understanding, not destruction! I could not worship a God who wants vengeance. Love has no part in that. We are all too frail to live with it."

"Polly . . ." Richard started again. "It is over with. Lena mentioned April when we spoke, and I assured her that she had done all she could, and there was nothing more to be achieved, but to move on. I think she accepted that."

"I am not one of your parishioners, Richard." Polly cut across him firmly. "And I do not have to believe as I am told to. There is no one else here but Mr. Frobisher, and he is free to believe or disbelieve me. I have no authority, and he knows it. But I believe that April will survive the judgment of God, as we all will. And the merciless and ignorant judgment of her fellow sinners will rest on their souls . . . not on hers."

Ian said nothing for a moment, but an idea was germinating in his mind. "Mrs. Rhodes," he asked. "Who else knew her? I mean, who else was involved?"

Rhodes drew in his breath, and then stopped. Instead of responding to Ian's question, he smiled gently and remained silent.

Ian saw the vicar's expression as half apologetic, but the set of his jaw was determined.

"Richard," Polly began, but stopped when she saw her husband's face.

"Please, my dear, let us not raise that tragedy again. It was over long ago, and there is nothing we can do to change any of it. Let's return to a lighter subject. Inspector, would you like another piece of shortbread? It's the best I have ever tasted. Our cook has few dishes at which she excels. She overcooks the cabbage, and rarely gets all the lumps out of the porridge." He smiled and shrugged apologetically. "We keep her entirely on the strength of her short-bread. That and her pie crusts. Her apple pie melts in the mouth."

"Yes please," Ian replied. "Another piece . . . but it's the last one!"

"You are young," Rhodes replied. "You'll exercise it off. And you are going back out into the cold and, no doubt before long, the rain as well. I most definitely am not."

"Thank you," Ian accepted. He could think of nothing more to pursue with the vicar and his wife. He did not want to push them for more details of the tragedy they had referred to. He needed to think about what he knew before he took it any further with them. When he could find the right words, he would ask Bremner what he thought.

He leaned forward and slipped another slice of shortbread onto his plate.

Twenty-One

DANIEL WOKE EARLY, his body already tense. This was the day before the trial of Nicholas Wolford would begin. Daniel told himself that he should not be nervous about it: he was fully prepared.

His first task was to go and see Wolford. He must make sure the man was still level-headed and reasonably calm. At least, as calm as possible. How could he fail to be aware of the possibility of losing? Juries were composed of twelve individuals, all with their own beliefs, perceptions, and understandings. They were not always predictable. Daniel had learned, often painfully, that individual jurors' beliefs and emotions could override reason. It was imperative that Wolford keep his emotions under control. Even if he did not give any evidence of his volatile temper, the jury was going to be watching him. They would see anger, fear, violent emotion in his face. And whether they intended to or not, they would make judgments not easily overridden by anything Daniel could say to them.

There was no time to waste with public transport, or walking through the rain. He took a taxi. Sitting back, he prepared for what he would say to Wolford, hardly noticing how the taxi driver negotiated the traffic.

Wolford opened the door seconds after Daniel knocked. He looked tousled and had missed a patch on his right jaw while shaving. There was no need to ask him if he was worried; it was only too obvious.

"Why have you come?" he demanded, without any greeting or preamble. "What's happened?"

Daniel forbore from criticism. He could see that Wolford was not overdramatizing, or indeed being rude. The man was frantic with worry.

"Nothing," Daniel replied, stepping inside and forcing Wolford to back into the hallway. "I came to reassure you, and to go over one or two details, just to be certain."

"What details?" Wolford demanded.

Daniel moved past him and into the warm sitting room. Whatever maid service Wolford employed must have been there recently: the sitting room was immaculate. Only two books were off the shelf and resting on a side table.

Daniel sat down and waited for Wolford to do the same, which he seemed to do reluctantly.

"What?" he demanded again. "What details? You've got them all!"

"Not about the writing," said Daniel. "That's clear enough. Any allegation of plagiarism is quite obviously a case of misunderstanding—at least, that's the kindest interpretation."

"Kindest!" Wolford's voice shook. "Have you no idea that—?"

Daniel interrupted. "Not the charge," he corrected. "The fact that Tolliver thought it at all. You are clearly not guilty. You both drew your facts from the same sources. Obviously, that resulted in your saying the same things. I'm talking about bringing the accusation at all. Why do you think he did that?"

"God knows! He's . . ." Wolford stopped. "Are you saying he did it to provoke me?"

"Why else?" Daniel asked.

"I thought . . ." Wolford did not complete the sentence.

"You thought he did it for the publicity," Daniel said for him. "And I believe you're right. Then it got out of hand. He lost his temper and took a swing at you. Don't forget, this is what you're charged with. Assault. Not plagiarism. You did not plagiarize anything—and that is obvious enough not to need proof—but you did injure him quite badly."

"He swung at me first! And he accused me, publicly, of plagiarism. A charge like that would ruin my career, my life's work—"

"If anyone believed it," Daniel cut across him. "No one with half a brain would." He leaned forward a little. "Has it occurred to you that this is exactly what Tolliver wanted? Not to get his jaw and nose broken, but to provoke a fight and end up in court. And look at all the notice it will bring. You are twenty years older than he is. When he swung at you, he expected to win. I'm quite sure it never occurred to him that you would be faster, and heavier, not to mention more accurate."

"Oh . . ."

Wolford's response suggested to Daniel that either he had not considered that at all, or the implications were coming to light only because Daniel was pointing them out to him. In either case, Daniel thought his response odd.

"I've tried to make his lawyer see that, and accept an apology," Daniel explained. "And I thought I'd succeeded, but apparently Tolliver is determined to make a case of it. I suppose if there's no case in court, there's no publicity. And publicity is what he's after."

Wolford swore.

Daniel nodded, agreeing with Wolford's words. "But that doesn't get us anywhere, and it doesn't win over juries." He leaned a little further forward. "You are in the right, Professor, and don't forget that. If you lose your temper in front of the jury, you lose the case. Remember that! He is the young hothead out for publicity, at any price, while you are the older, wiser man who did nothing more than defend yourself. And, unfortunately for Tolliver, you're a lot better at it than he is. Remember that he swung and missed. If he were better at this, you could be the one with the injuries!" He stared at Wolford. "The jury needs to understand that you are sorry he was so badly injured, but it was his own fault for making false allegations and then losing his temper. All out of a desire for publicity. Such a violent and essentially stupid way to get it. So, you will sit there looking innocent and sorry, and leave me to do the talking. Right?"

"Yes," Wolford said slowly. "Yes, I understand."

"I'm going to see Cobden."

"Who is Cobden?" Wolford demanded.

"Tolliver's lawyer."

"Why don't you—?" Wolford registered the weary patience in Daniel's expression. "Oh. You have to do it this way. I see. Good. Perhaps it will all go away?"

"With luck, yes. If you consent to pay a good deal of his dental and medical bills. The dental ones would be the worst."

"But . . ."

"Do you want it to go away, or would you prefer arguing it in open court? Possibly ruining his reputation, and your own?"

"But . . ." Wolford stared at Daniel. "I see, yes. Make it go away. I can afford it."

"Thank you." Daniel stood up. "I'll keep the cost as low as I can."

"Good. I mean, thank you."

COBDEN WAS IN, but although he pretended pleasure at seeing Daniel, it was clearly far from what he felt. Daniel did not take it personally: after all, Cobden had an awkward client.

"Come in, come in," Cobden said, with a brief smile. "We have not long to wait now."

Daniel understood that he was referring to the upcoming trial. He went into the office, as invited, and sat down in the newly upholstered armchair, as Cobden indicated.

Cobden closed the door and took his own seat behind the desk. "Beastly weather," he commented. "Sorry you had to come out in it, but glad to see you."

To Daniel, he looked anything but pleased.

"I think we can settle this without the expense and unpleasantness of going to trial," Daniel began. "My client is willing to admit his fault in injuring Mr. Tolliver, and he will make a substantial contribution toward his medical and dental expenses." He stopped. There really was nothing more to add, except the acknowledgment by Tolliver that Wolford had not copied any of his material, that they had simply drawn the same conclusions from the same sources. That was openly acknowledged. If Tolliver pursued the plagiarism accusation, he would look foolish and unusually spiteful. Before he could go on, there was a look on Cobden's face that stopped him.

"That would have been a very satisfactory conclusion," Cobden said unhappily.

Daniel felt a sudden chill.

"But I am afraid my client has made up his mind," Cobden went on. "He might have to settle for that in the end, as long as Professor Wolford is still of the same mind. But unfortunately, Mr. Tolliver wishes for his day in court, regarding the assault."

"You can't press the charge for assault without mentioning the reason why they quarreled in the first place," Daniel pointed out. "They had no other issue between them. In fact, they have never met, other than over this. And if you remember, Mr. Tolliver was the first to lash out. He didn't hit Professor Wolford, but only because his punch went wild."

"I know that, sir." Cobden shook his head. "But the fact remains, Professor Wolford landed a blow, and it was very considerable. He broke Tolliver's nose and jaw, while remaining untouched himself. That is what the jury will see."

"That is what you will instruct them to see," Daniel corrected. "I shall endeavor to make them see an irresponsible young man, losing his temper and lashing out at an older man, who turned out to be far more controlled, and far better at self-defense. The attacker lost his balance, and with the force of his own blow, he overbalanced and was an easy match for an older and, as it happens, stronger man, who struck him with the combined weight of both his own strength and Tolliver's impetus. The result was more devastating than either of them expected."

Cobden looked unhappy.

"And the cause of the quarrel," Daniel went on, "was Tolliver's quite unfounded accusation that Wolford had plagiarized his work. That is very easily dismissed. They use the same sources, so naturally they've found the same answers. Doubtless, what they wrote was word for word. And taking it to the court is not going to benefit anyone. Professor Wolford has agreed to contribute generously to your client's medical expenses, but he will not sit by and allow this accusation of plagiarism to stand."

"I know it isn't reasonable," Cobden replied. "But I must do as my client instructs. He has two reliable witnesses. And I have spoken to them myself, of course, to verify their accounts."

THE DAY OF the trial arrived.

Daniel did not want to leave anything more to chance than was absolutely necessary. He collected Wolford in plenty of time, and was relieved to see him ready, dressed in a dark, well-tailored wool suit, a crisp white shirt, and a conservative tie. He looked sober and miserable, nervously clenching and unclenching his hands.

"Don't worry," Daniel said, as the taxi drove away from the curb and into the traffic. Between Wolford's home and the courthouse, Daniel talked over various possibilities, and how to react to them.

Wolford repeated his innocence: the man was finally understanding that trials should never be taken for granted. There was always a possibility of something unforeseen arising.

Despite the conversation, it seemed to Daniel that the journey was interminable. The rain varied between a drizzle and a lashing storm. When they finally pulled up outside the courthouse, Daniel paid the driver, got out, and the men raced up the steps before they were soaked by the rain.

From then on, it was all formal.

Before Daniel and Wolford could take their seats, Tolliver's attorney, Cobden, gestured to Daniel.

"Wait here," Daniel told his client, and then joined Cobden in a corner, where they could not be overheard.

"I told you yesterday I was going to call two witnesses," he reminded Daniel. "Last night, my client agreed to settle without questioning them."

"Excellent!" declared Daniel, relief washing over him.

"Not so fast," Cobden said. "This morning, he changed his mind."

Daniel looked at the man. "And . . . ?"

"And I'll be questioning the doctor, the dentist, and the two witnesses to the incident."

Whether Tolliver, and his attorney as well, had always intended to do this or not was something Daniel did not know. He preferred to think that Cobden had been caught off guard by his client, rather than intentionally misleading Daniel. Unpleasant as it was, he had no argument that would change Tolliver's mind.

Daniel returned to his seat.

"Well?" Wolford asked, fear in his voice.

"Just a few loose ends," Daniel said, offering what he hoped was a reassuring smile. When Wolford didn't press him for more, he was relieved.

The jury was seated and the trial began. The judge presided over the opening formalities with no apparent emotion.

Wolford was fidgeting, and Daniel was grateful that he remained almost calm. He gave wordless thanks that Wolford was, so far, silent.

On the other side of the courtroom, Cobden sat motionless. Beside him sat Tolliver. It was the first time Daniel had seen him. He was taller than he had imagined, but wiry rather than athletic. His hair was fair and a little too long; his features might have been good, but they were marred at present by plaster on his nose, over a wound possibly not entirely healed. But since this hearing was about his injuries, he would have made sure they were prominent, anyway. At the moment, he was sitting silently, but if he spoke, which he surely would do, the dental damage might be both visible and audible.

Daniel knew that Tolliver would be a sympathetic figure. He was so much younger than Wolford. Would Cobden play on this? Daniel would have, in his place.

He glanced at Wolford, and saw that he understood the seriousness of his situation; he appeared more nervous than before. Daniel debated whether to comfort him, and decided he would play it as if he were not surprised by what was coming next, and certainly not worried.

He sat silently through the reading of the charge, but was aware of Wolford's discomfort and how, now and then, he stared at Daniel. He refused to meet his gaze. There was nothing to say, and he didn't want to encourage his client's visible anxiety.

They sat quietly as Cobden began to question his first witness. It was not one of the men Cobden had mentioned earlier, but the editor who had worked on Tolliver's book, a Mr. Edison James.

He was a young man for such a position, barely forty, judging from his appearance. He was thin, and of average height. He had an unremarkable face, with large horn-rimmed glasses giving him the appearance of a studious man.

Cobden walked him through the process of establishing his position and responsibilities, revealing a string of academic qualifications and books he had previously edited. Daniel had heard of none of them.

Cobden asked him about Tolliver's book. James waxed enthusiastic about it, promising it would not only enlighten many people about the importance of the French Revolution, which had foreshadowed the revolutions throughout Europe just over half a century later, but it would do this with an exactness that had not been seen before, and in a most vivid and exciting way. He believed it would replace all other such works so that, in the future, students would be able to grasp the essence of the period. This book was, in his words, "a great step forward."

Cobden thanked him and sat down, leaving Daniel to cross-question James, if he chose to.

Daniel rose to his feet. He had little choice because Wolford, beside him, was seething with anger. To remain seated would lead Wolford to believe he did not have the courage or ability to fight, and Daniel knew this would only encourage him, and he would not be able to refrain from interrupting. Added to which, he really did want to take issue with the arrogant young Edison James.

"How do you do, Mr. James?" he began politely.

James stared at him.

"I have read the book in question with considerable interest."

James smiled with obvious satisfaction.

"Part of my job," Daniel said coolly. "And, indeed, you and my client have frequently used the same references. But the events were over a hundred years ago, and there is a limited number of contemporary sources. I was fortunate enough to attend Cambridge myself, and as an additional subject, heard quite a few of Professor Wolford's lectures. I began with one, but was so fascinated that I took the opportunity to attend several more, though they had nothing to do with my subject. Which, of course, was law."

There was a slight murmur, the movement of jurors fidgeting and shifting their bodies in the courtroom. Daniel warned himself; he could not lose their interest.

He smiled. "Therefore, although you put your information in a slightly unusual format, nothing in it was new to me."

Now he had their attention. Even the judge leaned forward, fixing him with a steady stare. However, to Daniel's relief, he did not interrupt.

James opened his mouth, then closed it without speaking.

"Tell me," Daniel continued. "Why did you accuse Professor Wolford of plagiarism? You did, did you not? Indirectly, of course, but you backed Mr. Tolliver in his charge, and you are here now to testify on his behalf." That was a statement. To this, he added a few well-formed questions. "You encouraged him to believe he was justified in that claim, yes? And you were also present at the altercation where he attacked the professor?"

James looked startled. Quite clearly, this was not what he had expected. "I was . . . no . . ."

"Surely you would not encourage him in his charge of plagiarism against Professor Wolford if you did not believe it to be true. Am I correct? And you certainly would not encourage this, just for the sake of gaining considerable publicity for the book? And I grant that there certainly will be a lot of it—publicity, that is—with this charge of physical violence brought against a man of such wide repute. Which is far more than your client has. As yet."

"That's a monstrous accusation!" James protested, his face flushed red with outrage. "How dare you suggest such a thing?"

"I did not suggest it, Mr. James," Daniel corrected him. "I said surely that would not be the reason. Unless persuaded otherwise, I shall suggest that you encouraged him in the charge because you believe the plagiarism to be true."

James relaxed visibly. He had made a fool of himself and he was aware of it. He let out his breath slowly.

"Let us address it," Daniel went on. "Give us four or five instances where you believe it was plagiarism on Professor Wolford's part, rather than merely a reference to the same source."

James was stuck. It was obvious to Daniel, and probably to most of the court, that he had not such a thing in his mind.

"I . . ." he began.

Daniel stood wide-eyed, and appeared to be waiting patiently.

The silence stretched out, and became painful.

Daniel rescued him. "You cannot bring to mind any quote you believe was taken by my client from your author's book? Or possibly someone told you so, but you have no word of it to offer us."

James looked wretched. He started to speak once or twice, but ended in saying nothing. Daniel was sorry for him. Apart from the humiliation, it was possible that the man's job was now in jeopardy. But he had undertaken to smear a man's reputation, possibly at someone else's behest, and was now unable to back it up.

"Thank you." Daniel smiled and returned to his seat.

Wolford was smiling. It was the first time Daniel could recall such a thing.

"It's only a beginning," he warned. "The prosecutor failed to see that James is out of his depth. I don't say he was put up to it by someone else . . . yet."

"That's the plagiarism charge dealt with," Wolford whispered. "You are brilliant. Frobisher said you were."

"It's only the beginning!" Daniel warned again. "Don't jump the gun." He glanced sideways and saw Cobden earnestly talking to his assistant. He needed to repair the damage Daniel had done, or at least mitigate it as soon as possible.

The next witness Cobden called was one of the two young men who had been present at the event where the fight took place. He was a plump, agreeable-looking young man, and clearly uncomfortable being asked to give evidence.

He swore to his name, Roland Dixon, and to his presence at the time and place of the event.

"It was totally absurd," he said unhappily, in answer to Cobden's question. "But yes, the professor gave poor Tolliver a helluva whack. Sent him sprawling, and when he got up—or to be more exact, when we helped him up—he was covered in blood."

"And was Professor Wolford injured?" Cobden inquired innocently.

"No, not at all," Dixon replied. "Except perhaps his knuckles were bruised. Teeth are hard."

"So, he struck Linus Tolliver in the face?" Cobden asked, again innocently.

"Something like that," Dixon agreed.

"Like that? You said teeth," Cobden reminded him. "Surely the blow had to be to his face, then?"

"Yes."

"Thank you. And you testify that Professor Wolford was unhurt? Mr. Tolliver did not strike him at all?"

Dixon said nothing.

"Mr. Dixon! Did Mr. Tolliver strike professor Wolford at all?" Cobden repeated.

"No," Dixon replied uneasily.

"Thank you, that will be all." Cobden turned to Daniel, indicating that it was his turn to question the witness.

Daniel thanked him and rose to his feet. "I'm sorry to press you any further in this unfortunate matter. But just to be clear: Professor Wolford walked up and punched Mr. Tolliver, already in a rage, striking him in the face, injuring him badly, and knocking him to the floor. And Mr. Tolliver was too hurt, dazed, or distressed to strike him back. So, apparently, this was seen by you and your friend? That is, you were not alone, were you?"

"No, that's . . . not exactly right," Dixon replied.

"Then perhaps you would tell us exactly what did happen, and the order in which it happened. Because, so far, it does not seem to make any sense."

"We were talking," Dixon began.

"Who is *we*?" Daniel asked. "You and Tolliver?"

"And Michael Jackman," Dixon replied. "The three of us were talking."

"And without any warning, Professor Wolford walked up to Mr. Tolliver and hit him hard. In fact, punched him in the face?" Daniel asked incredulously. "No wonder you were shocked."

Daniel caught a cautionary glance from the judge.

Cobden began to rise from his seat, but then sat down again.

"Then please tell us exactly what happened, Mr. Dixon, so we do not jump to any mistaken conclusions. It really is very important," Daniel said.

Dixon swallowed. "Yes, sir. Jackman, Tolliver, and I were talking when Professor Wolford came out of the door a few yards away from us. We all stopped talking and looked at him. Tolliver said something about plagiarism, I don't recall exactly what. But it was offensive. It was meant to be." He took a deep breath. "Wolford came over to us and a few sharp words were exchanged. I don't remember exactly who said what, but it was very unpleasant. Professor Wolford seemed to get the better of the exchange. He more or less proved that it had not been plagiarism, but he was very angry."

"Go on," Daniel urged.

"He said something very offensive about Tolliver's scholarship. Tolliver was furious. He lost his temper and took a wild swing at the professor. He missed completely. I . . . I think it was perhaps one too many glasses of sherry, if you know what I mean?"

"We do," Daniel assured him. "Perhaps he lost his balance?"

Cobden rose to his feet.

Before he could speak, Daniel turned to the judge. "I'm sorry, My Lord. I did not mean to put words in the witness's mouth."

"You know better than that, Mr. Pitt," the judge admonished. "Please proceed."

"Mr. Dixon?" Daniel invited the witness.

"Tolliver swung at Wolford, but completely missed, and Wolford hit back at him, and did not miss it all. He connected. Pretty hard. And Tolliver went down. Jackman and I went to him. He was in a mess. The professor's fist must have struck him on the nose and mouth. He—"

Daniel held up his hand. "Thank you, sir. I believe Mr. Cobden has a doctor and a dentist who will tell us what damage was done. Were there other blows, or only that one?"

"That's all there was, sir. Just that one."

"But that first blow would have been from Mr. Tolliver, if he had not overbalanced and, for whatever reason, missed. Is that correct?"

Dixon looked relieved. "Yes, sir, that's right."

Daniel thanked him and sat down.

Cobden hesitated, then seemed to decide it would serve no purpose to take this witness any further. He called the doctor who had first attended Tolliver after the assault.

The man swore to his name, Dr. Albert Rand, and his medical qualifications.

"And you have attended many emergencies in your professional capacity?" Cobden asked.

Rand agreed that he had.

Cobden drew from him not only his professional actions, but his emotions regarding the incident, and the damage to Tolliver's face. It was dramatic, and damaging.

Daniel had only to look at the faces of the jurors, whose imaginations were filling in what the doctor did not describe. Cobden gave plenty of opportunities for emotion. It was all proving very effective.

He glanced at Wolford beside him, and saw that the color had drained from his face. In the course of the doctor's testimony, the sympathy of the court had disappeared. Daniel put his hand on Wolford's arm. It was rock hard, and he was shaking. Daniel gripped him harder. He tried to think of something to say, but he knew Wolford was not listening. His mind was totally absorbed in what he believed the jury was thinking.

"See!" Wolford hissed. "They all hate me. You can see it in their faces!"

"They don't like you," Daniel contradicted. "They're imagining what it would be like if it was them. We must expect this."

Wolford raised his arm, only an inch or two, and banged it on the chair seat in a gesture that was so violent it made the seat rock.

Daniel tightened his grip on Wolford's arm. "Wait for our turn!" Daniel said sharply.

"Can you undo the doctor's testimony? Don't lie to me. You said you could defend me, and you lied! You can't undo this. Look at their faces. They are all against me."

"Be quiet. Get control of yourself. Do you want Tolliver's team to win?"

"They are winning, can't you see that?"

"Be quiet!" Daniel said, fighting to keep his voice low. "And try to look innocent, for heaven's sake."

Now it was Daniel's turn. He stood up and walked forward, hoping to take the jury's eyes as far away from Wolford as possible.

"Dr. Rand," he began courteously, "I gather, from Mr. Cobden's introduction, that you have attended a good many scenes of violence, both intentional and accidental?"

"Yes, sir, I have," Rand agreed.

"Is it usually possible to tell the difference, medically speaking?"

"Not from the injuries themselves, no. But you can tell in most instances by the circumstances. For example, if someone is found in the wreckage of a motorcar, or a carriage, or near a damaged bicycle, then one assumes that this was the cause."

"Or if the victim can tell you?"

"Exactly. But there are usually corroborating witnesses, and they are not always reliable. They are horrified, grieved, frightened. On occasion, they have a personal interest in one conclusion or another."

"I understand. But in this instance, you had both? That is, witnesses on both sides."

"Yes."

"And Mr. Tolliver was conscious?"

"Oh, yes. But because of the injury to his jaw and teeth, he was not able to tell me a great deal. It is a shock to the mind and to the body to break a bone, and to see so much blood."

"And the injuries you described were to the nose and three teeth, and the jawbone?"

"Yes. The nose was broken."

"Does that happen often to people involved in a fight?"

"Yes, I'm afraid so."

"And the break in the jawbone?"

"It could be more accurately described as a crack, but painful. And three teeth were badly enough broken that they had to be extracted."

"A lot of blood? Difficult to stop the bleeding? Frightening?"

"Bleeding is often frightening, but it usually looks worse than it is. It is internal bleeding that is dangerous."

"Was it internal bleeding in this instance?"

"Good heavens, no! As I understand it from witnesses, there was only one blow struck, but it was hard."

"So it has been testified," Daniel agreed. "And no one has suggested otherwise. Apparently, Mr. Tolliver struck first, and missed. Had he not missed, would he have inflicted the damage you described to Professor Wolford instead? In other words, whoever had received the blow, accurately aimed, would have suffered the same result? Possibly Tolliver was overtired, stressed, a little the worse for indulgence, so he struck first, and missed. And Professor Wolford, possibly acting in self-defense, and facing a much younger man, landed his blow accurately? Is that a fair judgment?"

"Yes, I would say so," Rand agreed. "He was also sober," the doctor pointed out. "Totally sober. Even being a little worse for wear makes a difference to a man's balance."

"Thank you, Dr. Rand. So, it is fair to say that had the younger man been sober, it would have been Professor Wolford's nose that was broken, and his mouth full of blood—if he had not succeeded in disabling Mr. Tolliver." Daniel drove the point home.

"Possibly."

"Would you take that chance, if faced by an enraged man twenty years younger than you are? I do not mean to disparage your abilities, Doctor," Daniel said apologetically.

Rand gave a half smile. "I am glad I have not been put to the test, sir."

"So am I, Doctor," Daniel answered. He glanced at Cobden, who seemed in no rush to cross-examine his own witness, as if he knew to leave it well alone.

Daniel made an instant decision. He turned to Wolford. "This will be a good time to offer to settle," he said quietly. "Stop this while we are ahead."

"We are ahead? Then push forward!" Wolford said, with growing eagerness. "We could win? Why would you pull back?" He looked hopeful for the first time.

"Because we won't win eventually," Daniel explained. "Cobden will put Tolliver on the stand, mumbling through his wired jaw and broken nose. He would have to be a complete fool not to win back the sympathy of the jury."

"But you said we were winning!" Wolford argued. "I can see it."

"We are now," Daniel agreed. "But this is a trial, Professor. It can go one way or the other. Now we are winning. It's time to get the best bargain we can."

"But we're winning, you said so!" His face darkened.

"Now, yes, but will you win in the end?" Daniel pointed out. "As I've explained, it could very easily slip the other way. Let me speak to Cobden, offer a reasonable amount of money and an apology. We'll not have a better chance. Leave it and the legal judgment could very well be theirs. Settle now and you could come out of it with your reputation intact. Is that not what really matters?"

Wolford's eyes narrowed. "Why give up when you're ahead? Whose side are you on?" His voice was harsh and his face growing redder.

"This is not a race, Professor. Being ahead won't last, once Cobden gets Tolliver to testify. He has a broken nose and broken teeth, and you are untouched. Whose side do you think the jury will be on?"

Wolford remained silent.

"Do you want to get this over with? Paying a small, fair amount in costs, and preserving your good reputation? Because that's what I'm aiming for. If you can't accept that, then find yourself another lawyer."

"Then I suppose I must settle for that, or you'll just leave me," Wolford said grudgingly.

"That's right," Daniel agreed. It was a gamble: he would not have left Wolford. The man was potentially a walking disaster. "I'll go and talk to Cobden."

Cobden seemed to have expected him. "I would in your place," he said. "What are you offering? Money? An apology?"

"A reasonable contribution toward medical and dental expenses," Daniel replied. "And reciprocal apologies."

"Reciprocal?" Cobden said incredulously.

"That's right. Wolford apologizes for injuring him, and Tolliver apologizes for accusing Wolford, falsely, of plagiarism. Fair?"

Cobden smiled. He held out his hand. Daniel took it.

Daniel told his client about the agreement.

"I suppose that's fair," Wolford said, rather bitterly. "Or it's the best we can get."

Daniel swallowed his irritation. He could see that Wolford was exhausted by emotion. He had been badly frightened and such deep terror did not evaporate instantly. He had feared he was going to lose his reputation, the most precious possession he had.

"All right," Daniel said gently. "Did you have breakfast?"

"What?" Wolford stared at him.

"Come and have a late lunch," Daniel offered. "Bacon and eggs, toast, tea, we've earned it. I know an excellent place."

"Yes," Wolford agreed. And then, as the good news that the trial was over began to sink in, "Yes, thank you."

Twenty-Two

WHEN DANIEL LEFT the restaurant, where he had had a late breakfast with Wolford, he was immensely relieved. There was always the possibility that Wolford might lose his temper at some slight made by the other side, a word, a gesture or an inflection that could cause him to lose control, interrupt the proceedings, and show the jurors that he was, indeed, capable of violent assault. Now that it was over, and considering that they had agreed on terms quite amicably—with a very reasonable financial settlement, but more importantly, Wolford's reputation not only intact, but possibly improved—Daniel could stop holding his breath.

He said goodbye to Wolford and took a taxi back to his chambers. His first duty was reporting to Marcus on the successful conclusion of the Wolford case. Then he sorted through the incoming mail, where he was pleased to discover nothing that needed his immediate attention. He said goodbye to Impney and declined afternoon tea. He wanted to escape, have time away from cases of any sort, to sit beside a roaring fire and not care if it rained or not.

"Go home and relax, sir," Impney said, with a smile. "Shall I call a taxi for you, and tell you when it is here, sir?"

"No thanks," said Daniel. "I'll walk down to the main road. It's not raining yet."

"The wind is pretty sharp, sir," Impney warned.

"I know, but I can daydream in the fresh air. I can let my mind wander."

"Indeed, sir. I understand," Impney agreed. He held Daniel's coat for him and then opened the outer door. "Goodnight, sir."

Daniel thanked him and went out into the slicing wind, sharp as a knife. All warmth had faded out of the afternoon and the air was bitter with cold. He walked quickly to the end of the street and turned the corner into the main road. He nearly bumped into Miriam, which made him feel immediately warmer, as if the wind were not edged with ice and they were not standing in the middle of a wintry London street.

"How was your case?" she asked.

"It went better than I thought," he admitted. "I won. Or more accurately, they agreed to settle for an apology for the injuries, and a substantial contribution to the medical and dental costs. And in return, we got an apology from Tolliver for falsely accusing Wolford of plagiarism."

What he really wanted to tell her was how pleased he was to see her. "Is Dr. Eve better? Are you going to chambers? It's too early for supper." He glanced at his wristwatch, which was so much more elegant than a pocket watch. A pocket watch made him feel like an old man. "Oh, it's early, only just after four," he finished. And then he chastised himself for babbling on. Why did he do this, and only in the presence of Miriam?

"No, before you ask, you cannot take me somewhere elegant for afternoon tea. I was coming to see if there was any news yet, and clearly there is. So I will take you! You won! You should be treated to something special. How about chocolate cake? We could take a taxi and go to the Ritz. Would you like tea at the Ritz?"

"I would like to eat anywhere, if I'm with you," he replied honestly, while at the same time wondering if he could afford such a luxurious place. She had offered to pay, but would that be correct? Proper?

The heck with it! He would worry about stretching out his finances later.

THE RITZ WAS lavish. No expense had been spared to make the enormous lounge seem like a glimpse into another world. The carpeting was thick, so all footsteps were muted. The chandeliers reminded Daniel of crystal mountains of light hanging in the air.

Waiters moved about soundlessly, carrying trays at shoulder height, and as easily as if they weighed nothing. They had the grace of dancers, even though they carried heavy silver teapots and hot-water jugs, silver dishes with different kinds of sugar, and plates piled with sandwiches, none of which was more than two mouthfuls. And there were individual cakes of many flavors, all of them promising a sweet and delicious delight.

There were many tables around them, and each one was festooned with huge cascades of flowers. At this time of the year, nothing was blooming except in hothouses. It was too late for even the last of the asters and chrysanthemums, and too early for the bravest daffodil. Daniel nearly quipped to Miriam that it cost shillings just to stand in this room and wait to be seated, but he realized that would be clumsy. And it did not matter, as long as he was in her company.

The wait turned out to be less than two minutes. They were shown to a small table, where it would have been impossible to seat a third person. Wondering if he was going to be in debt for the rest of his life, he ordered tea for two, with sandwiches and cakes. He was actually very hungry, when he thought of it. But it hardly mattered.

They talked about the case until the tea came. Miriam told the waiter that she would pour. She did so, passed Daniel his cup, and then poured one for herself. "Do you mind being toasted with tea, rather than champagne?" she asked, with a smile.

"Champagne in the middle of the afternoon would be a little excessive, don't you think?" he asked in good humor. "It was not a major trial."

"No one would hang," she agreed. "But Professor Wolford's career would have been ruined, if it were not for you. And he would probably have lost his job. I know he won. Or . . . you did, on his behalf. But I was in the public gallery for the start of the trial, and he looked dreadful. It must have been a fearful ordeal for him."

"Yes," Daniel agreed. "He took it very hard, both the trial and his victory. He's very fragile, and belligerent in trying to hide his emotions. As for the plagiarism that provoked the assault, he was innocent, and he knew it, so I'm surprised how hard it was for him. He thought it was deliberate malice, and it must be awful to believe that anyone hates you so deeply that they would set out to destroy your career, your reputation."

"But he does, doesn't he? Believe that it was intentional, I mean," she said.

He looked at her and then concentrated a little more seriously. For a moment, he forgot the elegant luxury around him, the strange whispering silence that washed around them. He thought about what Miriam had said. She was right: Wolford was deeply frightened, almost to the point of losing control.

"Yes," he admitted. "He cares intensely. That's probably natural enough, and he is so good at his job. He can think like all those ordinary people he writes about: hunted, poor, frightened, and angry. It's all real to him, the French Revolution, and the High Terror and all that's tied up with it. And he cares desperately, as if it were his own life, his own people going through the horrors of it all. But I know he can become impassioned by other periods as well. You should hear him on our civil war, and the trial of the king." He smiled at the memory of Wolford's lectures, seeing the professor in his mind's eye and wanting to share his impassioned oratory with her. "Wolford was marvelous, mesmerizing. Listening to him was as good as going to the theater. In some ways, better."

"As if he lived all the parts?" she asked.

Daniel saw that she was very serious, more than the situation seemed to demand. "Why do you ask?"

"He worries me," she replied. "From what you say, he's in trouble."

"True, but he's been through a hell of a time, and he's free of it now," he tried to explain. What did she not understand? "He's a very intense man. He loves his work and he's exceptionally good at it. But it would all have been lost if he had been found guilty, and plagiarism was at the center of it. Who would listen to him any longer, if he were convicted of a crime committed because he had copied someone else's work?"

What was that look on Miriam's face? He wasn't sure. Certainly, she could understand how disastrous a loss would have been. Were she not so intelligent, her confusion would not surprise him, but she was a professional woman, prepared to make extraordinary sacrifices to build her career. Like Wolford. She had given her whole youth to the pursuit of professional qualifications, and much of the time her abilities were not recognized, much less rewarded. How could she not understand Wolford? Surely, she could not be so blinkered that only her own discipline mattered? He tried to deny the rush of disappointment he felt, but it remained, leaving with it a strange and painful loneliness that swept over him. It hurt. "It matters to him. It's his entire world!" His voice was louder than he had intended. "Miriam, he's put his whole life into it, everything."

She put her hand on his, gently. "Daniel, I know that. It has nothing to do with his being concerned for his academic reputation; he's brilliant. All the people who have listened to him agree, and they say so. And I would have taken your word for it, anyway. But I'm not talking about what he feared he would lose."

Daniel listened carefully, relieved that he had misinterpreted her words.

"I was there in court, for a little while. And I was worried for him." She seemed to be struggling to find the right words. "He looked in pain. But more than that," she rushed ahead, before Daniel could respond. "Not physical pain. He was . . . it's hard to describe. What I'm saying is that I believe he's ill. Not just tense or nervous about the trial, but . . . ill. Mentally ill. Of course he was afraid of what the jury might decide: that makes sense. Even the most obvious cases are not over till the verdict is in. And to lose must be appalling for anyone." She stopped trying to explain and looked at him earnestly.

He was overwhelmed with relief that she understood. He felt as if something infinitely precious had very nearly slipped out of his hands. It took him a moment to find the words that sounded rational, as if he were in control of his emotions. "He's very passionate," he began. "And he really did fear he would lose the respect of his peers over the plagiarism allegation, even though he knew he had made all the footnotes and attributions. I don't know if he's missed something in the past, or—"

Miriam interrupted. "I don't suppose there's anything you can do, anyway," she said, leaning back into the luxuriously cushioned chair. She smiled, but it wasn't joyful, more wistful. "Maybe he'll be better tomorrow."

"I suppose I should go and see him," he said.

Miriam smiled again, all vestige of anxiety banished for the moment. "To present your bill?" she suggested, eyes wide with feigned innocence.

Daniel could see a gentleness in those eyes that was so precious he was afraid to say or do anything to break the moment. It spread through him like a warmth in the blood. He must take hold of it, but gently, very gently.

THEY WERE BACK at fford Croft and Gibson when they saw Impney standing outside on the pavement, clearly looking for someone. It was dusk and the sky was heavy with impending rain.

"Ah, Mr. Pitt, sir," he said, with evident relief. He nodded at Miriam, then back at Daniel. "Inspector Frobisher was looking for you, sir. He called on the telephone. Mrs. Rhodes has gone missing, in the rain and the dusk. And he's frightened for her. At least . . ." His face filled with distress. "I think, if you will forgive me, sir, he is afraid that the Rainy-day Slasher may strike again."

"Attack the vicar's wife?" Daniel said incredulously. "For heaven's sake, why?" And then the obvious answer struck him. "Could she know who he is? Did she somehow put the pieces together?"

Impney did not answer immediately. The hesitation was only a second, no more than that. "Not exactly, sir."

"Then what, Impney? What is it!"

"I think, sir, the inspector is afraid that Mrs. Rhodes . . . *is* the slasher."

Twenty-Three

DANIEL FROZE. HIS first thought was that the very idea was absurd. Then the darker, stronger truth swept over him. Ian was afraid that Polly Rhodes was the slasher? Was it so unbelievable? Did this explain why they had not been able to catch her before? And did Richard Rhodes know, or at least allow himself to understand, that such a terrible truth was possible? If there was a worst nightmare for a man, Daniel was unable to envision what it could be.

"What does the inspector want me to do?" he asked Impney.

"He was wondering if you could go to the vicarage, sir. The vicar is alone, waiting. He must be desperate. And, of course, if she returns, she . . ." He stopped.

"Yes, it would be a terrible thing, the worst imaginable," Daniel agreed. He could barely grasp the possibility of such a horror. If Polly Rhodes really was insane, might she go so far as to hold Ian and the vicar hostage? Or even kill them? No! That was absurd. As was the idea that she crept around during the rain, knifing people to death! But somebody did! And if they looked insane, wild and murderous, then they would have been caught after the first crime.

Daniel tried to think it through. If it were Polly, it made no sense. She must be insane, and that insanity had to have its roots so far back as to be nearly untraceable. And impossibly tragic. He was relieved when his thoughts were interrupted by Miriam's voice.

"Of course we'll go," she said decisively, speaking directly to Impney. "Give me Father's car keys, please."

Impney fidgeted. "I think, Miss Miriam, that—"

"I know what you think, Impney," she shot back. "And I'm sure you're right as to what Father would say, if you asked him. So, don't ask." She held out her hand.

He stood frozen on the spot.

No one spoke. No one moved.

The first heavy drops of rain fell.

Impney turned and rushed into the building. He was gone little more than a minute. He emerged and put the keys in Miriam's open hand. She smiled at him, briefly. And then, before he had a chance to reconsider, she turned and marched down the street to her father's parked car.

Daniel came to life and caught up with her. He knew he should try to argue with her, dissuade her from joining him. She would be safe at home. And he was perfectly competent to drive Marcus's car, albeit without his permission. He also knew that Miriam was a very good driver, and if there should be an ugly situation at the vicarage, she would be strong, and likely able to deal with it. Even if it became violent. His stomach churned. This was the time to accept her help, not to argue—or, worse, push her away.

Miriam settled into the driver's seat and then leaned across and unlocked the passenger door for Daniel. Without speaking again, she started the engine and pulled out into the stream of traffic, driving with confidence, and with ever-increasing speed.

Daniel remained silent, as did Miriam. At this point, there was nothing left to say. It could be a tragedy for which there was no answer, no bearable explanation. Nothing seemed to fit with what they understood or could believe.

Miriam was staring ahead as she wove her way through the traffic, overtaking wherever possible.

Daniel reached out to put his hand on hers where she grasped the wheel. Her muscles were hard, tight. The words were formed in his mind, and he discarded them.

"Do you believe it could be Polly?" she asked. "Really?" There was derision in her voice, but real, sharp fear, as if she could hear his thoughts.

"No," he said, without hesitation. But that was the answer he wanted to believe. It was meant to convince himself as much as he could. But inside he knew it could be Polly Rhodes, and he had no idea how to deal with it. What monster hid inside her? If she, of all people, could be so utterly unlike what she seemed, who could he trust? What could he believe in?

It was now fully dark and raining steadily. The surface water on the road flew up in a spray as the wheels plowed through, bright-edged where the droplets caught the lamplight.

They were a good distance from the chambers in Lincoln's Inn Fields. Miriam drove with fierce concentration, following Holborn, and then right up Tottenham Court Road. She headed north toward Chalk Farm, then west along Adelaide Road.

After what seemed like an interminable drive, she pulled the car to a stop in front of the vicarage. In a clear sky, there would have been a shadow thrown by the church's spire, but there was insufficient light for even the faintest demarcation between light and shade.

Miriam switched off the engine, opened her door, and stepped out into the rain.

Daniel climbed out as quickly as he could, feeling the icy chill carried by an increasing wind. He closed the car door, and together they went swiftly up to the vicarage door and knocked. There was no answer. Miriam waited only a moment before trying the handle. It opened. Either someone had forgotten to lock it, or they had intentionally left it open.

She glanced at Daniel, then went inside. The hallway was warm and dry. The maid was standing at the far end, just outside the door to the kitchen, with the entrances to the larder and storerooms visible beyond her. The woman's face was filled with dismay. Clearly, she had been hoping it was Polly walking in through that door.

"I'm sorry," Daniel said to her. "We came to be of any help we could, practical or otherwise. The vicar should not have to face this situation alone." He forced himself to give a slight smile. "Nor should you."

She, too, gave an uncertain half smile. "Yes, sir, thank you. Would you like a cup of tea, sir?" She turned to Miriam. "And you, ma'am?" She blushed momentarily, trying to think what she should say. Or more difficult still, what she should do.

Daniel did not want tea, but he saw the necessity of giving her something to do, to distract her from the enormity of the situation. Her world was on the edge of disintegration. "Thank you, I think we would all like that," he answered. "But first, would you be kind enough to ask the reverend if we may come in?"

"Oh, yes, sir!" She was clearly relieved to have an errand to run, if only to approach Reverend Rhodes and announce the visitors.

In no more than two minutes, she returned, holding open the door leading to the sitting room.

"Thank you," Daniel said, before she could speak. He went straight in, knowing that Miriam was on his heels.

The room was stuffy, but it was not warm. The fire had burned low, the curtains were drawn tight. Richard Rhodes sat in his usual chair, but he was slumped, appearing to be uncomfortable, but not willing to move. He shifted and faced Daniel, turning only his head. "Mr. Pitt?"

"Yes, sir," Daniel replied. "And Dr. fford Croft."

"Doctor?" Rhodes said apprehensively. "I'm not ill."

"I'm not that kind of doctor, Reverend Rhodes," Miriam said, stepping forward, her voice low. "I had been to afternoon tea with Mr. Pitt when we heard what has happened. I came with him to see if I could help in any way at all."

Rhodes took a slow, deep breath.

It was obvious to Daniel that the man was under an almost unbearable strain, too close to what must be his breaking point.

"Thank you," Rhodes said a little hoarsely, his voice strained, as if he were speaking for the first time in hours. He cleared his throat. "It is very kind of you. Time seems so much longer when we are alone."

Miriam walked further into the room and sat in one of the big chairs.

Daniel went to the hearth and stoked the fire. There was still plenty of wood and coal there, and he was grateful not to have to go outside and search for it.

"Is it raining?" Rhodes asked, addressing his question to nobody in particular.

"Yes," Miriam answered. "But then, it seems to rain most evenings."

"But he's never killed when it wasn't raining, has he?" Rhodes pressed.

Daniel dared not look at Miriam. The man's use of *he* either meant he couldn't believe that his wife was the killer, or he knew and didn't want to admit it. Not even to himself.

"No, he hasn't," Miriam replied, throwing a quick glance at Daniel. "Did Mrs. Rhodes go to visit a parishioner?"

"Yes. She said who, but I can't remember. It isn't unusual for her to go from one to another, depending on who needs her attention. She goes even in the rain. If someone is in trouble—"

"Yes," said Daniel, and then he hesitated a moment. "It's a part of your job shared by both of you. I know that Mrs. Rhodes comforts many people just by being there, and believing in God's goodness and mercy." He did not want to sound as if he thought she did her husband's job for him, but he did want to acknowledge her good work, and how much it was appreciated.

Rhodes managed a smile, as if he understood what Daniel was doing. "I don't know who she went to see. That is, after Mrs. Henderson. The poor woman lost her mother last week, and she's feeling a bit adrift. She's a widow, you know. Two sons, but they live quite a long way off. Manchester, I think." He was talking, but he was not really speaking to either Miriam or Daniel.

Daniel suspected that Rhodes was filling in the silence, or the empty space left by his missing wife. And that he probably did not realize that his fears were so clearly visible.

Daniel looked over to Miriam, and she returned the gaze. In her face, he read her growing concern, both for this suffering man and for his missing wife. And then he wondered if Rhodes was afraid for Polly because she might meet the slasher in the dark and the rain, or because his beloved wife, his helpmeet and partner, might actually be the slasher herself. He wondered, too, if they should sit here talking about nothing in particular, with no one saying what they really meant. Did that help? Daniel had to ask himself about his own motives. Was he being polite because he wanted to avoid having to be alone with his thoughts of violence, even death—a potential tragedy that he could do nothing to prevent?

"Did you speak to Inspector Frobisher earlier?" he finally asked. It did no good to sit here and wait. Perhaps Rhodes could provide even the smallest detail that might set them in the right direction.

"Today?" Rhodes asked. "Yes, briefly. He came to ask a few questions. That was his first visit. He came again after my housekeeper called him about Polly's . . . absence. I didn't tell him anything useful. I don't know anything useful."

"What were you discussing with him the first time?" Miriam asked. Her voice was gentle, but very insistent.

Despite the intrusive question, Rhodes hesitated only a few seconds. "He wanted to know more about a tragedy that happened a long time ago. Many years. And then Polly suddenly remembered her promise to visit Mrs. Henderson . . ."

Miriam leaned forward. "May I ask—?

"A young woman named April," Rhodes answered. "She died years ago."

"How?" Daniel asked. "Or . . . why? Did it have anything to do with all these murders?"

"I'm sure not," Rhodes replied, but the tremor in his voice betrayed the lie.

Daniel waited, watching Rhodes's face, the confusion and the grief in it. And more than that, the fear.

Miriam spoke. "She had an idea, didn't she? Is that what you fear, Reverend? That she realized who the killer is?"

He looked up. "I think—yes, maybe she did."

"What did she say just before she left?" Daniel asked, his body suddenly so tense he could feel his muscles like tightly coiled springs.

Rhodes drew in his breath to answer.

At that moment, the maid knocked on the door and came in with a tray of tea and cake. Daniel thought that this was the last thing they wanted, but he rose to his feet and helped her set the tray on the table. He put it in front of Miriam, thanked the maid, and said to her that this was all they would require for the moment.

Miriam told the maid that she might go ahead and make dinner, but something that could be eaten at any time, or even kept for another day, if necessary.

The woman thanked Miriam and went out, closing the door behind her.

"You were saying?" Daniel prompted Rhodes. "A tragedy?"

"Yes, well," Rhodes answered. "It was a young woman named April. She died in the most terrible circumstances." His voice caught in his throat, as if the effort to speak the words choked him. He hesitated for so long Daniel thought he was not going to continue. Then he drew in a shaking breath. "She was with child. Don't ask me who the father was. I don't know, and I prefer not to. She had a backstreet abortion. She bled to death, alone, in a filthy bed." His voice cracked. "None of us knew about it until it was too late."

For a moment, the silence hung heavily, then he continued, his voice rough, tears on his cheeks. "She had no family. It's so easy to fall in love when you need friendship so much, the need to feel someone cares. You can mistake appetite for love. And, of course, there were those who said she was a tart, even pointed the finger and called her a whore. Some blamed her for taking her own life. She was buried alone, with no one to grieve for her except Polly . . . and me." He wept for her unashamedly, the tears distorting his face.

"Pointed the finger," Daniel repeated slowly, not daring to look at Miriam. "Reverend, is that what this is about? The pointed finger?"

Finger. The word filled Daniel's mind. Suddenly, he was choked with the meaning of a mutilated hand, a pointing finger, a digit hacked off, flesh and bone. Was it the meaning of the gesture? A pointed finger of blame at a young woman in distress? Even if indirectly, it might have been pointed at someone believed to have caused her destruction. He felt the anguish of pity himself, and he had not even known her.

He finally looked at Miriam and was convinced that she understood what he was thinking. He lifted his right hand and pointed.

She nodded. "Reverend, can you get in touch with Ian Frobisher? I don't want to alarm you, but we need to call the police—now."

"Why?" Rhodes said sharply. "What do you think she . . . ?" His face turned ashen. "Don't frighten her. She . . ." He stopped.

Daniel was not quite sure what Rhodes feared, but he was certain Polly knew something that was lethally dangerous to her. "Where did this happen?" he asked, his voice insistent. "Does it have anything to do with Haviland, or Sandrine Bernard, when she was younger? And what about Lena Madden? And how does Mrs. Rhodes know about it?" He was searching for something, anything, because he still did not understand how the pieces fitted together.

"Cambridge," Richard said quietly, as if the memory had suddenly surfaced. "I forgot all about that . . . until now." He spoke in little more than a whisper. "A musical group. Most of the time, there were four or five of them. Age and gender didn't matter, only that you could play. And were willing to join, and to practice together. They all loved music, and they were amateur, but gifted. And again, there is no use asking me who was responsible for April's situation, because I don't know—"

"I understand," Daniel interrupted. "It makes sense. Your wife, with her love of music, would have known this group—and this young woman, April?" He stopped when he saw the pain in Rhodes's face, and it hurt him to look at it. "Can you tell me where Mrs. Rhodes is likely to be? On what street? Any place in particular?"

"I'm sorry, no." Rhodes spoke so quietly he was barely audible.

"May I use your telephone, sir?" Daniel asked.

"No! I—"

"I'm sorry," Daniel apologized, and he meant it. But then he stood up and went to the table where the telephone sat. He picked it up and asked for the police station. When the call was answered, he asked to speak to Inspector Frobisher.

"The inspector is out on a call," said the man at the other end. "Can somebody else help you?"

"He's still out? Do you know where he went?" Daniel asked. "I need to find him. I have information about the case he's on, the slasher case. And it's urgent."

"Would you like to speak to someone else, sir?"

"No, damn it, I—" He was being unfair to the man, and he knew it. He had probably had dozens of panic calls about these murders.

"This is Daniel Pitt," he said more levelly. "I'm working with Ian Frobisher."

"In that case . . . if he calls in, I'll tell him you were in touch. If you give me your number, sir?"

"I'm at St. Wilfrid's vicarage, on Adelaide Road . . ." He was still holding the receiver when there was a shout, followed by a high-pitched sound, almost a scream. He dropped the phone and swung round.

Miriam was on her feet. Rhodes rose as well, and then turned slowly to face the direction of that cry.

It came again, slicing through the darkness and into the warmth of the sitting room.

"This way!" Rhodes called out sharply, and started toward the door.

Miriam followed on his heels.

Daniel caught up with them at the front door and they all went out into the rain and the dark. There was more shouting, now clearly two voices, and they rushed toward the sound.

They had moved only yards from the door before they were in utter darkness, the light from the house no longer of any use. Miriam and Daniel followed Reverend Rhodes. For him, all was dark, even in the sun. But he had trodden this path often, and it was as familiar to him as his wife's voice. He knew every step of it.

They followed him out of the gate, along the footpath in the patch of light from the streetlamp, and into the shadow again, onto the path through the graveyard, leading to the church.

Miriam and Daniel followed as closely as they could, watching Rhodes's black figure as he wove his way through the graveyard, dodging gravestones, knowing exactly where every one of them lay, protruding above the wet earth.

"There!" Miriam said, her voice hoarse. She pointed to a corner at the far end of the cemetery. The beam of a torch became clear as soon as they passed the lower branches of the heavy, wet yew trees.

A few steps more and they saw Polly Rhodes. She was backed against a huge gravestone. It had a marble angel carved into its top. The woman was clearly terrified, struggling to keep control of herself. In front of her, torchlight glistening on the blade of his long, curved knife, was Nicholas Wolford.

At the same time, Daniel and Miriam reached out to stop Reverend Rhodes from proceeding.

"Wait," said Daniel, his voice a low, harsh whisper. "It's Wolford, and he has a knife."

"Please, stop!" Polly begged, her voice high-pitched with terror. "I didn't hurt her," she said, pity now in her voice. "I swear. And I never repeated what the others were saying: that you were somehow to blame. I didn't save her, I couldn't. But neither could you! And I know, God knows, you tried."

"I did! I tried," Wolford said, desperation in his voice. "But now I've avenged her and she can rest in peace."

"Not if you kill me!" Polly cried, her voice almost cracking on the words. "I was her friend!"

"Then why didn't you stop them, speaking those ugly words against her? They would have listened to you! Who was the father? Who took advantage of her?" His voice choked in a sob. "Why didn't he save her?"

"I don't know. I think it was Haviland, but I don't know. I tried. I did, but I was too late, and they wouldn't listen to me!" Her voice was rising again. "I swear to you, I tried!"

Daniel saw Wolford lift the knife a little higher.

"Don't!" Polly cried out.

Richard Rhodes moved a few steps toward the voices. "No more, Nicholas, please . . . let her go!"

Daniel stepped forward, his voice shaking. "This is the end of the road," he said. "I don't know why you did this, but perhaps I can guess."

"You have no idea," snarled Wolford.

"But I do," Daniel said. "Being accused of plagiarism broke something inside you. Was it because you were not believed, just as April was not believed?"

Wolford stood motionless, his eyes staring as if was seeing something no one else could see.

"It's over now," Miriam said. "There's no need to hurt Polly, no excuse to hurt her. Please, Professor, give me the knife."

Daniel stepped between Wolford and Miriam. If the man lashed out, he would have to strike Daniel first.

Wolford stared at him, then slowly lowered his hand and relaxed his grip. The knife fell soundlessly onto the wet earth. He looked dazed, as if he could not remember where he was.

Polly Rhodes stumbled away from Wolford and into her husband's arms. He held her and they both wept.

At first, Daniel did not see Ian Frobisher moving along the path, trying to feel his way between the gravestones. Bremner was on his heels.

The inspector walked right up to Wolford, ignoring the others. He nodded to Bremner, who put handcuffs on the man.

Ian Frobisher spoke quietly. "Professor Wolford, you need to come with us. It's cold and wet here, and a graveyard is no place to discuss what we need to do."

"Need to do?" Wolford repeated, as if these were words he did not understand.

Daniel thought that he was like a man newly come to consciousness after a fall, or a lengthy coma. He turned to Miriam. "Did you know?" he asked.

"That he was the killer? No, but I did begin to wonder if he could be paranoid. If he is, Daniel, he's a sick man. Does the inspector know that?"

"I think he does," said Daniel. "Judging by the way he's treating him. Not roughly, but with kindness, as you do when someone is beyond your reach."

He looked through the rain to where Ian was guiding Wolford

carefully and slowly along the path, Bremner lighting their way with a torch. They moved through the grass, toward the gate, careful not to push ahead too fast. Ian looked rather dazed, too, as if he had just been awakened and did not fully realize where he was.

"Can you think of anything worse?" Daniel asked Miriam quietly. "The poor man is really lost, even to himself. How terrible, to feel your mind slipping away from you. In his paranoia he lashed out at the people he felt had betrayed April, blaming them for failing to save her reputation, and even her life." When she slipped her hand into his, it felt good. Cold from the rainy night, but strong.

Reverend Rhodes and Polly moved slowly toward the vicarage, his arm around her shoulder and holding her close to him in a protective embrace.

Daniel and Miriam followed, picking their way carefully through the gravestones and back to the main path. The lamplight on the pavement seemed far away, and of little use. The rain was getting harder, more insistent.

Daniel heard the click of the vicarage door closing. Richard and Polly Rhodes were safely inside.

"Can I think of anything worse?" repeated Miriam. "No, I can't. It must be terrible to trust no one, and always feel alone." Her voice was filled with sadness.

Daniel stopped. Despite the pelting rain, there was something he needed to say. "You won't be alone. I promise. Not ever."

She blinked, and then her eyes grew wide. "Do you . . . promise?"

He realized what he had just said, and how deeply he had meant it. "Yes, I do. I promise. I'll always be with you . . . if you will let me. Will you? Please?"

Miriam leaned closer to him. "Yes, Daniel, I think I will let you. Yes."

He bent forward and kissed her, and then kissed her again, and she clung to him, both of them no longer aware of the rain.

THE
FOURTH ENEMY

A DANIEL PITT NOVEL

by Anne Perry

Daniel smiled at his wife. "Your father might forget people's names, if he doesn't particularly like them, or office meetings entirely, but he's never late for dinner." He passed by Miriam and did not even try to resist the desire to touch her, kiss her cheek again and feel the softness of her hair before leaving to go upstairs to wash and tidy up a little before dinner.

Marriage was still a new and wonderful adventure for him, a happiness so intense he found it hard to accept. He and Miriam had known each other for some time, but they had only realized that their relationship went far deeper than friendship, or even collaboration of their separate skills, in the past year. He recalled the end of the last case on which they had both worked and how, as they had stood in the torrential rain in the graveyard, he had finally understood that it was love. Now they were together, and this was rich, new and infinitely sweet to him.

As expected, Miriam's father, Marcus fford Croft, arrived exactly on time. He was standing on the doorstep, smiling, when Daniel answered the bell. At this time of year, it was still full daylight, and Marcus practically glowed in the slanted rays of the evening sun. He was wearing a yellow-gold velvet waistcoat under his light jacket, and his bow tie was a deep bronze. He was smiling with sheer pleasure.

"Come in," Daniel invited him, standing back so that Marcus could step into the hall.

Once inside, Marcus paused for a moment, looking at the paintings Miriam had brought from his house, where she had lived all her life. It clearly pleased him to see her old childhood possessions here in her new home. It was a sign that she felt this was now where she belonged.

Miriam came out of the kitchen and greeted Marcus. She hugged him quickly, met his eyes for a moment, then turned and led him into the sitting room where she poured him a glass of sherry. They kept it especially for him, knowing how much he enjoyed it. The doctor had said that one glass was acceptable, but since Marcus's first heart attack, not more than one—and definitely none of the much stronger brandy he preferred.

Miriam brooked no argument. She loved her father deeply. Her mother had died long ago, leaving the two of them behind. But Miriam was strict about him obeying orders where his health was concerned. It was the only issue on which she always prevailed.

Marcus settled in his chair comfortably, glancing at his daughter and then back again at Daniel.

Daniel could see that he had something to say. It was there in the way he sat, a certain tension in his shoulders.

It was Miriam who broke through the pleasantries. "You have news." It was a statement. "Tell us, before dinner spoils," she said with a smile. "Don't put my cooking to the test. Please." It was a sincere request.

While she had lived in her father's house, she had never concerned herself with any domestic tasks at all, including preparing meals. All her time and her passion had gone into her study of pathology. Daniel had learned by trial and error what to say regarding her culinary skills, and what to leave unsaid. But Marcus had never learned, nor, indeed, had he tried to. But then, Miriam would take a lot of criticism from her father because they adored each other, and she was secure in his acceptance of her eccentricities, as he was secure in her acceptance of his.

Daniel was still discovering how easily he could hurt her, sometimes without realizing it until it was too late. She was older by fifteen years, and his admiration for her was immense, but admiration was quite different from love. Their marriage was new, exciting, frightening, and comfortable, all at the same time. It touched emotions he had not known before.

"I have news for you, yes," Marcus said, breaking what had been a few moments of silence. He was smiling, as if he was anticipating their surprise . . . and pleasure.

Miriam inhaled, as if preparing to speak, then apparently changed her mind.

Marcus said, "I have decided to retire. I think perhaps, finally, it is time."

Miriam drew in another sharp and audible breath, but Daniel saw that it was out of relief, not apprehension. She was only too aware of the danger of another, more serious heart attack—perhaps fatal this time. After the first one, she had come home from Holland, interrupting her studies, and she had not gone back until her father was out of immediate danger, regardless of the lectures she was missing and the exams awaiting her.

Daniel looked at her and saw her shoulders relax.

Whatever might happen to the chambers of fford Croft and Gibson without her father's leadership, Miriam regarded it as secondary to his health. She was smiling now. She glanced only briefly at Daniel, then back again at Marcus.

"Good!" she said firmly. "They will have to learn to manage without you. And you must let the new head of the chambers—

whoever he turns out to be—take the lead." She smiled, as if to soften the words. "You must not lean over his shoulder and second-guess his actions. Let him make the important decisions, as if you have complete confidence in him. He will not do everything as you would, but that is not necessarily a bad thing. He must be allowed to have his own ideas, or he will not be much use."

Daniel knew that she meant every word; she was looking at her father sternly, despite the gentleness in her face. He knew, too, that she was thinking not only about Marcus, but also about whoever would be taking on the extremely difficult task of following the brilliant, erratic and eccentric man who had led the chambers since its inception. There had never been a Gibson. The name had been added to bolster public confidence, so people would think there was more than one man at the helm.

There were undoubtedly several extremely competent barristers, some of them well established. Daniel could not think who Marcus would choose to succeed him. Toby Kitteridge, Daniel's closest friend in the chambers, was extremely able; he was far cleverer at the law than he realized, and he was very good in court, but he had a long way to go to develop the assurance required to lead. Maybe, one day Daniel would become head of chambers, but not for ten or fifteen years, at the very least—and possibly not ever. His chief ability was leading in court, as well as carrying out the detective work usually done by one of the solicitors. It was an area of expertise in which he hoped to become known.

Daniel was watching Miriam, who seemed to be waiting for her father to go on. Instead, Marcus turned to Daniel, a flicker of uncertainty in his eyes. Surely he was not going to ask for Daniel's opinion? That would be absurd. Daniel had been with the chambers for no more than a couple of years. Marcus might not ask his opinion regarding his successor, but perhaps he would want his support for whatever decision he was going to make. No one would be particularly surprised by his choice, with several very skilled men in the chambers, but they might be disconcerted. At the same time, his staff would be relieved. Marcus's health was of paramount concern to all of them.

Whomever Marcus appointed, it would be a big change. And it would be a hard job at first, no matter who took over.

The silence dragged on too long.

"Who are you going to choose?" Miriam asked. "Have you decided yet? Or are you asking Daniel's view?"

"Or yours?" Marcus said, his smile now a little less certain. "Neither, as it happens. I have thought about it long and hard, and I have already decided. Although it is too late for you to disapprove, I value your opinion, and your love even more. But I will not change my mind." He took a deep breath. "You may, of course, disagree with my choice. But it is a fait accompli. And—he has accepted."

Daniel glanced at Miriam's hand resting on the arm of the chair and saw that her knuckles were white. He let out his breath very slowly. "And who is he?" he asked. "Do we know him?"

"The new man?" Marcus raised his eyebrows.

"The new head of chambers." Daniel was wrong-footed. Surely Marcus was not bringing in an outsider to lead them?

Without answering, Marcus said quietly. "Well, we need a new barrister also. You are good, Daniel, but we need a King's Counsel, a silk! To make a splash. You will do that one day, but you are not ready for it yet."

"Then who?" Miriam demanded, her face tense. "Who have you invited in as King's Counsel?"

"Oh, you will know of him," Marcus replied. He was smiling, his voice slightly husky, as if his mouth were dry. "Gideon Hunter KC. He has been second at Mitchell Dawson for years, but he will never be a member of the family—and they are a family chambers, and a trifle stuffy. I found he was looking for something more . . . more adventurous." He smiled again, seeing the tension in their faces. "We will suit him excellently."

"And who will be head of chambers?" Daniel asked. He was confused, even worried. Was that going to be someone new also? It was too much change. He liked everything as it was, and he was comfortable with the familiar team.

"I think Toby is ready for that," Marcus replied. He lifted his shoulders in a slight shrug. "Of course, he did not think so when I told him, perhaps he never will. Daniel, I wish for you to help him. He trusts you. Perhaps more than he trusts himself." His face was intensely earnest now. "He has the skills. He is very clever—far cleverer than he knows or accepts—but he hasn't the confidence or the courage that you have. Nothing in his life has yet given it to him."

Marcus appraised Daniel before continuing. "I expect you to take on a leadership role in the future. You can, and you will! The position of senior barrister will be yours one day. When you are ready. You are an actor, a crusader! You are not an administrator." He stared at Daniel levelly. "Do I have your word?"

Daniel was stunned. Marcus leaving was one thing—he had expected that, and wanted it, for Marcus's sake—but hiring a new barrister, to take all the leading cases? An ambitious man. A silk. A King's Counsel! Daniel had heard of Gideon Hunter. Everyone had. A brilliant, erratic, yet charming man. But coming into fford Croft and Gibson to take the major cases? Of course, Daniel was not yet ready for that, but he would be one day. At least, he aimed to be.

And Toby Kitteridge! Quiet, often painfully shy Toby must have been horrified at the thought of leading the chambers. But could he do it? Was Marcus right? Toby Kitteridge was awkward, clumsy, wrists always poking out of his sleeves, hair falling over his forehead. But yes, clever, seeing further ahead than others could, recognizing details they missed, understanding their significance before anyone else did.

Marcus was waiting. So was Miriam. They were both looking at him.

"Yes," he said. "Of course. I'll give the new appointments my full support."

Marcus stared back at him, meeting his eyes quite candidly. "Good, I want fford Croft and Gibson to retain its distinctive character. Gideon Hunter will either be a great success, in which case you will all thank me for my perspicacity, my daring and my wisdom, or he will be a disaster, in which case people will say that no one could follow me! Or they could also say that I lost my wits and made a catastrophic mistake." He smiled, and there was both humor and tension in his expression. "But if you help Toby, have confidence in him, and make him believe you do, then he will be rock solid. He will make mistakes, as we all do. But they will not matter. His achievements will outweigh them."

Daniel forced himself to smile. "It could be brilliant," he said, although he did not sound as sure of it as he wished to. "And the new lineup will certainly attract attention!"

Marcus nodded. Suddenly, his eyes were as sharp, bright, and forceful as they had ever been. "Precisely," he said, almost under his breath. "Everyone will sit up and take notice. It is up to you to make the most of it. Do your best. Take chances! Now is the moment when everyone will be watching you. Be seen! Don't play everything safe, as if I were watching over your shoulder. Throw yourself into it!"

"You are doing this on purpose," Miriam said quietly, but with certainty. "Striking out to where it's roughest, to see whether you will sink or swim!"

Marcus nodded his agreement. "You are young enough to take chances. If not now, you never will. If you only do what is safe, you will eventually become boring. You must wear velvet waistcoats so people know who you are!"

"If I wear a waistcoat, people will think I'm trying to be you," Daniel said immediately, with a half-smile.

"And aren't you?" Marcus asked, his eyes wide.

"Oh, yes," Daniel said, now smiling fully. "But not yet. I want to be myself first!"

Marcus hesitated for a moment, then burst out laughing.

Miriam relaxed into her chair, her clenched hands letting go of the arms.

"You will approve of Hunter's wife," Marcus went on, turning toward Miriam. "You have much in common. She is an ardent fighter for women's suffrage. Indeed, you will agree with her about a lot of things. And disagree on some, no doubt."

"I hope so," Miriam said fervently. "I shall learn nothing from anyone who already thinks as I do." She looked at Daniel with a smile. "Not that I'm in any danger of being bored."

He felt warmth burning his face at the memory of their rather heated differences of opinion the evening before, and the intense pleasure of making up afterward.

Miriam turned to Marcus, a slight blush on her cheeks as well.

Daniel knew with happiness what she was remembering. He recalled it also, vividly.

Marcus relaxed even more, sinking down farther into his chair and taking another sip from his glass. "Good," he said. "Very good. So, are we having supper?"

Two

THE FOLLOWING DAY, Miriam worked at the government laboratory and morgue as usual. She had done so since her return
from studying in Holland, now accredited as a fully qualified forensic pathologist, an ambition she had held since the age of eleven
or twelve. While in Holland, she had missed England, and above
all she had missed her father . . . and Daniel. The time had finally
come when she'd admitted to herself that she was in love with
Daniel, but still dared not consider that he might feel the same
about her.

Miriam was painfully aware of the fifteen-year age difference
between them. It would have been nothing if he had been the elder:
Such matches were quite common and thoroughly approved of.
But she was the elder, and it hurt her more than she cared to admit;
it created a deep sense of futility and pain, knowing that all that was
most precious to her, this source of her real happiness, could so
easily slip away.

Not that she looked her age. She was in her early forties, but often mistaken for being a decade younger. She was a striking woman in her own way. For better or worse, her hair was the same flaming auburn as Marcus's had been in his youth. But of course, now his was dazzlingly white. The kindest thing she could have said about her own face was that it was "individual," that it showed her intelligence and registered every emotion, whether she wished it to or not. Daniel had more sense than to tell her she was beautiful, for she simply would not have believed him, although she had always felt she had lovely eyes.

Before leaving for Holland, she had worked under Dr. Evelyn Hall, whose guidance had not only added to her sense of confidence but had actually enabled her to go to Holland to study further. It was Dr. Hall—affectionately referred to as Dr. Eve—who had insisted she pursue her studies in the one country in Europe that would grant forensics degrees to women.

In Holland and in Britain, Dr. Eve was highly respected. Miriam knew that it had taken time for her to prove herself, but the scientific community had come to consider her a leader in her field. With her cropped hair, husky voice and rather shapeless body, she struck Miriam as the epitome of the eccentric scientist. Dr. Eve was forthright, candid to a fault, and brilliant. That the woman not only liked Miriam but also believed passionately in her ability was of no importance to the British authorities, but to Miriam it was the highest possible accolade.

Since her marriage to Daniel three months ago, Miriam did not often work the long hours she had before. In those days, she had had no particular reason to hurry home to the house she shared with her father. Now it was different. Daniel often worked long hours too, so their evenings at home—time to talk, or to just sit together and watch the waning light in the small garden, hearing the whispering of the leaves in the wind—were infinitely precious.

This evening, Miriam wanted to be home early to hear from Daniel about the new barrister, Gideon Hunter. They had never met him, as far as Daniel could remember, but he knew his reputa-tion. Everyone did. There were not so many lawyers who attained the title of King's Counsel, the highest of honors bestowed by the Crown on outstanding barristers of fifteen or more years' experi-ence. Like the best of his peers, Gideon Hunter had both prose-cuted and defended cases in court, as many barristers chose to do. He was spoken of as clever, unpredictable, highly articulate and, on occasion, even colorful. Which was almost exactly what had been said of Marcus fford Croft when he was in his prime.

Miriam wondered if Gideon Hunter was actually like Marcus. She resisted the thought. No one was like her father! He was the only relative she had known since her mother's death when Miriam was still a child.

Now, of course, there was Daniel. Please God, let that last for-ever! She could hardly believe it when she woke in the morning and felt his warmth beside her in the bed. Once she had even woken him, just to make sure it was not a wishful dream. Of course, she did not tell him that was the reason. It sounded so insecure, even demanding.

Now she was coming in from the soft summer evening to make a quick supper and hear what he thought of Gideon Hunter on what was the man's first day at fford Croft and Gibson. She was eager to learn how Toby Kitteridge was handling his sudden and extraordinary rise to leadership as head of chambers, a position she believed he had never dared to imagine for himself.

She must remember not to give advice to Daniel, but to listen. And not only to his voice, but to his choice of words, his intona-tion. And, of course, she must watch the expressions on his face.

She thought of her father's relationship with her husband. Mar-cus was not only Daniel's father-in-law, but his friend. He liked Daniel very much. He had given Daniel a position in the chambers, his first real job after university, at least in part because Daniel was the son of a man Marcus had known and liked for years. Sir Thomas Pitt was now head of Special Branch, the department of the government that dealt with terrorism that came from within the country rather than from abroad. Special Branch tackled violence and the threat of insurrection and anarchy, which seemed to be on the rise all over Europe. Miriam felt it all around her, and read about it: Civil unrest was growing, along with calls for overdue and desperately needed reform.

But for now, her concerns were closer to home: this new barrister at chambers, Gideon Hunter, and how he reacted to Daniel, the son-in-law of the founder. She was anxious to know how Daniel had fared on this.

She turned in at the gate and went up the path quickly. She had her own key, of course. She was later than she had meant to be. There had been some tidying up to do at the lab. Dr. Eve had said she would do it, but that was a pattern Miriam was not willing to set, as it would be all too easy to fall into. Dr. Eve was her benefactor and her superior, and she should never take advantage of that unless it was absolutely necessary. And even then, she should never take it for granted.

"Hello!" she called from the hallway

"Hello!" Daniel replied from the kitchen.

Miriam felt as if her heart skipped a beat. She was a pathologist and knew very well that her heart did no such thing. And if it did, it was a happy skip, not a lurch to be feared!

She wore no coat. It was high summer and the sun was warm. There was nothing to take off except a light jacket. She hung it on the coat stand in the hall, then hurried on.

Daniel met her in the kitchen, where the sunlight was streaming through the windows. She walked straight into his arms and hugged him hard. It was no surprise to see him, but it still astonished her that she could walk into his arms and be hugged, deeply, softly. It was such an exciting thing to do. And always would be. Perhaps for a very long time.

"How was your day?" she asked, not yet willing to let go of him.

"How was Hunter? And in particular, how is Toby dealing with it all?"

Daniel leaned back and looked into her face. "Hunter did not come in until quite late," he replied. "I think he was tidying up at his old chambers." A shadow crossed his face and he stepped away. "But Toby is pretty shaken." He breathed in, and then out again slowly. "I think he's amazed that Marcus imagines he could possibly do this. He wants it to be true, but he's terrified of failing." He smiled ruefully. "It's one of those things that you dream about, and really want, but not yet. I don't know if he will ever feel he is quite ready for it."

"We can't pick the time," she said quietly. "Marcus needs to go now. He says he's feeling fine, but I know him well enough to see through that. He smiles and comes into the office, but it's getting harder for him." She gave Daniel a steady look. "Please, help him to believe you can all manage without him, even if you don't really want to."

She knew she was asking a lot. She was expecting Daniel, who was only twenty-eight, to convince Toby to take command before he felt ready to. Because if Marcus did not believe his firm would be all right, he would have to stay, even if it exhausted his strength and brought his death much sooner.

"I know it will be a heavy burden," she went on. "But if Marcus has another attack, it could be fatal this time. You will feel dreadful. And so will Toby. He won't be able to forgive himself." She saw in his eyes the understanding of everything that she was saying—and even what was beyond her words, to what was implied. She did not bother to finish the thought. There was no need to spell out the future. "You'll help him. If anybody in the office gives Toby a hard time, you will rein them in, won't you?" she urged.

"No," he answered. "But I'll tell Toby to do it. I'm not going to look as if I'm the real boss. That wouldn't help anyone."

She knew he was right, but she wanted to protect all of them, and she felt Daniel was the least vulnerable. Was that unfair? Or wishful thinking, because she did not want him ever to be at fault? Loving people was so very complicated.

"And Hunter? Tell me more about him," she said aloud.

He smiled a little ruefully. "I don't know what I expected, but he wasn't it. He looks . . ." He reached for the right word. "Aristocratic. And bland. Until you look at him more closely, and you stop noticing his pale hair and his elegant face and see his eyes. Dark blue, steady, and very bright. I don't know what to make of him. He has a sense of humor, which I didn't expect. And he's cleverer than I expected—" He stopped, as if he had discovered that he was surprised at his own thoughts. "I don't know," he admitted. "At least it won't be boring."

"That's what you're worried about? Being bored?" It was not that she believed him—she certainly did not. He was being flippant, so as not to worry her.

"No," he admitted. "I thought he would fall into one of the categories I understand. At least mostly. But he doesn't. And I think I might like him."

"That's a start." She touched his cheek, then withdrew her hand. "Supper?"

ANNE PERRY is the bestselling author of two acclaimed series set in Victorian England: the William Monk novels and the Charlotte and Thomas Pitt novels. She is also the author of a series featuring Charlotte and Thomas Pitt's son, Daniel, including *Death with a Double Edge* and *One Fatal Flaw*, as well as the Elena Standish series, including *A Darker Reality* and *A Question of Betrayal*; a series of five World War I novels; nineteen holiday novels (most recently *A Christmas Legacy*); and a historical novel, *The Sheen on the Silk*, set in the Byzantine Empire. She lives in Los Angeles.

anneperry.us

To inquire about booking Anne Perry for a speaking engagement, please contact the Penguin Random House Speakers Bureau at speakers@penguinrandomhouse.com.